Children of Stone

Going Forth By Day

Revised Edition

*Merry Christmas Cheryl,
Mary R Woldering*

Mary R. Woldering

This is a work of fiction. Names, characters, places, and incidents are the product of the author's imagination or are used fictitiously.

Copyright © 2020, 2015 by Mary R. Woldering

All rights reserved. No part of this book may be reproduced or used in any manner without written prermission of the copyright owner except for the use of quotations in a book review.

ISBN 13: 979-8-6806-9832-7 (Paperback)

ASIN: B08GZSMY6C (E-Book)

Editing by: Thomas Woldering

Cover Art by: Thomas Woldering

Map by: Thomas Woldering, based on a map by Jeff Dahl

Independently Published

To my parents and my family, who nurtured my creative soul.

To my son Thom,

for being my editor and formatter for this volume.

To Annette Taylor -

first with me on my journey,

without whom this story would never have been told.

Author's Note

To all of you returning to this series after reading Volume 1 of the Children of Stone, <u>Voices in Crystal</u> - thank you! I'm glad you're here to continue the adventure with me. For new readers, this story is a work of visionary fiction set in the time period around 2500 B.C. in the ancient Middle East. I have used many proper names for places and peoples in this story which are believed to have been used historically. I've included a glossary with this novel to explain the locations visited and terminology used throughout the book. I sincerely hope that you enjoy this story, and that the extra material provided allows you to better understand the historical setting in which this novel takes place.

When we last left off, Marai and his companions, Ariennu, Deka, and Naibe-Ellit had been separated by the schemes of the now-aged prince who has hounded Marai since the day he was gifted power by the unearthly "Children of Stone". Having seemingly defeated Marai, the Prince now seeks to use his influence in the royal court of Khemet (Ancient Egypt) to control Marai's companions. However, in each of these women lies great untapped potential, which they are only beginning to discover. This is their story. Join them on their journey to wisdom as they independently grow to understand their own powers. New alliances will form, loyalties will shift, and the comfortable lives of the royals will be shaken to their cores. And what of Marai? Has he met defeat, or will he rise up and Go Forth by Day?

Enjoy!

Contents

PART 1: DRIFTING AWAY 1

    Chapter 1: Pronouncement 3

    Chapter 2: Things Fall Apart 13

    Chapter 3: Two Princes 25

    Chapter 4: The Arrangement 35

    Chapter 5: The Choice 49

    Chapter 6: A Mysterious Grandson 69

    Chapter 7: Naibe's Charm 81

    Chapter 8: Visions and Memories 91

    Chapter 9: "A Curse be on Your Houses!" 99

    Chapter 10: His Spell 109

    Chapter 11: A Royal Concubine 117

PART 2: LOOKING BACK 131

    Chapter 12: Going Forth By Day 133

    Chapter 13: The Unexpected 147

    Chapter 14: The Veil 163

    Chapter 15: A Priest at your Altar 171

    Chapter 16: Away from Here, to Where? 181

    Chapter 17: No Ordinary Man 191

    Chapter 18: The Sacred Cow 201

    Chapter 19: Lilitu 215

    Chapter 20: Another Departure 225

    Chapter 21: Intermission 233

    Chapter 22: Ariennu and the King 237

    Chapter 23: Naibe Brown Eyes 251

    Chapter 24: Bakha Montu 267

PART 3: SENDING FORTH 279

    Chapter 25: The Wdjat 281

    Chapter 26: Preparations and Discoveries 297

    Chapter 27: Arrivals 313

    Chapter 28: The Dance 333

    Chapter 29: The Competition 343

    Chapter 30: Theft and Shadow 365

    Chapter 31: Crossing at Night 379

    Chapter 32: Image in the Water 393

EPILOGUE: THE LAND OF THE BOW 403

MAP 405

GLOSSARY 407

MARY R. WOLDERING

Part 1: Drifting Away

GOING FORTH BY DAY

Chapter 1: Pronouncement

Six days and nothing from you, Marai. I'm tired of lying to Baby One and Bone Woman. Ari sat on the edge of the well, shrouded in her invisibility until the alleyway furor dissipated. *I think they've even started lying to each other about not being worried, like me. It was good the first half moon and some. Talking through our stones, you saying it's alright. Then just nothing? Something bad's happened.*

"You see which way that sorceress went?" a voice followed by several gruff-voiced companions emerged from an alleyway and headed toward the well. Ari hunkered down tightly until she appeared to look like either a shadow or an old woman who had risen for goddess knows what.

I'm good at this now. They won't find me, she tapped the place where the dark stone in her brow lay. *His fault anyway.* She thought of the drunken male who had come staggering out of a tavern not long ago. Ari hadn't been able to sleep. Leaving Deka and Naibe in their apartment, she had stomped along the waterfront, looking in on the tavern where she had enjoyed some of the patrons before Marai and she had become intimate. *He'll sense me taking my own pleasure like in the old days,* she thought. *It'll make him want to speak to us.*

She had been standing in the doorway watching the revelry inside. Men were singing some discordant tune about the King being the best drunk in the land and adding verses about some of the women they knew lying with him. Others were gambling over a senet game.

One of the girls who wore a badly fitting bobbed wig bent over near a man and ground her hips suggestively.

Somehow, Ari had lost any interest in finding some fun.

Well would you know – she mused. *It's not this stone doing it, it's you after all, you big fool.* She had looked up into the night sky. *Girl can't go have a good time without thinking about you. You know I was that girl all my life not so long ago and my mother before me was nothing but a low waterfront kuna.* She sighed, disinterested. *Might as well go back and try to get some sleep before sunup.*

She had taken a step back and felt hands on her waist drawing her into an embrace.

"Pretty, pretty! Pale girl," a male voice whispered in her ear. "Got something for you."

"Not impressed. Get off me," she snapped, but the grip tightened.

"You out here at this hour? You're looking for a big *hnn* to fill you up. Don't lie to me, ka't."

Ari knew it was the last thing the young man had said before his friends found him addled, bleeding from a gash on the throat that taught him a lesson in blood, but didn't do anything fatal, and nurturing a swollen groin.

As she fled, shrouding herself, she had heard him jabber about sorcery but he couldn't recall anything about her and how or why his injuries occurred.

Damn. She shook her head after the group of his fellows passed, searching for the woman who had hurt their friend, then trotted up the steps to her darkened apartment to find Deka and Naibe lying on their pallets.

Hope they're asleep. No mood to talk about it.

Deka stirred, an almost-scowl crossing her face that showed in the lamp Ari had lit before she left.

Feeling better? came from the Ta-Seti woman's thoughts. Ari rebelled at her unspoken sarcasm.

Not what you think. Had to teach one fool a lesson. She held up her little finger, measuring a knuckle, indicating the size of the "hnn" he'd been bragging about.

Deka snorted in amusement, then sat.

Ari noticed her staring at her pale kalasiris and then saw her expression shift to something she couldn't comprehend. She used to see it when the men in N'ahab's band would fight and cut each other.

Blood, sister. You kill him? Deka silently asked.

Ari looked down and saw the rust-colored splatter across her breasts and on her laced vest. She dimly remembered a hot spray of fluid, her cursing mightily, and then touching to heal it into something not so fatal.

He lived. You know me. I know how to make a messy cut that won't kill. She unlaced her vest and removed it, then took her place on her pallet. Naibe lay between her and Deka. When Ari settled the youngest of Marai's wives began to quietly talk in her sleep.

"He'll be home, MaMa. Tomorrow. We'll know something tomorrow. My heart says tomorrow." She sighed and settled again. Ari smoothed the young woman's night-colored hair and nuzzled her neck affectionately.

"Shh, Baby One. Go back to sleep," she whispered, still unnerved by the clarity of Naibe's words – as if a spirit had been speaking through her. "Hope you're right."

Ari wanted to believe the former shepherd who had ushered she and her sister-wives to Kemet over a year ago would be home from his studies with the priests across the river.

She lay sweating on her pallet, thinking of carrying it up to the rooftop to sleep, but knew she'd likely wake the others. After long moments, she rose, stepped outside onto the landing outside their door, and strained to seek Marai across the river. Her thoughts bounced back at her as if they hit a wall the first time and then the second.

Must be too tired to pay attention, she sighed, then startled awake with the greying sky of day.

Fell asleep in the doorway? Odd, she reflected, taking in her surroundings in the courtyard below.

Still early. I don't hear anything except for birds on the river. Better get up and get the days water before it gets crowded. The cistern water is even getting tainted now. Throwing on a loose shirt to guard against the dawn mist, she took the water jar down in hopes of being earlier than the other women who took their own jars from the well. Barely able to see the stone-lined sides, she lowered the jar in its rope harness until it paused on the surface of the water, gurgled, and then sank. When Ari felt it was full, she tugged and drew the jar up. As she did, a sound from the apartment made its way down to the courtyard. The eldest of Marai's three wives pushed her russet curls out of her eyes and tasted the water, then spat and cursed over its condition. *Still better than the river. Might have to start boiling it to get the filth to settle out. And there's Deka – chanting her tune again. Means she's worried. Hope she can keep it from Baby One. I'm in no mood for her night terrors to start again.*

Trying to distract herself, Ari sent a mental signal: *Deka! Stick your head out here!*

In moments the woman's face emerged from behind the dark drape. She made a gesture of rubbing her eyes as if she had been crying, then pointed at the floor inside the window.

I guess I thought about that too late. It's nightmares again, Ari shrugged. *Like a child, sometimes. Always the fear of a storm coming or about being lost from the rest of us. And it's up to me to put on a brave face and tell them not to worry – wrap the secrets in rainbows like always. Because I was a sneaky kuna and a thief, I now keep secrets so tight only Naibe can get in them and when she does, they give her nightmares.*

She sorted over the concerns that had developed when Marai's little messages stopped.

He said he'd be taking his trial soon and then come back to us, but I thought he sounded tired. She wondered now if he'd been trying to tell her something. Once more she mentally reviewed the images he'd sent of himself seated at the feet of an old man in a sunny plaza. He appeared to have a smile on his face as he sat in contemplation.

After her first suspicion of something not being right, she busied herself with Deka and Naibe as they worked for Etum Addi and sold candy, herbs, and cinnabar cedar bark that "came in through Ra-Kedet by way of the Great Green Sea" as she used to declare to passing shoppers. Now, six days later, the doubts were back.

Something's up, Ari sighed and pushed more of her curls away from her face and positioned the filled water jar on one of her wide shoulders. *Even Etum Addi was grumbling that he thought you wouldn't come back after he came up from the coast and saw you weren't here already. Probably wonders if his business will flounder when he and his family work it alone the way they did before. Funny man. Reminds me of old N'ahab, except with a real soul.* She looked up the path into the market area and saw women with jars approaching. Soon the crowd of wives and daughters ringed the cistern well, squeezing past her with pleasant enough greetings. Normally she wanted to stay and catch up on all the latest gossip, adding her own findings, but today was different.

Should have gone up already. I don't feel like talking.

Taking the jar from her shoulder to at least seem friendlier than she felt, Ari chatted with the women about the weather, the coming festivals of Ptah, and local gossip.

Satisfied she'd said her piece, she hoisted her jar to her shoulder again, but almost froze and almost dropped it.

The meddlesome inspector-priest who had visited before Marai left and had cast a spell on them all was suddenly standing in the group as if he was one of the women himself.

What the pus sucking – where did he come from? Wasn't there. I know he wasn't.

He was there, magic indigo cloak at his shoulders and backed by four peacekeepers who stood at a distance ready to protect.

Goddess. Get away. She whirled on instinct briefly creating her shroud of privacy in a glimmer of light-chased rainbow color, but backed it off when one of the women gathering at the well gasped at the sight of her winking out and then back again.

As soon as she gathered her wits enough to glance back at the Inspector, she saw his flat expression that made everything in her own vision blur.

And he's blocking me now. She quietly bowed her head, but as she did, she saw she was alone with the five men. The other women at the well had melted back into their homes, some even leaving their water jars. *Cowards. No sisterhood, I see. They know the last time this one showed up Marai left and hasn't been back.*

"May peace be with you this early day," the man spoke a formal greeting in perfect Kina.

Ari watched, distracted by the slim man's dark cloak that billowed as if it had its own will. He looked up the stairs to the cloth draped door of the apartment. "Are your sisters still asleep?"

Ari felt a vortex of terror begin to spin and suck in the back of her head when she heard the man's words. A freezing sensation crept over her heart. That feeling quickly became a clammy, sinking sickness which made the world at the well dissolve into blurs. "Something's wrong, isn't it?" she stammered. "Something's happened to Marai. That's why you're here, isn't it?" The priest looked down at her remark, any kind of expression well hidden. She couldn't tell if he agreed or disagreed with her.

When the Inspector looked up again, she found his face even harder to read than before.

"It is time for your audience with The Great One of Five," his voice remained quiet and even. "The tests have been completed and as promised, we have come for you and for the carved box the man Marai has left in your safekeeping," he folded his hands and waited for her response.

He. Done. He. You saying – her thoughts raced and her face screwed up in confusion because part of her wanted to scream, another part wanted to slap him, and yet another wanted jump for joy, kiss him, and run up the steps with the greatest news. She returned only a dumbfounded stare.

"If you could hurry and pack your things, we might cross the Asar and take care of this matter quickly."

Ari looked deeper into the man's dark eyes in a last-minute attempt to wrench out any deeper meaning to his words but met nothing beyond his bland face. She saw him notice what she was doing and slip his hand up to touch the glimmering crystal amulet that had been hidden in the folds of his travel cloak the last time he visited. Today, he wore it proudly so that it peeked out from under his beaded pectoral, as if he dared her or any random thief to take it.

The nerve of him, she lowered her eyes again. *Watch him try to cast on me and me not able to do more than call my power to start a bigger fight with all five and then what?*

Putting on a visibly false face, Ari replied: "I see. I'll get the others." She set the full jar down by the well then broke into a run toward the worn sun-brick steps, squawking: "Deka! Naibe! Get Up! Get Up! It's time! That priest is here!"

Ari zipped past Deka who had just emerged from the draped door. She skidded across the floor to her basket of things. Digging deep in the folded cloth shifts, she lifted a carved wooden box. Snapping it open, she quickly saw that all the Children of Stone were still tucked safely inside.

Really? Will we see him? Her thoughts sighed out to the crystalline and smooth stones as she waited for their glimmering response.

They have come.
Take all here but eight
You will choose
Take those apart from the others.
Remember how to live
It is time.
Remember, Remember Wise One
How to live!

Ari didn't like the way the Children's message sounded. *Remember how to live? I said that to Marai in a dream, I think. I'm not sure.* She slapped the box shut.

"Is it time?" Naibe sat up from her mat, no longer slow-moving or sleepy. "Did Marai speak to you in the night? Did he say something?" She fastened her shift and patted the loops of her braided hair, lamenting that they were scrambled from sleep.

"The priest who came to us before has come back," Deka answered her, then stuck her own head out of the window to look. Ducking back in, she announced: "This time he's come with men!"

GOING FORTH BY DAY

"Men?" Naibe rustled, but Ari paid little attention to her comment or the growing atmosphere of uncertainty and hurry in their little room. She sighed and slid down the wall. *Is everything alright?* she opened the box one more time, sending her thoughts through her hands and into the stones. Once again, the Children pulsed faintly in recognition.

Truth waits for all
There we must go
The ones who do not know us
Must not touch the eight
That see —
Keep these safe
Keep them hidden

The voices that sounded like children hushed through Ari's heart. She knew the answer.

"We have to go to Marai now. The men are going to take us to him," Ari smirked, trying to look cheerful and winsome. "The Inspector said to take our things. The men are here to help us carry them to a boat, I guess. Nice, eh?" She set the box down and poked her head out of the door to see the Inspector and the men milling about in the courtyard below. One of the peacekeepers was halfway up the steps and another was at the foot. Ari knew they had been commenting about the rabble's frantic sorting.

"We're dressing. We'll be ready soon! Just give us some more time!" Ari called out to the men, hoping they wouldn't barge in just as much as she hoped neither Naibe nor Deka would sense how uneasy the Inspector's sudden appearance had made her. Tucking any misgivings into a silence so deep that even Naibe would not be able to see it, she drew her head back inside.

"Marai's teacher sent this man to get us and he told us to bring the Children of Stone. It's time to go. Just move yourselves!" Ari paced in the middle of the floor as Deka and Naibe dressed, lined their eyes, and dabbed some light rouges on their lips.

Realizing they would be gone a while, they rolled up their mats and belongings, stuffing them into baskets. While they worked in silence, Ari secreted herself into a rear corner of the apartment, turned her back, and opened the Children's box. She sorted out the first eight stones that appeared to glimmer more brightly than the others, then quickly closed the box again.

The eight. What in the goddess name? These? Why? she asked herself and the stones, but there wasn't an answer. *Hide them. How?* She strapped a braided leather belt around the box to keep it fastened, then found a slim leather bag for pins and fasteners which she emptied into a larger basket. She put the chosen stones into the bag.

"Hide these in the bottom of one of the baskets. I don't want anyone but Marai touching these. You remember that stupid boy on the way here that got his hands burned off." She handed the box to Naibe to hide in the bottom of one of the baskets. Dressing next, Ariennu dropped her wide work apron around her ankles, stepped out of it, and changed into a better shift. While the other women were occupied with the last of the packing, she hid the bag with the eight stones under her skirt and bound it securely to her midriff with a large sash, pressing out the bulge in dismay.

Won't work. I should stick them up my kuna but for the misery it'd bring every time I took a step, she smirked, then sent her thoughts through the child stone in her brow: *You want these hidden and safe, you'd better inspire me.*

"Mama," Naibe's voice sounded small with concern. She returned from the window where Ari assumed she had been spying on the men below and the effect it was having on any of their neighbors. "I saw that man talking to Etum Addi and then Etum looked like something was bothering him."

"Oh, we can't worry about him right now, Baby," Ari responded to the 'Mama' nickname in kind. "I'm sure when we're back he'll tell us all about it."

But then, another thought surfaced. *Except maybe he won't even be here when we get back. Heard him talking about Ra-Kedet the other day, like he wanted to stay there. Marai thought we might all go together when this is over.*

"Some kind of writ the Inspector showed him, I think," Naibe added, making Ari wonder if she had pulled some of the thoughts from the men.

"I wouldn't worry," Ari decided to distract the young woman. "Besides, the Children sang it to me that we have to do this. And – we're going to be with Marai soon!" she beckoned for Naibe to help roll up the last of their things.

Within the hour, just as the market began to open for the day, the women presented themselves. Their apartment had been stripped bare, except for a few baskets just inside that the peacekeepers would carry. They left only the curtaining they had made from the tent that sheltered them when Marai and they had first made their way on the Copper Road to Ineb Hedj.

Walking down their steps one by one, they each carried a brightly painted basket with their personal things inside. Ari, the last to leave, pointed up the steps as they eased past the peacekeepers and quietly mentioned the few remaining baskets. Soon, the men brought the rest of their possessions down the steps.

With a sad but proud look in his eyes, Etum Addi embraced and kissed each one of the women as if they were his own daughters being sent away to meet their bridegrooms. When he came to Ari, he paused and gave her a big hug that spawned only one thought: *N'ahab. There's a cruel joke. Used to wish he'd been a better man. Wonder if the gods were listening – sent him back to me. Over now though. Goddess! This has even made a lump in my throat. Wonder if the others have thought it too?* She sought Deka's expression, then Naibe's, but they were hugging the women in his family. Even Raawa and her baby came out, thanking them again for their help in her difficult birthing.

Naibe stood on tiptoe to kiss the tip of Etum Addi's nose. He tousled her hair and whispered in her ear: "now you go on, little goddess. You go make him some fine sons and daughters. And if that thing across the river doesn't work out, you four come down to Ra-Kedet and look for old Etum-Addi, eh?"

"Oh, you got the writ? Then –" Naibe turned, but Ariennu quickly tugged her away and pushed her along to catch up with Deka and the Inspector before the peacekeepers noticed she was lagging behind.

Chapter 2: Things Fall Apart

Ariennu of Tyre, known to those close to her as Ari or Red Ari watched every move the Inspector made as he led their parade to the downstream dock area. He held his head high as he walked in front of her, Deka, and Naibe. Behind them, the peacekeepers pulled for the duty followed. One of the lightly armed men silently accompanied the indigo-robed priest while the three others moved behind the women, carrying their baskets which had been filled with everything they owned. In the top of one of the baskets were packages of honey and date candy to be used as gifts for the royalty when they met. In another basket, hidden in the bottom, sat the carved wood box containing the Children of Stone.

When everyone arrived at the water's edge, the men helped the women climb onto a modest sized wooden boat that was moored to a stone post along the dock and under more guard by attending oarsmen. The task of boarding complete, the men pushed off into the murky water. Ari thought about Naibe's joy and the sheer innocence the young woman exuded.

Excitement. Look at her, happy like a child on a new adventure!

"Oh, MaMa Ari," the girl whispered. "A real wooden boat, not a straw and reed one." She ran her fingertips over the brass fittings on the rail near her plank seat. "See how bright these are? I know someone polishes these every day. The boat even has a name. See these markings?"

Ari glanced at the characters painted on the bow. She'd read enough of the Kemet writing, but never studied it.

Simple name, she thought, momentarily distracted from her suspicions. *Sun's Wisdom.*

"Says Sun's Wisdom she whispered back to both Deka and Naibe.

Sun's Wisdom, she heard Deka repeat in her thoughts. She sat beside the Ta-Seti woman in the midsection of the boat and Naibe sat on the other passenger plank.

GOING FORTH BY DAY

Peacekeepers sat in front and behind them. When he saw everything was in order, the Inspector moved to a shaded cabin-like area near the bow.

As the men pushed away from the mooring with the long steering oars and the other men began to row to a light rhythmic chanty praising the sun, Naibe giggled as if truly giddy in expectation of both the coming reunion and the finery in which they now travelled.

Naibe marveled aloud at the black-green water churning past the dark bow, leaned over the edge, and carefully stuck her hand in the river. She giggled again, shook the water off her hand, and wiped it on her dress.

Laughing! Look at her! Ari shook her head in disbelief at the changed mood. *And last night Deka says she was sobbing for our Marai. She's so much like a little girl. Even with everything harsh that's happened in our lives!* Ari's thoughts briefly reviewed her life before Marai had come into it.

From a childhood full of fending for herself as her mother drifted between men in the coastal and Tyrean towns of Kina-Ahna, Ariennu had learned many lessons about life long before others her age.

Mother tried to kill me for catching the eye and el of a man she had in mind. From that day I learned I was better off alone. Still ended up with some mean-hearted humps and hangers on. Thought I was going to die that way but, you Marai? She silently addressed the air. *You changed that. You and these Child Stones I guard did that.*

Drifting in the morning sun that had begun to get hotter, Ari remembered the early morning when Marai had been brought as a captive into the camp where they lived. He stood there, tall, full of muscles, and beautiful. His hair gleamed like the bright moon; his skin shone like new copper.

You were such a pretty thing, looking like a god. I was about to die of yellows and the other two of us weren't much better. Why you would pity us still gets me. Why you would even want us to be whole and walk with you. She shook her head, wondering why these thoughts were coming to her now. They felt like finality.

Ariennu patted the narrow purse she had nestled under her upper skirt with some concern. *Didn't expect to fall for you. I've had too many people in and out of my life and once I used them up it was always on to the next prospect. I didn't think it would hurt like it does not having you beside me at night and loving on me the way you do. Lots to think of these three weeks you've been over here studying with these priests. Something's not right.*

What's wrong? Is it something about Marai? Naibe-Ellit's thoughts interrupted her musings.

Uh-oh. She saw through it. Hard not to. That Inspector himself is trying to bury something. Ari glanced at Naibe, then at the Inspector seated in his cloth draped cabin. She saw his hard stare in the direction of the white walled estates and followed his line of sight toward the causeways that spilled out to the river.

Shh. Don't worry, Brown Eyes. We'll be with him soon. Ari clapped her arm around the young woman and tried to reassure her when every part of her except the part that sent that thought wanted to shout: *No! You need to worry. Something's wrong.* She knew that if everything had been perfect, the Inspector would have been open and at least as friendly to them as he had been three weeks before when he first came to them. He might have spoken about the festival, his boat, even expected modes of behavior in front of royalty. Instead, the boat trip was silent except for the cadence chant sung for the rowers by their leader.

Once the boat had reached the opposite shore, servants quickly secured it and lowered a plank for the unloading of the women and their baskets.

As the equally silent parade approached some high wooden gates, the Inspector instructed the women in the necessary homage and forms of address for both himself and his senior: "Great One" and "Lord Inspector of the Ways". *So formal,* Ari sniffed. Two gate guards on duty ushered everyone through the tall, carved cedar gates of the estate. Her heart rushed again because this was the vision of the place she'd seen Marai sitting while he studied.

The nearly bare, shaded alcove opened out onto a spacious and sunny plaza that surrounded a wide-but-shallow lotus-filled reflection pool. Woven mats and soft, pleasant cushions adorned the tile-edged pool. The setting and surroundings invited one to take a refreshing dip on a hot day.

The old man. Ari thought. *That's the one connected with this Djedi that Marai was told to find.*

The elder sat under an awning in a dark stone throne stuffed with pillows. From his vantage point, Ari knew the man could survey his plaza and pool as if they were part of his miniature peaceful kingdom.

She opened herself for any sensation of Marai as they waited, but found herself glancing at Deka. She clearly heard the woman thinking: '*Long ago, when I was wealthy –*'

Naibe broadcast no further thoughts, but she stroked the white pearly walls to see it some of the crushed lime surface would come off on her fingertips.

Yeah, lime dust walls. Ari's memory flashed with visions of her much younger self slipping over walls like that in her days as a thief to charm whoever was inside. She almost giggled. *Got that stuff all over me back then. Had to dust off before anyone ever saw me or they'd know.*

Her thoughts were interrupted by the sight of Deka, followed by Naibe who studied and copied her moves, going to her knees on the mats between the pool and the dais where the elder sat. Ari half-stumbled, smirked in embarrassment, and knelt with them. No sooner than she did, more feelings of uneasiness swept over her.

Where's Marai? I can't sense him, she thought. *I understand when we were across the river, I might not have been able but if he's here, I should.* She couldn't sense Marai anywhere near.

Marai, she tried again. *Damn you, Marai, show yourself. Make a noise. Do something.* She felt her heart pounding in her ears but remained bent over in respect. The Inspector whispered something to his elder, then the old man spoke:

"As I speak your names you may rise and look on me."

Perfect voice. No old-man warble, Ari thought.

"ArrEnu, DhKa, NaBtd-EyT," he spoke the women's names with a thick but elegant Kemet accent.

Ari felt Naibe's hand tremble as the young woman slipped it inside hers for reassurance as the old man addressed them.

I can't feel him, Ari. He's not here. He was supposed to be. Where is he? Naibe's thoughts sought her.

I know, Baby, I know. Somewhere else, maybe. Let's just get through this part and maybe then they'll take us to him. Ari answered her thought, even though her doubts were about to choke her. If Marai had been there, she knew nothing on Earth or in Heaven would have prevented him from striding into this pretty plaza and taking them in his joyous arms. *Why isn't he here? What's wrong?* she glanced around the open area.

Then, once the women looked up, the elderly man in the chair pushed himself into a standing position. The Inspector moved toward him instinctively to steady him, but his elder waved him away and faced the women directly.

"We of Great Djehuti have news of your husband," the old man began, gently and almost quietly. "He did exceptionally well in the offered trials. This man Marai astonished all of us that he was able to learn our truths so easily. We instructed him to the best of our ability. When our part had been completed, he did inquire as to what normally lay next and we answered to him that there were certain tests and trials to undergo. We told him that it was not necessary to take them, that he was free to return, but he stated those who had sent him wished his heart unlocked fully." The elder paused as if scanning them or at least pausing to breathe. "We warned him that the final test would be far too dangerous for a mere sojourner to undertake."

Ari heard the old man's voice chattering and saw his mouth moving, but she already knew what was coming next.

What? He's dead? Goddess, you bastards murdered him! The blood left her face in a rush and her heart felt as if a cold hand gripped and wanted to tear it out by the roots.

"We did all that we could to dissuade him as we knew the dangers, but it was not enough. I'm quite afraid your husband has left this realm to drift in the Field of Reeds," the elder priest and his Inspector bowed their heads in a solemn moment of respectful silence, giving the women time for their words to sink in.

Ari glanced helplessly at Deka's bowed head and watched as her cinnamon-colored arm went around Naibe-Ellit's waist. Naibe's face paled to the color of sun-bleached wood. Her eyes cast up to the sky, showing only the whites as her mouth gaped.

Gonna faint. Catch her. Goddess, God! Ari groaned internally but saw Deka had a good grip on the young woman.

A high-pitched whimper like a dreadful keening of the first syllable of his name, issued from Naibe's throat and chest. "Ma… Ma… Ma…" her gasping voice caught on each painful syllable as every part of her nightmares shot through Ari's and Deka's Child Stones. Her knees buckled. As Ari stood, hard and unmoved she saw the Inspector take a step forward to support Naibe. The elder's dark arm snapped out to stay him.

"Where *is* he?" Ari felt words come out of her mouth, but she couldn't feel them form in her heart before she spoke. "Where – Is – He?" she shrieked once. She didn't care *where* she was or *to whom* she was speaking. Pulling herself up as tall as she could, she sensed herself becoming as tall as an avenging giantess, but knew it was an illusion. All the hatred that raged in her stopped as if her Child Stone blocked it.

Listen.

The voice inside Ariennu whispered, but she didn't want to hear it.

Damn you! You let him kill N'ahab. Let me kill.

Listen

To what they tell you.

"Where does he lie? I will see him *now*," Ari ordered; fists clenched at her side. Tears started, then stopped, but the pit of her stomach heaved almost as badly as when she suffered from the diseases brought on by drink and lack of care.

I won't cry. Not now, and maybe not ever again. If he's dead, then so is my heart!

"I – I'm afraid you cannot see him, my poor dear." the elder man's demeanor became paternal and even meek.

Ari simmered just below seething rage at the man's words.

"You vile – I'll rip the sweet off your face, throw it down and step on it. Lie! Both of you lie!"

With a slight stammer as the only indication his demeanor had changed, the elder explained once more.

"You *must* understand. We warned him! There is just nothing left to *see*," he held forward the torn shirt Ari had woven for Marai and handed it to her.

Ari snatched at it, then reverently untied the red sash on which Naibe had embroidered little gold bulls. It had been nicely washed and folded. For just a moment she studied the way it had been torn across the shoulder, then let the tunic fall loose in her hands

Oh, not too bad. I could sew this, and he could still – Her thoughts stopped dead as she suddenly realized he would never wear it again. Lovingly smoothing the place where it had been torn, Ari envisioned Marai transform into an image of a Bull-Man the moment it had torn. *Why, Marai? Was that when it happened?* she groaned still asking his hopefully lurking spirit: *Why'd you do that in front of these bastards?* As she saw the shift, she tried to visualize him consumed by mystical and godly flame sent by the men in response to his act, but instead she heard the Inspector's thoughts:

See how they loved him, Great One. This is so very sad!

The elder gestured for him to keep his thoughts silent as the sash with the little gold bulls slipped from the tunic in Ari's hands.

"Care? Act like you care, murderer!" Ari hissed under her breath in Kina. Deka seized the sash before it touched the floor, as if allowing it to drop would have been a sacrilege. Naibe took it in her trembling hands and clutched it to her breasts.

"No –" she moaned "I –don't– feel him," her mouth opened and choking noises came from her throat.

Damn, Ari knew the young woman was about to sink into the same sleep she had embraced the day the Inspector came. *You promised him you wouldn't but – yeah, go to him,*

GOING FORTH BY DAY

Baby – I'll be sent along to join you after I send some of these devils straight into Sheol!

Deka added in sympathy. "No, Brown Eyes, you promised him, you promised him – stay with us." she gripped the young woman tightly.

Ari, who had been standing half-paralyzed over the idea of the priest's audacity in bringing them across the river merely to confront them suddenly broke free of her spell.

They're gonna kill me, but good if I make them! Wanted to go this way before you came, you big ox, and at that point she strode up to the elder priest and spat in his face. The peacekeepers fell on her, seized her, and slapped her soundly, but when they tried to bind her arms behind her back, she wrenched arms, kneed balls, and bit ears until more guards came to hold her down.

Somewhere in the middle of the fight, Ari sensed more than saw the old man raise his hand carefully and gesture. She cackled hysterically, but as she did she felt agony building inside her head. She was almost too angry to notice the pain, but soon she sagged in the men's arms and stumbled, unable to control her hands or feet.

"Kill you all!" she screeched, struggling, but the pain in her Child Stone immobilized her.

Triumphantly, one of the peacekeepers gripped a war mace and waited on a nod from the elder that would order Ariennu's death.

Instead, the old man's expression changed to one of bewilderment. He smiled, the edge of his worn teeth showing.

"Now, I don't wish to end you, dear woman. But you must simply –" the priest took a step forward "calm yourself."

You're smiling at me, you sick little keleb! her thoughts screeched. She struggled in the men's grip, working against the paralysis of the elder's spell. Then her eyes fogged, and she lost the power to see.

My stone. No. Ari felt no voice or surge of energy. Her legs tripped under her body as the guards dragged her.

Heavy. I'm too heavy for you, she sagged hard in their grip to resist them.

"Go on! Beat me, you fools! Harder! Put in some good ones," she mocked, twisting her body so she could see.

The old man's attendants rushed forward with a linen towel to wipe his face. She stumbled and tried to kick as the Inspector and another attendant brought their baskets of clothing into the clear area. The box containing the Children of Stone was almost too easily found and handed to the elder priest.

The pain in Ari's head eased when the elder looked at the box and then nodded in approval.

One of the guards lifted Ari's bound arms high enough behind her that her body bent forward.

Listen

A sudden internal whisper alerted her. The clutch of the stones tucked in her sash had loosened.

There.

Ari felt the surge of comfort move partway and wanted to chide the tardy child voice, but stopped. She understood what the Children's message had meant earlier.

Listen to what they tell you.
Hold the others in your hand.

She paused in her struggle and remained bent over, taking in the rest of the scene she'd been too angry to see. Deka clung hard to Naibe, as if gripping her fast would somehow keep her from sinking into unconsciousness. Still in pain from the scuffle and blows she received, yet no less enraged, Ari noticed the elder priest clear his throat. He sat down in his chair that seemed more and more like an imposing black throne. With a calm and somewhat indifferent expression, he sipped at a cup of liquid a third clustering attendant brought him.

A tremor in the plaza's atmosphere distracted her as a silent and catlike snarl came from Deka who still held a quickly fading Naibe.

Old man who plays at being a god. I see you satisfied at the pain you bring. Soon you will see me and know that what beats in my heart and soul is far older and waits for the hour when it will destroy the last of your hope.

Bone Woman? What? Ari valiantly wriggled in the peacekeeper's grip watching as the old man frowned. She knew he had received the Ta-Seti woman's message. His expression implied first that he was amused and ready to dismiss her thoughts as madness and demented boasting, but then his look sobered.

"Take these women to the dry storeroom near the garden until they have gathered their wits, Dear One." the elder gestured at the air with his fingertips to the Inspector. "Have the guards stay with them so they do not run amok and cause any more distress. When they have managed to calm themselves, I will put them in the women's common and have our sweet ones attend them properly there." Then, he sighed in a manner that seemed almost petulant as he indicated for his assistant to lift a chair to the wide dais and sit next to him. "I must meditate on what to do with them. Now however –" he turned his attention to the box that had been given to him.

As Ari saw the old man lift the box, she shouted one last time: "Liar! Both of you! There *was* no trial. No gods punished *anyone*. You both did it all. You stink of evil. Cursed black vomit from the Baal you eat."

Then, she stopped, heartbroken.

But you were fooled by them, Marai, you poor stupid man. I should have been with you. I warned you. Every part of her soul ached along with the bruises the men had given her. Marai's messages to her had never portrayed anything but his confidence in the men.

This was all about the damned box, Ari sighed inwardly as the peacekeepers led them away. *He didn't bring the Children with him. That's the only reason we were brought across the river – the only real reason.* Summoning more vitriol, she added:

"Why don't you go and open the box, you greedy old seed sucking *keleb*," she shrieked at the old man. "Take 'em all out and play with them! I dare you!"

Take the eight

The breathy interior child-voice that sounded almost like Naibe whispered to her, reminding her again.

The eight. I know, but what do I do? She remembered the errant and uncomfortable thought she'd had about inserting the slim bag of stones between her legs. *Make a kuna case? Women raiders like me needing to hide something, then we just claim it's a sponge for the moon blood. But they're putting us with other women. They'd find out. I'd end up hurting someone.*

On the old man's signal, the guards pushed, shoved and kicked her down the hall. Though she didn't even want to look at the others, she knew Deka and Naibe were being pushed along behind her.

Done! No more sweet little merchants. Goddess this wasn't supposed – she shifted between half-thoughts directed and Marai if his spirit still roamed near enough to hear them. *We were supposed to be un-killable, but if they found a way to kill you, Marai, then Naibe's dreams were right. It'll only be a matter of time, once they get tired of playing with us. No better than N'ahab and the boys with a band of desert rats. Tricks, traps, and tortures, then leave them for the dogs. I just thought it was going to be different for us.*

GOING FORTH BY DAY

Chapter 3: Two Princes

"Over here now, Wse dear —" Hordjedtef prodded the Lord Inspector of the Ways after the guards hustled the women down the hall to the dry storeroom. "— and do not concern yourself the females' welfare. No harm will come to them, but they must contain themselves before I speak to them again."

Prince Wserkaf stepped back away from the hall and the rabble moving down it, then faced his elder who added:

"Now that we have these neters, we shall look at them, shall we not?"

The Inspector bowed, then took a seat beside Hordjedtef, who held the wooden box on his lap.

"Perhaps we should wait, Great One. There might be a spell. The woman Ariennu certainly tried to cast one."

"A weak attempt when I have words and a nau stone in this brace." The elder smirked and held up his left hand with a dark leather "x" brace on it. Where the two pieces joined there was a fitting bearing a thumbnail-sized polished chunk of desert glass. "See?"

Wserkaf had seen the piece rarely and had heard it was one of two pieces that had belonged to his teacher's own mentor, Great Djedi. There were secret words of an enchantment in some dead language too. He didn't like to use force when confronted, personally. The Inspector preferred illusion or confusion as weapons rather than pain. Hordjedtef had used that on the tall woman and had mentioned to him that he used words and the nau, once, on the man Marai at the start when the big man had disrespected him.

"But because you have warned an old man like myself, perhaps if you will recite them in tandem with me, copying each word I say and we lay both our hands on them in one movement?"

Wse notice the mischievous twinkle in the elder's eye that told him he knew no harm would come to either of them, but that they could make a show of it.

Together on the elder's cue the men carefully spoke the words:

Little stars —

Soul's embodiment of light and truth

Cast in crystal stone of Earth,

Understand us —

We bring you no harm,

You need not fear us.

Or selves defend

"What a charming verse!" Wse smiled as a thrill raced through him that felt like chattering children. He'd felt it a few times when he had been talking with the man Marai. Today, he knew he needed to keep silent because it seemed his teacher felt little if anything.

"Isn't it?" Hordjedtef beamed and eagerly threw open the box, grabbing Wse's hand and placing it on the stones inside.

Their thoughts were filled with peaceful images of sun and the calm, beautiful River Asar as they touched, so that these stone creatures would be reassured and not bring them any harm. A gentle purr emanated from the stones, as if the beings inside them read the hands that caressed them. The Inspector knew at once that something wasn't right about the sensations he and his master felt. Instead of a flash of light or some mysterious energy signature, the so-called *Child Stones* or neters lay inside the open case like a heap of ordinary river or quarry rock. The only difference was the barely noticeable hum.

"Humph," Prince Hordjedtef shrugged, moving his hand independently to paw through the stones. Nothing happened to him.

"*These* can't be the keys. The Set-haired ka't must have switched them out. I think we've been taken for fools again, Wse," he picked up one of the stones that was the size of a small nut and examined it. "And yet –"

As Wserkaf watched, Hordjedtef held an unpolished looking piece of ore that didn't glow.

"Warm," he said then quickly chose stone after stone remarking how each 'felt' different from the other.

"Take these and talk to me about them Wse," the elder scowled then quickly asked one more question instead of waiting for the Inspector to speak: "Now, *how* would one use these to unlock the secrets? If this is more code –" he fretted, thinking aloud. "I suppose these *could* indeed be of the heavens, but our ancestors knew of such stones. We've gathered them and shaped them into simple charms and beads for years. I presume even this piece I've worn today might have come from Tjemehu land."

"Perhaps we shouldn't have gotten rid of their messenger so zealously," Wserkaf muttered loudly enough for his mentor to perceive and choose to ignore. "Now we'll need a soul-binder to find him and compel him, *or* we'll have to force the women to show us more if they *will*." The Inspector got up from his cane chair that had been beside his elder's chair. "Now that their beloved one has been dispatched; I somehow don't think they'll want to."

"An astute observation, Dear One," Hordjedtef paused, "but as we both observed, we dealt with no easily worked simpleton. His rudeness, which I entertained at first, would never have been tolerated in earlier times. In the end, I felt such behavior would never be modified and might prove threatening to Our Wonderous Majesty. Those few of my brethren with whom I discussed it agreed."

But you didn't discuss it with me, after assigning me to become more accommodating to the brute, which I did and discovered a high sense of nobility about the man. Wserkaf bowed his head in false humility, realizing what Marai had said to him on one of his last days. Hordjedtef, after a lifetime of teaching him and shaping his every thought, kept him at arms distance and didn't give him the level of trust or credit he gave others in the priestly ranks.

"I understand, Great One," Wserkaf nodded. "Shall we then use trances and the wdjat I wear to unlock these keys?"

"That, and in time we shall reopen the box where the Akkad's body lies and harvest the small shining stone imbedded in his forehead once his unprepared corpse has withered." He paused to take another sip of his tea infused with restoratives he'd developed over the years.

Wserkaf wanted to stop listening and to open the box in the privacy of some unappointed chamber. *There's something,* he thought and the unspoken other thought returned.

That never was here before.

"So, Great One, how will taking the neter from his skull help?" the Inspector asked.

"If there is sense under the universe and these are indeed the true neter stones, and not some mere group of baubles fit for a jeweler, one would think our diligence in obtaining the knowledge of the gods and sorting truth for Goddess Ma-at from scores of lies would point out that we were the intended recipients of them all along, wouldn't you think?" the elder offered another cup of the medicinal tea to his assistant. "Something to gladden the stomach and sooth the heart?"

Wserkaf obediently took the drink, knowing there would be some herbal calmative containing mostly garlic sweetened with date honey. As he sipped, he knew the teacher's thoughts were racing about his next step. The women had been brought over and had been given their worst possible news. The Inspector and his mentor knew the women also possessed neter stones and might be more resilient to influence than common sojourned women. He opened the subject first.

"The women. That's the next thing, isn't it? We have them here, have these stones they were keeping, and now they blame us for the man's death, as they should. I wouldn't think we should cut them loose at this point, should we?"

"Exactly. I'd say it is *highly* important that we show these women some respect, despite their scorn of us, shouldn't we, Wse?" In silence, he folded his hands so that his forefingers touched his pursed lips. "Allow me to think about this very briefly."

Wserkaf bowed and placed the empty cup on the table. He meandered in the plaza and did a few stretches designed to promote the release of tension, then noticed Hordjedtef beckon and clear his throat. When he had returned to his teacher the man related his ideas, beginning with:

"You *did* know they were the lowest of women at the start of things, didn't you?" the elder beckoned for Wserkaf to sit again.

"Not sure. I know only what I saw that day and reported. I saw nothing of their past."

"They were trader's ka't, no value to them and apt to allow any sort of treatment of their bodies as long as they might be fed. My senses tell me their keepers never saw to their welfare and they had become mad or sick or both. Our most unfortunate sojourner told me that himself."

Wserkaf noticed a slight expression of disdain filtering over his master's face as he continued to speak of the women. He tried to relax. The garlic potion helped, but he still felt ill at ease listening to the sorting of his master's thoughts.

And it used to be a joy to listen to you old man, he sighed inwardly, now wishing to find any sort of emergency that might cause him to need to leave.

"Evidently, he pitied their lowly and humbled selves regardless of how many men had plowed their overturned fields," the elder continued to muse while the Inspector carefully took the box containing the Children of Stone from him and placed it safely on the pedestal nearby.

"Great One," he interjected. "I don't see why we can't offer them a widow's pension as we do our sojourned workers. They might return to The Poors to work with the gentleman who had employed them," he strained his ears to pick up sounds from the direction where the women had been taken. He knew they were skilled in some forms of heka and hoped they weren't back there casting some of it on the guards placed over them.

"Oh!" Hordjedtef paused as if he was truly amazed his second in command would suggest that. "Didn't you see to the spice seller as I asked?"

Wserkaf nodded.

"Then you *did* give him the King's writ to take his business to the seacoast, Ra Kedet I believe, Mmmm?" The elder inquired; his ancient eyelids, thin and almost translucent, drifted over his half-shut eyes. "Didn't you open it and read it yourself? If it bore no seal, you know it's allowed of those in our discipline to do so – especially under the circumstances." He smiled in such a wistful manner that Wserkaf instantly knew there was another layer of intrigue.

Circumstances. The man had made request to barter on the royal side and to check on moving his business to the coast. Wserkaf recalled he had wanted to read it before he handed it to the merchant but had been so upset over having to fetch the women that he forgot.

"Our ever-forward-thinking Majesty simply offered to pay the man's expenses, if he could leave to set things up in that city within the week," the elder began to sigh in exasperation. "Which brings us back to our three *new* guests," Hordjedtef's lips pursed. "As widows of a usurper, or at best a storied man, and not an honest sojourner worker, they will likely be *shunned* in any neighborhood they attempt to visit and soon will become destitute without our protection." After only a moment's pause, he suddenly added: "So, then, they are far from their homes and have no family or friend to return to? I believe they are at the mercy of our decisions," the elder's eyes blinked shut once. "If we turn them out, they go back to our lesser subjects and soon enough will need to make their way bartering their flesh as they did before this Marai bin Ahu harvested them – a shame for ones so comely, wouldn't you agree?"

Wserkaf nodded mutely, amazed at his teacher's instantly crafted manipulation.

Incredible. They have committed no crime for us to hold them but that's what you suggest – the crime of associating with questionable company. He had at one time admired the old man's skill. Now, it shocked him.

"What about their heka?" Wserkaf asked. "As you have agreed, they have it through their own neters and could turn it on us out of vengeance."

"Yes. True. I did think of that. They could be quite dangerous," Hordjedtef continued. "Let me chance that they haven't gained full strength; certainly not as much as the man Marai and he was stunningly naïve." Hordjedtef paused, licked his lips, and then lightly touched a small gong at his table, signaling another attendant to refresh his cup.

As soon as the youth walked out on quiet feet, bowed to the two men, and then set the cup before the elder, he left. Hordjedtef continued. "So, I would wager this: what if we were to give them an uplifting and positive direction for the applying of their beautiful and magical skills? As we teach our own daughters, beautiful women foster greatness in their brothers and in their sons," he sipped. "Treated as high-born ones, they might even find love again among some of our esteemed ones, wouldn't you say?"

Wserkaf said nothing but nodded as if he was contemplating the wise words.

I hope he's tired. He seems tired. I know he wanted the use of the neter stones to be both obvious and easy but it isn't. He really hoped the sojourner influence would be done with.

But you see, now.

A quiet but musical whisper entered the Inspector's thoughts and then left them just as quickly. Without being noticed, he looked toward the hallway where the guards had hauled the women to see if one of them had returned. No one had. He was alone with his thoughts and his senior was alone with his schemes.

After a few moments, Hordjedtef reached for the box, opened it, and began to pick through the stones.

"This one. A lapis I think. And there is this dawn colored one and a pale crescent moon shaped one – this malachite one reminds me of something. I think they are coded – as if we are meant to find out about each one. They purr like a sunny day miw – very comforting, I must say."

"But you see, now," that voice said. He didn't hear it. See? It just gives a little more credence to that tired old legend my parents tried to spell into reality – that I was a son of Ra. So much dung. He shook his head while Hordjedtef continued pawing and sorting the various stones, as if he was looking for a special one.

But then the tall woman with the red-kissed hair taking up my mother's spirit? It made me wonder if part of this was true. Not the son of Ra part. I was sired by Userre and my mother was Princess Neferhetepes, Priestess of Hethara and Mistress of the Sycamore. This was about finding the keys of wisdom inscribed on lapis, crystal, and emerald stone tablets. Father had even called her Redjeddet, the name spoken in the legend, as the woman who would bear the triplet kings and would alone be able to lead the wise to the unlocking of the keys. It had been a good-hearted jest. She didn't have three sons. She had me and then miscarried twin boys so many years later. I studied at Father's temple in Per-A-At and was expected to go into the cult of Ra, but I preferred mystery and healing and then went to study in the discipline of Djehuti. Somehow, it was the beginning of the end between father and I and then my mother died not long after. So much for faith in legends.

The elder cleared his throat. "Thoughts, Wse?"

"Oh, nothing. I was just thinking about my mother. About how looking for these artifacts like they and Djedi did, consumed them."

"She was a great woman, Wse. I know she looks in on you sometimes," he added and then closed the box. "We can study these later," Hordjedtef whispered. "You have guessed correctly. I need to rest – to bring myself level after that – that wretched woman insulted me. I'm still tempted to send a wraith to strangle her draggle-tailed self and that wouldn't be entirely helpful. I have a plan and will send runners right away with the messages for a gathering tonight where they will be presented." The elder rang for another attendant to help him to his quarters.

"I need you to go to the dry store-room to check on them, would you? That first," Hordjedtef spoke quickly to the Inspector again, running a verbal rapid-fire list of things that needed to happen. "I will meet you after I pray upon the Countess' maids to get those creatures washed and purified according to a more civilized custom. I'll ask the Lady Countess to supervise them as they bathe, if she would, and get her sister to play soothing music for them. Do see they are given calmatives to drink and intoxicants to inhale. We need them to be in an excellent state as quickly as possible," the old man had reached into the folds of the cloak which he had bundled up behind himself as extra chair padding. He drew out a curved dagger, not as glorious as the one he used in ceremony, but still sharp and useful. Handing it to Wserkaf, he continued: "Take this, and don't be afraid to use it if you have to."

"Great One, are they now our captives –" Wserkaf asked, thinking: *That was fast.*

Secretly he planned this all along? A gathering of the elite? "– or will you allow them some freedom in the women's rooms until they are level?"

The Inspector assisted the old man in rising and steadied him with his attendant and his canes.

"So compassionate you are, Wse, but do you *truly* care about them?" Hordjedtef stared up into his protégé's eyes, then smirked. "Perhaps the young Shinar woman has continued the charm she wove over you those weeks ago?" he dropped his gaze. "I was thinking she might actually be the one to brighten the mood, as Hethara did for elder Ra, of our Great Majesty. Some other arrangement in one of our many noble houses could be made for the others," he turned and continued to reflect and plan as he did. "I'm sure His Majesty will want to meet them *all* this very evening if we can get them calm. Go, Wse. Tell them that. Speak to them about their options, and get the tall old girl to shut her disrespectful mouth for once. Once they are situated – comfortable –" his old eyes silvered just a bit in anticipatory greed. "Go, now."

So this must have been his plan soon after we dispatched the poor man; gather the women and somehow coerce them into reading the stones. Spoil and flatter them, dote on them and put them in noble houses as handmaidens or perhaps even concubines if they should catch someone's eye. After a while, then, he will convince them of his good intent. It's the way he has always worked. Wserkaf knew his senior well. Hordjedtef possessed the coldest intellect and discipline, laced with necessary honey-coated charm for all subjects in his realm. He was a true master of people, and of granting their desires bit by bit. *Charmed even me,* Wserkaf wondered suddenly how much of his flight to the Cult of Djehuti had been his own idea in the first place. *How much of my own thoughts and beliefs have been the old man's manipulation of the future of the Two Lands? Why did he need to lure me from study with my own father?* Wserkaf thought as the image of his mother's resolved but sad face the morning he left came to his mind. He wondered back then, as he did today, why the old man *really* needed to bring him under his *own* power and instruction. *Perhaps now that you have those stones in your presence, your true plans will be laid bare.*

GOING FORTH BY DAY

Chapter 4: The Arrangement

Ari couldn't bring herself to raise her eyes from the smooth brick floor in the empty, windowless storeroom. The guards had snatched the rope that bound her hands when they threw her headlong into the room in disgust. They were milling around and joking outside the doorway. As she listened, she heard them making occasional comments about bending her over something.

They might try, she scoffed, *and maybe this worthless rock in my skull will wake itself up and give me the power to burn their balls to nubbins when they do.*

She didn't know how long she had been lying there. She wasn't even listening for the voices of Naibe and Deka, although she thought she heard Deka gently singing to the younger woman. Outside, she heard voices of other women and knew they were coming to check on them. Further away, she heard the elder priest's voice rise and fall in an argument.

After another short while, she heard someone enter and recognized the nearly imperceptible footfall of the Inspector.

"Ah! You. You make me sick. Go away or I will get up and hurt you," she spat without looking up.

She guessed it was mid-afternoon. Before the priests spoke to them she had assumed it was the time of the high sun. Neither she, nor Naibe and Deka had eaten. In their excitement of coming across the river to be reunited with Marai, they simply forgot.

If he's brought food, though, he'll leave wearing it. I'd rather starve than look in his eyes long enough to take anything.

Over the slow hours of waiting, she had tried to calm herself. She no longer felt raving rage. Now, her emotions transitioned into grieving and memory.

Yeah, you were wonderful to me. That just makes it harder, though. Better you had been a strutting ass like N'ahab. Didn't cry over him, did I? she mulled over her life a little more.

GOING FORTH BY DAY

Everything she had made hard in herself throughout her life of danger, adventure, and ultimate disappointment had become soft and pleasant in the light of Marai's unquestioning love. With him gone, she felt everything inside her would become hard once more. Ari stroked her own face, bidding farewell to that brief softness he had engendered in her. She sensed all the tenderness floating away as if it had been forever lost in a dream of him. It had stayed only long enough to soothe the slap the guard had given her when she spit on the high priest and screamed at him to open the box of Child Stones. Almost amused, she touched the swollen places on her face and her split lip only to discover they were already healing. *Oh, the Children will heal me, but they couldn't save you Marai?* her thoughts trailed bitterly. *In just a little longer my split lip will heal and my black eye will clear, but what them getting you does to my heart? Who knows how long that will take?* She pretended her hands were Marai's as she caressed her face. Comforted by the thought of him, she hummed a little and remembered the good times, beginning with the first time she heard the whispery voices on the crystal vessel in the sand.

Ariennu born in the Kingdom of Tyre on the Kina coast
Know you that youth passes
Age is the voice of wisdom and experience.

I was dying of "yellow disease". I know now it was the drink and the men and then the heart seeds to keep the babies from getting started in my belly. They rot a woman from the inside out after a while. But you stayed with me when I was about to give up. You never looked the other way at my sickness or nastiness. A tear wanted to form in her eye then, but Ari forbid it. *No; Never more. I will never cry until I find whatever's left of him and weep it back to life like their goddess Aset who searched for and brought back Asar, piece by piece.* She remembered how he had consoled her in the middle of her agony, saying "Ariennu, you won't die! You'll see." *That's what he had been like – gentle,* the thought of him was stunningly clear. *Those were days and nights filled with joking and singing,* she continued to think back. Ari poignantly remembered that wonderful afternoon when she set out to soothe him from a momentary setback and found that she was the one getting soothed in such slow, elegant, and easy passion. *All only a memory now,* she lowered her hand mournfully and kept focused on the floor.

Maybe I should just go back to what I was, if I must be without you. There's no point in any of this anymore. You men want something from me, you just make sure I'm really drunk and then do whatever makes you happy. Just don't kid yourself into thinking you can bring me around cause all the while I'll be meditating on your death. What's the use? Child Stone would heal me. No going back, I guess. Maybe if I start to speak up again and long enough these men will cut off my head or bash it flat. Maybe that old buzzard will have me mortally wounded and this little Child Stone dug out of my head, she laughed silently, *bastard wanted to do that. Old man wanted to show Baby and Bone Woman what happens when one hacks a wad of spit on a "Son of Gods' Body". Wonder why he didn't make the order? He killed Marai, why not us? It's not like having these Child Stones is any use,* Ariennu smirked as she continued thinking. *They always want to just watch calmly. They only really helped us fight when that boy tried to steal from us, or when they helped Marai kill N'ahab. They were so brutal then. Why can't they be brutal now for us?* the bereaved woman questioned, resentful of their apparent powerlessness. *Maybe they're right, though,* she suddenly thought. *Maybe it's going to be best for the three of us to appear unmoved – and begin to work whatever life we can manage while we make plans to settle this.*

Ari raised her head and saw Deka out of one side of her field of vision. The woman hugged her knees as she sat in the corner of the box-like room. Her expression ranged from hard to forlorn. *See her sad look* – Ari felt hot tears try to come again and fought them again – *I will not cry. My tears were for only for him. Damn him. Oh, sweet loving damn. I'm lost again, why?* Ariennu asked as one tear fell despite her struggling. *There. That's done now. My mourning the best man ever will be my lack of weeping. My soft, sweet heart that you held in your hands, Marai, she's become a stone once more. Let your ghost see how much you meant to me by growing powerful in the lives of others, should I speak of you.*

Ari resolved to stop her self-misery and turned her attention to Naibe. When they had first been placed in the room the youngest of the "wives" had been held by Deka, but the Ta-Seti woman had let her go and had drawn into herself. Now Naibe sprawled on the floor gripping the red sash with golden bulls and weeping inconsolably.

She'll take it worse than me, I guess. I've always been the tough one – strong and ready to bounce back after my moment. That thought was distracted by the sensation they weren't alone. Ari remembered the Inspector had come in, but she had been so wrapped up in her own thoughts that he had seemed to vanish. He, however, had quietly remained in the room with them.

You the enforcer? her thoughts asked, hoping that he heard her accusation. She remembered Chibale the Kush heka-wielder who had fallen on bad times and had come to N'ahab dragging a very malformed and docile Deka on a chain.

But you're different. He was cruel and deserved his death. You sense pain where the old Kush enjoyed it. You feel sorry for what you did, don't you? Good! I hope you suffer with us! Take it in, bastard! Let the pain in us be a part of your days and nights for the rest of your life! No one, not wife, not concubine, not even your gods will be of lifelong joy to you, because of your weak hand in this!

Ariennu had never cursed anyone before or even wanted to inflict a curse. She preferred a fight with her fists whenever she needed to make her point known. Just at this moment, however, the growl and snarl of her silent curse launched at this wiry looking Inspector felt so good.

As she quietly watched, the man approached Deka, who rose from her seated pose, but continued staring at the floor. His hand went forward in what could only be interpreted as sympathy, but she hissed and leapt back like a mad cat.

Goddess — Ari's eyes leapt open because for the briefest of instants, she saw a dark lioness instead of a woman. She crouched, scrambled backward, and growled, baring her teeth; her eyes blazing in fury as flames appeared around her. Instinctually checking her surroundings, Deka backed against the wall. Unable to flee, she threw her hands up in front of her face to claw at her adversary.

Bone Woman? Can that bastard see? Ari sat, fascinated and almost delighted that Deka had at last seemed to show some misery at Marai's fate.

The priest took a step back in shock, but with a simple and elegant hand gesture, he advanced again, whispering very quietly to her: "Hke SkHt. Na Hke. I see you there, inside this woman. Abandon her or be calm. Do no harm," he brought his hands down slowly. As he did, a spell wafted through Deka's attack. She sagged down the wall then settled into a sitting position on the floor. Rocking back and forth, she looked inward started to keen the chant Ari recognized as "Hagkore –" for summoning and strength.

It is as it should be, flesh of my flesh, a gentle man's voice filled Ari's thoughts and by her expression she knew Deka had heard it. It wasn't the Inspector's higher-pitched tenor, and it seemed to bear a different accent than one typical of the natives of Kemet.

What? She thought, but when the Inspector moved to her leapt to her feet, turned and paced the floor as if trapped.

"Don't you come over to me," she held her head high and began to stomp around. "I knew you were standing there watching to see which one of the other women was safer than me, but I guess she shocked the piss out of you." She made a sharp turn to find the Inspector standing behind her. "You stop following me, you gutless dung-licking keleb. You get on your hands and knees and go crawling ass-first back to your owner! Leave us to our grief!" her voice lowered until it was a bare whisper under her breath as another wave of grieving filled her.

"Will you *please* be still, woman," Wserkaf seized her arm forcefully, tightening his grip until she felt the pain and froze her response to it in silence.

He's this strong? Odd. She gritted her teeth and raised her other hand to strike him.

Listen.

The voice beneath her thoughts reminded her.

"Shut up!" she shrieked hands grabbing her head and ears to blot out the gentle voice. "I don't want to hear it. I don't want to listen, damn you!"

No, but I'm supposed to listen. Why should I? she asked herself, then realized the Inspector might be worked for advantage so she could get away and kill both he and his mentor.

"Why are you here? To torment us?" she asked earnestly, but her wit had different ideas and she no longer cared if her words got her in trouble. She turned and stepped toward the man.

"Ah, Lord *Inspector*. Hmph! Inspecting the goods, eh? Well!" she forced a fake laugh. "That's what this is about?" she furiously pulled her breasts out of their binding straps. "Want these? Have a look at them, you gutless bastard. Suck on one, big baby.

My milk will grow some hair on your little boy twig."

The Inspector's eyes steadied. She knew he was ignoring her taunts but continued.

"See? Still nice and firm, *and* I have all my teeth. Good knees too!" Then, with her head tipping to one side, she whirled around. "Oh, I forgot. No guts and no balls *either*. I suppose nothing I have could move you."

The Inspector loosed his grip and walked to the door which led to the hall adjacent to the kitchen stair.

Nothing I said, she laughed inwardly. *Maybe no heart like his master. And they want me to listen to that?* She remembered the spirit of his mother entering her the day they met and it only gave her something else to say when he re-entered after several moments carrying a basket of things.

"Back so soon? Want more? Did your mother beat you and make you come to like it? Is your dream of her the thing to make your el stand like the rest of you royal monkeys leaping on your mothers and sisters?"

Again, he ignored her, but indicated the basket he brought as if he wanted her to look inside it.

Ari dug through folded modest sheath wraps that looked like open coats. The triangular scarves could be fashioned into skirts. Deeper in the basket, were chains of tinkling bells, beads, and fringes. There were dance girdles and pots of cosmetics.

What? Ari stared at the basket contents. *Dance outfits?* She felt shock make the back of her head feel cold. She dropped the items back in the basket and looked at the Inspector disgusted and horrified. *You bastards had this planned all along! You knew what you were going to do with us before –*

"Your Highness," Ari began, feeling almost defensively. "These are dance clothes. If you are trying to help, just let us leave and go back across the river to work with the Sanghir. We are not helpless."

"Oh, I don't think you understand," Wserkaf answered, but his voice remained flat and even. "As you prepared to come to us, to bring what you promised, our great and wise Menkaure had passed along a writ commanding the Sanghir, Etum Addi is his name I believe, and his family to an opportunity in the sea town of Ra-Kedet far from here, at no cost if he would hurry."

Ariennu paled. She remembered somewhere in her haste at getting ready to come across the river that Etum Addi had received a scroll of from the Inspector. He had appeared upset at first, but then almost relieved.

Goddess, that's why he told us to come to Ra-Kedet to work if it didn't work out here. He knew he'd be gone if we came right back. He was saying goodbye. Now the rope these men had placed around them had just been tightened. *That's what all of that was about*, she shook her head in disbelief.

"Well you have the stones," she mumbled. "Marai's gone. If you let us go right now we might catch them." She sought Deka and Naibe to see if they had heard any of her conversation with the Inspector, but quickly realized they hadn't. Deka buried her face in her hands and sat by the wall. Naibe still lay prostrate in the middle of the floor.

Slowly and wryly, the Inspector shook his head. "I don't think you understand what we are attempting to do for you, Lady Ariennu, is it?" he looked up, face fully sober. "Your husband. Well, as a sojourner, and an –" the priest put on an air of sympathy, but in his attempt to be direct, he stammered.

"What are you not telling me?" Ari took a fearless step toward the slim man, all her attempt at calming her rage gone in an instant. "Let me come over there and slap it out of your mouth along with your teeth, Prince or not."

"Insurrectionist," Wserkaf sighed. "Word has already gone 'round that he, as a sojourner coming to us, had no good intent but to insert himself in our schools so he could take away our secrets. No one in Ineb Hedj will accept any of you now for fear of being viewed as accomplices."

"You *executed* him. You planned this from the start, and you *killed* him. I don't believe this," Ari took a step back in shock. "Insurrect – a god-cursed lie!"

"We extended courtesy," the Inspector snapped back. "He was rude coming in, and even insulting to my senior and to his high office! His Highness could have stopped his nonsense right away but decided to humor him and to see into his heart! You search the spirit of memory in these halls! You'll see,"

She saw his hand go to his wdjat, yelped in defense and hid her forehead with her arm. "No you don't!"

Instead, he merely raised his hand in a blessing pose.

"I don't want to talk to you or anyone else on this side of the river," she protested but then felt a gentle wave of relaxation come over her. It apparently extended to the others. She noticed Deka looked up with a more sober expression and Naibe curled into a ball like a child rather than remaining sprawled.

What? You're an odd duck! I'm scorning you and you aren't fighting back? You send blessings, not curses? her conscious thought responded but then she felt a memory being fed to her. She saw Marai in the presence of the high priest and saw the way he would not bow or bend his knee; that he treated a royal son as if he was a peasant. *Oh Marai, why – Why? You proud old fool. Did you learn that from me? The taking a stand or did your Abu teach it?* Ari shook her head, dismayed. The hardness returned to her heart as the weight of their futures sank into her soul.

"So you tell me we are *shunned?*" she thought of her own life of checkered businesses, thieving, procuring, and seducing before she had known Marai. *They didn't have to seed everyone with that news. It could have been unsaid unless they intended to make it impossible for us to survive out alone.* Evidently, these men assumed she and the other women would probably go back to such a livelihood. "That no one would wish to trade with us, because you took it on yourselves to ruin us all? That there's nothing but – Ooh!" Dismayed, she stared at the dance outfits again. "I hear you, but it won't be. Not *this* time," her eyes shut as she smoothed the front of her rumpled kalasiris. "So tell your *owner* I will not soon be opening my legs for his nasty twig or any other," she picked up the basket of cosmetics the Inspector had brought in, took one of the little pots and flung it against the wall. Picking out one after the other she laughed as, she watched each one bounce, splatter, and roll on the floor.

"Would you stop! Must I force you calm?" the priest stepped in front of her, extending his hand toward her throat.

Ari ducked back, dropped the basket and turned to confront him. "You see me? I'm not afraid of any of you, especially now, so go ahead and put a hand on me. Choke me. You say I've got nothing to go back to. So, what's the difference," she took enough of a step that the Inspector was forced to move back. "You say what you're offering me is better?" she asked. "Dance for you? Maybe do some *tricks*? Bit of bending over, too, maybe? Who but your kind would think it's all sojourners are good for?" she turned her back. "Sick bastards, all of you!"

"And if I were to present you to the King himself?"

Ari looked over her shoulder at the Inspector, who had calmly walked over to the heap of bottles and color pots and bent to examine them. "Would you not enjoy the offer of a god's bedchamber? A woman of your fine skill?" he stood up again, having found the two jars that had burst.

Ari felt the sardonic laughter rise like bile in her throat. *Skill. Of course! Is it that damned obvious? The gall of him – and suggesting the King to me? Over the bodies of how many noble maids with gods in their eyes, much younger and ripe, who feel they've already gained the right to that royal couch?* Her eyes narrowed. "Oh, I don't think so. Is that so I could tell lies like your own mother did and say I have bedded a god and not some handful of faceless vagrants traipsing past the bedchamber door?" she stared him down, face to face. "I heard her truth and sad story when I allowed her soul to come into me. Truth is –" she smirked, "– I *have* bedded a god, and *often*, and you know it. So what did you think a mere *king* that I do *not* accept as a god can do for me that *he* has not?" She turned to the wall, shutting off her thoughts quickly spinning out of control again. That lasted until she felt herself grabbed by the shoulders and slammed into the wall, followed by pain that leapt from her brow through her right ear and into her knees.

Calm. Sweet.

Harm not.

The words of yet another calming spell, this time spoken by a woman drifted through Ari's ears but she knew the message wasn't for her.

"And you can't hurt me, coward. You can try," she added to the child stone voice, then laughed. "Go on beat me! Try."

She felt him ram her shoulders into the wall again, but this time she wriggled her hand loose. Reaching backward she stroked the joining of his shendyt, mimicking how she might stroke him in pleasure. At first the Inspector ignored her. As she mockingly caressed him, he responded by making gentle circles with his forefingers over the tops of her arms, forcing a sense of pleasure into her.

"Nnnh," she groaned a little, hating the pleasure she felt. "So, you know touch magic," she grunted through her teeth. She envisioned where their mutual hand play was leading and realized how disgusting the idea was to her. The fight went out of her like a sigh, but the rage stayed. "I suppose maybe I shouldn't even care about *what* you do with me. Just show me where the bath in this miserable place is and then I'll make ready." She forced a seductive huskiness into her voice that became as forced as it was breathy. Her arms encircled his shoulders in a lascivious embrace and kiss. Her tongue dug between his lips and she rubbed against him, hands reaching and caressing insistently.

She felt his hands release her shoulders, reposition themselves and then hurl her to the floor in disgust. She rolled onto her back, cackling, and stared hard into his horrified eyes.

"Go on, get it. I felt you stiffen. You know you want something." She widened her knees, laughing. When he backed away, she felt a sudden wave of nausea sweep over her. She wanted to vomit, preferably on the Inspector, but could only retch and bring nothing forth. That failed, she got up and looked around the confined room once more.

She was about to sit by Deka, who was humming her self-consoling tune, hugging her knees, and rocking but she stopped short.

"Priest," a low, almost sweet voice sounded behind her and the Inspector.

Ari froze. Naibe had spoken. Her voice had become hoarse from weeping. Ari and the Inspector turned to see the young woman standing directly behind him. Her light brown eyes were dark and hollow as she stared up into the Inspector's eyes.

Casting her glance down, suddenly, she spoke as if she was overwhelmed with shyness.

"Come to me. I have something for you," she huskily croaked. Something about the tone of her voice both seduced and commanded. Naibe beckoned to him and enchanted him, but her sweet, passionate face had grown hard.

Inspector Wserkaf took a step closer to her as if he had become involuntarily curious, but he stopped in shock to see her pale right hand turn palm up and then extend to him in a backhanded caress down his side. The knife in his belt jarred loose from its place, then magically floated with a half-turn into her hand.

Naibe paused as if she was reflected on what she'd done, turned the blade and grasped the hilt in both hands.

"No!" Ari shrieked.

In the instant that she plunged it towards her heart, the Inspector seized the dagger and flung it aside. It skidded on the smooth brick floor, but no one paid attention to where it had been thrown. Her breath came in gasps ending with:

"Kill me, priest. End my day of agony, if my Marai is gone." She sobbed bitterly until it seemed she was about to stop breathing.

Both Deka and Ari rushed to take her in their arms.

She'll go get that and use it before he can stop her this time. Dunno, maybe I should just let her, but we're all suffering. If we end ourselves, they win. Then, she sent a thought to try to calm the young woman. She knew she was already too angry to do it herself.

Deka embraced her and whispered into her wild hair. "Shh Brown Eyes. Shh"

"No! Send me to him, *please*. *Somebody!* Let me sleep with him forever!" she struggled and attempted to move toward the place where the Inspector had thrown it. He carefully picked it up and paused as if he was about to say something. Instead, he fled the room.

As Naibe continued to suffer like one on the brink of madness, Ari saw women come to the doorway and stand somewhat timidly among the guards.

"You three," one of the guards addressed them. "These women will lead you to prepare. If you even think of causing them grief, you will not be killed even if you so beg, but you will suffer the rest of your many days."

Ari thought of many tortures she had seen in her days with the traders, but despite their cruelty the men or she herself usually allowed begging for death and mercy as part of the process once they'd had their fill of hurtful pleasure. *Cutting off fingers and toes? Cutting noses so no man would ever want us? Breaking bones and forcing them to heal badly so moving about is agony? That bastard Inspector knows we would rather die and now they've decided to keep us living.*

As the maids came in to lead them to the women's area, she whispered to the others in Kina: "Let's just *do* what they want. I'll think of something, I swear I will. We'll make them suffer; if I find a way, we'll kill all of them for this. Just let them think we've reconsidered." Ari got on the other side of Naibe and half-dragged her with Deka, who agreed in a soulless sigh. They followed the maids out of the storeroom and the guards closed behind them.

The guards. Wonder where they were when I was explaining things to that priest?

It seemed to her as if they walked forever crossing an area between plazas, and then entering a separate building with a steamy water-filled pool in the middle.

Marai bathed here, she thought. *He sent those messages to us from this place.* She paused, sensing something. *Marai?* she silently asked the air. *Is that your ghost? You watching us? You hoping we can be strong? It's Ari you're seeing. You know I'll get us all through this. Would help if you could send some righteous devils to help us get these bastards for what they did to you, though,* she shook her head and noticed once again how tired and hungry she had become.

The maids left the area, then returned to cast oils and crushed flower petals in the warmed water. They also brought small amounts of finger food. When the girl carrying the tray extended it to Deka the other maids chimed in choral tones, followed by giggles.

"For health, sweet ones, rest and food to come soon."

"Wasting your time," Deka hissed. "I will not eat your food," she stared directly at the serving girl, then pushed the pretty red dish of stewed meats and grain back into the girl's arms. Ari knew the woman must have made a dreadful face because her mouth twitch in delight as the girl shrank back in terror.

No, Deka, you eat that. We must be strong if this is going to work at all, Ari shook her head.

The Ta-Seti woman ignored her, then helped Naibe undress. She removed her own clothing and eased the younger woman into the hot bath with her.

Ari, the bowl of food now in her hands, greedily dipped up a small portion of the food and ate it.

"It's fine. Not poison. I just wanted some of it while it was hot," she remarked, but stopped eating when no one responded. She set down the food and then undressed, watching the sweet smelling, steamy fog. Deka held Naibe's head above water so she wouldn't be able to drown herself, then splashed a little water up onto the young woman's face. As the two women started to bathe, Ari searched the darkened room for a place to hide the bag of eight Child Stones until they had finished. A tiny space in the brick in the darkest of the corners caught her attention. She slipped the bag into the crack and then climbed into the bath. With a gentle wave of her fingertips over the place, she cast an illusion of solid brick over them. After they finished their bath, she would get the Children of Stone and hide them again.

GOING FORTH BY DAY

Chapter 5: The Choice

As soon as Ari sank into the warm water of the shoulder-deep pit pool, the maids hovered and attempted to assist her and the others in cleansing.

Any other time, she thought, *the luxury I'd love. Today* – Today their well-trained, dainty manner nauseated her.

"Go!" she hissed at them. "Just go! Get out of here! I know you've been sent to spy on us – bring a story of our plans!" her voice rose to a shout. "Get out, before I come out myself and put you under this water!"

The girls startled, looking at each other with shocked expressions, then backed up and left the steamy little room, more frightened than insulted.

"If I need something, I'll call you," Ari cautioned the girls and then whispered to Deka to either hand-talk or speak only in Kina to her. For a few quiet moments, the only sounds were the occasional splashing noises of their bodies as they moved around in the warm, fragrant water. It was almost peaceful.

Soon, an older, medium-brown-skinned woman with penetrating black eyes and a blue beaded cap that covered her entire head entered the bathing room. She stood near the edge of the water with her arms folded across the pale straps of her informal day gown. She wore simple jewelry in the form of armlets and bracelets on her arms. A plain amulet of Seshat rested in the hollow of her throat. When one of the maids brought her a folding, three-legged stool, she sat on it at one side of the deep, hot pool and quietly observed.

Ari knew the fleeing maids must have told her about being sent out. She sensed the woman had kinship to the high priest and couldn't resist a taunt. "Oh. *Look,* sisters, he has a *daughter.*" Ari's mocking voice trailed up, even though she instinctively knew the elegantly dressed woman was probably Hordjedtef's wife. "Oh, pardon me, his *wife.* What a curse your life must be, poor thing, to service the old man in his infirmity. His faltering el must disappoint so."

GOING FORTH BY DAY

At first the older woman showed no reaction, warm or cold. Her expression remained aloof and imperious as her voice rose slightly in an introduction.

"Countess Lady Saeteptah."

Ari nodded to the others in silence: *Don't speak back. Don't welcome this.*

The Countess leaned forward on her seat and added: "*Do* be grateful, sojourning women. It could go *far* worse for you."

Glad she had been able to hide the bag that contained the eight stones just before she had entered the water, Ari thought about the Countess and realized ugliness had not been the right approach. In the past year of living in Kemet, she learned that the Seshat emblem the woman wore meant she was highly educated in writing, calculating, and other wisdoms. She was no mere nursemaid or concubine.

Might be able to read my thoughts. Having her here is worse than some spying and silly handmaids. Read me through the water, then. She took a deep breath and ducked under the water, pretending to wet her face and hair. The moment she was underwater, she sensed the small voice whispering in her brow.

Charm her

Be kind

Guide and lead those who grieve.

Do not give in to weeping.

Ari heard the small voices and answered as secretively as she could while she held her breath under the water. She kept her communication brief, before the countess decided she was drowning herself.

How could you let this happen to him? Is there nothing that lasts between you and Marai? Between you and us? Were you amused to bring us so far only to watch as we are brought down? When the Children's voices didn't answer her question, she sighed in defeat and let her head come above the surface of the water. She knew she would have to face the Countess alone.

As she had ducked under, the maids had returned to refresh the water. They dipped out a cauldron of cool water and poured in hot, perfumed water to replace it. Next, they brought in a smoldering brazier and lit lumps of incense on the coals which quickly filled the air with an intoxicating sweet smoke. The whole time they were sing-chanting something vaguely reminiscent of Deka's "Hagkore" chant. It was close enough that the Ta-Seti woman joined them in the chant while she cradled Naibe.

"Worse for us?" Ari asked, wanting to make the woman explain so she might use it against her later. "Please explain, Your Grace," she whispered in her own slightly halting Kemet speech.

"His Highness told me that he has sent word out to men of the highest rank today. We have advised them of your presence and your situation and have asked for them to come into our home to sup with us this evening," she spoke officially, but avoided direct eye-contact with the women in the pool. Covering her nose with a wisp of cloth to keep the odor of the incense from making her dizzy, she continued. "They will appreciate your company and perhaps a dance if you would do that for them," she attempted an artificial smile. "I understand one of you is quite –" she began, but Naibe struggled away from Deka's hold and began to shriek:

"No! I will *never* do it. My dances were for my beloved! Only for him! There is nothing *left* in me!" she broke into more sobs, her cries echoing around the small, quiet room.

Ari made her way to Naibe and Deka.

This isn't going to work. I can put on a polite face. I think Deka can too because we've been in noble houses as girls. We need to get Baby One under control.

Ari's self-preservation instinct had kicked in.

We need to show we're level for now. We can let it go after tonight. I'm sure it's dawned on them that we're miserable. They're looking for ways to call us mad and cast us into the wild. We must at least consider *this.* Ari knew that the high priest must have called in some mighty favors to get a meeting with the nobles set up so quickly. Her doubt re-surfaced. *Planned this all along they did. I need to do this to see how we kill them.*

"Shh, Baby One," Ari tried, both arms holding Naibe tightly. When she glanced back over her shoulder, she saw the countess leaning forward, watching all their reactions carefully.

"I know it hurts," she hugged Naibe fiercely but couldn't mask the dullness in her heart as she lied with all her skill about her feelings. "We have to try, though. He would want us to, Baby. He would want it."

"Dear ones," Countess Saeteptah underscored that sentiment. Ari knew the elder wife was taking a hint from her and now attempting a sympathetic approach. "You are so blessed!" her lips stretched wide in a rehearsed smile. "I'm told that even Our Father King Menkaure himself, in his great charity, has been moved by your story! He will *indeed* ask for one of you to come into his house, I am told – honored to bring him joy."

Ari nodded to the woman, but the Countess attempt at sympathy was less genuine than her own attitude of compliance. Ari sensed the woman had been disappointed at Marai's demise, but had wanted her, Deka, and Naibe pitched into the wilderness after the box of stones was located.

Because you know the havoc that women can wreak from the bedroom, having done so yourself as a girl and obtained your own prize. Nothing we haven't done and something we might do as soon as there is a way – you know the dangers.

"I understand, Great Lady," Ari nodded so the Countess would believe her to be accepting.

With Ari's agreement, the conversation between the four women ended. A harpist set her instrument up next to the Countess and began to create gentle chords to calm the women as they bathed and washed each other's hair. Ariennu and Deka paid little attention to either woman at the side of the pool as they took turns holding and caressing Naibe-Ellit, who was still overwhelmed with grief. Ariennu whispered tenderly to her: "be still sweet one. Our hearts are breaking too. Let us be one heart together," Ariennu tried, but instantly realized her error. "One heart" was the phrase Marai had used for all of them moving and thinking together.

"One heart, one heart. Oh, goddess in me, why? I loved him," young Naibe-Ellit cried out again and again.

The elder countess eventually shrugged, got up, and left, apparently worn down by her fruitless watch and no improvement in the younger woman. After a few more melodies, the harpist left too. Very slowly, over the course of the late afternoon, Naibe regained a semblance of inner quiet. She was a pallid shell of herself, constantly rubbing her eyes and shaking her head 'no' from time to time.

One heart, her inner voice called out to seek an answer from the spirit world.

One Heart, my sweet one, the air shimmered between her and Ari, who paused dumbstruck. Marai's voice, or the memory of it, seemed to be sounding among them.

I took a lesson from sweetest Naibe…
Woman, you taught me
That I can escape death!
I believe you, my goddess!

The sound of his voice meandered among them as if it was about to take flesh and walk.

Naibe bowed her head against Deka's arm. "I hear him. I *hear* him," Naibe-Ellit snuffled. "Don't you hear him speaking to you, Ari? Don't you?"

Ari nodded because she thought she had heard his voice even though she instantly decided it was just a wish. She wanted to shake her head "no", but in reality she *had* felt his dreamlike spirit. *Perhaps,* she thought then addressed him silently.

You here, Marai? Is Naibe really hearing you? she asked a particularly dense portion of the vapor. Not hearing a reply, she sighed defeated and looked at the others. "I guess we'll just have to do this."

The maids returned to the room as Ari was speaking. She swallowed her words in case any of them understood her tongue. Gesturing for Deka and Naibe-Ellit to listen to her thoughts, she hoped that the countess had gone far enough away that she would not pick up on her next thoughts. *I know you want to kill the men who did this. I do too!*

GOING FORTH BY DAY

Let's just do what they want and soon we'll find ways to avenge Marai and more! her thoughts whispered, *let's just see what comes next.*

As they finished with their bath and the maids returned to help them with grooming, Ari tried to keep her thoughts from Marai. It didn't work. She heard his voice echoing in her heart. When she closed her eyes, she felt as if Marai was in the water with her. Although they had never bathed together in a pit pool or even in a wadi hole on the entire journey to Kemet, she felt him reach through time in a fantasy of them bathing. *When did he weave this dream of us?* She imagined him gently pulling her back against him in the darkened warmth, planting evil-sweet kisses on the back of her neck until she begged for more.

When the three had been ushered into another area and their belongings had been returned, Ari allowed the soothing oil massages and the general pampering provided by the maids to continue, but her thoughts drew her further and further away.

When the maids left, the women lay quietly and finished the simple meal brought down from the kitchen. Still later, the maids brought out henna paint mixed in bowls, with paddles and brushes of various sizes for applying it. Deka used it to brighten her hair, Ari laid it on thickly to make her own hair shimmer like brighter fire, and Naibe painted it on everyone's nails followed by dreamy lacework patterns with symbols of protection on everyone's hands and arms. Adding to the artwork, Ari stained everyone's lips with the paint. Following this, Deka put the kohl and the green color on everyone's eyes and then painted her own patterns over the tops of her hands and on her breasts and torso. In silence, they anointed themselves with spicy smelling oil. Naibe-Ellit braided Deka's hair in tight rows along the sides of her head. The Ta-Seti woman returned the favor by pinning up Naibe's hair and twisting Ari's hair into rows that swept over her ears in a band. When she had finished, her bright hair looked like an elaborate headdress.

That's good, Ari thought. *Maybe if we work together – keep talking through the stones, we'll get through whatever their plans are.*

As soon as she could do it without being seen, Ariennu went back into the bathing area to retrieve the stones from their hiding place. She buried them deep underneath her things in her own simple burden basket which had been placed with the other women's possessions. *They already searched this. They won't do it again. It'll go with me wherever I go tonight. Once I'm there, I'll find a better hiding place for them. Bigger thing though: get us all back together, because I know we'll be separated, and then get the Children of Stone in one place. Then, I'll see who in the universe I give them to, because these bastards can't be the right ones.* Ari hoped the Children would tell her what steps would be next, now that Marai was gone.

Outside, she heard the bustling sounds of the setup of a fine evening gathering.

"He didn't lie," she moved toward the doorway and attempted to peek out, but the hallway was too long and filled with guards so that they wouldn't escape. "There's something going on out there. I can hear the servants going on as if the world is about to end." Turning back to Deka and an exhausted-looking Naibe, who sat on some large floor cushions the maids had brought in on their last visit to the room, Ari's shoulders sagged and she sighed. "Better try to rest. Maybe if his spirit sees how we are trying to make good of this mess he'll speak to us." She sat and embraced Naibe, kissing her throat and then her lips gently, more in comfort than in passion.

The women lay quietly together and then, as if he had heard their desire, the stones whispered in Marai's voice.

Oh. I hear him MaMa, Naibe's thoughts traveled to the elder woman first.

I do too, Baby One. It's for you, though, Ari stroked the young one's brow and knew the message was really for all of them. She swallowed hard against her own emotion as they listened to the voice.

Naibe, beloved, I love you…
Know you are my goddess walking
once more in earth.
If I have truly died,
go on and do what you must.

GOING FORTH BY DAY

Do not fail of grieving on my account.
You showed me once
how wrong it was for me to grieve my onetime bride Ilara.
Do not weep for me too long.
Live, beloved woman.
Love again, and be happy

"Oh!" her tears started, but Deka rose quickly and dabbed at her eyes before the tears ruined the kohl lines they had drawn. "I can't," Naibe-Ellit sighed, knowing Marai was watching them and that she needed to get control of herself.

"It's not like we haven't done any of this before. The men, that is."

Naibe heard Ari talking, but knew this time it would be different for her. She would understand so much more about the nature of passion and love; not just how good it felt to her body to have a man inside her. She realized that the gift given her through the lapis-blue-colored stone the Children had buried in her brow was not only full intelligence, but a godly capacity to give and feel greater than human emotions of purest love. She could reach into a man's soul just by talking to him and by offering him a pair of arms in which to whisper and weep. That power opened men's hearts and told her all their secrets. She could see people better than they could see themselves. In return, she knew she gave that love to and then evoked it from Marai when they had been together.

They might use my body again, but they won't be him. She felt the storm roll through her eyes. *I can't see me lasting long, knowing what I have known now. If the goddess would strike me ugly and idiot again.*

I know what you feel, my sister.

Naibe paused, because Deka sent her a thought. Most of the time she had been closed to everyone.

I now have some memories of this when it happened to me, Deka went on in a quick explanation. *For me it was different, though. I was never a common one. I was created to be different. I was kentake – of goddess blood.* Then, as if she wanted Naibe and Ari to understand every word she added aloud:

"Try not to think about it too much, Brown Eyes. These men will at least be *clean*. You must learn to fly away from them. Fly away. Do not allow yourself to give love to any of them, ever! They are *unworthy*. Fly away, in your heart, and let your flesh do what it wants, but do not *think*. We must *never* give our hearts to them."

Ari groaned internally as if this insight from the Ta-Seti woman had been too much. *And that's why you couldn't be with Marai, eh? You think of him as a father, some high all-father? The one who dropped you made some raw wounds then. For you "what the body does" and "what the heart feels" can never be joined? I thought so too at one time and took a hard lesson from the man.* Marai wouldn't have even *thought* of dividing women's pleasure from love and passion. *And now we're all alone? Seems so unfair.*

Another noise at the doorway distracted her thoughts. Ari raised her head from the pillow and looked up to see that the countess and the harp player had returned to check on them. This time they walked in tandem but remained aloof. The servants followed the two noblewomen to a more private room detached from the common handmaidens area. When they left, Deka whispered:

"This is a second wife, I think."

"Mmm. So, I knew one of them had charmed her way into the old dog's life. Thought it was the older one," Ari remarked. "Take deep breaths, ladies. It's about to be time," she breathed. Shortly, the wives emerged fully wigged and adorned for the fancy dinner.

Servants attended Hordjedtef's wives quietly, making the last preparations for the evening.

Ari watched the two wives whisper instructions to each other. As she watched the women, she realized she also heard their thoughts and the instructions they were giving the maids as clearly as if they had been speaking to her. *When you check on them, make sure they drink this spiced wine*, the elder countess ordered. *It will calm them. I cannot have any of them humiliate me before my King. It is your duty. Fail me and I will see you punished.* Ari saw Countess Saeteptah push a small pot of something into a serving girls' hands and saw her glance quickly at Naibe, who continued drawing spells on her hands with the deep green henna paste. *That one especially. See the spells she's casting? I want that stopped.*

Yeah, Naibe's going to need that. I think Deka and I can manage, but we'll drink some too. Baby One just needs to fall asleep and wake up somewhere else. Ari put on a stiff, false smile when the nervous handmaiden brought the jug to her. Before Naibe could think of objecting, Ari offered it to her.

"Baby, drink this. It'll help you sleep better," she lied. "We've all had some of it."

Naibe gulped most of it and went back to making her henna patterns.

Ari continued to listen to both wives converse privately about them. They mentioned each one's suitability back and forth, giggled and joked. Then, they left to join the dinner guests. Ari, Naibe and Deka remained behind in eerie silence.

With the drugged wine and the incense in the room, Ari felt their hostesses wanted to make it easy for them to stop thinking about any fate awaiting them. *Royal men,* she drifted, already hazy and admiring the wine they had been given. *Proud of their bodies, most of them. Even the old ones – even this nasty Count: wiry, but not much sag to the flesh. The Inspector: smooth muscle and slim, but very strong. Walks like he's floating or gliding on a cushion of air where you don't hear his steps; not the filthy pig dogs that went flabby and unwashed as they did in the wilderness.*

As darkness settled, the women were brought back to the dry storeroom where they had first tried to calm themselves earlier in the day. Ari gawked at the once plain room that had been freshly cleaned and filled with even larger woven cushions placed on the floor.

Not so much like a dungeon now, she sniffed the different smoke in the air and nodded. *Dream incense, too.*

Servants brought them more wine to drink. Deka quaffed plenty of it, as did Ari, but Naibe had as much of it as she could take down earlier. She started to whimper again.

What is this stuff? Ari frowned. *Tastes like wood. Strong though. If they wanted to poison us, they would have done so earlier. Must stay sober enough to get all of us out.*

The women sat in silence, listening through the open doorway to the distant sound of men as they talked and enjoyed their meal in the wide plaza, punctuated by occasional comments from the "Countess". Musicians played instruments. Someone rattled a little sistrum again. Ariennu laid back on the bloated cushion, holding a now dry-eyed Naibe. Deka had scooted back against the wall and drew into herself. They drifted in thought as the time before their introduction dragged on.

After a while, the Inspector came to the doorway of the little room. Ari decided he must have returned to his home at some point because he was wearing a longer, more formal shendyt and two gold and pearl-shell wristlets. The crystal amulet he had worn had been attached to the middle of his collar, and his head was adorned with a plain dark khat.

She watched his expression as he paused to slowly regard the three of them. He seemed clearly stunned at the way their appearance had risen from that of ordinary, but well-dressed peasants to women of extravagant beauty. Ari smiled up at him, almost haltingly, sensing his thought that she and her sisters in kind would be *truly* at home and at ease around nobility.

"*Very good*, ladies." The Inspector turned directly to Ari, who propped up on her elbows. "You are feeling calmer, then?" he asked.

Ari blinked, wanting to launch a thousand curses, but she felt giddy from the drinks and detached enough to see how asinine this all seemed. *Should have just let us go our way. Someone must have a death wish.* Then, she answered the question.

"I do, Your Highness." She beckoned for the others to get up.

Deka's arm stayed around Naibe, who got to her feet for no other reason than to get away from the Inspector.

"Just so you know," he spoke softly after a brief and respectful pause, "I am nothing if I am not truthful. Our King, Great Majesty Menkaure, is here to see you. Son of his Body and Overseer of the Northern Army, Crown Prince Shepseskaf, is here also. Finally, the highly esteemed grandson of Great One and Overseer of the Southern Army Prince, Maatkare Raemkai, is here." The Inspector paused for a moment, then after a thought he added: "If it puts you more at ease, I will not choose one of you as a help maid, nor will the Great One. It is his express wish that none of you remain in his home for the evening," the Inspector paused, waiting for his announcement to sink in, then added: "you should feel honored that these godly men could put the business of their position aside to come and meet with you." With an abrupt turn, the Inspector stood in the doorway to wait for someone to escort the women to the party.

Aye, I hear you saying the same thing the Countess said to us, you weak and simpering wretch! Ari's thoughts muttered loudly enough to cause the man to pause as if a gnat had entered his ear. *The old man must have told you exactly what to say and how to say it.*

"What is *desired* of you is companionship within the houses of these godly men," he explained. "You will be asked to assist with entertainments in the household, to honor them, and to serve them. In return, you will be protected and may, in time, advance in status and independence."

"Oh, you *dog*!" Ariennu hissed under her breath, unable to pretend civility any longer as she moved toward the man. She gritted her teeth, even though the expression came out as a grin. "I know what this *really* is! You're *selling* us as slaves! King and princes will bid on who takes which one."

"No," Inspector Wserkaf inclined his head to her with his own desperate whisper. "You are *not* slaves. You are guest workers, much as those who sojourn to work in the farming or building trades in our land. Just understand an effort to find the right household for your best protection and growth is being made! *Please*," his voice urged the women to quiet themselves and to regain the composure he had seen when he entered the little room.

Protection and growth, Ariennu grumbled a little. *Still, might as well be slaves.*

Wserkaf turned away again and stood with his arms folded across his slim brown chest. Patiently, he waited at the entrance for a few more minutes.

When the Countesses returned from the plaza and brushed almost rudely by the Inspector and the women, Ari noticed they were whispering and laughing about some unseen but naughty thing that had just happened. She tried to follow their thoughts, but the Inspector nodded that it was time for them to come out and to present themselves.

"Honor His Majesty then by coming to your knees, eyes turned down, and remain so until he speaks to you and gives you permission to rise." The Inspector paused, then added: "Don't be afraid. Our Father is feeling kindly tonight. Much so," Wserkaf sighed, seeming to Ari as if he was nervous as an unwilling bride. He lined them up: Ari first, then Deka, then Naibe.

The eldest of Marai's women felt a chill as they stepped into the plaza. She knew nothing of their humble background remained. Even though the wine and excitement made it hard for her to see any of the faces of the guests, she knew they moved elegantly enough, as if they were conquered but still proud god-wives. They knelt as they entered, then bent at the waist and remained with their heads down until the Inspector motioned that the King had gestured for them to rise.

Ari focused her sight on the two men who were seated in her line of sight.

Is that the King? her heart skipped a beat. *The nemes has all the stripes and his circlet has the snake. He's sitting lower than the old man though – looking up at him. Something not right about that.*

The King sat to one side, relaxed, in an ebony and gold wooden chair. An old man she hadn't seen before moved in a little closer to whisper a few words to the King as he beckoned to each woman to rise, walk, turn, stretch, and to make some demonstration of her sturdiness and good health.

Displaying us like cattle, Ari thought, leveling a cold but emotionless stare at Hordjedtef. *And I see you acting the part of king, sitting high like that!* Ariennu hesitantly turned her palms upward to show her hands to the three men.

"What is your name, woman?" the King asked as he beckoned her to come a little closer.

When she moved toward him, she noticed his breath had a sick honey-ish odor.

I see the rumors about the King being a drunk are true. Smells like he's had much to drink already. It's the troubles he has making him want to drink them away. I used to have that odor before – she thought of Marai and the healing love he gave her – and would never give her again.

You hide it mostly, like I did at first, but tonight it's harder. Did they tell you who we are? Did they tell you of Marai and what they did to a god?

The hurt and quiet rage about Marai's death stole over her once again. She fought it, not wanting it to shine through her expression. *I could work this king and end him easily, the way he drinks, and yet there's something so pitiful about him; like he's almost helpless.*

"I am Ariennu of the Kingdom of Tyre, Your Majesty," she lowered her eyes.

The vizier addressed her next as he situated his smallish, plump self in front of the bowing women. "We understand you have learned something of women's mysteries. You have been selling spices and remedies for illnesses? You have also assisted in births. You are a priestess of Bes?" the elderly vizier asked.

Ari considered her response as she noticed yet another man in the plaza; a scribe who was seated by the King to take note of everything she said.

"No, Your Majesty. I am not *trained* as a priestess, but have learned much in my travels," she shied back but kept her hands extended. "See my hands, Your Majesty, if I may be trusted to touch." She kept her voice humble and quiet, even though the desire to shout every vulgar curse at the entire room likely came through. Great One Hordjedtef tensed and Ari sent him a thought.

Look, you old sucking hound, I'm not stupid or crazy. There's no foolishness or trick in my touch tonight. I know my future in this cursed place is at stake!

"You may touch *me*," a different man's voice sounded from behind her right shoulder.

Ari had worried about her ability to stay out of trouble long enough to get out of the sight of Hordjedtef and his simpering protégé, the Inspector. She turned to see a man who appeared to be a little younger than the Inspector of the Ways. He stepped onto the dais casually, showing a quick but informal reverence to the King, which seemed more out of habit than respect.

Shorter than the other men here – shorter than me, she snorted inwardly. *Meaty, though.* His face was round, but he was thickly boned and powerfully muscular under his plumpish exterior. Ariennu turned slightly and bowed very low so that her breasts displayed well, but she didn't dare to fully turn away from the King. Her instinct told her the man was some sort of royalty, so she once again only moved when the new man beckoned for her to rise and move behind him. As she took her position behind his back, she noticed his half-striped nemes. *Half-stripe. Prince. He does look a bit like the King, but not too much.*

Pushing aside any hostile thought or desire to cause trouble, Ari began to work on the Prince's thick, corded shoulders.

Hmmm. He has a nice, manly feel to him, she began to hum gently and sway side-to-side, giggling knowingly as she played her fingers lightly on his upper back.

Hmm. If he picks me, I'll jump him. Might be a pleasant enough distraction. Been needing one.

Her movements were seduction, not healing. Everyone in the plaza saw it. When she glanced at the elder priest's face, she noticed even it had softened.

Ari knew he was truly shocked that she, whom he'd viewed as incorrigible, had apparently calmed and was attempting erotic touch in front of the entire assembly. *Or so you think I have calmed. Make no mistake, though. Since I know what any of you will expect of a new maid in the house, why not show some of it now?*

The Prince reached up to Ari's hand and stopped it. He smiled, beaming with happy satisfaction over her demonstration. "Come to me, gentle woman with hair of blood and fire," his head turned to look over his left shoulder and his black eyes softened as they looked up into hers. "Come sit with me by the wall for a while. Come to know me. Your look pleases me," he patted her hand.

Oh. And I thought I was fast, the elder woman smirked, amused the man had come straight to the point of the evening and didn't coat it with any honey either.

"I am grateful, Your Highness," she whispered, quite puzzled that this man had apparently chosen her without even *looking* at the other women. It seemed as if he had been *told* to choose her. Putting her observation aside for the time being, Ari bowed again to the King as the Prince rose and went to Menkaure. The two men exchanged whispers, fondness, and an embrace. Then, the King patted the Prince's shoulder to congratulate his choice.

*Hmmm,*Ariennu thought, *that* is *the Crown Prince. Not bad old girl, not bad.* But then, she found another question forming. *He likely has a beloved one or two at home, so I don't know what he wants* me *for. I'm not a cleaning woman and he doesn't look like he needs a healer.* Putting those thoughts away, she put on her best false face of adoration and let the Prince lead her to a stone bench by the wall enclosure where the torchlight wasn't so plentiful.

From her place on the stone bench, she saw the Prince beside her, the Great One, the Inspector, the King, the musicians, the scribe, and the elder vizier to the King. The King appeared even more drunk, sleepy, or bored. As she surveyed the plaza, Ari wondered if she had been mistaken in understanding that some grandson of the old priest was supposed to attend this selection process. *Wonder where the other man is, if he is a man? Probably wasn't man enough,* she thought.

Ari visualized a new youth of perhaps fourteen or fifteen years. *Maybe the Count wants one of us to school the boy in the sensual arts. That would be interesting,* she mused, then laughed at herself. *Ari, stop it. These children of kings are born old and need nothing of the sort. Any number of maids looking to catch a royal mate will have done that. And only a grown man would be a General of the Army in command of a division. Maybe he stepped out for a moment. Maybe this is why this prince made his decision so fast. Maybe they are rivals and he doesn't want the missing man snapping me up first.*

"Again, bright-haired one, tell me your name," he asked, holding her at a slight distance as if an embrace was too close before good introductions.

"I am Ariennu, Your Highness, of Tyre but many years in the regions of the wilderness and one year in Kemet." She spoke as elegantly as she could. "It is also Red Ariennu or Red Ari if it is your wish," she laughed and bowed her head toward his in a little tease. "I promise you, your choice will not be regretted tonight," the woman promised as the Prince wrapped his arm around her waist and pulled her close. The Prince's signal delighted her at once, but at the same moment and for perhaps the only time in her life, she hesitated.

Marai's voice sounded in her heart as surely as she heard it every night and as surely as she heard the voices of the Children of Stone.

I must make him believe he's won.
I will need you to be open to me, Wse,
in case I need help.
Go tell my wives what's happened.
Tell them to be ready to leave Ineb Hedj at a moment's notice,
before the old bastard can get his claws in them.

Ariennu trembled at what she heard, puzzled. *Why was Marai talking to the Inspector as if they were friends when the man betrayed him? Were those his last living words? Did he cry for help and get none? Is he truly dead and now speaks as the spirits and the ancestors through these stones we have?* Her hands wandered inquisitively over the Prince's chest as she tried to make sense of Marai's ghostly words. *Am I wrong to go about my life and take on whatever comes next? Am I to go with this prince?* Ari *knew* she could seduce this prince and keep him interested in her for at least a few days, if not longer, but the pain of being without Marai for the rest of her life still nagged her. He had given her freedom. He never complained if she dallied or flirted with other men. He even teased her about it before they became intimate just as much as she had teased him for waiting so long to bed her. It was all part of what made her love him and hearing his voice at this moment gave her noticeable pause.

Death. That was it then. *Laugh at me and tease me if you know I love you best, but death tears us apart forever.* She didn't realize she had bowed her head in thought until the Prince caught her chin again and raised her face so that she looked into his dark, but sympathetic eyes. She blinked, and then stared at the double-banded coronet clasping his nemes to his head again.

"You have had tragedy come to you and your sisters today, I'm told," he brought her chin forward and then kissed her mouth gently in an almost father-daughter way. "If I trouble you, it's not my intent," he added. He reflected on her situation and the enormity of what lay ahead of her as keenly as she felt it.

Intent? Ariennu smirked inwardly. *No mistake what this one wants. Hired as a healer, but what illness is he wanting cured? Crown Prince, eh? Never had one of those*, she thought as she returned the kiss. It pained her heart again. *This man isn't Marai, and this isn't love. It will never hope to be more than work.*

> *Wise Mama Ari,*
> *that you are and always were*
> *Teach wisdom.*
> *Be not hard or vengeful*
> *Learn and never forget.*
> *Remember how to live!*

Ariennu, the wild girl of Tyre's squalor-filled fishers' hovels, trembled and fought back the tears when Marai's voice filtered through the whispers of the Children of Stone. All the sweet and gentle memories of her days and nights with him played again: the day he found the three of them after he killed the thieves who harbored them; the way she had been so close to death; the struggle to the mysterious vessel in the wilderness where they all slept and had become renewed and beautiful; her mocking and teasing him because he would not be her lover at first; and finally the beautiful afternoon when he not only took her up on the offer, but also traded hearts and souls with her too. He was gone now, and it was an unbearable loss.

The Prince frowned as if he sensed Ari's disquiet.

"I'm sorry, I've rushed you," he held her out from his chest at arm's length to check her expression.

"No, Your Highness," she lied. "It's just the light of your goodness to my wretched state. My poor heart —" she drew him close again, burying her head on his arm.

"Lady Ariennu, I am Shepseskaf, Grand General of the Lower land, Chosen Bodily Son of the Most High. It's *my* honor to be chosen to help you re-find some joy. Know you will be at peace and no one will pursue you if that is your wish," he kissed her brow and nuzzled her face in affection.

Chapter 6: A Mysterious Grandson

Deka, her eyes cast down, feigned humility as she moved into the open plaza. Even when the man wearing the King's nemes gestured his permission for her and the other women to look up, she glanced up only briefly.

Without ever having focused her eyes on the King, she lowered her gaze again, then sat on her heels and tried not to stare at the King, the other men, or Ari and Naibe. Instead, she closed her eyes and began to feel herself "flying away" up and far to the south. She sailed in her soul over the grassland and into the tawny, rocky hills where the waters of the great river boiled over huge, elephant-shaped stones. As she flew further south, she hovered above the bent, brown backs of those who toiled in the fields and sang the same song in the grass that had always burst from her lips in her own times of trial.

A man stood in the distance within her thoughts; gold clad arms crossed majestically over his wide, ruddy chest.

Is it Marai's ghost? Deka asked herself. *Are you, my king, destroyed by these ingrates once more? I will help you rise. We will end them.*

The man she saw was about the same height and size as Marai, but he had redder brown skin and bright copper hair. His hand stretched out for her, but then she saw a sudden shaft of light drop down about him. It was like the one that had surrounded her on the vessel of the Children of Stone when the mysterious entities there had cleaned the surface of her skin.

Are you my Man-Sun? Was it not you who restored my beauty? she asked the vision in her head. *I wanted to love you as we had once loved, but you shunned me when I was ugly and again when I was beautiful. Why? Did the eons make you forget as I forgot? Did you no longer know you were the bringer of red things; blood, life, and fire? Did you not know you had returned to me in another form, that you are* not really *a shepherd?*

Saddened, she told herself she would accept no man until Marai woke to the truth hidden inside his heart, or until Man-Sun returned in his true form to claim her.

GOING FORTH BY DAY

They killed you. She looked down, but felt her heartbeat increase for some unknown reason as if something called her. *Or did they? Can one kill a god? Perhaps you are not dead, as they say. Maybe you are hidden once again in Ta-Seti, in your secret cave beneath your crystalline dome waiting to take me with you. I must prove myself worthy for you to remember, but how may I do that?*

Tonight, when Deka flew, she felt a voice calling out words and knew they had been her old names:

Ha-go-re! Akh-go-re Neter Deka Nefira Sekht. Mother. Mother of lions, call to me, the call came in a young man's voice that grew old and unanswered. In response, she heard laughter that roared like the wind and rolled like the water. Those images faded suddenly as the reality of the gathering to choose her keeper returned.

Another test, Man-Sun? One with Marai when neither of us were ready. I will be polite. I will go with whatever man chooses me. I will put aside my pride, because Marai no longer exists. I will be as I was in the days before my sweetest Man-Sun plucked me from the wilderness. The men assembled here will pay for their sins against me. I will make *them pay, once I have learned the quiet places in their hearts. If planned well –* Deka thought of Marai once more. She thought of how she had resisted him because to love him when she wasn't entirely sure of *who* he was would have changed everything about her. *Wise MaMa just doesn't understand, and Baby One was so, so god-smacked by him she could only think of his loving. What if I and Marai, my Man-Sun, had loved? What if I was wrong?* Deka pondered, feeling almost winsome at the thought. *He's gone from life now, just like before. Only there's less of me to remember him or the man big as the sky in the season of the storms.*

No, she whispered again to herself, *he showed me the greatest love on Earth by not making any demands of my flesh. He told me again and again that he would not take me by force; as so many had done before. He would wait for me to give myself to him. In his honor, I will do the same. I will not give my heart, unless I am truly loved. I must never give all of myself, body and soul, to another until that day when he returns through death to claim me.*

Out of the corner of one eye, Deka saw Ari in the arms of the crown prince. They were seated on a stone bench in the semi-dark by the plaza wall, enjoying "bird-kisses", nuzzles, and then even deeper kisses.

One taken, me and Baby One to go. Will I ever see either of you again, once we go away with these men? We've been thrown together for so many years, like scrap thrown out into the same heap. We were changed together and we chose to be with Marai in our gratitude, but now he's gone. Now all is changing again, she reflected. *Maybe it's best for us to look into another pair of eyes and then fly, fly away!* Deka sighed. She accepted her coming fate and yet cursed the purity of her love for Marai, who had asked for nothing from her in return.

After some time, she felt dragged back out of her darkening reverie by a peculiar and invading presence. *Is it the King?* she asked herself. He had looked at her more than steadily, approving of her movements. *I don't want Menkaure the Great to choose me tonight.* She knew there could be a chance of it. For generations, the kings of Kemet had chosen at least one Ta-Seti wife or given them status as a high-ranking concubine. The land of Ta-Seti was the source of women's wisdom and the birthplace of the woman-gods. These women taught the kings and princes, ensuring their knowledge and respect remained in the right place. *Of course, a god of men would desire a god among gods.* Calmer, she seriously wondered *is it you who I sense?* as she looked at the King.

The King remained seated in his ebony wood chair, seemingly unmoved by *any* of the women. Feeling bold from the thought that the King might choose her, Deka tried to sense his thoughts and discovered they were leagues away from this quickly thrown together dinner party. Tonight, he was seated as a man and not as a god or even as a king. He looked tired as he presided over this sordid entertainment and seemed much more interested in sipping the mulled honey wine from his cup. The weight of his kingdom and his life as a god had suddenly become too heavy. Something else troubled him, but Deka couldn't sense what it was.

Next, the dark-skinned woman regarded the inspector-priest, the King's vizier, and the high priest in dismay, hoping that they had not lied about their desire to choose a woman tonight. Any of those three men choosing her would be unbearable to her after everything they had put upon her today. Seeking their intent without probing them enough to be noticed, Deka felt no focus upon herself from them. Relieved that it wasn't, she continued to wonder who it possibly could be. Someone else was watching her, and they were watching her in the same pointed manner as a predator stalking its prey.

GOING FORTH BY DAY

Deka did not have to wait long for her revelation. Soon, a man moved forward into the light of the dozen or so strategically placed torch stands. *This man must have gone into another room to refresh his cup or to relieve himself before we came in,* Deka thought. He was younger than the other men. If the crown prince was about thirty years of age, this man was likely under the age of twenty-five. His color was darker than the other men's skin, but lighter than her own. He was average height for a Kemet man, and his broad, heavily-muscled chest tapered to a small, hard waist and flat belly. His massive arms, fit with a showy and glittering collection of golden jewelry, were undeniably powerful. Emerging below his flawlessly-pleated shendyt kilt were even fitter and mightier looking legs. *His face!* Deka shook her head in dizzy disbelief. Marai, her Man-Sun, had a beautiful, calm, and loving face. This man's face was lovely too, but severe. Its expression spoke of a cold but sensual and arrogant rage that bubbled beneath its surface. An animalistic wildness that seemed as much a part of him as his own skin lurked in his expression. *Who is this man? Was he the one I felt watching me?*

After a quick salute to the King, the young man slumped into a vacant wicker chair near the high priest's dais. With a spoiled and petulant sulk, the newly arrived man studied her, approving yet predatory. He briefly glanced at Naibe, who still wandered near the pool, then snapped his eyes back to Deka. In a sudden movement, the man sat forward, pointed directly at her, and then beckoned for her to come closer to him.

Something, she thought calmly, but almost involuntarily moved in his direction. *He knows something,* Deka rose from her seat on the floor. She moved demurely at first, toward the man. With a turn to the side, she stretched her slim arms high above her head to display her shining henna-patterned breasts and torso. If this man meant to watch her intently, she would give him a show.

As she displayed herself, she felt a warm tremor course through her chest and out to the flanks of her arms as if the young prince had sent something that sought out and then fed on the energy in her body. *A spell?* she tensed and was about to defend herself, but she found all her desire to fight the feeling had fled.

Deka's hands spiraled up into shadowy dance movements, mimicking her dance that had started *everything* those many months ago. She had shown it to the young sesh priest from the house of Djehut because she recognized their kinship through the faraway land of Ta-Seti when she looked at him. With a graceful twirl, she brought herself near the two priests and then stood directly in front of the young man who had motioned for her. She hovered over him briefly and then grinned down at him, eerily confident. The energy in her arms ran quickly back into her heart and out of her chest toward him, it's seeking done.

The man cocked his half-nemes-draped head to one side: a slow, amused smile dotting his full and pouty lips. Deka recognized that same cautious half-smirk under those glittering but watchful eyes; she had seen it in the older priest's visage this morning.

This is the grandson; the General? Deka mused, knowing he was also a prince but one not as close to the throne as the man Ariennu entertained.

Something else in the man's eyes begged her to take an even closer look into them. The eyes of most people she knew were a deep variant of black or brown. The exception was Marai, whose eyes bore a silvery overcast to their natural black color. Her own eyes were a dark olive color once, but the Children of Stone had given them a cat-like green-gold overtone when they remade her. They had given Ari's eyes a black starriness and Naibe's light brown eyes a delicious golden flash that filled them with goddess stars. This man's eyes were a rich combined light brown, golden *and* green color almost like her own eyes in the plaza light. They seemed enhanced by something not entirely human, just as hers; a thing that quietly tugged at her memory. *Is he one of us?* her thoughts asked, but the Child Stone in her brow remained silent.

"Ta-Seti," his sultry voice spoke to Deka in the language of the upper lands and beyond. It had a kind of growling, rusty catch to it. She froze, hands raised, unable to move them any further. Without a blink or a change in expression, the man then whispered directly into her thoughts. *Will you dance the rain and wind? I know you, woman. I know you inside. I know what you like,* he pushed his thoughts at her again as they reverberated in her heart, descending in meter, volume, and pitch. In a way, his inner voice spoke to hers the same way she, Ariennu, and Naibe spoke to each other before the Children of Stone were part of her world. He spoke to her heart the same way Marai used to speak to them all.

With his words, however, came an instant spell. His hands, ringed and immaculately groomed, caressed the air briefly. They re-played her gestures as if he knew the answer to the question her dance asked. She gestured the unknown question again, approaching him closer, but he leapt to his feet and seized one of her hands firmly as she drew near. He twirled her under one arm, nodding at the old priest's pleased expression. The face of the Inspector, however, darkened in appalled concern over the younger man's actions.

Deka gasped a little. *Will you dance the rain and wind? Had he really said that? Wind and rain like a storm. Dance until the wind circles up. Laugh and run back and forth deep in madness until the rains come. Does he know about the rain?* she tensed. *Is he one of us?* she asked herself again. *How can he unlock my heart the way Naibe did on the way to Kemet so long ago if he is not one of us?*

Naibe had quite innocently blurted out, over a year before this day, that she thought Deka must have been the plaything of a god who had dropped her, bent and broken, to the earth when he had tired of her. The youngest of the three women had intended for her revelation to be a good-hearted tease designed to impress her sister in kind with her newfound ability to draw out secrets. She had no idea until it was too late, that her gentle wit had come far too close to the truth.

Golden-eyed Naibe had never owned more than one undimmed wit before she had been changed into a young goddess by the Children of Stone. She had been a drooling idiot with a heart-sickening sexual madness. That Naibe uncovered the truth before Deka herself could learn it, hurt rather than delighted the Ta-Seti woman. Something so angry and wild-hearted inside her had struck back at her instead of thanking her. To punish the young woman, Deka created a pathway to the night terrors which plagued Naibe that night and still bothered her to this day.

Shall I punish you for this? she wordlessly asked the Prince, *for daring to say you know me?*

"No, you shouldn't," he replied aloud and then whispered almost gently: "but you *should* come with me, for a walk." The younger prince tugged at Deka's hand and she stumbled a little closer into his semi-embrace. Catching her, he nipped at her ear then whirled her around to look at the elder priest. "Why *thank* you, Grandfather. A Ta-Seti piece, too! You *know* I like them so much," his gruff chortle echoed throughout the open plaza.

The King winced ever so slightly at this outburst, then with a tired, annoyed sigh he gulped at his cup of wine.

"See. This one's a stray out of old Akaru-Sef Metauthetep's house, I'll bet," the young prince continued. Taking Deka, who now couldn't hide her shock, by the chin, he turned her head to one side so the men could see the swept-back line of her brow. "Look at that profile! The old lion tamer's been holding out on me. Been hiding a granddaughter from me down here! She'll be *just* what I need for my journey next moon, if she's a decent piece at all," he grinned in increasing excitement.

"I *was just* thinking…" he turned to the King with an almost audible chuckle, saluting and bowing. "*If* I may take my leave, Excellent Majesty and Father God…" he looked up slightly enough to catch the King's expression of irritation, then lowered his eyes again humbly. He then sent a thought to the high priest so clearly that Deka sensed it and started to shake in a combination fear, rage, and delight. *You watch me, grandfather, while I solve all the problems here. You know I can.* With his head still bowed as if to receive the King's blessing, he spoke aloud: "I've had a delightful evening. I would stay, but I was thinking of showing this one my *boat* tonight, now that we've met, just to get better acquainted." He emphasized the word "boat" and then paused, suddenly sniffing at the air like some odd sort of hunting hound finding a scent. After a moment, he tilted his head down, looking fully human again. "Hmph! Might even make it rain a little drop or two, I see," the younger prince stared into Deka's green-brown eyes and then spoke into her thoughts. *Wind and rain, eh? You doing this for* me, *eh? Wind and rain it is, then.* Remaining bowed until the King nodded absent-mindedly to dismiss him, the young prince half-dragged Deka toward the cedar entry gate in the high white wall that surrounded Hordjedtef's noble plaza.

Ari stopped caressing the crown prince when she realized Deka hadn't resisted the younger prince in any sort of way. When she heard the tardy young general's boldness and salty wit, she maneuvered the man in her own arms so she could witness the expected fire.

GOING FORTH BY DAY

That man certainly has nerve to be so at ease in front of the King. They're both drunk. Must be, she thought. She knew the man was speaking to Deka in the tongue of her birthplace but knew that until that moment the woman hadn't recalled much of the language herself. He spoke with thought too. That felt like buzzing in her ears, but she didn't know the language they shared. What he had said *aloud* to his King about what he intended to do with her, however, was perfectly clear.

"Oooo-eee," the elder vizier giggled like an old woman as he paced back and forth on the edge of Hordjedtef's marble-stepped dais to still his own merriment. It was clear that everyone else in the plaza understood the young prince's intent.

Boat, eh? No pretty manners or even a hint *of respect there, I see.* Ari nearly burst in laughter herself as she continued to think about the comment. *He's not just bragging. He meant to say that. Should have set Bone Woman on fire, but it hasn't.* "Show her a boat" was a euphemism for a quick gash in almost any language *she'd* ever heard.

Ari wondered if the Ta-Seti woman was completely drunk or stupefied by the wine and the intoxicating incense the serving women had provided all afternoon. *Well she was drinking quite a lot of it. Maybe she thought being drunk would help her "fly away" from this man. I don't know. Maybe she saw something she liked.*

That she would put off Marai and then appear to eagerly go to this young man merited Ari's attention. When she focused on his look, her heart began to pound. *Whoa, goddess! That is so not fair. Not fair at all!*

She knew the Prince was aware she was sneaking a look. As if he had been prompted, he made a gesture that caused the muscles in his arms to glisten and ripple as he tucked Deka under one arm and stood with his back turned and his legs slightly apart. She traced the line of his lower back around the tight curve of his linen-shrouded buttocks and then lost herself in a fantasy of what she expected to find if she had reached to the front of his loin.

The young prince looked over his shoulder at her and raising one slanted eyebrow, he returned a thought to her:

Oh, I see. You don't fret, Red Sister. You can have some too, in time. After that, the Prince jerked Deka to his side. Ari saw his smile, but thought it resembled that of something undeniably hungry and about to bare its fangs. With another deep look into Deka's eyes he beckoned with his free hand. As if ordered, she straightened, stood aloof, calmly smoothed her skirt, and walked straight from the plaza with him. As they walked, he towed her by the hand as if she were a naughty child or a dog on a leash.

What was that? Ariennu wondered as she watched them leave. She remembered years before when Chibale had dragged Deka into the camp on a chain. Her departure like this seemed little different.

"Does something trouble you still, my pretty one?" the Prince in her own arms paused, taking notice of her staring and thinking she was upset again.

"Sorry, Your Highness," Ari spun a lie that was filled with half-truths designed to inspire the crown prince's confidence. "You are my savior from this tragedy, but my sisters and I have not often been apart since we were thrown together years ago. Is he a good man, this other prince?" she began, betraying that she *was* anxious. In truth she was an *aroused* sort of anxious.

So strong and outrageous enough, Deka? She knew everything in a glance without even trying to read him. Everything about him had climbed atop a mountain and shouted itself. *He's a killer. I can smell the death rolling off him.* She knew it was a more than suitable trait in a general or a warrior. The Prince in her arms wasn't like that. The crown prince was polite and seemed caring, even sympathetic to the thought that her heart might be broken. *I know that other man's kind though,* she reflected. *They get pleasure and pain so braided together that they become the same thing. N'ahab-atal was like that. I used to like that kind; lost boys. When they get old though, they are still boys and get greedy or disrespectful when they don't get their way.* The young general was no lost boy. He had wealth, sumptuousness, title, power, and a pretty face and form; all of that was topped with the ability to speak to her heart the way Marai and the Children of Stone could speak to it. The entire package made her ache so fiercely that the crown prince noticed. She knew she would have to cover her instant lust with something.

"How caring and sympathy-filled you are," the older prince patted Ari's arm. "That man is Prince Maatkare Raemkai. He is an excellent general and a powerful young man, beloved by the troops he commands in the Southern region; in Ta-Seti. Your sister *could* do well by him," he blinked calmly, then unfastened some of the pins and ornaments in her hair so that it flowed brightly into his hand. "Such a pretty color hair on you, not wretched as it is on a man."

Ari knew the crown prince had carefully guarded everything he said about the younger prince. His words felt tinged with sarcasm. He despised the other prince and the comment about Deka "could" do well implied she likely would not. Whether brother, cousin, or nothing, princes, as Ari had learned through listening to local gossip, considered each other rivals. They often plotted against each and considered killing any contender for the crown. Maybe the sensation she felt between the King, the crown prince, and this younger prince was nothing more than such a rivalry displayed.

Too late to think about that. I'm sure she'll contact me through our bond if it goes bad. For now, though, this one. If I can charm a crown prince, this king won't live as long as I will. I won't be any Daughter of the god, but the influence – Ari pushed away the quick thought that Marai, though immortal he'd told them, was apparently dead. Or was he? Maybe that was why she sensed no loss from the Children of Stone.

"I like you, Lady Ariennu," the crown prince spoke again. "I welcome you to my household tonight," he smiled. "You'll rest and be refreshed. In the morning you'll begin again. I'm certain my beloved will agree to you and you'll find naught but joy in being part of our family," the Prince stood up, then helped Ari stand with him. Together, they went back to the presence of the King and knelt before him for a blessing.

The King gave a vague, intoxicated smile that appeared sober but lost in thought, so the Prince took his gesture as permission to sit on the dais for a few moments in silence before leaving.

Ari worried about Deka, but now her thoughts went to Naibe. She glanced at the youngest woman, still unpaired, while the King and crown prince whispered to each other in a ritualized farewell. Naibe sat by the sesen pool, her hand swirling back and forth in the water. Ari knew the girl still considered tumbling face forward into the pool to drown herself.

Won't work, Baby, her thoughts consoled. *They'd just drag you out again.* Ari wanted to stay a little longer to see that the young woman would be going to a good situation, but Prince Shepseskaf stood up with her again then bowed once more to his father.

He moved her to the entrance of the open courtyard to await the arrival of his bearers and ready men with his sedan chair.

Ari followed him quickly, whispering under her thoughts to both of her sisters as she left. *It begins. Be strong and let's find our way back to each other when we can!*

GOING FORTH BY DAY

Chapter 7: Naibe's Charm

The memory of the morning plagued Naibe as if the announcement of Marai's death was still ringing in her ears. It swept over her like a wave of dark, falling night. She cried and ached inside until there was nothing left but hollow dullness. When she first heard the old priest say the words about his demise, she wanted to leap out of her skin; to somehow fly to Marai's ghost, never to return.

MaMa and Bone Woman thought I would die standing there. I wanted to. It would have been the greatest gift ever. She sat by the sesen pool, staring into the water. *It's all falling apart. Everything in my life is suddenly gone like it was' ripped out, dog-shredded, and broken. I don't want their help. No. No solace but his arms, and if not here, then perhaps I shall join him beyond, where gone from skin we can be one forever. I'll find where they laid him down and lie down with him; that's what Ari wants too. But, I can't – body destroyed by the light of wisdom. Was he burnt by the sun? Then, let me find a scrap of an ash. I will consume it with the finest wine so – Oh no, no, no. If he is nothing, I am nothing.* Naibe-Ellit thought of how she had panted and gasped, her breath growing short. Her sight had blurred and greyed, and then finally her legs failed when she heard the old priest speak. She knew it was wrong to allow a man to overtake her so greatly, but Marai had loved her and she had loved him back. She knew it would take too much effort on her part to ever love another man. Perhaps she would fly away after all, as Deka suggested. She hoped whoever chose her tonight would at least be considerate, so that she could dream of Marai when she lay with him.

Deka's gone with the youngish muscle-y one. Ari's out of this evil place with the crown prince. Who do I get? Is it one of these old men? Even the King is old, handsome though, she thought. *The Inspector? I will die before I allow his touch. Goddess you would punish your vessel for my dance to trick him. Why?*

Naibe's fingertips felt the gentle healing flow of the water through them and imagined even the sesen flowers, now closed and submerged for the night, extended their sympathy. The King watched her as she sat, but even a chance that he might choose her tonight no longer mattered to her. She planned to lose herself in the memories of Marai's touch, his mouth, his wonderful shining eyes, and the secret ways that had grown between them in their year together.

GOING FORTH BY DAY

Naibe and he had fallen together on too many journeys through each other's hearts. She had wanted to have his child and had been waiting for his time with the priests to be completed. For a time, right after he left, she thought her womb had awakened and had begun to swell; but her red moon came. Now, all her hope of having his child was forever lost.

She overheard the men talking; snickering about the young man who had just taken Deka and remarking that the crown prince might find his beloved wife not too appreciative of Ari since they had sought a fertile concubine. The red-haired one had no proven children.

Is that awful high priest daring to speak about me? she felt another sob rise in her chest. *Is he speaking of me as if I'm a brood cow when he says the older prince should have chosen 'a ripe thing like me'? Does he dare make sounds in my direction after destroying everything good in my life? I will see him dead. He will die choking on his proudness, drown in my vengeance, and all in his house will be evermore cursed,* Naibe swore to herself as she swirled her hand in the water of the pool again.

"Young NaBt," the elder priest cleared his throat as if he had just discovered an idle servant in need of an assignment, "would you dance for us?"

Naibe sat up straighter, turned and looked at the men. She was so stunned she couldn't focus on their faces in the flickering torchlight. *Let him speak. I won't hear him until his guards come at me,* she sighed, devoid of any care. *The young man who left with Deka said something about the rain. Is the wetness in the air they felt rain, or is it my tears? I could make them come from the sky because I weep. She, too, weeps; the goddess within me. We cry out for our beloved, my Marai and our very own Dumuzi the shepherd.* Naibe-Ellit knew the kohl on her eyes had run, and that she had smeared it all over her face.

Dance.

The sad little voice inside the stone in her brow whispered to her as if it finally understood the depth of her grief. When she heard it whisper, it sounded like Marai's gentle voice. For a moment, the sound of it comforted her. In the next instant, it broke her heart again because she knew it was only a spirit voice. She knew it would be her only link to him for the rest of her days.

Know, beloved goddess, that I want you to.

Naibe almost let a sob escape. Then, with her eyes cast down, she struggled to her feet. One of the attendants shook a sistrum again. A musician resumed pulling the strings of his harp. Somewhere, she thought she heard the voice of another man whisper: "I think she was his favorite."

His favorite, the words echoed in her heart. *Then, I must give my dance back to him, as he has asked – once more before I die.*

Naibe-Ellit twirled and swayed, moving toward the men. Her arms began to roll and play as the seductive music of the harp and the jingle of the sistrum reverberated in her body. Her naked breasts trembled and shimmered, the spirit glow of pure and healing love rose through her lion-gold skin. With a quick flip, she loosened the gaily woven scarf that had been tied about her hips to reveal a dark, snug-fitting loin belt with golden beads dangling in the front. The music drove through her body and soul as she danced and began to call down the spirit of a woman's ecstasy.

Oh, Goddess in me, please! Let this be for my beloved to see it from where he is, so that he can come to take me with him to his world. Let death come to take me too, she shimmied on among the smiling men. *Ah, look. The King is smiling. He has no right to desire me,* she affirmed as she arched her back until her forearms brushed the floor sweetly behind her. Her knees parted as her buttocks poised above them. They tightened until she could gain her balance on her arms and kick one leg over at a time. She slid into the floor, then rolled on her belly with her arms extended in front of her. She reached toward the King. Her hands implored as he leaned forward for a better look. She knew, as if by instinct, the next step she needed to take.

King.

Naibe looked up. She whispered into the thoughts of the man with the full nemes who sat in front of the spot where she lay. Her soul spoke to his:

GOING FORTH BY DAY

You looked the other way,
While my beloved suffered.
Yet, you have suffered.
Remember,
I have seen your sorrow in my heart.
The precious one who has died
while, again, you did nothing.
The curse you bear within your heart
which the oracle told
was your failure to protect your beloved child
from the hidden one summoned by another.

Her head tossed and arms traced the floor as she arched her hips forward slowly, becoming a woman merged with a serpent. Her movements undulated to the beat of the sistrum.

Are they murmuring at my skill? Are they whispering that it's good? Of course it is! Has the King felt my thoughts? Then he should listen to these:

I am the serpent of earth.
I am temptation to life,
To birth through my sacred womb.

The King shifted uncomfortably in his chair. The other men snickered uncomfortably, like young boys, as they watched her moving in joyous rapture while she balanced above her own ankles. *Do they see the serpent in my heart? Do I care? I will bite them with my poison one by one! The dance isn't for them. It never will be for them. Only my vengeance will they take from me!* Her eyes closed and mouth opened in a gasp of pleasure, knowing once again the memory of all Marai's touches and caresses. *Oh, Marai, please be here. Be with me, sweet, again. Be part of me. You see how I need you so much.* She felt movement at her feet. Someone approached her. *Is it you, my beloved?* she asked the hot air above her.

A hand went under her arched back, but the owner of that hand tottered and slipped. Naibe collapsed backward in a heap on the polished tile, a man who was *not* Marai lay sprawled on top of her. Instantly sobered, she sobbed helplessly; her dream shattered. It was the high priest, Prince Hordjedtef. He had risen from his chair and advanced to seize her. He had been drunk, half-dazzled by the dance; convinced she would fall into the pool if he didn't grab her. She felt his wiry, ancient frame weighing down on her, aroused. It was too much.

"You? No! Murderers!" she clawed at him, fought, kicked, scratched, and bit. "Marai! Help me! Let me die! Now! No! Get off me!" she screamed.

Elder Prince Hordjedtef scrambled up from the young woman, shocked. He leapt back a full step, infuriated at her rejection but also amazed that he had even made a move toward her.

Inspector of the Ways Wserkaf darted to her and grabbed her up into his arms. He touched her shoulders, then pressed at her neck to calm her. Clapping her firmly to his chest, he accepted her grief-weakened fists as they beat at his arms.

The King frowned, sitting straighter in his chair. "Uncle?" his voice rose in bewildered surprise as if what he had heard the young woman cry out instantly cleared his hazy thoughts. "Did she just call us *murderers*? I know my Kinacht, now. What *is* this? Is there something you're not telling me?" The now-sobered man bent forward in his chair again, then nodded to Wserkaf to keep a fast grip on her as he extended his hand. King Menkaure turned his ringed hand palm upward and gestured to the Inspector of the Ways that he wanted Naibe brought forward as soon as she stopped struggling.

Hordjedtef shook himself out, clasped his hands behind the back of his neck, and hissed something under his breath about sorcery and fiery winged *seref*. He quickly praised Goddess Seshat that he had *not* been on duty when he had been caught in the young woman's demonic spell.

"No, nooo. Please let me end it," Naibe-Ellit continued to quietly struggle against the Inspector's chest as he moved her toward the King. Her right hand slipped to her side, afraid at first to grasp the King's extended hand.

"There, poor one," the Inspector consoled as he pressed and massaged the back of her neck until her head lolled and relaxed against his chest. "Your king wishes that you —" he started to remind her she needed to obey Menkaure's kindness. He did not need to finish. Naibe let the King take her trembling hand in his.

The tense moment lengthened, punctuated occasionally by her light sobs. The King stroked her hand gently, trying to calm her. "Poor thing's heart is really broken, it seems." King Menkaure sighed as his own voice drifted.

Naibe felt the King's secrets enter her heart. Her power to read emotions and unlock hearts had been heightened by her sorrow and by her dance. At first, she thought his reaction to her was due to the cups of wine he had gulped all evening, but even through her misery she saw more of his heart than she wanted to see.

In King Menkaure's eyes, Naibe saw his memory of being crouched by a young woman who lay dying on a pale, polished floor. Naibe knew the woman lying there was the King's daughter, even though she knew nothing of his family through the rumors she'd heard. A strap of the woman's torn kalasiris was twisted tight around her neck. The King wrested the fabric from her neck and stared, horrified at the growing bruise that had been uncovered and the way her head sagged unnaturally as he lifted her close. In the distance, frantic servants pointed to a place above him; it was an upper balcony. She had jumped over the rail to hang herself. The King lifted her tearfully, imploring all the gods for her. He begged the Goddess Hethara to not depart the vibrant body in which she had so artfully walked these twenty years.

When she saw the King's own sorrow, Naibe remembered it was her own call for vengeance a few moments ago that must have made his sad memory come forward. That she had gained such a power made her cry even harder.

"Yet —" the King's voice soothed, "see how touching. She still tries to please us, despite her grieving," Menkaure continued, his manner so nurturing and un-kingly.

Naibe-Ellit felt a sudden sense of calm. *Perhaps this king, though older, might not be as these other men.* She allowed the Inspector to transfer her to King Menkaure's lap. As he did, she noticed the strength in his arms and the way they surrounded her like a warm blanket. He would have been a great comfort to her if this had been any other time. Overwhelmed by her misery, she tentatively lay her head on his chest. She sensed his heartbeat and felt the slight bite of the stones and glass beads in his wide collar as she put her arms around his neck. Naibe stopped being a woman who had offered herself to her King and became a little girl who wanted to be soothed. She tried to stop crying so that she could feel the gladness of the King's touch, but only sobbed harder because his warmth brought back all her thoughts of Marai and the way he would hold her so tenderly after they had loved. King Menkaure patted her back, waiting for the elder high priest to answer his question about murder.

"As we have said, Your Majesty, there was *no murder.*"

Even though she was secure in the King's arms, Naibe sensed more than she heard. Count Prince Hordjedtef cleared his throat. His thoughts were too easy to read. His embarrassment over her rejection trumpeted itself out across the courtyard to her.

Damn her. The girl is a heka-filled she-beast. First she tricks me into drinking too much, then dazzles me! But I was the quicker one to get on with the protection I spoke! Almost, young heifer, almost.

Without raising her weary head from the King's chest, Naibe knew he had returned quietly, albeit rattled, to slump in his dark stone chair.

"The man, their 'husband' as it were, demanded to learn of the sacred keys of knowledge before he was ready to undertake it," the Great One explained. "Your kind Majesty *do* recall this was the sojourner who claimed prior knowledge of the 'First Age'. When we, against our better judgment, admitted him to study, he progressed through all our lessons in a quick order."

The King looked up at the servant who had arrived at the left side of Hordjedtef's dais with a tray of cups that contained the last round of drinks for the evening. Sensing him shift, Naibe clung harder, but lifted her head to look at the King as Menkaure blessed the youth who had gone to his knees the moment he set down the tray. The King accepted some soothing honey-infused tea and nodded to the other men who were still present that they should try his uncle's new calmative brew.

"But, he had not entirely emptied himself," she heard Prince Hordjedtef continue. "He was neither master nor match for the light of Ma-at. As I had perceived, he understood only the physical and the sensual dimensions. He was able to parrot higher truths, but not comprehend them," he sipped again as he framed his next words. "His boasting of his readiness for final trial undid him," the elder breathed. "It was a tragic accident! We discovered too late how little he *truly* knew and figured him to be naught but a usurper. Because he had trespassed, we had little choice but to turn the matter over to the gods. So, we placed him in the preparatory ritual. He went mad and raged like a bull. Then, the *true* Bull of the Sky engulfed him and he self-immolated."

Naibe bowed her head again, distressed, but sensed the Inspector was even more upset by his senior's story. She sobbed once, saying to herself: *It's a lie. All of it. He knows that's not what happened.* The King pressed her again, but the young woman knew he thought of his daughter on his lap and in his arms.

"It's alright Meri, sometimes the things men do —" he started but stopped with an inaudible gasp. Clearing his throat, he took the cup and offered it to Naibe.

She sipped a drop or two, then shut her eyes and shook her head, not wanting any more.

"I read the report when the Inspector of the Ways brought it to me last week, Uncle," the King's voice sounded even wearier.

Naibe knew it wasn't the wine or the tea that tired him; it was sorrow. She almost regretted that she had cursed him now because she realized he was so broken.

The Inspector tried to hide his feelings but was only successful in blocking them from the high priest. Naibe didn't want to feel the Inspector's thoughts or anything else of him, but they had come through her so easily, like he was crying for help. Through the weight of her own emotions she saw that he *had* already gone on record the week before, but his notes stated he did *not* actually *see* the sojourner die; he had only learned of it through Hordjedtef. He had been assigned to go into a trance to locate the sojourner's spirit, to determine if it was of the realm of the living or if he had died. He couldn't find anything. Her heart sank again. *That part's no lie, but no god or goddess caused my Marai to die. He knows that. He wanted to speak the truth when he heard that man lie.*

She felt the King stroking her loosening hair and making it cascade down her back like a soft easy-curling black river. She didn't understand what was happening, but she felt safe in the big man's arms and knew he felt it too. In her darkest hours she could still comfort him, when he was supposed to be the enemy of all that she loved.

Does this sweet girl see my heart? Does she understand why I need to drink more than usual when that despicable wretch of a man attends me? Can it be that she sees *me?* She felt his thoughts enter her and ask impossible questions.

Naibe didn't want the King's sorrow to enter her already broken heart, but it insisted on invading her. She sensed the King's daughter who died and knew somehow that she had been paired with the young general who had taken Deka away. Without wanting to know about it, she became painfully aware that after a tempestuous and often scandalous year the young princess hanged herself. Though the Prince and King had quickly cut her down, her neck had snapped. She died in her father's arms.

My uncle, Count Prince Hordjedtef's, grandson. I trained him and took him into my home for her, to ease our anguish when my son young Kuenre died. She had been so vibrant and joyous, but so stormy and wild-hearted as well. I thought Prince Maatkare might settle her with his own hot-blooded nature. I never denied her wishes to have him as her royal consort, but she could have been so much more, the King lamented the past as he continued to hold Naibe.

When Naibe felt the King's conflict over the young man pass through her, she quietly cried again. Her thoughts filled with bitterness at the condescending way the high priest had spoken of Marai. Now the King spoke about her beloved too.

"Ah, but I have seen such a thing, Uncle," she felt the King bow his head to hers again. "Sometimes the comeliest of all, like this one here, are smitten beyond words by the villain or the madman. The dear daughter out of my body –" he began, Naibe knew her being with him had made him think of his daughter and that had made him incurably miserable. In a moment, when he had regained his bearing, he looked at the Inspector politely. "I can't accept her like this, though she is honey-sweet," he helped the young woman stand and guided her back to Wserkaf. "Take her into your own home. Perhaps she might serve there until she comes to her senses. Our kindest

Khentie will tell me when she is ready to move on." The King then turned away and accepted another cup of warm wine from the old man.

Wserkaf bundled Naibe into his arms and hushed her tears.

"Hush there, sweet one." He whispered, but knew instinctively those were the wrong words when she called out and started to struggle:

No. No. Don't want. Then aloud: "No!"

Hordjedtef nodded curtly, still apparently humiliated by his own action during her dance.

Remove that sorceress from my sight at once, Wse. She will not set foot in this house again.

Her struggles increased to the point where the Inspector found the relaxation point above her shoulder and cast stillness on her.

As soon as the fight went out of her, Wserkaf carried her to his sedan chair. As they were borne toward his estate, the Inspector hoped she would find peace enough to heal there.

Our Father is right. My Khentie is an excellent counselor and no stranger to grieving. She'll be more than glad to help ease the girl's sorrow. It'll be restful and easy for her, and there'll be no demands on her. I owe that much to Marai. I couldn't save him or convince him to save himself. Maybe redemption is through this child-woman — if she can bear to accept our help. Maybe in time she'll even be able to again find some of the happiness she had shown in the presence of her beloved Marai.

Chapter 8: Visions and Memories

Relax. This is not real. Say it to myself once again: he can't beat me, if I do not accept defeat.

Marai remembered how confident his thoughts had been as he sank into the trance needed for the ritual of scrutiny. Now so much time had passed. *How long?*

I do not accept this as defeat. I am stronger than this. The dull ache of existence had wrapped him in its tentacle-like grip so tightly that he couldn't sense how long he had been lying in the tomb. He only knew that he was still there and that he was alive.

One more time, the words. Maybe it will be enough. He felt himself gradually slipping away.

Be not unaware of me, O God;
If you know me, I will know you.

And the answer returned in gentle voices – blended tongues of Kina, Shinar and Kemet; all gently intoned by the women he had come to love more than his own existence. The whispered sound in his thoughts had buoyed him in the bad moments and sustained him. He would not accept defeat, but it was growing harder for him to remember who spoke it or what the women looked like.

Get through it.
No matter what it takes.
See it to the end.
You are strong enough.
You always were.
Come back to us, my love
My love remember how to live.

I was too sure of myself with your help "little child stone in my head". He spoke to the blackish metallic stone that lay under the skin between his brows. *You were something to know, old man. You convinced every one of your followers to believe falsehoods of me and never question. To ask them to curse me before their Gods, though? Now I lie here floating in the solitude of my own thoughts for ages, but how long?* To pass the time he always found solace in the ritual words that echoed through every miniscule cell of his body locked in eternal and suffering chorus:

He lives. Your servant lives.
Wepwawet opens a way for me,
Shu lifts me up,
in order to reach the Above,
and Nut puts her hand on me
just as she did for Asar on the day when he died
You go, this sojourner goes –

G-goddess it hurts. Another spasm bored through his body. *But if I'm suffering, I'm alive because the dead don't know pain. When will there be no more pain? Will I know the last one?*

Naibe, my sweetest one, Marai's thoughts whispered into space in the hope her soul could hear his cry. *I need you. Teach me. Heal my soul.*

He felt consumed by the thought of just slipping away. He saw himself dangling suspended in midair over the stone coffin in which he lay. That image twisted into something else – a raised well with no pit at the bottom. Only the roar of empty space formed beneath him, and then he realized he was waking into a vision of a long and endless fall into nothingness. His consciousness tensed, but the image changed again until he saw himself hanging upside down by one leg with his arms bound behind his back like the image of the hanging man, and the tomb had transformed into a vaulted cave.

As if seized by a fresh onslaught of fever, he concentrated on the words of the incantation again:

The doors of the horizon open themselves, the bolts slide –

At his concentration, the cave around him vanished as the open starry sky appeared above.

May you allow this wise one to seize the cool region.
standing over the places of the first ocean –

With this, he now saw himself flipped upright and unbound, enveloped in cold blue fire, yet burning inside with a hotter flame as he now straddled the well over the void. The stars above his head became waves beneath his feet. *One false step,* Marai thought about his impending doom.

Then, remembering the coolness of Deka's dark cinnamon-colored hands placed on his hot brow, he was filled with renewed hope. He had not thought of her so far in his interminable time suffering, but she, the second of his three wives, would be the one who could calm Hordjedtef's poison. She would sing her healing song to him in her beautiful Ta-Seti tongue, even though he couldn't understand the words. With the thought of her, Naibe, and Ari, the whirling visions subsided and he was left again in the empty blackness of his trance.

Wives. Not by ceremony or writ, not all by flesh. We simply lived and worked together, caring for each other – a family. I call them all MaMa. MaMa, help me through this. Help me. His thoughts scattered, wanting to weaken. He didn't know if the blackness that engulfed him was true relaxation or death at last.

Then, a point of light formed as if some invisible hand placed it in the distance. A pattern of intersecting circles formed and grew until the pattern became a living and breathing entity. It radiated majesty and glory. He heard the distant roar of a lion mixed with the voice of a man: *Believe you can, and you will prevail.*

The flower. H-Hordjedtef showed – the Children inside – hollow crystal filled stone. He thought of the bed in which he and the women had been changed. *I want to lie there with them forever. I hurt.*

GOING FORTH BY DAY

As if his wish had been granted, he lay there, but the shape had changed into something else with him at the center. Now there were two rondels of the pattern. He didn't see or sense it, but he knew an invisible third pattern above those two began to turn. As it did, the lower two changed shape into cones shaped like two of the Eternal Houses for the dead kings set tip to tip. Moving together, these two shapes began to intersect such that the tips of each aligned with the open squares at the bottom of the other. This final shape, for which Marai had no name, rolled towards him and halted as if he was expected to step into it. The sharp, harsh edges of the shape softened then, beginning to resemble the glowing sleep pod in which he had rested for so many years among the Children of Stone. The sojourner stepped up, turned, and sat in the shape as it transformed into a flying throne. The weightlessness he had felt in the faraway sleep pod all those years ago returned to the forefront of his thoughts as the throne closed around him. A spinning sensation overtook him, and all worry, terror, pain, and time fell away. Rays of light sifted through the shape, bending through and inside him, and then streamed out of the other side of his body in rainbow colors. He felt as if he had grown large enough to incorporate all of life and time itself in his heart.

> *"O beautiful one, Asher-Ellit;*
> *Immaculate one of the goddesses,*
> *Come bless me this starry night.*
> *Shine for one who begs to serve you.*
> *Come bless me this starry night."*

Marai heard himself singing the song he sang to his goddess Ashera for fifteen years to atone for the death of his wife and child. It came to him as clearly as if he was still singing it to her on that starry night when what he thought was his goddess came to him.

> *Come and see me…*

He remembered how the Child-voices had sounded like the tinkle of a hundred tiny rings and bells on a dancer's swirling skirts, luring him in search of her across the scrub-filled wasteland where he had lived. He thought he would find her a chariot drawn by flaming lions. Instead, it had been a fallen star.

There is something here

The Children of Stone had been on that star. It was their boat of the places beyond his sky, they told him. He never saw them, but he felt their words inside his heart. He never understood why they had come to the wastes of the land below Sin-Ai, or Place of the god Sin. He never knew what their goals truly were, only that they needed his help. As he rode above the heavens in his own mind-born boat, the memory came to him as clearly as the words he had sung to his goddess.

Perhaps I was a fool after all, Marai thought as he continued to traverse the wonderful imagined starry depths, *a fool to be amazed by those little glittering stones. But then, they can think and act and they even flew through the sky to come here. Why shouldn't I be amazed?* The man accepted that even if the children were not his goddess, they were certainly worthy of being called gods. *They gave me so much as well,* he continued with the thought of how sun-burnt and overworked his aging body had been before the children arrived.

Now his body was godly, and so were the bodies of the three women he had decided to help along the way. The four of them were now beyond human, marked by the "Child Stones" left in their brows like small unreachable eyes. *Why me? Why was I chosen for this?* he had asked the Children of Stone. They had told him that as their song seduced him, his song to his goddess had come into their restless souls to teach them about the nature of man, and the power of devotion. *Devotion?* he asked himself as he lay trapped. *Foolishness and madness!* He wanted to shake his head in grief, and with that impulse, the horrible cursing thought which had come to him when he first entered his trance returned:

You will not escape them.
They will use you until you are gone
and nothing remains of your simple shepherd man but an empty shell.
Pray you die tonight.
Pray to the gods,

GOING FORTH BY DAY

if you have any left who will listen to you,

to take you from this,

lest what they create goes on to animate your dead flesh forever.

Great One's thought sent to me at the end like a bad spell. I know. Rage that the gifts the Children had brought were wasted on a mad peasant such as myself.

No one's coming back to see how I am. I will die. He knew, but didn't want to know that he would be left to rot in this stone box in the depths of some forgotten tomb. For him, there would be no Going Forth By Day.

His inner voice answered the curse:

They chose me for my devotion, for my ability to continue despite all odds. I may not know the way to return, I may not know how long I will suffer, but I shall endure. Laughing to himself, he returned once more to where he had begun. *Relax, Marai. This is not real. He can't beat you, if you don't accept defeat.*

Men should have come to check on me, but I think no one has. Return? Where is Wserkaf?

The first evening he had been entombed, Marai had sent a thought to the inspector-priest, telling him he had survived the initial onslaught of Hordjedtef's herbal preparation. Now, whenever now was, he sent another thought.

Wserkaf. Code name Wseriri… were you coming to check on me? Was I wrong? The old man didn't turn you again, did he? he implored the ether in the hope that his thought would reach the inspector-priest. *Maybe I'm wrong about the time passing. Maybe it hasn't been more than a few hours in this cursed stone box, and this is still the middle of the first night. Wserkaf will come. He is a man of his word. He'll get to me, I'm sure. Hard to tell.*

His urge to escape; to somehow turn on his side so he could worm his legs into a bent position then turn again to press his feet against the lid, never stayed in his thoughts long enough for the action to become more than a flight of fancy. The sojourner imagined he had tried that, and failed, many times. Sometimes he thought he had only dreamt of doing this, because he knew it was impossible to push the lid up and off the box even with his superior strength. Gradually, something magical began to happen to the sojourner in his deep trance. Each time he willed something, Marai became part of whatever he willed. He sensed all things and became part of everything he knew. Soon, it became harder and harder to identify himself with anything he remembered of his waking life either in Kemet, or the Sin-Ai wastes, or even from his wandering childhood. As time passed, new visions swarmed through him. Eventually, except for his stubborn periodic risings, he began to lose interest in "Going Forth by Day."

Marai vaguely remembered this same sort of oneness had come to him on the Children's vessel that had come down years before. Somehow, he had forgotten most of what he saw. Once he woke from his 'sleep' on the crystalline vessel, the dream world quickly became a vague and fleeting memory, like he was forbidden to remember such illuminating and wondrous sights.

Now in a trance again, the doors to the dream world were open and he remembered those things which had left his waking mind. This time, Marai understood so much more of what had happened to him when he slept. Most of the images in his dreams the first time had been lulling and gentle; something to observe and learn. The second time, when the women were healed and re-formed, the images had been about *them* and how he might best go from the life of a solitary hermit to a man who would take three women as wives. Were the children directing his visions and memories, or were these thoughts coming to him because he willed it, the sojourner wondered.

Random images flickered through Marai's thoughts and filled his body. There was a woman whose face was obscured by a veil. She stood and beckoned to him, then she shrank through herself and became a little girl again. A faceless demon's hands reached from behind a curtain to touch her and then to fondle her. The vision repeated through his expanded thoughts again and again as if it was on a seamless loop of rope. He tried to blot it from his thoughts. He had never possessed the madness of sexual desire for a child, so he wondered why the nightmare pursued him. Whenever other visions had become too peaceful, evil scenes like this crept in like unbidden demons. Slowly, the image of the man behind the curtain became the darkness that had perched on Deka's shoulders when the Inspector first visited them.

Deka. Something's happened to Deka while I am here. A sick feeling filled him that all the women teetered on the brink of disaster.

Why can't I see them? he asked, creating a vision of their happy apartment in Little Kina-Ahna and becoming part of it. *Where is Etum Addi and his family? Why can't I see everyone working at the market? Why can't I even visit them as they sleep… as part of a dream?*

Try again! his thoughts rang. He imagined that if he had been out of his trance, he might have gritted his teeth hard enough to break them at his effort. *We've had a not-bad life together, my beautiful ones!* He thought in a disheartened whisper, not knowing if his message had reached his loved ones.

Ari, Mad Red Ari, as tall as the sky, who wove the clouds about her breasts and rainbows into her hair appeared in his thoughts, bent to him and whispered sweetly:

I'm your secret keeper. One day I'm gonna unlock the rest of this thing the Children started with us. I might not look the same… be the same… Her belly churned like the goddess of creation, birthing out her varied shapes and colors from so many different times, only to suck all of them back into herself until they lay superimposed on her basic form, giving her extra arms and heads.

A monster is coming for me. He's hidden in the dark. Marai cried out in his mind as he sensed another nightmarish vision beginning. Longing for the comfort of his beloved ones, he whispered to them to keep the nightmare at bay if they could. *If this is it. If I die here and I will never touch you again, I will return in another shape. I think I'll always find you, no matter who you are, or if, when we meet, you even believe me anything but mad. And on that day when we meet again, our hearts will touch once and say: Yes, I knew you well, my love. Yes, I knew you well!*

Chapter 9: "A Curse be on Your Houses!"

Wserkaf, who had been cradling Naibe in his arms as the men bore him to his nearby estate, rocked her like a suffering child.

You caught my teacher into his cups and with his guard down so that he reached for you and became an old fool. The situation had made him almost laugh except for the tragic nature of the evening. If the "old fool" hadn't been Hordjedtef and the King hadn't been there, he might have.

When he felt her sliding from his arms, he secured her more carefully and whispered: "bless this night and the stars above us."

"No," the young woman gasped and struggled again. "No. Please, don't take me! Haven't you done enough to me already? Leave me. Just let me find my own way across the river," she protested.

"Shhhh… " the Inspector tried, holding her fast on his chest. "Nothing's going to happen to you. Not tonight, not *any* night, unless you wish it," he whispered. Wserkaf had hoped this would reassure the girl, but as the bearers moved away from the estate and down the path, she cried even more heartily.

"He said that. He said that," the Inspector heard Naibe mumble against his chest. As if her tears created a magical window, he heard her thoughts: *Not any night unless you wish it. How dare he use those words my love said to me. How dare he!*

Wserkaf tensed, and then noticed her tearful face had nestled on his pectoral collar and had moistened the wdjat crystal fastened to the underside of it. He touched the side of it and then patted the back of her head again.

She's right. I remember Marai telling me that he said that. Poor thing doesn't know I opposed my senior over Marai's final treatment. I'm the enemy to her.

"Let me go," she stated flatly.

"You need to rest; to grieve your beloved in peace and quiet. I've offered you my

GOING FORTH BY DAY

home to have as a safe place for now," Wserkaf urged. "It's nice there – peaceful. You'll see. My dear wife Khentie can help you through your sorrow, she's good at that." The Inspector was truly at a loss for any *other* way to console the woman, but he knew every word he spoke stabbed like a new knife plunged into her heart. Wserkaf stroked the back of her neck gently as he sent another wave of healing energy through her. He knew she was exhausted from the day. The rhythmic sway of the chair borne on the shoulders of four men had almost lulled her to sleep when the men turned and entered the gated area of the Inspector's estate. They brought the chair through the double wooden doors and into the plaza. The Inspector helped the woman down and started to guide her forward into the open area when Naibe suddenly went to her knees.

"Oh goddess, he's gone! Leave me alone! Let me die!" she shrieked.

Instantly, the Inspector's entire household was in an uproar. The servants and guards ran toward the gate to see what was going on.

Wserkaf bent down and tried to pull the young woman up, but she was rooted to the spot.

"Kill me! Kill me, priest! I can't *be* in your world. Stars. I must go home! I must go to the stars! To my El Anu, my Father! Kill me! Let me go!" she screamed.

Instead of being able to help her up, Wserkaf found Naibe-Ellit had tucked herself into a tight rocking ball. She would not move from the threshold of his front courtyard.

"Wse. What's this?" the Inspector's wife rushed across the courtyard toward him. Behind her was her serving girl, along with the women's personal attendant. The three women clustered in the gateway, then bent down to assist the strange young woman clad only in a dance shawl and belt. "Is she the Kina woman? She said a Kina god's name as her *Father?*" The woman smoothed her own curly dark hair, and then reached forward to the sobbing creature.

"A curse is on all of you!" Naibe snarled, burying her face in her loose and billowing hair that had spread itself out on the tiles. "You knew it was wrong, but you did *nothing* to save my beloved. *Death* is in this house!"

Wserkaf's wife hissed a quick protection under her breath, and then admonished her husband: "Wse, she *cannot* curse our house. *Show* her!" she stepped back quickly, averting her eyes from the young woman's now upturned glance.

Wserkaf seized Naibe's heaving shoulders and shook her hard.

"Die! Murderers!" the girl howled.

The Inspector cuffed her in the face with his open palm, mostly to distract her.

"Stop it!" he roared. "Stop it *now*, I command you!" his hand seized the wdjat crystal on the gold chain around his neck so he could show it to her, but she collapsed in a motionless heap on the floor. Everyone who had come to see what was going on moved back a worried step. "Huh?" the Inspector bent to the woman crumpled before them, shocked. He touched her throat to check her life signs.

"Wse, is she… ?"

"I didn't hit her *that* hard, Khentie!" the Inspector stammered. The thought that he might have killed her so effortlessly unnerved him. "I think she's just fainted," he turned to two of the bearers who had brought the chair in. "Here. Bek, Resh, stretch her out on the floor here," he pointed to an empty spot in his plant-filled interior plaza. Darting to his reflection pool, he gathered some pillows from a wicker couch to place under Naibe's head.

"Something to cover her –" Khentie suggested to her maid, but as soon as Wserkaf put the pillows under Naibe's head he unfastened his travel cloak and laid it over her. "Poor thing." She asked: "is she one of those women you were telling me about?"

Wserkaf bent to fan her face, but she didn't stir. After a few silent moments, he checked her signs again and sighed in relief.

"She is. She's alive but her signs are slower and weaker than should be healthy – as if she is playing dead as some beasts do when in danger. She's the one who danced for me that day; the youngest wife."

"Well, why would you bring *her* here? Were there not *three* of them?"

GOING FORTH BY DAY

Wserkaf moved aside to allow his wife to kneel beside him. The woman smoothed Naibe's hair, then paused.

"I think you must have struck her, Wse. There's a blue mark on her brow and her hands are so cold. I should send someone for a healer." She started to get up again, but he stopped her.

"Not yet," he looked into her eyes earnestly. "Let me try to explain. The blue is something else – a stone in the head. The man I told you about and the three women each have them and call on them for godly powers I think."

Khentie shook her head and grasped her Hethara token at her throat, whispering her own protection.

"Godly powers? Is this poor thing a priestess in her land? Why are we even *dabbling* with this sort of risk? And you never said anything about the foreign god part to me? Do you have more I need to know as Daughter of the God?"

Wserkaf noticed her tone grow imperious.

"It's not like that, Khen. The girl is barely aware of her powers. None of them had training; not the man Marai and I think the women had even less awareness. Don't worry," He held her arm in reassurance. "The other two found homes to go to," he checked the girl again. "One is in our brother's house; the other went with Maatkare Raemkai to *his* house. I had hoped our Father-God would take this one to gladden his heart, but she was in no shape for his holy house. He asked me to see if you could help her mend her heart with your gentle counsel, then perhaps send her to him when she is better."

The Inspector lifted Naibe's head and examined the blue spot, then took his wife's fingertips and encouraged her to smooth the place. When the spot seemed to purr beneath their fingertips, he smiled.

Kindness is the cure, and the undoing

A small voice whispered in the man's thoughts. He knew Khentie heard it too and was about to ask because it generated more questions than answers, when he saw her sigh and shake her head.

"You know Our Father far better than I, Khentie. A woman *this* distraught – with all the tragedies and curses he's had to endure. He couldn't gain any joy from this one."

"This is truth, Wse. Two years ago, recall Mother Khammy even chose to have her own apartment. They appreciate each other well and come to official functions as one, but she cannot bear his sadness, nor he hers, without one or the other taking a knife or powder to end things. And if that beast attended, I still have no understanding of the reason Our Father was there."

"I think Great One coerced him to come to this evening. It's that simple," he answered. *Being in the same room with Maatkare was enough of a risk even though the man has matured considerably since he called him "son",* Wserkaf reminded himself.

"So, help her through her grief because I console Our Father and have the scar of tragedy on my own heart?" Khentie's face went calm and unlined as if the emotion drained from it. "Well, if he asked it then I am honored, Wse. You know that," Khentie hesitated, as if another thought was forming in her heart but never found its way to her lips.

"Perhaps the guest room can be hers for now," Wse suggested. "She'll need a close eye on her through the night. Then, tomorrow, she can move to stay with your women in *their* room if she feels better." Wserkaf gestured for the men who had placed Naibe-Ellit on the tiles to carry her to the little room that overlooked the edge of the pool. Mya, Khentie's little handmaiden, and another servant moved the unconscious woman's basket of things from the set-down sedan chair to the guest room. "And go get some wet soil from the cattle pen… some that's strong-smelling, to shock her senses back to us," Wserkaf ordered the men to go to the back yard of his estate, where a few head of cattle were kept. Still very worried, he gently tucked his arm around Khentie and brought her to the guest room behind the men who carried Naibe. The men carefully set her on the padded bed once they were in the room. The maids set her things down along with two folding stools for Wse and his wife.

"Smell that, Wse?" Khentie looked up from the resting woman, astonished. She clasped his hands affectionately, as if she expected he would magically calm the strife that had entered their estate with the weeping woman.

Wserkaf recognized the smell; it was that of a coming storm. He thought about the little bit of rain that might come before day. *Maatkare, talked about it. Sniffed it like a dog, he did – teased the Ta-Seti woman he took about making it rain, too.* Wserkaf nodded.

"Rain, in the distance," Khentie whispered, settling beside her husband and looking up into his eyes. "What an odd time of year for it. Do you think it's a sign? This woman cries to the stars as if she commands them to aid her. Now, rain comes to soothe her hurting heart." Khentie reached forward to hold Naibe's hand, blowing on it to warm it.

Wserkaf looked up from the girl and Khentie. The servants had returned from the livery. They carried a strong-smelling sponge soaked in bull urine. He blessed it of any impurities and placed it under Naibe's nose. When he waved it her head jerked, but she remained senseless.

Khentie jumped slightly as Naibe's head moved. Wserkaf knew she was worried the girl would come awake and continue the curse she was casting before she fainted.

"Here," he caressed Khentie's hand to sooth her and pecked at her forehead. "I'll sit with her first. Perhaps a cleansing blessing, beloved, so that no ill befalls our house," he suggested.

"Well, give her this, then. I think it's hers," Khentie handed the inspector-priest a red sash. "Our man, Bek, passed it to me. She must have dropped it in the carry coach. It's lovely work, don't you think? Bulls, like *El Anu*. I'm afraid all I took from her words earlier was the name of the god and that she was making an evil utterance." Khentie got up and then called to her attendants and maids to come assist her with the purification. They bustled around silently and in moments had returned to move with their incense and prayers all around the house and yard, until they had covered and chanted over each place.

Wserkaf had accepted the sash from his wife's hand before he recognized it. The man, Marai, had worn it as a token every day until the start of his final ritual. For a long time as the women went singing and waving cedar bundles from room to room, the Inspector sat in silence. He contemplated the sash in his hand. *El Anu,* he mused, *and Hordjedtef told me he became a bull. He said it had been a sacrilege because it was the Bakha Montu. El Anu's not the same thing. He would have looked* different *if he had been El Anu. Wonder if this sash protected him from harm until his last trial when he couldn't wear it,* he thought. *When this poor child saw it, did she think it could have protected him in his final hour?*

He draped the sash over Naibe's hands, weaving it through her fingers so she could grasp it. After that, he sat quietly and tried to reach into her thoughts so that he might be able to ease and heal her.

He saw the sash being sewn. The young woman who lay before him gently handled the fine copper needle, couching the gold and yellow thread. Her nails were tinted rust red from henna paint. She was laughing merrily. Big hands reached down along her arms in a loving caress that turned into an embrace.

"What's that, pretty Brown Eyes? A bull?" the deep-but-sweet voice asked her.

"Oh!" she startled, covering the pattern. "It was supposed to be a surprise!"

The Inspector heard Marai laugh.

"There's a row of them, though. You've made a herd of young bulls on there," Marai sweetly encouraged her.

"Oh, I plan to bear a herd of young bulls like these for you when you are done with these priests," she replied.

Wserkaf knew he was looking at the daily life of two people who loved each other very much. The image blurred and then cleared. This time, he heard passion shared and glimpsed very briefly at Marai and this woman lost in each other's arms. He ached at their tender whispers, because he knew they would not exchange them again and there would be no herd of bulls born for him. The Inspector knew he had been part of the reason they would not. Once again, the image changed and showed him a monstrous and mash-chinned, pop-eyed girl. She laughed so hard that her fat shoulders shook. Her stubby hands were twisting a strand of her frazzled black hair.

She drooled, then stuffed something into her mouth to stop it. The priest had remembered the big sojourner telling him the women were in a terrible state when he found them. The woman in his vision was the same as the beautiful creature before him. He knew that, but didn't want to believe she had ever been that imbecilic little toad of a woman he saw in his thoughts.

He knew she wanted to die. As he meditated, he worked to stabilize her life force by sending her thoughts of tranquility. As he continued, he understood more and more how unfair the suffering of the women and the death of Marai had been.

After some time, Khentie and the women returned to their starting point in the front plaza by the guest room.

"Not awake yet?" Khentie entered the small room and asked, seeing that Naibe slept peacefully. She clutched Marai's red, bull-embroidered sash.

Wserkaf stood, stretched his arms tall, and embraced his wife.

A sound came from the bed a moment later. Both the priest and his wife looked, thinking the girl would wake. Bending down to tend her, they braced themselves for an onslaught of her emotions.

"Marai," she whimpered.

Wserkaf listened carefully so he could translate her words for his wife.

"Don't leave me, the storm is coming," the girl mumbled then drifted.

"Look, Khentie. I think she opened her eyes a little. I saw her look into my eyes for and instant before she rested. She said: 'Don't leave me, the storm is coming,'" the Inspector whispered. Wserkaf had just related her words when he realized a light, wet wind had begun to blow. The tip-tapping of the first drops of a gentle rain sounded in the plaza.

The servants, who had settled to rest for the evening, roused themselves. They called to each other and pulled out open vessels, bowls, and pans to catch the fresh water that was blessed to come from Nut, goddess of the Night Sky.

Wserkaf and Khentie stared open-mouthed at each other as the droplets began to splatter on the tile roofs and awnings in the estate. *The Goddess weeps…* They both thought simultaneously.

Khentie got up, then yawned. She was about to go to her room, but paused and pulled her husband to the door to whisper a question: "This girl. Are you truly going to send her to Our Father or are you thinking to have her as a concubine when I am called away from you?"

Wserkaf frowned, because the thought had genuinely not occurred to him. He knew his wife was gifted in far-seeing and had tried to sound unaffected, but she couldn't hide her concern. It was routine for noble to have a secondary younger wife to create additional offspring. In all their years, he had never mentioned that he might want another woman in his household.

"I don't think I need one, do I, Khentie? We have healthy, grown sons. Our legacy extends beyond us. We meet each other well in sacred union. We both have our duties now, so when would I be able to take time to attend or entertain another without neglecting you, my best beloved?" the priest whispered tenderly and ushered her up the stairs to his own bedchamber. "Later, before we both sleep, one of us ought to check on her. Maybe young Mya can come in here and bring a mat. I heard her outside moving some water pans." Wserkaf kissed his wife's head and felt her hold him tightly. Something in the way she embraced him worried him, but he couldn't quite name it. Something in the future, perhaps a coming event that wanted to leave its hint tonight, plucked at his thoughts ever so gently.

GOING FORTH BY DAY

CHAPTER 10: HIS SPELL

Deka lay on her side, remembering the Land of Grass. For several quiet moments she rested, and then she saw even more of her life parade through her newly awakened memory. She had flown so far away that she thought he would never be able to pursue her, but he was relentless. Once again, she had seen herself as a young girl held close in the arms of something great, powerful, and dark red. A hand stroked her arm.

"Tired?" A man's voice sounded almost tender in its rich seductiveness.

She shook her head.

"Come here," the man pulled on her shoulder. "Come on, sit up," his wistful suggestion became a command when she didn't move. His irritated sigh became a low and half-hidden growl. "I told you —" he began as if he intended to seize her forcefully, but then he stopped to stare at her.

Deka looked up at the man who gripped her arm. They lay together on a bedding–and–cushion-strewn tile floor in his low-lit bedchamber. The distant rumble of thunder she heard meant the young man's earlier prediction of a strange off-season rain had been right.

The young general was incredibly beautiful to look at. Everything about his body was firm, muscled, and hard, yet it was smooth-skinned and refined to the touch. She had felt only a few calluses on his hands when he seized or caressed her. *From the spear and the bow, not labor, not a prince,* she thought. His soft skin, scented with perfumed oil, showed meticulous grooming. The close-cut black hair on his head felt like fine animal hide when she touched it. A peaked pattern in his hairline mimicked his straight, upswept, brows. His broad, Kemet nose was not typical in that it turned down like a hawk's beak, rather than rounded in a slight ball to the lip. His ears were sharper than most ears as well – almost pointed. Coupled with the line of his plucked brows, which had been arched into smooth, straight black wings, his expression took on a permanent scowl. When he smiled, his perfect teeth flashed over his full lips and firm jaw, showing that the teeth on the side were unusually long – like dog teeth.

"Drink this to refresh yourself," he reached over her to fetch a cup of beer that had been set out for them on a table between the mounded-up goose-down pillows and the wall.

This isn't real, she kept staring at everything: the man, the room, the flickering lamp, then shook her head, "no."

"Hmph? Cold to me now, my Ta-Seti *ka't?*" His voice sighed, more disgusted than disappointed.

Deka flinched a little at the word ka't. Alone, the word, which meant "woman" was no insult. The inflection he used, though, made it a scornful label: 'vagina', specifically 'walking vagina'; a term meant to objectify.

"It's not like you didn't like it," the Prince looked away from her, his manner having grown suddenly dismissive. "Not a while ago you couldn't get enough of it, or was that someone *else* shouting my name and begging to me?" He took the beer for himself, drank it in a single gulp, and then moved beside her.

"Maatkare, please –" Deka spoke just above a whisper. She *was* tired, and *very* confused. *Ta-te, hidden from me, will he not drift to sleep now?* she prayed silently. She knew she needed time to sort the whole day and this evening out. It would be dawn soon. Maatkare was still awake and seemingly unmoved by any of the passion they had shared. It appeared that at any moment he would regain himself and mount her again, without any consideration for her exhaustion; he would simply expect and command her eagerness. Worse than that, she knew she would obey because something about him had reached into her heart and throttled it until it was dry and aching, yet she dreaded his release of it. *He is a hungering demon who steals my soul for his food in lying with me. He consumes me. I said I would not fight a man tonight, because Man-Sun had died and I must lift myself up, but this is not a mere man. My heart cries now and she's so weak. I cannot fight him, only desire him. See him sit, hear him mock my desire and call my weariness cold.* Trembling, she whispered a further reply to Maatkare: "I – I just can't. This is…"

The young prince slid behind Deka, as if her last statement had finally reached him. He leaned against the wall and took a last sip of beer, then pulled her up against him, her back to his chest. One of his hands lazily stroked the dark sunburst tattoo that surrounded one of her nipples; the other hand held his empty cup. In the distance the wind stirred and the thunder rumbled softly again, showing the rare but brief early morning shower had moved closer. He shrugged again and put away the cup. Lying back with her locked in his arms, he soon faintly snored and sank into a sound sleep.

Deka lay awake in the Prince's arms, trying to piece together everything that had happened that evening and to somehow fit it with the rest of her life, because *none of it fit. He is going to my homeland, to Ta-Seti,* she reminded herself. *If I am strong enough to match him, I will run with him as a mate. He will take me with him. Once I am there, I can free myself of all that binds me; even him.* She had overheard him speaking to the men at the party that he would be returning there soon on an annual campaign of inspection. *That's why I let him take me,* she told herself. *Then, the only thing that binds me to these others with stones is this little red one in my brow and maybe my Ta-Te will either explain it or allow me it's full use.*

Somewhere in the middle of letting the body do "what it does" and flying away into the dreams of her childhood, she woke to find that the bird of her soul had flown straight into a hopeless thicket. Although the sensibility of it made her nauseous, she *wanted* this man Prince Maatkare rather desperately.

She went over the evening she had just spent. With an almost horror-filled shock, she watched herself as if she *had* flown away and seen everything that happened from a distance. She shuddered, but felt compelled to relive everything from the moment the Prince had tugged her past the gate of his grandfather's open courtyard.

He had been silently walking her toward the interior lake and harbor to "see the boat", or so she thought. They moved peacefully and in silence, but as they did she sensed something peculiar about the way he held her hand. At first, she thought she was just intoxicated from the horrid day and the wine she had consumed all evening. She stared up at him, puzzled by the warmth of his hard-looking face, then saw him glance away. He scanned the horizon ahead of them.

Is the fierceness I see something from his warrior soul? From many battles? she asked herself.

GOING FORTH BY DAY

A peculiar vibration that seemed to come from the palm of his hand drew the energy out of her body. She couldn't look at his hand, as if the thought wouldn't stay or her eyes got distracted each time she tried.

Wearing something on his hand that feels like a stone. Is it? She tried to look again, but couldn't. The sensation had been a good one at first, but it quickly became alarming. Deka suddenly rethought going home with him but knew she had nowhere else to go without calling on the feline energy that engulfed her whenever she was upset. She had promised herself she wouldn't do that unless he hurt her. She pulled her hand in uncomfortable protest, worming it almost free from his tight grasp.

"It would be rude of me not to give my name," his deep rasp of a voice announced. "I am His Royal Highness Prince Maatkare Raemkai, General Overseer of the Upper Lands, but *you* will use only 'Your Highness' or perhaps my simple birth name, 'Maatkare'. The right to say all other names or titles must be *earned*," he emphasized.

The cold ire that had crouched, hidden inside her heart leapt up at the man's announcement. *And I am not your pet,* she wanted to hiss and break away, but she fought that urge. "Ma-at-ka-re" she twirled her free hand in a summoning gesture, not sure of what force or who she called to aid her at that moment. "Deka", she replied, knowing her deep brown-green eyes must have begun their feline glow.

Suddenly, Deka found herself forced up against the wall and ambushed greedily. The Prince's mouth devoured hers as the weight of his massive upper body pinned her flat on the wall. He sought out her breasts, raked the sensitive skin on her back with his oddly sharp nails, and then found the opening of her dance belt. "The name *Deka* means pleasing," he insistently caressed her increasingly moist mound, gasping in a delighted but momentary pause of tittering, low laughter. "Will you be that to me, Hmmm? We shall *see*, Ta-Seti, shall we not?" he spoke eagerly, his phrases punctuated by heavy breath as his mouth and tongue sought her jaw-line and throat.

The instinct to push him away overwhelmed her. She knew she was strong enough, but at that moment the will to pry his hands loose, to knee and kick his hardening groin suddenly fled. She became tense as a wooden plank despite her arousal.

The Children, she whispered inwardly, but the red stone pulsed a little more quickly as if it had become eager itself. *They want this, just as they wanted Marai – They want me to.* Deka remembered how the Children of Stone had always enjoyed these tense emotions, particularly lovemaking, but this man was rough and unquestioning enough for her to think of it only as rape.

"You *fighting* me?" he paused only briefly in his torrent of hard and biting kisses on her face, neck, and shoulders. "No. Trust me. You don't *want* to do that!" A pause followed, and then another deep and searching kiss. "Well, not *too* much..."

"Stop! Not *here!*" she croaked, weak and giddy in his arms. Desire and need welled up and overwhelmed her, against everything in her nature. *Augh! No! I am being betrayed by them. Why?* Deka thought Maatkare would take her in an instant, like a dog would, out in the open and against the wall. He really *would* rape her, and then leave her scrambling to right herself from a humiliated heap as he went on his way to his home. Something about that, though repulsive, thrilled her.

Then you fight me! Make me do it. Win me! she felt her thoughts screech in a strange voice. Something inside her froze because the voice, though male was not the Prince. It was the same dark entity that had visited her dreams throughout her life of misery and had always eluded her, but steadily hovered nearby. It had come into Marai when he went up against the thieves to slaughter them. It returned the night Marai took Naibe into his arms for the first time. Their act together had called forth all the wrong kinds of magic through the Children of Stone, distracting them. She knew in that same moment that this magic had burned the young thief's hands later that night. It had sat on her shoulders the afternoon before Marai went to the priests, when Naibe almost died of fright.

Ta-Te! Here? Her thoughts leapt again, sensing that the force smiled. It seemed proud beyond telling, as if it had waited for her to be caught in this passionate moment. *But why have you come now? Is this man more than he seems?*

As if the young prince sensed her inner turmoil, he whirled her around and boosted her away from the river, suddenly going in the opposite direction. He wound through the white walled corridors with her. As he raced, he stopped her frequently to drink in and savor her mouth and breasts with more fierce and brutal kisses. Quickly, he urged her along the narrow path to the back entrance of a two-leveled building. Once they were inside it, he rushed her in a flurry up a set of brick stairs to a wide room with a porch that overlooked an open plaza. Servants, who had appeared to tend to the Prince's needs as he arrived, scattered. A woman paused and shouted angrily, but he turned to her with a snarl that wasn't even human.

Once they were in his spacious bedchamber, he released her briefly while he threw the bedding from his carved ebony bed to the floor. Deka trembled with excitement as she began to remove the pretty dance kilt the Inspector had given her, but the Prince seized her arm, pulled her back to him again, and tore it from her hips. She felt herself being lifted into the air, and then deposited on down filled mats on the floor. Maatkare showed her no tenderness or even a hint of anything beyond reddest lust. As he scrambled on all fours to her like a ravenous animal, he didn't even give her time to admire his nakedness. For the tiniest of moments, she felt fear and cried out in a breathless whisper: "No. Don't."

"Don't?" the Prince stopped his insistent grappling. "What lie is this now?" his voice growled as if he had become a wolf or a wild dog that could still speak as a man. In the dimmest light of the room she saw his silhouette now seemed other than human. In so many ways it matched that snarling voice. "Say one thing, beg for another. See this? You know you want it so bad, so very bad," he sat on his heels and caressed his erection with a tenderness that showed he *might* either be gentle or just in love with his own hugeness. "Get away from me," he snapped. An agonizing, stony silence followed as he turned his back to her in disgust.

Deka panted, winded from running and trying to catch her breath. *He's making me weak. I can't hide. I can't fly away. Oh, Mama Menhit! He would shame the fertile god, Min. He means to hurt me, not please. Run. Get out. Escape,* cried her thoughts.

Stay. I can smell your fear, woman. Good, his inner whisper flooded her beneath the whispers of the Children of Stone. *It is good you are afraid of me. Your fear makes your hunger all the more desperate, cos you know you want it. I've seen your eyes craving it, all of it to the root deep inside you.* He repeated what seemed to be a mantra he had begun earlier: *Beautiful fire, I know you inside. I'll sit here. You'll think about it for a while.*

Deka felt ill and weak. Her upper body fell forward behind his back. *No.* Her heart wanted to burst. Every breath hurt because she wanted him. Worse than that, she wanted to be owned by him. *You can't do this to me. Don't overtake my thoughts. I am god-blood. I remember, now.*

She heard him sigh, expressing his own needs while his back was still turned to her.

I already know what you are. I told you that.

Deka studied the small of his dark back and the gentle swaying curve out into his hard, muscular buttocks. She saw no evidence of fat whatsoever. Her hands wanted to grip them hard, to guide him. Everything about his shape made a statement about raw and untamed power. Another rumble of distant thunder sounded. The pitter and patter of gentle drops of water struck the outer tiles. A gentle rush of wind caressed her as she lay behind him, like the gods of wind and rain she'd called were blessing this moment.

"Nnnggghhh. Nnngh… " Maatkare emitted at a faint moan that sounded like a whine of a beast that was suffering for something sweet.

At that moment, Deka knew she could not deny him. With trembling fingers, she reached to the inner curve of his arm.

"See?" he whispered, then turned to her again almost tenderly. A low, hoarse chortle accompanied his voice. "You see?" his eyes closed then re-opened. For a moment, she thought they flashed a different, greener color. He crossed his legs and gently stroked her thigh, stopping just short of her mound to frustrate her into gasping and bucking in needy struggles.

"I know what you are… and *who,*" he chuckled and lifted one of her feet to his lap, then up to his lips. Breathing out gently on her toes, he lapped at the arch of that foot, then glanced toward the wall. Deka turned her head so she could see too. Above the piled-up comforters was a small wicker table. On it stood drinks and a medium-sized jar with a brush inserted and leaning to the side. "I could take you and break you before you knew what had come upon you, like a bitch in the tall grass. But, because you have decided to obey me and perhaps learn a little of me, I will take you slow and sweet." He abandoned her foot and lunged forward to get the jar. Maatkare pulled out the brush, and the golden, rich sap on it formed a bead and dripped back into the jar. He wiped the excess on the inside lip, and then took up her foot again. Slowly, he began to paint her toes with the substance.

"I saw it in a dream once, that in another world I am a painter, an artist. So, I will paint you now. It's honey, because I like something sweet with my meat."

Deka felt him slowly lap at her left foot, then pause to seek her expression with his own smoldering eyes. They had turned a mysterious greenish gold from their olive color. She gasped, unable to speak, gripping the comforter on each side of her body, with her fingers like claws, as she panted with the anxiety of expectation.

"Say it to me," his husky, deep voice growled again. His side teeth seemed somehow longer. "It will go better for you if you do."

The enraptured woman felt the brush and his mouth moving to her other foot, then up a little higher, lapping the honey he had applied gently before continuing upward very, very slowly.

"No words, sweet brown cinnamon woman? None? Too overwrought to speak already?" he teased. "Then, *sing* for me as I play your instrument better than it has ever been done before," she heard him laugh.

Deka wanted to struggle but couldn't. She lay so spellbound with anticipation that any movement on her part would break the magic. The Prince tittered like a jackal. "And know this about me, my sweet sister Ta-Seti. Know that I will take what I want, *when* I want it, and as *often* as I want it," his voice grew darker and then quieted. With that, he licked and kissed ever so slightly higher on her inner thigh.

"Please," Deka's whisper escaped.

"No, not yet, perhaps not even tonight," he moved upward, drizzled a little of the honey onto the dark fur of her mound, caressed it to spread the sweetness evenly and then settled gently alongside his prey.

Chapter 11: A Royal Concubine

He's finally asleep, Ari smiled, turning to lie on her back for only a moment's stretch. She had held the crown prince in her arms until he slept. The man who had taken her to his palace two nights earlier and who had claimed he would be compassionate to her situation ultimately sent for her the second night. *Odd man,* she thought, *almost plump and soft like a big child but there's muscle underneath. Acts like one in a way; sweet and matter of fact.* Not vain or haughty – she sighed, misty about Marai again. Ari didn't want to think about the evening she had just spent with him, or the day of preparation and indoctrination that had preceded it, but the memories played in her thoughts. Despite her efforts to push them away, she couldn't.

When she had arrived at Prince Shepseskaf's home the first night, she shared some late-night kisses at the entry to the women's quarters with him.

Servants politely bowed as they approached and quietly led her to a freshly prepared, wonderfully cool and perfumed bed. It was set up in a large room with a shallow central bathing area, some storage chests made of cane, leather, or wood stacked against the walls, and five linen draped beds with other women reclining in them. They gazed at her with passing curiosity, but, as it was late, they said nothing. She lay on her new bed that first evening, contemplating her future for only a few moments, but the exhaustion, the wine, and the stress of the horrible day sent her into a fitful sleep.

After a few hours, she woke and found herself tossing and turning even though the bed was excellent until dawn lightened the sky enough for the rest of the household to stir.

What followed her brief meal of honeyed breads and fruit was a full day of instruction in the behavior expected of a royal concubine.

Ari spent the next part of the day practicing dances and walking through the gardens of the estate posing in elegant grace. There were certain areas for serving women and concubines and other areas which were private.

Except for me. I'll get in and see some things once I know this place. A woman's got to put a few things by for trade. She snickered inwardly, comparing this lush place to some in Kina where she had lived a noble life until her thefts were noticed. *Ran from a few of them. Those were other towns and wilder times.*

The various maids and servants instructed her in personal grooming, service, deportment, and public behavior. She was matter-of-factly informed that she was "on observation" as a potential concubine. The only difference between her status and that of a maidservant, she learned, was that her "duties" included sexual entertainment if the Prince desired it. Her teachers were extraordinarily close-mouthed about any emotion or desire their employers might have. Although she wanted to ask a dozen questions, she found quickly there would be few answers.

Ari rested in the shade of an awning in the women's area after their midday meal. The two instructors in deportment chatted with each other but left her out of the conversation. Feeling glum and abandoned, she thought about her life with Marai and the others as a merchant in Little Kina Ahna.

The pain of it is, I can't speak freely about any of this or I'm a threat. Fine by me if they pack me out of here or cause me to leave from the roof. Princy is nice, but the rest of them here are sour, she huffed. *Just makes me want to learn faster and find out what happened to Bone Woman and Baby so we can get together and get out of this cursed land.*

She was so lost in thought she almost didn't notice the two tutors gasp and scramble to attention as a small woman arrived.

"Her Highness. Stand up. Now." One of the women whispered, grasped Ari's arm, and yanked, which would normally have merited a swat, but Ari stopped with only an uncomfortable glare. Once she was standing, she looked down at a simply dressed young woman in a pale gold travel cloak. The woman quickly dismissed the tutors, but her soft brown eyes commanded Ari to stay.

"So, you are called Lady Ariennu, I understand," she began. "Know that I am Bunefer, who sees Horus and Set. I am prophet. She held something fluttering and pale in her hand as she beckoned for Ari to come to her.

Ari bowed as she took a step, answering:

"I am Ariennu, of the Kingdom of Tyre by birth, but I call no place my true home."

"But now you are here in my house," the quite tiny woman with a heavy indigo wig approached. "Come with me, Ariennu… Arry-*Yen* noo. I will learn of you some more. My King is impressed by your look and your apparent good health. Walk with me awhile, no speaking. I have ways of seeing that need to be surrounded in quiet." The young woman cracked a pert and artificial smirk. Her unspoken works were clear as water from and unsullied fountain: *and I will learn your spirit as we take some air.*

Ari padded quietly but warily near the woman, tucking her thoughts in secrecy and looking down at her as they walked out to the gardens where an abundance of fig and date trees were starting to fruit.

She's twenty-two? Ari thought quietly of what one of the maids had told her as she dressed this morning. *So grown and somber. Must be the prophecy running through her. Hope I can talk to her. She acts like a God's Wife already – distant like that, higher than others.*

The woman's pale hands caught Ari's attention again. This time she saw the woman wore a pale linen mitten on each hand.

Leprosy? Illness? Ari wondered. *Hardly,* she answered herself, pondering. *Why the mittens?* Ari wanted to ask her a question but decided to nod and smile, accompanying the Princess in silence. As they walked, she noticed the woman had no reserve about touching or petting one of the hounds or cats or allowing one of the trained falcons to fly down to her arm as they walked.

If a person approached, they waited until she had donned her glove. No one seemed to think her little private ritual was out of the ordinary.

What's she afraid of? A spell from someone touching her? Time, she knew would have to give her the answer to that question. For now, Ari smiled in all the false demureness she could muster. "I am grateful his Highness has chosen me to come to his house, to be your companion perhaps, Your Highness," Ari answered. That was the sort of exchange the maids had told her was allowed: demure, subservient, but friendly in tone.

"And if you need one, perhaps I could be a nurse to your daughter," the elder woman suggested.

"Oh, I think you do not truly understand, Lady Ariennu. Young Princess Khamaat has seven years and will be married to a prince who is now studying in the temple of Ptah and will be our vizier when the time comes. She is away at training to be prophet," the little woman's eyes averted. "But as she may also emerge as Daughter of the God, it would be helpful for her to have a brother, despite the age difference, to be her divine twin." Then, the woman looked away and seemed in Ari's thoughts to be upset. She knew her conversation had strayed into forbidden territory.

"I'm sorry, I –" she felt uncomfortable and though she thought the luxury might have solved many problems, Ari wanted to be anywhere else in the world than in this garden.

"Do continue to walk with me in peace. I have need of counsel beyond those who listen.

They walked together in silence out to the perimeter of the estate to a well-kept hut for garden tools. Ari had no idea why the Princess would take her into confidence so quickly and immediately raised her secrecy level.

She's toying with me. Maybe trying to trap me. I don't like this.

As soon as they were seated on benches outside, the Princess gestured to two guards Ari hadn't noticed. They had been trailing them at a respectful distance, ready to pounce if something went wrong.

"I know you are uneasy and do not yet trust me – and that is good. To trust easily is foolish, but I believe you already know this."

And – I think she just read about my past. Ari cleared her throat, hoping that past only extended to her time in Ineb Hedj and not back to her days as a thief and a raider.

"I understand you sold medicines for women in your marketplace, our cousin who is the Inspector of the Ways has told us this. Is it true?" her mitted hand shaded her eyes from the sun streaming over Ari's shoulders.

I already know the Prince is going to try me on but if he thinks I'll make a child for him, that's just not possible after the Children of Stone sealed my womb. Another fine example of me doing myself unfortunate. First, I wanted to get one for Marai just because I'd be able to raise a good one now. And now my status depends on me making one for the Prince. Urghh!

Then, Ari had an idea. *If the Princess divines that I'm infertile, perhaps I can be a healer and seek training in the temples for Aset.* With the perceptiveness radiating in the little woman's aura, Ari knew the Princess would find out soon enough.

"I did, Your Highness," Ari said.

"Then, hear me. Although my beloved may have chosen you because he found you fascinating, I have need of your services as well."

Ari paled.

She wants bed sport too? Ari tried not to grin, but her eyes still widened. There had been women in her life as well as men, but her dalliances with women usually began as comfort and progressed to lovemaking, whereas with men it was always the other way around. As reserved as the Princess seemed, thinking of her lost in pleasure wasn't easy. *But she's Hethara; all about drinking and dancing and pleasure. I shouldn't wonder.*

In the next moment the Princess put all the speculation to rest.

"Lady Ariennu, I have not come with a child for his Highness in five years and I am still young. I have not sought a physic yet, because tongues wag that ought to be cut and are not. Tell me what customs are used in Tyre, or any part of Kina-land to increase a woman's fertility," the Princess inquired.

"Uh, I am not certain what you mean," Ari lied, reduced to stammering. *I know what she wants, and I know she's going to see too much of me, when I was the secret keeper. Children – I need to do better than this. I need her out of my thoughts.* Bunefer was reading her, despite her burying her life in secrets. "Oh," she started again, struggling for a better lie. "Well, Your Highness, no one has approached me with such a request since I have been here. I sold love charms for lonely women; merely that." She tried to laugh, but her humor was lost. "Maybe I – Don't worry so –" she started and stammered, then gave up, turning to face the sun.

In that moment she learned one more thing. Bunefer lied and she caught her. The young woman had not been to a "physic", but she had been through many rituals that were guaranteed to produce a child and had been told by her sisters in Hethara and many other seers that a child would be born of her womb, and that one more would come from an unexpected source. She was obsessed with becoming pregnant. Telling her to relax would have been like telling the River Asar to cease flooding in its season.

Obsession was only part of the issue. Exhaustion from the multitudes of royal and temple duties was another.

Never had to worry about that one. All I had to do was walk by a man and I would come with a child. Not coming with one was my interest.

"Well perhaps the blame is not yours to take, Your Highness," Ari suggested but regretted it the instant the words came out of her mouth. At that point, the conversation nearly ended.

Clasping her mitted hands in anger, the young princess scolded. "*Could* you insult our kindness?" she asked. "The Count did inform us of your undisciplined mouth. So, watch what you imply," Bunefer stayed seated but turned away again as if she were contemplating a gentle breeze then began to hum a little song of praise.

"Oh, I apologize, Your Highness. I didn't mean –" Ari felt her heart skip because the one time she was actually trying to offer some help it turned insulting.

The Princess sighed, balefully shaking her head and getting to her feet with a beckon to the guards.

Great Goddess, Ari sulked. *Now she'll order my execution, but I won't be a lamb for her headsman's blade or trust the Children to get me out of this, like I'm sure Marai did.*

"Don't fear me because of your loosing a careless word or two, Lady Ariennu," she consoled in an off handed way. "Just understand when you speak wrongly of things you know little about; I will be compelled to correct you. If you fail to learn from our daily encounters, well —" Bunefer closed the afternoon walk and talk, but before the guards arrived, she added:

"Just understand that His Highness is very much in control of his manly urges and entirely beloved of me. He doesn't crave the *variety* of flesh as some in my extended family do."

What is she talking about? The grandson? Ari frowned, sorted through recently met royalty, and decided the Princess was referring to the delicious-looking man who had been at the high priest's house the night before. *That one looked like he could pound through quite a few servings of flesh without breaking a sweat. Lucky Deka,* she thought then reconsidered. *No. Unlucky for her and quite possibly deadly for the fool if he mistreats her or comes to deceive her before she is finished with him.*

The guards flanked the women and walked them back to the palace. When they arrived, one guard broke off and sent Ari to the women's quarters where she sat on her bed and sulked.

Well that was horrible! she sighed. *What was I thinking? I know why she hasn't come with a child. I'll lay odds the problem is as much this prince as it is her, or handmaidens would have brought one forth. He's a prince and a healthy male. If he sees a kuna out to charm him he's not going to look the other way. At least — I wouldn't expect faithfulness is taught over fertility here. If I can't find something to give hope, I won't be staying more than a few days. I won't even have to wait for my barrenness or that I was past bearing before I was changed to come out.* She felt emotion welling up again, but it was self-anger this time. *How am I going to get to do anything for Baby and Bone Woman if I'm on the run again?* Such thoughts brought her to one more subject. *And this prince. I already decided I wouldn't want to love him; that it would be a mistake to tease him away from his princess, though I think I could if I tried. She isn't going to stop trying to read me now that she knows I have secrets. I'll bed him, if he wants, but it's just a place to stay like in the old days until I can do better. No joy in it at all.*

Weary of the weight of everything, Ari lay back for a before-dinner nap.

GOING FORTH BY DAY

In the evening of the second day, after an excellent dinner and plenty of spiced palm-heart wine, the Princess danced and sang for her beloved, inviting Ariennu to join in the dance with her. She was pleasant and seemed to bear no ill will about Ari's earlier remark.

Bunefer's song was sweet and joyous; it affirmed her young womanhood and glad heart. She sang of praise and gratitude for Hethara, and of the goddess' great love for her wonderful king.

Ariennu paled. She had learned temple dances as a girl and knew the so-called "good-health" salutations to goddess Malidthu for a good birth. These dances involved dipping, swaying, waving and turning, but nothing as rhythmic or ritualized as the Princess' dance. The dances were supposed to be inspired by love of the goddess and the desire to birth a healthy child, but Ari wasn't feeling inspired this evening. She never paid much attention to gods or goddesses except to use their names in vile oaths. She needed the evening to wind down quickly, and for the Prince to get up and whisk her away to his bedchamber so she might make a respectable impression on him. Ari hoped the Prince would enjoy her enough by the time the Princess discovered her illusion that he would ask her for a show of mercy.

Instead, the evening wore on. Ari danced for the Prince, but when she danced, she thought of dancing for other men, or for Marai in the first days of the journey when it was part of her teasing him mercilessly.

Princess Bunefer danced a short dance after that, then stopped, whispered to her beloved a sweet good night blessing and a prayer for fertility, then left the open plaza where they had eaten.

The Prince slid over to the spot at the dining couch where Ari reclined and put his arm around her. "Feeling any better today?" he asked.

"Some, Your Highness, but my heart is still quite heavy," Ari paused to reflect on Marai for just a moment. All the fragile composure she had woven over herself today was about to vanish as she envisioned the sojourner's shining black eyes that flashed silver light, and that self-assured, wicked-but-crafty-and-teasing smile. *Watching me do this, silly bastard, you. You had to go and get yourself killed, didn't you?* her thoughts echoed.

Oddly enough, as soon as she gave her inner voice to that thought, she felt an answer: a rolling, desperate prayer of a man who sounded as if he was in fervent torment.

Shu lifts me up,
the Souls of On set up a stairway for me in order to reach the Above,
and Nut puts her hand on me
just as she did for Asar on the day when he died

The words grew thin, fading into nothingness.

Marai's ghost, she paused, almost gasping in horror. *His soul is in torment in the underworld, but he sounds so alive; so –* she looked at the Prince, trying *not* to think of the man who had brought her from her own nothingness eons ago.

"You are comfortable here?" he asked.

"I suppose, but still sad." And then she spun the seductive part of the lie: "and in need of your kind understanding," her voice caught, and he hesitated.

"Forgive me, Lady, but how can I, who do not know you?" his hand patted her shoulder and he pulled her into an embrace.

"Did you meet him when he was here?" she asked. Partly stunned that the conversation, which was supposed to be building up to him sweeping her off her feet and toward his bedchamber, had taken a different turn.

"I did not," the crown prince answered. "The Great One of Five was very private about him and had, I've learned, ordered any who saw him to speak nothing of it. Not even Our Father met him."

Hopeless. I can't go on thinking of him as a god of some kind. I must push through this, Ari moaned internally, rubbing her arms as if she was chilly.

"He was a good man. You've been told he was bad; evil, but Marai was our savior. I was dying when he found me, and he healed me. It just seems so wrong that he's really *gone*," she shut her eyes, hoping a tear wouldn't form.

"I hope I might lighten that heavy heart then," he suggested, helping her rise from the now vacant table.

Instantly, servants, who always seemed within hearing distance sprang into action behind them, tidying and cleaning despite the late hour. Ari assumed some must have even slept in the day so they would be ready to attend, feed, clean, and fan any member of the nobility or visiting guests through the long, hot nights here.

Someone had always been watching her for the short time she had been there; privacy didn't exist at all in the house. Even as Prince Shepseskaf guided Ari up a strangely narrow stairway to his bedchamber, she saw servants casting a casual eye in her direction as they cleaned the dining area.

Everything she remembered while lying next to the sleeping man made Ari's head ache. Their walk up the stairs had only been hours ago, and now the Prince was asleep.

Well that's that, she sighed. *I should go now before the chamber guard tries to see what I'm up to and wakes him.* She remembered the pointed instructions from the tutors earlier that day:

"When your entertainment of His Highness has reached completion and he dismisses you or rests, you do not remain. Gather any items you have brought with you and retire to the women's area with the attending guard. Speak to no one of the evening."

Well he wasn't a bad *time, but the rules! How miserable is that? It could suck the joy out of most anything.* Her time thinking about the evening served a respite, reminding her that this was just work. She threw a shawl over her shoulders and wrapped her flowing dance skirt around her hips. Exiting the Prince's bedchamber as instructed, she tiptoed with the servant to the women's quarters.

On her way back across the plaza, she wondered how the evening and these last two days had gone for Deka, and *who* had chosen Naibe. *Wonder if it was the King, after all. I should have heard something by this time, but I've heard nothing from either. It's like the link between us is just smoke now. Started with us not knowing about Marai and now it's spread.* She sponged herself in the pan of scented water left for her and settled to sleep on her bed, ignoring the snores of the women in the room.

When the maidservants had returned to their own chambers for the evening and she was certain they would no longer be checking on her, Ari sat and dug into her basket of things and found the small satchel of eight stones she had hidden under a false bottom.

With all her practiced quiet of thievery, she made her way up to the second level of the women's area to a wide upper porch outside Princess Bunefer's room. Checking to see if the young princess and her attendants were asleep, she used the power of the Children of Stone to cloak herself in invisibility. Feeling the relief of instant freedom from anyone's watch, she crept out to the upper walk rail.

Cooler up here now, she held up her hand and stylistically wiggled her fingertips as she made an arc up one side of her area and down another to deepen the illusion of secrecy. *But do I dare use them to see? Even Marai didn't do it that often. I guess he didn't want any of us getting dependent on them for everything – to allow our own senses to grow.* When she spilled the stones out in her hand, their light came up instantly, as if they had been waiting to speak to her. She placed them in the shape of Inanna's eight-pointed star formation on the wide stone rail that overlooked the plaza below. She tried not to laugh in delight over the gentle vibrating sound that soothed all the thoughts of the horrific last three days.

Be at Peace.

The voice in her thoughts spoke with an unfamiliar man's voice. It was gentle and almost as if several childlike voices had joined in a chorus.

Know you are loved and
that you will always find love.

What? her silent thoughts scoffed. *This prince here? Oh, I don't think so. But tell me this:* Are *Deka and Naibe safe?*

GOING FORTH BY DAY

Bodies are safe,
The will intrigued.

The voices whispered as an image formed in the middle of the lit formation. Ari saw Naibe sleeping peacefully, still clutching the long red sash with the golden bulls she had embroidered.

That's nice, Ari thought. *Someone must have seen to it that the sash stayed with her.* Her vision of the scene expanded and Ari saw the young woman lying on a frame bed in a small private room. The room wasn't open and airy. *That's odd. It's not big as the room I stay in here. I would think the women's room at the King's house would be huge.* A man in an evening drape was sitting on a stool by that bed, watching her. Before Ariennu could clear her thoughts enough to recognize him, a woman beckoned to him from the door. He stood and embraced the woman.

The inspector-priest, Ariennu shrugged, wondering how Naibe-Ellit had come to *this* man when he had said he would *not* be choosing a woman and when the King had seemed to have at least a passing interest in her. *At least she is cared for.* Ari watched for a while then drew a deep breath to focus her thoughts more clearly. The Inspector was speaking to the woman. She heard the woman's answer:

"*So, help her through her grief because I console Our Father and have the scar of tragedy on my own heart? Well, if he asked it then I am honored, Wse. You know that.*"

Ari's worry calmed. *Naibe is cared for at least, but how long will that last? And Deka? What of her? Will her prince do right by her?*

The images shifted at her question, they did not come through clearly at first. Faintly, she heard a woman's voice screeching and cursing in the distance:

"*You bastard! You dare insult me, the mother of your children* again? *You bring your monkey-girls into the same bed you ask me to lie in? Answer me! Am I still nothing more than one of them to you? After all we've been through? I hate you! I hate everything about you!*"

Ariennu frowned. *Is that his wife?* If so, she wryly snickered, *Deka will certainly have a rougher time than I'm having here with all of them watching every time I go to the privy day or night.*

She might get a knife in the ribs just passing by.

Next, an image of the pretty young general who had drawn such a rage from the screaming woman formed in the light emitted by the rays crossed upward from the Children of Stone. He was naked, his back turned to her vision.

Ari felt the corner of her mouth twitch in admiration. *Oh, oh, oh, oh, oh! Look at that!* Her eyes traced the line of his muscular buttocks, then around to the front. *Oh goddess, have mercy on me! Bet she doesn't hate that.*

You know,

Ariennu suddenly felt a growling, almost dog-like human voice bark back at her.

I can tell someone is looking into my world.
If you like, you can stay and get you spirit's eye full of me.
Enjoy the view, but don't bother me while I work on this one,
or I will have to bind you.

Ari's eyes bugged at his comment and she hastily scooped up the stones, ending the farseeing. *Gods, he could sense me? Even with all my magic shielding and from this far away? What is he?* Almost embarrassed, she hurried down to her bed in the women's area. Tucking the bag under the false bottom in her basket, she flopped onto her bed and lay contemplating what she had seen as she tossed, turned, and tried to find some sleep.

GOING FORTH BY DAY

Part 2: Looking Back

GOING FORTH BY DAY

Chapter 12: Going Forth By Day

The sojourner's thoughts wandered. He had felt a monster coming for him so many times that it seemed as if it was the precedent vision to other things he saw. The monster never arrived. It remained outside the tight, airless box in which he lay as if it waited to catch his spirit as it shuffled loose of its body for the last time. At times he thought he sensed an animal, a lion, pacing outside the box and guarding him. Despite this animal spirit's efforts, Marai knew his end would be soon. His visions had become convoluted as he felt his body gasp from lack of air. The dark stone box was too tight; his body during his time inside had spent most of what was breathable

In another vision Deka transformed into a harpy and flew right through his heart. She had become the benu of flaming plumage. Then, she was human again and cowering at his feet. When he looked away though, she snarled and leapt up with a dagger. Her dagger never hit him. His dream moved on to one in which he was a god.

It began as a sweet dream of lying in Naibe's embrace, but her face constantly changed into other faces he didn't know. They were women who worshipped him and offered their bodies to him, eager to steal his precious seed so they could fashion demi-gods and heroes in their bellies. Then, the dream began again. Each time he would be in a different place and time. Centuries and eons passed as he lay trapped in the stone box. He would emerge from time to time, renewed and seeking love, but he would receive only strife. The box became his pod from the ship of the Children of Stone. Sometimes it flew end over end, tumbling and turning. After a while, he moved on to other lands, living whole lives in those places. He never had the chance to stay in one place long enough to see the outcome of the children he fathered. It was always over some foolish misunderstanding. Abandoned, the women blamed him, claiming he had raped, seduced, and deserted them. Legends grew up about him possessing a certain lack of empathy. *It's not true. If it is; if I wake and become this god then let me sleep forever. Love. I did love them*, he felt of these envisioned future wives. *I loved them just as I loved my three wives of the wilderness. This new fiction is just that – fiction. A lie repeated often enough soon becomes the only truth available. When something, even a lie, becomes truth, there are no further questions. I cannot let this ever be the truth!* he told himself.

GOING FORTH BY DAY

Where are my wives, if these women come to me at all? Were they not immortal as I am? I want to be a man of peace, maybe the patriarch of a clan; not a man who becomes a god. I don't want to start uprisings and conquests, or lead warriors into battle and then drop, half-dead, into a throne atop a mountain to recuperate until the next outrage occurs.

The kingdoms he knew rose and fell a thousand times in his future-vision. Ineb Hedj was gone and lost in the dust. The years fanned out, overlapping as if he had become a single element in the heart of the lotus he had been taught to contemplate: the flower of life with layers of flowers extending and turning so that he saw through all of them at once. Those unheard-of places and lands winked their crystal spires at the heavens. Their citizens reveled in the self-assured pride that they were indestructible. They, too, sank beneath sand or wave, forgotten; ravaged by war, disease, and starvation.

All time pulsed like a heartbeat. Nothing ever changed, whether he became a god in each land or not. He saw all the possibilities at once and grew immeasurably sad. *Why am I even here?* he asked himself over and over.

To observe and know.

The quiet whisper of blended voices from his Child-Stone answered.

Then, tell us.

Marai saw his wives, but *they* were made of stone, having turned into the footers of an ancient monument in a green, green land that was itself, over time, consigned to dust and tumbleweed.

Something's wrong, he thought, *the Children's voices have changed. Everything's fading; distracted.*

Free yourself of that which has become evil.

Their voices struggled to emerge from an increasing crackly distortion.

You are strong enough.

Wait. The unlocking. Wasn't I supposed to be unlocked! His own thoughts suddenly burst through the confused fog and he understood that truth and wisdom were never something to seek. Nothing had *ever* been locked inside his heart for others to open with some magic formula, as Hordjedtef would have had him believe. Truth had only been hidden.

I know... I am a god,
who is ever and is never a god.
I am the messenger,
the ever born,
the earthly witness,
the gatherer of the sane who live as madmen.
I reveal the Hidden
Oh goddess mine, save me,
I don't want to do this.
I just wanted to know
your sweet love
and to give it back to you again.

The passage of time had finished its parade. He rose as the sun in splendor. The monster he had sensed waiting for him fled in horror of his brilliance while he watched his glorious body in the distance below. It self-immolated; burned to ashes.

I'm really going to die, he thought. *I can't. I must save them.*

You do not save that which can save itself
They are strong as you are strong
Allow them their trial and their own victory
Deny that and all fail.

The voice he heard seemed inherently evil and in nature. He wanted to shriek: *I am a shepherd, I must tend my flock. It is what I do.*

A shepherd you never were

A messenger

A guide

Until you accept this truth

It will evade you

He rose like the benu of the sun, but he struggled in his rebirth. Falling back to his body, he felt the painful heaves of complete suffocation and slipped into an even deeper sleep, unable to move, unable to think, unable to rise again. He knew the voice now.

Wserkaf. I'm done. I know it. He couldn't feel his heart beating. *Take the Children and put them with your mother's keys. Your wife will know where they are. Naibe, my love, go to him. Go. Go. So sorry, so very sorry.*

He felt a slight breath begin, as if he was rising to consciousness in his last moment. With each suffering heave his chest made, he grew weaker. *One last try before oblivion.* Marai pushed himself up towards consciousness. He could not open his eyes or his mouth, but he tried to move his legs. He had thought of kicking the lid off the coffin before but was only desperate enough now to try it.

There was a grinding sound, stone grating on stone. *It's moving? Heavy. Heavier than anything. Push. Grind. Push.* He could not stay to find out. Blackness took him — and silence.

When Marai became aware, he felt a gentle but fidgeting weight on his chest. Someone whispered in the dark. A hand delivered a soothing touch that pressed upward in a massaging motion toward his neck. The points it pressed tingled to the point of numb pain and then stopped. A voice inside his thoughts rushed.

Ease

His eyes twitched under his dry, sealed lids as someone rubbed a greasy substance into them. If he could have screamed in pain he would have done so. His eyes felt as if they had been adorned with jagged rock where his lashes had knit shut. When he cracked them open just the tiniest bit, he saw a soft, red light against a black void the way he assumed a blind man might see shapes and light moving without definition. The shadows of two men moved near him.

Who? he asked himself. *What was the person's name? Someone was supposed to get me out. W? Wes? UsRkf?* he noticed weight on his chest. *Sitting on me?* the sojourner sensed the presence of the man he had first known as The Inspector and later as Prince Wserkaf straddling his upper body as he lay in the stone box. Marai remembered more now. *Asleep. Long time. Children not here. Long ago.* His thoughts were broken. None of the images made sense, and his thoughts about them made even less sense. The man in the box with him attempted some sort of healing procedure. He worked on him breathlessly and feverishly. Although his whispered phrases were clear, Marai had forgotten the language the man spoke. The words sounded like lyrical gibberish. The sojourner tried to move his lips. Panic filled him, because he *didn't* understand the words and knew he *had* known their meaning at one time. The man above him realized it.

"Do you know my words?" the man asked, "nod your head."

Marai tried but couldn't move his head. The man repeated the words more slowly. Gradually, the sound of the language cleared, and the intonation of the man's utterance rang true.

Frozen. Things going dark. Lost. Dying. He sent thoughts: *Too late.*

"Awake!

Turn yourself over!

So, shout I –

Oh, elevated one stand up!"

Then quietly, as if he was begging him, the man urged: "Come on, Marai. Breathe!"

"Feel the light of Holy Ra in you.
Feel the truth of Ma-at in you.
Around you."

"Breathe," the voice trembled in a kind of terror as it spoke the utterance. Marai remembered memorizing the words in a hot, sunny plaza. Some old man or a kind of bird-demon with a long, curved bill and scrawny legs picked over nearby muck. The bird-demon was there to overwhelm, confuse, and dazzle him with huge amounts of rapid-fire, coded knowledge, but the sojourner had committed to memory each exact word and phrase he had been taught. Marai heard the squawking bird lecturing him, his tablets tucked in its white wing.

This isn't right. There was no bird. There was something else.

Someone grasped his stiffly folded arms from their position across his chest and bent them out straight. He knew the odd sensation of movement would have been excruciating if his arms had not been entirely numb. The constant rhythmic pushes on his chest continued as more pressure was applied. Suddenly the pressure was joined by a new agony. It burned like lightning strikes at various intervals from his shoulders to his thumbs and then into his fingers.

Places on the body. What are they called? Lotus points. He's working them. He showed me them once, but they didn't need to teach it. I wasn't supposed to wake up.

Something greasy was rubbed into his cracked lips and them while the man on his chest intoned some more words. Something opened his mouth.

A finger? To gag me? he startled and wanted to bite, but couldn't. Drops of a fiery liquid of some sort were squeezed out into his open mouth.

No! Stop! His chest heaved as the liquid went where breath ought to go. He couldn't cough it up.

"Marai,"

the voice commanded again.

"Raise yourself up to me.
Take yourself to me
Do not be far from me
The tomb is a barrier against me"

The priest's voice continued, becoming clearer each time he repeated the phrase. "Quick. The waters –" Swiftly, the priest instructed the other person in the chamber.

No more, Marai silently begged. Although the first bitter drops had cleared his throat, he worried the next might drown him.

Marai felt drops hitting his lips. This time the wet, though cool, liquid burned his mouth and trickled onto his face. Cramping in his gut renewed itself. He remembered it hurt before, so long ago.

This is worse. Poison. I was given poison to drink. Why is it still in me? Have I been here only three days? Warped and twisted blurs swam through his slit-eyed sight, spurred by the pain. Every conscious thought was scattered and walking around the dark red and black chamber, as if it had its own pulse and set of legs. The thoughts were locked in step behind the infernal bird. He wanted to reach forward to grasp its neck and wring the last tinny squawk from it, but the pain kept him in place.

The men continued their utterance, speaking the phrases together.

"I have cut heaven"

The voice whispered, urging him directly: "Say it with me when you can, Marai."

"I have broken through the horizon.
I have travelled the earth to his footsteps."

Marai heard Wserkaf whispering in his ear and pressing on his chest rhythmically. The person assisting him, continued working pressure on the intervals along his arms.

"Highness, he has died but is not corrupt. He will not wake. Leave off from him," the man said.

"I cannot accept that, Rekenre. A few moments more."

The Horizon is split for a weeping Warrior.

The Children said that before they rested. Now they speak again. Why? Is he really lying on top of me? Marai tried to focus on everything that had begun to happen, but couldn't decipher the myriad of sensations sweeping his body. He felt the rhythm of the words and knew the pattern of the pressure the men were exerting on him. He heard the Inspector's whispered but desperate chant:

"O One, bright as the moon-god Iah;
This Asar Ani comes forth among these your multitudes outside,
Bringing himself back as a shining one.
He has opened the netherworld.
Lo, the Asar Ani comes forth by day."

Marai felt a thump inside his chest, followed by another after some moments.

What is that? he asked, but noticed the rhythmic pounding had increased in tempo and that it eased some of his suffering. An involuntary gasp struggled through his chest, followed by a wheeze and a weak cough.

"Blessed Truth!" the Inspector's voice startled in astonishment. "See, he breathes! Get him up before he strangles on his own phlegm!"

Marai felt the two men prop him up and drape his upper body over the side of the stone box. They pressed and slapped his upper back, then rubbed the outer sides of his arms with rough, ointment-filled toweling.

"Can you speak? No, no. Never mind. Don't!" The man broke away from his ritually chanted tones. Marai remembered the Inspector was supposed to ask him if he was well, but he wasn't. He shook his aching head.

The man with the Inspector offered more sips of watery liquor. The Inspector continued working the back of the Marai's neck.

Stop. Hurts. Then the flood of miserable sensations caused him to heave and retch.

"Good! Get rid of it. Oh, I can't believe this! Oh blessed, *blessed* witness!" the Inspector cried out.

Marai opened his eyes a little more, but they still felt like dried, painful slits. When light was brought near his face, it was too harsh. The pain made him vomit up a few drops of fluid they had poured into his mouth.

The assistant gave him more liquid, this time with a bitter herb infused in it, but his arms and legs trembled violently. He knew he would have voided if he had not been entirely dry. He felt the men raise him up, but he still felt powerless.

Marai opened clearer eyes after long, silent moments. He focused on Inspector Wserkaf, whose face was taut with worry, delight, astonishment, and awe that when combined spread over his face as an expression of horror. An assistant, perhaps a sesh from one of the other priesthoods, was with him in the chamber.

"H-Ha lo…" Marai tried to say '*How long*' but couldn't make his lips form the words around the sounds his throat uttered.

Wserkaf shook his head violently.

"Don't try to talk. Don't think too much. Save *all* your energy for standing up and walking out of here. I can put you in my chair once we're outside."

"Hor…" Marai tried to say Hordjedtef; another name he remembered.

"No! Gods, no! Don't even *think* about him, or he'll *feel* you. Let him believe you are vanquished," the Inspector urged and then muttered under his breath again. "Oh, by Wisdom, this *can't* be happening! Drink more of this, now," he held a small beaker up to Marai's parched lips, letting some of the fluid soak into his bearded chin. He felt the men making him lean forward and then pushing him up and out of the polished stone box, but then he felt himself slipping from their grip and pitching forward to land face downward on the floor. For several moments, Marai lay next to the box panting and coughing in the ashy dust at the bottom of the stone chamber. Slowly, he got up on his hands and knees.

The assistant gave him more sips.

Each time Marai took some of the liquid, his thoughts cleared a little more. He raised up and remembered there were ritualized stretches and breath-sequences to perform in the wakening phase, but he couldn't do them. Every part of his body that wasn't numb was on fire with pain. He stumbled and slid into an exhausted squat at the wall, then fell heavily to one side.

After moments of agony he tried again: standing, swaying dizzily and then moving, heavily supported between the men. As the men walked him forward, he began to fall again, but the men struggled with him each time until he could stand upright.

No, leave me, his thoughts whispered. Somewhere in time he remembered a yellow-skinned, scamp of an old woman. There was a lot of sand. Other women were with her. She said the same thing: *No, leave me*. He remembered he wouldn't hear of it and urged her on. Now these men, he knew, weren't going to leave him either, despite his misery.

All along the way, Wserkaf whispered bits of the "Going Forth By Day" sequences.

He's saying them. He knows I can't, but they must be said by someone before we leave the chamber. So, I can rise. It's wrong. Not the right order. He's just doing this. Marai's thoughts had begun to race to the point where his heart was now pounding and dizziness was surrounding him again. He stumbled, but heard the words echoing and filling him like mystical song.

> *"I am the lion-god who comes forth striding.*
> *I have shot.*
> *I have wounded; I have wounded.*
> *I am the eye of Heru.*
> *I have spread open the eye of Heru on this day.*
> *I have reached the riverbank.*
> *Come in peace, Asar Ani."*

The blast of the hot night air outside of the subterranean temple engulfed the sojourner in instant sweat. He felt the air rush out of his lungs as he fell like a tall tree, faint from exertion and the sudden temperature change. The air inside the hidden chambers had been almost chilly, even though it had been close and stale. The night air outside, by contrast, was brackish, smelly, and hard to breathe. He felt as if he had sunk beneath slime in a bottomless pit for the moments before he moaned once and lost consciousness.

I'm not going to make it, he thought, but felt even more hands seizing him and dragging him as he tried to rouse himself. Relaxing, he let the Inspector and however many men had joined him struggle to lift him into a draped litter.

"Here. Knees tight at your chin – eases the cramping. I'll walk beside you. When we get to my estate, I can get a physic who will not speak of what he sees. We'll get the rest of the poison out then."

Marai coughed, wheezed, and gasped, almost crying out. *Goddess, I don't care.* He wanted to roar in pain as the bearers began to move. He dimly made out Wserkaf's hand on his leg in reassurance as he walked beside him.

Taking so long. Didn't know where it was when they brought me here; don't know now. Just Gah! The pain with every uneven step or shoulder shift. I'm too big for these small Kemet men.

Finally:

Doors. Not like Hordjedtef. Not betrayed. He sighed in some relief because the two journeys there and back had been close in feeling.

Instantly, he heard a woman's voice chime up as they entered and passed the outer walls.

"Wse! What's going on? Is it someone, again?" A woman came up to the covered sedan chair as it was set down on the ground.

Marai only saw blurs. He tried to stand up, but stumbled groggily. The bearers moved in to support him.

Marai's ears made rushing and roaring sounds through his head. He felt pain at the sound of rising concern in the woman's voice.

The Inspector didn't answer her question at first.

"Is it? It's not – Oh Blessed Goddess what have you *done*, Wse? Have you lost your wits? Have you cursed us *all*?"

Even though Marai reeled at the sound of the woman chiding the Inspector, he felt comforted by her gentle hand as it touched his face to inspect it.

"Is that green paint? The Sed? What mockery! Oh no, no, no…" her voice edged toward tears of horror.

"Shh. Beloved. I'll explain it to you later. "You know I couldn't *know* until I went into the chamber to see about your dream."

"But – But. You lied. *Again.* You lied to me and to our gods! *Why?*"

"M- M-" Marai tried.

The woman's voice stopped suddenly at the sound of his effort.

"Mother is Iat…" He gasped, trying to wake fully, but exhaustion overtook him and he missed several words of the verse he needed to speak. "…nourished me. I was c'nceiv… night. Born at night," Marai felt the dark consume him once more and he went limp. Once again, strong supportive arms stopped him from hitting the ground.

Wserkaf. A softness of some sort of bedding touched his sprawling form. The cane frame beneath it groaned under his weight.

Rest.

GOING FORTH BY DAY

Chapter 13: The Unexpected

Marai slowly came to his senses. *Still dark*, he thought. *Knew it. I'm still stuck in this thing. It was a dream.* A slight breeze stirred over the top of his face. At first, he thought it was his own breath, then pain returned and with it his memory of the previous evening. *Wserkaf. He said something about a physic to get the poison out. No one yet. Don't want one, anyway. I think its morning before the sun.* Still feeling very weak and ill, he remembered being jolted awake by Wserkaf but more than that he remembered the stone box, the chanting, the partial Sed initiation and ritual that had been strangely disjointed and false, the agony.

For now, he knew he rested on a lashed cane bed in a small room, likely at the Inspector's estate. Opening his less-stiff eyelids, he peered around in the dark relieved that his extra-human had returned. The room where he lay was sparsely furnished, but somehow nicer than the guest room in Hordjedtef's estate. He tried to lie still, enjoying his freedom and beginning to pick out his surroundings: a chest high window on the wall opposite the bed where he lay was netted with sheer linen to keep out flying insects and afford a small amount of privacy. A low lamp on a stand burned, illuminating a cup that would contain flat honey water. Near the bed, in easy distance, was a night jar. Beneath the window was a folding chair where he knew someone had been watching him.

The sojourner lay quietly for several minutes, trying to make out the source and kind of sound that might have wakened him. Suddenly feet were scampering. There was chattering, hurrying, moving closer, and moving further.

Odd. I know in a royal house someone is always awake on watch, but they are usually quiet. This is too loud for hours before the sun. Then, he recognized the sound.

Women are weeping? he questioned as the sounds neared and became clearer. Marai struggled to his feet, lurching to the window to look through the edge of the curtain out into the plaza. Servants darted here and there across the open area in the gradually lightening dawn. They threw dark drapes out over various things in their path, lifting and transporting other objects to several litters that lined the outer walls.

GOING FORTH BY DAY

Straining his still blurred and painful eyes in the dimmest of morning light, he saw carved trunks and baskets. These were stacked on the litters. A draped sedan chair waited for its rider. The bearers shuffled about solemnly. They spoke in low, reverent tones to a good-sized crowd of soldiers and peacekeepers who had apparently come to help with all the items that had been gathered.

Marai remembered a woman's scolding voice when he had arrived even though it seemed as if it been only a few moments ago.

Wserkaf's wife, Marai remembered he had imagined her once. He had seen her a little later as well when he had been on a spirit journey. *Was she so angry over me she is divorcing him? There are a lot of things gathered up, like a journey being prepared.*

Then, he saw this same woman pacing anxiously back and forth in the open plaza beside the draped chair. Her servants attended her with whispers and something that felt sad to him. *Has something happened while I slept?* he wondered.

The woman wore a dark, hooded cloak that was pulled up over her head, even though the morning promised to be too warm for such clothing. From time to time, he saw her quietly whisper orders to those around her. She pointed to various baskets and chests they placed on litters. A very young female servant, possibly a handmaiden, bowed to her and then rose, embracing her. The girl appeared to be crying while the Princess comforted her.

He saw Wserkaf, clad in the same deep blue travel cloak he had worn when they met, entering the plaza area. When he tried to embrace the woman to soothe her, she shrugged him away. In the rising morning light, Marai noticed something about her proud and aloof face, but could not place what he saw.

Wserkaf, Marai sent a thought.

It resonated. The Inspector looked toward the window and then scampered over to it.

"What happened?" Marai asked.

"You're better?" the priest asked, astonished but oddly narrow-faced.

Marai nodded slowly, trying to determine what was happening on his own before the man had a chance to answer.

"Great Menkaure Kha-ket, our God and Father, has died. It was just last night; just after you rose," he sighed. "We received the word just before day. We must go to him before he is taken to the House of Life. His son and all our children are already with him," his face dropped. "By all the *gods,* I hope this is not my wage for cooperating with my senior over what was done to you. This is – This is *too much.* Not *now,*" his whispered words became increasingly distraught.

Marai recognized the Inspector's wife's face and understood why it had seemed so familiar. It mirrored the images he'd seen of the King's face. "Your wife was his daughter then?" Marai asked, his voice still hoarse from thirst. He saw the loading of the litters had increased in speed. Bearers and porters worked feverishly, loading the royal litter which seemed so much more ornate in the rising dawn even though it was draped in dark shrouding material. He watched at the sill of the small window, feeling helpless and weak as the Inspector went back to the men to assist them, without responding, but Marai didn't need an answer.

In a few moments, the Princess, her handmaiden and the rest of their entourage moved toward the gates and into the alleyway beside their private walls. The sojourner watched Wserkaf tie his cloak more securely as the last two chests containing his official garments were loaded. Marai overheard him state as the last in the procession was readied that he would catch up on foot and walk beside his wife's sedan as soon as he left duties for the servants ordered to stay behind.

So, King Menkaure is dead, Marai thought. *That's hard. He was loved by everyone in Kemet. They'll mourn for the rest of the year for him, and they'll do so willingly.* He had been taught that even though Menkaure's son, Shepseskaf, was considered king the instant the elder king breathed his last, he would now undergo months of intense preparations for his coming ascension with the rising sun on the first day of the New Year. *Must have been sudden. He seemed healthy when I saw him on my journey into the beyond world. Wasn't ill. Now the news drives them into an uproar.*

A vague queasiness distracted Marai from his thoughts about the King. In the next moment he realized what he felt was hunger.

GOING FORTH BY DAY

I'll just get a servant to fetch me something when they've gone, he thought then re-thought that idea. *Ritual. I should say damn the ritual, I'm hungry, but I'd better do this right.* Although he had not been taught this, he had read in the few texts left out on random tablets that it was of utmost importance to recite an utterance about food and eating as part of his waking ritual. Certain phrases and spells were needed for his spiritual as well as physical recovery. Marai was sure Wserkaf would have walked him through the recovery process this morning, but now any part of his ritual, complete or otherwise, was a poor second issue. He felt a rising sense of panic. *If I don't eat, I'll get even weaker. Maybe I won't even be strong enough to eat. Oh, this pain is almost as bad as the poison. Food. I must get out and go to a market, but I have nothing to trade and I'm sick to death with this.* The sojourner knew he wasn't strong enough to even consider going home across the river. *My ladies, I must get word to them that I live. They could come to me. They could cross, saying they were coming to mourn in the temples,* he thought.

Marai sent that thought to Naibe:

Sweet One, know that I am well and finally free, but the essence of thought rushed off into the air. *Odd. I wonder what happened. Ari? Deka? Is Hordjedtef blocking this? You'd think this with the King would have him too busy. He doesn't know I live. He can't know.*

Just when Marai leaned against the wall for support and tried to ease himself along the wall toward the door, Wserkaf walked back from the gates to the guest room window. Before Marai could ask him anything, he said: "I'll be back to check on this house and you by nightfall. Until then, everything I have is yours. It's just not safe for you to be about with green paint and Asar's garments fouled from your unwashed stench and still on you. You're still too sick from your journey as well," he looked sideways as if he expected some spiritual threat. "I *know* Count Hordjedtef will be looking for treachery now that Great Menkaure has entered his horizon." Wserkaf glanced over each shoulder again as if he thought his trusted servants or livery men might suddenly betray him. "He knows much, but not, I suspect, that you've drawn breath again. You should know he *will* attack you in your weakened state if he senses you walk and then turn on me as his chief suspect. He can still open my heart for grains of truth. Our fealty pact of mentor to protégé is still quite active."

"My ladies –" Marai heard the Inspector voice his concerns but he hadn't comprehended a thing other than the King was dead and he was in danger from Hordjedtef. That he couldn't reach them with his thoughts now that he was out of the chamber concerned him more than anything else. "I've tried to send a thought to them that I'm well, but I sense *nothing* of them," the sojourner leaned heavily against the inside of the windowsill. Weakness assailed him again and he felt increasingly faint.

"They're not here. They're no longer in Ineb Hedj," the Inspector answered without looking at Marai. He checked the progress of the work again. "It just wasn't safe for them to be here anymore. It's all I can say right now."

Marai looked about, feeling a rising wave of helplessness that wanted to strangle him. He snapped his head several times to clear the dizziness in it, but his arms and legs spasmed and buckled. The stubborn cramping in his guts from the hunger grew worse. Bending his head to the tiled sill at the window in his room, he braced against the pain. In the back of his memory he found the thought that he had talked to Wserkaf when he was trapped. *Has this been a dream? Am I still dreaming? Have I died?* Marai saw the scenario of his vision as if he had been walking around his neighborhood of Little Kina-Ahna in his everyday work clothing. It was night. He stood near the well in the open courtyard and gazed into the dark water. In the next moment, he whispered a phrase as if his voice had become one of the voices that belonged to the Children of Stone.

> *I must make him believe he's won.*
> *I will need you to be open to me, Wse…*
> *in case I need help.*
> *Go tell my wives what's happened.*
> *Tell them to be ready to leave Ineb Hedj at a moment's notice,*
> *before the old bastard can get his claws in them.*

The sojourner's thoughts continued clearing, but now the Inspector had returned to speak to him. Dawn had begun to break. The signal had been given that the rest of the entourage was ready to go to the King's residence.

"I've left a manservant behind to make your bath and feed you," Wserkaf's voice rose slightly as he began to turn. "He isn't an educated one, but he will do whatever you ask of him and keep silent to any who ask outside the walls. Remember the words you have to say about the food! It's part of the rebirth. Make sure you say them!" he shook his head. "If you move about too much before you replenish yourself, it will kill you. I'll see if I can get some word of your wives to you, but I have to go now," Wserkaf embraced Marai's head through the small window, patting it reassuringly.

Drawing up his dark hood, the Inspector gestured to the porters to start off. In the next instant, Marai watched the entourage, servants, and soldiers exit the brass and gold fitted cedar gates, heading for what he guessed was the King's residence. As soon as they were all gone, the manservant who had been instructed to stay behind pulled the latch into place across the closed doors and then walked toward him.

Gone? He said not in Ineb Hedj? Not safe? I remember — told him to protect, but where? The sojourner didn't care about the manservant, the ritual, bathing, or eating. He didn't care if he fell face down in the great river and became bait for crocodiles at that point. Worse than that, he instantly knew from the Inspector's tone, despite his other misery over the King that something else had gone worse than wrong. *I should have felt at least something from them,* Marai knew. *The Children of Stone and the one I have in my head is working even though I can feel it's become as weak as I am. I feel so alone, like it's in the wilderness.* Once again, his stomach began to feel like it was in shreds; he knew he had to eat.

Safe

a small voice whispered.

Worry not more.

Nourish and clean yourself.

Rest.

Repair.

Marai beckoned the manservant. He knew his Child Stone and Wserkaf were right for reasons other than religious belief. He had undergone something no human should have survived, and he was still in danger of collapsing and failing at this point.

It was foolish of him to assume the Children could revive him at any cost. "Some bread and broth, friend. A cleansing soak if he h – has –" Marai stammered as a wave of pain hit him, barely able to whisper.

The servant stared at him, a dumbfounded expression on his face, then quickly turned and left.

Noticing the stare, Marai rubbed the crackled surface of his skin, watching more of the dried green paint fall away. Although his entire frame ached and he felt as though he would collapse in on his own ribs at any moment, Marai made his way out of the guest room. He padded slowly around the open plaza as he waited for the servant to return. Stillness and silence surrounded him now that most of the household had gone. Marai took in the beauty of the empty plaza at daybreak until the thought of his wives returned.

I must shake this off. If they're not here, Wserkaf will tell me where he hid them so I can go to them. I must be in better shape than this. Marai held his head and groaned in misery as he moved toward the ladder up to the roof kitchen. His glance traveled the distance and he realized he wouldn't be able to climb at this point. *I scaled cliffs back in the Shur. The gods must be laughing at how I don't dare do it now. I'll just wait for someone to come back down.*

The few servants who had remained on duty had started to make the daily bread. Everywhere throughout the estate, their work continued without the usual chatter and lively gossip. The lack of sound diminished everyone's growing sorrow.

Marai tuned his ears to pick up any distant sounds out in the town, but even they were absent of morning clamor.

They must have sent the word out early, he thought, truly wishing his wives were with him as he walked around the open area of the plaza.

Oh, my love –

A voice, halting and full of tears, filtered through Marai's thoughts.

Naibe! his thoughts called back. *Naibe! Is that your voice? Naibe-Ellit… I feel you are near me, sweet one! Do you see me?* Marai paused in the middle of the plaza. He looked around, turning in each direction, but saw and heard nothing more. *A bird?* he asked, briefly fearing the bird was Great One and that he had been discovered, but silence followed. *Goddess not a ghost – Please, Sher-Ellit, call out to me. Dammit, I need you,* he looked up. When he did, he thought he saw something float by him on the wind, followed by a guttural cackle he knew as Ari's laugh. *What is that? A veil?*

It had vanished in the new light and he ached too much to search for it.

"Good man."

Marai heard the voice of the manservant calling to him. He turned and saw the smallish man beckoning from an area around the side of the main building.

"I have freshened the bath water and added heated water. There is food for you later. I have been instructed how to do this by his Highness."

Following the sound of the man's voice, the sojourner let the man lead him to the bath area. Marai stared, unable to move when he saw the water rippling as the man tipped another krater of fresh, heated water into it. The pool was smaller than the one in Hordjedtef's house – just big enough to soak day-weary bones – but the motion of the water unnerved the big man.

Something, he started, suddenly anxious. The servant beckoned, encouraging Marai to remove the sweat-sticky ceremonial shenti he still wore.

Marai's hands shook as he peeled the garments from his body and let them fall to the tile floor. His vision clouded again, and he stumbled.

Strong arms and hands seized him and wrestled him into a seated position by the water. He realized he would have fallen into the pool and likely would have bashed his head on the side, due to his height, had the servant not abandoned the water jar to run up and support him.

"Someone's here," Marai gasped, exhausted and unable to see clearly again. *Something in the shadow. A wraith watching me,* he panted, realizing it might have been a vision, but hoping it was some nuance of one of the women.

"No one, sir. You're here, and I. No one else. They've gone up to the royal house now. The rest of us will go later if we are needed," the man insisted. "You slip in now and soak while I get the sop," he steadied Marai by the arm as the big man eased into the pool. "Oh. These?" the man turned and pointed at the discarded linen as he was leaving.

"Burn it, I guess," Marai ached so much he wanted to sink into the water and drown. Only the thought of finding the women kept him focused on his recovery. Soon, he was alone.

In the warm darkness, just enough sun came through the woven roof over the bathing area that it made little star-lights dance on the rippling warm water. A feeling of ultimate relaxation rushed upon Marai and a distant, aching sigh, wandered through his heart again.

Naibe, Deka, Ari, he begged the air.

Oh, my love – why did you have to leave me? Marai *knew* he heard Naibe's whisper that time. He smelled her scent on the morning breeze as certainly as if she had visited him in spirit. That whisper became Ari's voice gently lulling over the sacred words from the Divine Utterances:

> *Take me with you, beloved,*
> *That I may eat of what you eat*
> *that I may drink of what you drink…*
> *that I may be strong whereby you are strong*

"Naibe, Ari! I'm *here*" he insisted aloud, wondering how Ari knew the words he had heard only in his study of sacred ritual.

More than that, he wondered how the link between their stones had stopped functioning in his time of greatest need and why it still seemed broken.

How could they not know it? Did they think, when I spoke, that it was my ghost? That bastard told them I was dead. I know it now. Why did they accept that? Why did they not question it? They knew as I did that the Children of Stone said we would not die easily if at all in the regular sense of the word. Marai shut his eyes in misery. *I must tell them it's not true without Hordjedtef sensing my thoughts.*

The memory of Naibe's sweetest touch, fingers gentle, like flower petals, ran around and through the resting sojourner. He felt all three of the women watching him, then saw them fade one-by-one like those same flowers withering in the summer heat. Deka appeared last and for the longest time, looking even more regal than ever before. A golden disc was affixed on her forehead and she spoke to his thoughts in a language he didn't know. The disc squirmed, then transformed into an *iaret*, the serpent that appears on the King's nemes; symbolic of "risen one". He didn't understand why only she appeared this way, but the return of the servant distracted any further contemplation.

The servant, a clean-shaven, dark man of middle years, knelt by the pool and gave Marai some strong wine, which went to his head and made him nauseous and instantly groggy again.

"I must do other work for when the Lord Inspector returns." The man put a little chime on the tiles along with the food he had brought. Use this to call me if you become too weak to stand." Then he remained as if waiting for Marai to speak. He appeared to be guarding the food as if he had brought it but didn't want Marai to eat it yet.

Marai puzzled and then realized why the man was perched so protectively. *The Words. Wserkaf must have told him I needed to say something,* he shook his head dizzily, remembering his words of the devotions that he needed to recite:

If emptiness flourishes
The elevated one cannot take his food
If the elevated flourishes
emptiness cannot take its food

After Marai whispered these words under his breath so the man would only know he had said the devotion, not *what* he said. It was enough to spur the servant into feeding him small amounts.

The food was a porridge made of beef and onions dipped in sop-softened bread. The sensation the food dizzied him at first but soon the sojourner felt strong enough to wave the servant away. The man set some bowls and a clay trencher by the bathing pool within Marai's reach. He brought out a small amount of bread over a bowl of hot stew then, and respectfully left the sojourner alone.

Marai couldn't bear the thought of getting out of the warm water to get the bowl of stew. His left arm trembled as he reached to dab up a little of the beef with a crust of bread. Slowly, he pulled the bowl closer. He ate a little more, tugged at the ceramic bowl, and then grabbed it with both hands so he could sip it. He relaxed again, feeling a little stronger with each passing moment.

If emptiness flourishes
The elevated one cannot take his food
If the elevated flourishes
emptiness cannot take its food

He whispered the required prayers from the re-birth sequence again. Once more, he tried to send more thoughts out to his wives. This time, he tried to access the energy in the Child Stone in his brow.

Little one inside my thoughts, he began, *take me to a place where I will find them, if they are not here.*

Leaning back against the edge of the pool, the sojourner felt his spirit soar away from his body with greater ease than ever before. He balked at first, thinking the shock of eating again after his entombment had overwhelmed him, but then he relaxed and let the vision take over.

He stood in the open area of this plaza again.

Ineb Hedj, right here in this house, unless it's a trick. He stood in spirit by the pool in the open plaza and looked down at the water. Somewhere in his thoughts he heard Naibe weeping.

GOING FORTH BY DAY

Sher-Ellit. Don't cry. Know that I live. Know it. Believe it, he started, but remembered Wserkaf's warning about the elder priest. He didn't care.

Let him try again. Let him. I'll freeze his heart! he paused, then sighed because freezing that heart would mean he believed the old man *had* a heart. The vision continued. Marai wondered why he was still wandering in *this* estate. Had the women been here? By the light of day the plaza seemed empty as if it had been stripped of its loveliness. In his vision, it was a different place.

The entire pool area was decorated with huge painted pots, filled with beautiful flowering plants. It looked as if someone had captured a bit of the great river had brought it inside the plastered white walls of this estate. A small stand of papyrus even grew at one end. At the other end, a trickling little water wheel was planted in the water. A hand crank in the side of the wheel could make water come over it as it was turned. Dozens of sesen the color of a moisture-laden dawn sky floated in the pool. Among the pots, large ottomans stuffed with goose down had been placed so people could lounge near the pool or go for a casual swim on more blistering days.

Although it was deathly quiet now, the sojourner sensed the memory of the laughter of the children who grew up here and the chattering of their pet monkeys. He imagined other sunny and lazy days with beautiful birds floating by and perching on the awnings. Cats crouched, eyeing them. All was silent and breathless, as if waiting for something new.

Why am I seeing this? Marai asked. *Where are they? Why do I look at these pretties instead of the places my beloveds now walk?*

Except for a wisp of a spirit, there was no hint of Ariennu, Deka, or Naibe.

Sighing again, Marai moved further in spirit. *Take me to them, little one, before I go mad in trying.*

The scenery flashed by him and became solid once more. Now he stood in a wide causeway, flanked by incredibly tall buildings on either side of that hard, black path.

Where's this? he asked himself. It looked nothing like any of the places he had ever seen. The Child Stone had made another mistake. It had focused on the city of Ineb

Hedj, not his wives. *Ineb Hedj, little one, but in another time. Why this? Have the ladies been carried here?*

We understand.
They are not here
But
See how it endures
But drifts and changes
Lion in the dust

The stone tweaked gently, soothing him. The city where he lived now was green and filled with lakes, palm trees and stands of papyrus. There were flowers; plazas of them. White walls wove among each royal city estate. It was a shining place, but then it changed. The greenery was sparse, and the tawny earth was full of windblown dust. Ka-Ro or something like it was the new name, he could sense. It was built quite some distance from where he reclined in a warm and soothing pool. It rose from many levels of ruins that had risen, crumbled, and were finally forgotten over time.

In this world there were no fine palaces as such. The city still teemed, but the part he saw was a wide place amid tall buildings surrounded by a stinking beggar-town, as squalor filled as the Poors' Market on the other side of the water next to the Little Kina Ahna neighborhood where he had lived before his ordeal.

Why am I seeing this? Take me to my wives. I need to see they are well. His thoughts raced so wildly, he nearly roused himself.

In the next instant he had moved to what felt like a different time. He was by the river. The beautiful, lush greenery, the fragrant, flowering trees, and even the humblest of shrubs had been replaced by a shack-filled stretch of sand and lapped by filthy, but ever-rich silt-laden water. Boats both huge and small, noisily growling and roaring, plied the river. They, strangely enough, had no oars and blasted loud horn sounds from time to time. From where he stood, he could see the Eternal House of Khufu. It stood in the distance, not nearby, as it did now. The Great Pyr Ntr and two more pyr monuments.

GOING FORTH BY DAY

How far in time have I come if I'm seeing them this way? he asked himself. All three eternal houses were complete, but they no longer gleamed. They were riddled by time, water, and wind, but, by the goddess, they were still of such magnificent size. The wondrously painted "Daughter of the God" as Sekhmet still fronted them. She was nearly stripped and destroyed by what he sensed were thousands of acts of ultimate disrespect. Wire fencing surrounded her, and oddly dressed men and women moved around her, holding up small, flat, rectangular amulets to their eyes for a moment before lowering them again.

What an odd way of worship, he mused, then shuddered that he had been distracted. *My frailty from the poisons must be misguiding me. Damn!*

The roadways and paths to and from were wider. Spires with odd shaped tops were not as fine as the three visible eternal ones. In these paths, things like the wheeled toys of children, but big enough to carry people, moved. They were much noisier, dirtier, and moved in their daily lives between walking people. A song of men blared from the towers in a tongue different from the one spoken in Ineb Hedj. He understood one or two words that had a Kina flavor to them, but the phrases were mixed up and changed around.

Nothing in any of this time or his own time came to him from Ariennu, Naibe, or Deka except a distant wisp of a disconnected thought. *Where have they gone? If I can't see them, has everything failed?* He touched his brow and a sensation of comfort spread through him.

I need to see them. He tried whispering to his own inner thoughts.

Rest

the voice returned.

Where are they? he asked.

You will see them again.
Love them.

Touch them forever.

Look inside.

They are part of you. One heart.

This time when he heard the thoughts of the Children of Stone, their voices didn't comfort him. He had gone on a great journey and seen the city in ages to come but didn't know why.

Touch them forever, eh? Even in that time when the Great Pyr Ntr stands ravaged? Are you just as weak and confused as I am?

The water had cooled even though it was midday. Feeling refreshed and stronger, Marai planned to get up, find some manner of clothing, then leave as soon as possible. The Great One or his protégé no longer mattered. He would just go as soon as he was able. Travel to Little Kina-Ahna would be impossible without a boat. For half a moment, Marai thought of Djerah, the young basket-maker turned stonecutter. He wondered if he could slip into the worker's camp to contact the young man without being noticed. Perhaps *he* would have heard a rumor of where the women had been taken. *No. If even the Children can't find them, Djerah or other workers wouldn't know. I won't be safe outside these walls and I'm not yet fit enough to confront anyone. The old man likely has eyes everywhere if he has come to suspect.*

Marai got out of the bath and dried himself somewhat sullenly at the thought that he had to stay put at least until Wserkaf returned. Looking around, he noticed the servant had been in at least once while he dreamt and had left folded linen for him. From it, he quickly fashioned a shenti and a simple shendyt covering. *I'll rest for now. Perhaps I can at least safely reach them in thought. Something, anything, will be enough.*

As he sat on the bench by the bathing pit and finished his food, Marai knew he owed his life to Wserkaf. He had cried out to the Inspector in what he thought had been his final delirium that first evening and had continued sending thoughts from time to time. *If the Inspector hadn't felt me calling, the Children might have wakened me in that place of the future where everything and everyone I knew would be gone the way Houra grew old and left me.*

After he took the carved bowls back to the servants' areas, Marai thought of exercising and then resting again. His stay here was going to be a lull in the middle of a storm. Resigning himself to wait for the Inspector's return, Marai left the bathing area and padded around, exploring.

Laughter, tears, and whispers – quiet little sounds and memories – wafted through the Child Stone in his brow, gently whispering acknowledgement of each sight, as he went from one glorious room to the next and back into the open area.

Chapter 14: The Veil

Something white glimmered in the corner of Marai's vision as he stood, freshly bathed and nourished, in front of the garden pool in Inspector Wserkaf's main plaza. It fluttered in the gentle breeze that rustled the little stand of papyrus that grew on one side of the green, moss-filled water. It was a white scrap of cloth with a red and gold edging that reminded the sojourner of something Naibe and he had seen at the market.

In his memory, he saw himself with his arm slung around his beloved's waist as they walked among the stands of trade goods. It was early in the morning. Etum-Addi, Gizzi, and Ari were still setting up their store for a day of brisk trading. It had been before the flood festival.

When Naibe saw a merchant set a white scarf out, she remarked that it was lovely, but that the trade value the man expected was far too expensive for either of them to afford that day. They decided to wait until the end of the day to see if the merchant could be talked down. Wserkaf's visit had distracted them from carrying out that plan.

Marai realized that the Inspector of the Ways must have seen it as he left that afternoon and picked it up for his wife. When she had been swimming or playing in the water, she must have left it so that a breeze pushed it into the reeds out of the servant's sight.

Marai walked around the edge of the sesen pond. Getting on his hands and knees, he fetched the cloth from among the tall stems. When he sat back on his heels, reveling in the soft feel of the fine and "sheer as royal" cloth, he saw more needlework had been added since he and Naibe had seen the piece in the market. It was Kina-Ahna and unmistakable in style.

Touching the veil to his cheek, Marai understood that it had somehow come into Naibe's possession. The little bulls on it were the same as some she had sewn on the red sash he had worn when he went to visit Hordjedtef. It meant one thing to the him: his wives had been *here* for at least a short while and that meant Wserkaf was *still* lying to him. The Inspector *knew* where his wives were, and he probably knew everything that had happened to them on this side of the river.

Marai touched the long shawl-like veil to his face reverently once more, kissing it, then stood and threw it over his shoulders. He kept out of sight of the few servants in the back areas as he walked through the rooms in the front of the estate. If the women *had* been here, he wanted to seek their essence and learn what happened without hearing more false stories. If he found the veil, he thought, perhaps Ariennu or Deka might have left something for him. A first, he found nothing. Finally, he entered a large upper room with a skylight and an awning over it.

The Inspector's bedroom, Marai realized the possessions here had not been packed and moved as had the items in the rooms belonging to the Princess. This room had a lion-footed bed in it with a carved and padded headrest, along with many other luxurious belongings.

"My love.

My love, my love. Noooo… "

Naibe-Ellit's voice whimpered softly on the breeze.

I've seen this room; this whole estate. It was while I lay trapped, when I was rising. I saw Naibe then, holding this scarf. He patted the white and embroidered fabric over his shoulder. When he did, he felt her sadness drifting through him. He saw her by the papyrus stand below where he had found the cloth. Her feet dangled in the water, her face was in her hands, and she seemed so very tired. He knew his vision, if he continued thinking about it, would reveal the story of how the beautiful piece of linen in his hand became tangled in the stems. Temporarily wrestling himself free from the vision, he left the Inspector's bedroom.

Wserkaf will be back before evening, Marai reminded himself, *and he will tell me the truth about my wives then.*

Trotting down the steps and out into the plaza again, the big man sat at the same spot where he had visualized Naibe sitting and weeping. As he was taken by the last remnants of her magic in this place, he felt the sad but wistful memory flood him. It nearly reduced him to empathic sobbing. Once again, a vision of the events began.

He didn't know what day his vision showed him, or how many days had now passed since this scene had taken place. As a ghostly witness, he saw it was late evening and the inspector-priest's household was preparing for bed.

Wserkaf was about to put his late-night work away. He had been working on a numeric formula for a repeating pattern, inspired by a grouping of stars in the early sky. It was a puzzle designed to sharpen the wits and reveal a prophecy. Marai saw that Wserkaf's groom approached to wash his feet and hands. After that the man who Wserkaf called Anre, massaged his master's aching shoulders with hot oil. Then the Inspector planned to retire to his bedchamber. His wife was already asleep in the women's quarters. Both he and his beloved had tired themselves out from their meetings and devotions so they could hurry home to check on the tragic young widow of the sojourner.

Marai's vision showed him Naibe again, little improved. He sensed she hadn't spoken to anyone in the Inspector's household. Though their conversations provided no details, he had the feeling she sat for hours staring with her hollow eyes into the water of the plaza pool. Servants kept checking and trying to get her to speak, thinking she might wade into the sesen pond and hold herself under the surface until she drowned.

He saw the Princess' little handmaiden come out to the pool to get Naibe to come in. She had brought out something to drink, but Naibe shook her head in refusal. When getting her to drink failed, the little girl went to the Princess to get further instructions. Unfortunately, she found the Princess already in bed and in no mood to be roused. Despite her weariness, the Princess, whom he had heard Wserkaf call Khen or Khentie affectionately, managed to mumble to the girl that she should consult the Inspector and then leave off to come to bed herself. Now, the handmaiden had come into the edge of Wserkaf's chart room. She stood quietly in the doorway until the Inspector looked up.

"Your Highness —" she bowed deeply because she had interrupted him from his calculations and closing meditation. "Forgive me, but my great lady wants you to know that the Shinar woman is still weeping for her husband. No one has seen her eat more than scraps today, for the third day. Now she will not come in to sleep and we think she is looking to drown herself. My great lady says she *must* get more sleep before her temple proofs in the morning. She wishes that *you* talk to her. It is her wish that you *order* this girl to eat and to be grateful of our care. She says she knows that in *this woman's* land women do not trust one another as women of Kemet trust our own. Perhaps a *man* is needed to give her direction."

Wserkaf sighed unhappily, blinking once at the girl who stood before him.

"Very well," he cracked a little smile at the maid. "Go tell Anre to bring some fruit, sweet cakes, and drink to us. Then, both of you go your way. I'll see her comfortable and then retire without the evening toilet. It's late. We should all be resting." The Inspector waited for the girl to bow again, then rose from his worktable as soon as she left. Rubbing his tired eyes with his slim fingers, he rolled up his chart and took the lamp he was using out to the pool.

Marai had the sense then that the Inspector was truly worried about Naibe. He'd been kind and ordered no jibes or taunts from servants, no shunning whatsoever. All his kindness and all his wife's attempts at consoling her had not worked. The sojourner knew that she, with each passing hour, wanted to join him in death. Though he was focused on Naibe, Marai had felt nothing dreadful coming from the households where Ariennu and Deka had been sent.

Sweet one, Marai's thoughts reached through time hoping his message would reach her and brighten her even if it had no power to change future events. The visions told him the original intent was for her to go to the King to brighten his mood with her dances, but she had been too broken. *Maybe that's good you didn't go straightaway, love,* he thought. *Now that he has died, they might have blamed you.*

Briefly sensing Wserkaf's own thoughts on the women, he knew the Inspector objected to the Great One's' quick and heartless behavior toward the women and heard their argument before they were separated that evening. Count Prince Hordjedtef disrespected them. He considered them *valueless females*, thus any assistance he gave them had been an undeserved honor. That he had to deal with them *at all* had galled the old priest. *'The unclean man has been allowed into my home and now his unclean ka't have brought their stench and disease into my place, no matter how cleaned up and painted they appear,'* he had said. "What I've arranged is a gift they will never deserve. They will simply ply the trade of their flesh which the man told us was how he found them. I want them gone and you had best comply before I change my thoughts and condemn them as criminals equal to the one they lay with."

Marai had learned that concubines were not often random beauties spied by the King and his men. More often, they were daughters and young widows of minor nobles hoping to move up in status by charming a high-ranking man. There were intrigues, fights, murders of children, and other mysterious deaths emerging into gossip. It wasn't a good place to be, but Ari and Deka would either be victorious in a fight or turn the arrangement into triumph. Naibe had no idea, having been an idiot-child who thought of men using her body in the past as little more than a funny and good-feeling game.

Marai ached as he saw her weeping nearly to death the first day, making it necessary for serving women to stay with her constantly so that she didn't try to kill herself as the Inspector and his beloved went about their daily appointments and devotions. By the second evening she seemed to have cried much of it out, but the third day she went through another gut-wrenching bout of ranting, running about, screaming, weeping, and had one seriously bad fainting fit in the afternoon that had servants scurrying for physicians.

When Wserkaf returned from his meetings, and his princess returned from a consultation with some of the prophetesses of Ptah, the maids suggested it might be more merciful to offer her some quick-acting poison than to allow her to suffer so.

Tonight, the Inspector sat silently beside the young woman at the pool. In the three days she had been with them, she had taken only a few sips of beer, a crust of bread, and a small piece of melon. Marai understood she was turning inward and losing touch with the living world. Soon, her fainting episodes would increase. She was making herself ill. At this rate, the man knew a fever would eventually take her and she would die in starving and suffering misery. He had to do something.

"I know you hate me, blame me," the Inspector began. "What you don't know is that I came to like your Marai. I know he was a good man…" Wserkaf ventured, "…and one I will never forget." Naibe turned her tearstained face up to his and he continued: "I will write of him and speak of him all the days of my life, as will my children and their children, too. It will help him live on, dear lady."

She was stony and silent, as if his words hadn't reached her. When she finally spoke, her words began as a soft mumble in Kina: "Oh, *why* did he have to go," then grew more audible as she repeated for him in the language of the king.

"Oh, *why* did he have to go," she pressed her eyes closed as the thought made its way through her heart one more time. "I told him of my dream. I begged him to take us away, and see…" she gulped hard, trying not to collapse again as her dizziness grew. "The night everything in me died, do you remember how it rained?" she suddenly asked.

The Inspector frowned, but added, shaking his head in what appeared disbelief. "You were aware? I knew you lay as one dead when the rains came. We knew that such a rain was likely a sign."

At that moment, in his vision, Marai sensed her heart lightened almost imperceptibly.

Oh, poor goddess. She's trying to heal herself the way she healed me – in talking to him. He hoped that moment he saw showed him she had begun a long process of recovery, but then allowed the vision to continue.

"Mmm. A little storm? It was in my dream, that storm, but now so many more will come." Her shoulders shook with misery as if she hadn't heard any of Wserkaf's words.

"I guess he thought he would live," the Inspector answered. "I don't know *why* he thought that. *I* warned him too."

Why is she saying that about storms? These folks will think she cursed them over me. Marai saw Wserkaf's consoling hand start for her shoulder, then freeze above her as if his touch her would have been the same as profaning a sacred object. Instead, he offered her some of the food. She shook her head, staying his offering with her pale and trembling hand.

"You *have* to eat. Would *he* take joy in the way you are suffering so? Try to think of something that pleases you – here." Wserkaf asked, edging closer to the pool beside her. He put his own feet in the water beside hers, then pointed to the other end of the pool. "See that wheel in the water over there?" he pointed at a vertical wheel. "See how it goes round and round like the seasons of life? See how it sends the water over the top if the wind stirs it?" he wistfully tried to distract her from thoughts of her beloved. "I can get up and make it go too," he pointed to the wheel. "In a vision once, I saw a place that was so very green with water running in rivers from mountains and through forests of great trees. The power of the water rushing in that river turned this great wooden wheel which then turned other interlocked wheels below to grind the grain into flour. No more servants grinding and wearing out their backs when they are old. Maybe a saw blade on it for cutting things. When I told my beloved of it, she wished for me to create one. Sadly, our pond doesn't flow, so I made the turning device to show how it ought to be."

Marai couldn't stand her not hearing him. He focused on that moment with all his might.

Naibe-Ellit almost giggled. In a moment, she quietly looked into Wserkaf's eyes. When she did, he thought he heard a gentle voice whispering inside her thoughts. He saw her gasp, comforted for only an instant by the power of the words and the sound of the sojourner's voice. Her eyes lowered, sadly.

Eat... I would want you to.
You know I would
So sorry. So very, very sorry
I just wanted to know love.
To take your sweet love and
to give it back to you again, my Goddess.

She nodded, too worn from weeping and hunger to continue. The corner of her mouth softened. Marai knew she had felt his words, but wondered if she would listen.

Speak to his heart, my sweet? It is a way we shared in my walking hours before the trial.

She took a small sip of the beer. Her thoughts went to the Inspector.

Tell me of him
And I will eat.
Whisper his words and
I will drink what you offer me.

In the stunned silence that followed, Marai knew Wserkaf had heard her thoughts in the same way that they had spoken and in the same way his mentor Hordjedtef had taught all to speak.

Her spirit voice was filled once again with an odd sense of power that had recently evaded her. It evoked, like layers of the same dissonant soft whisper laid over each other and filled with smoky, seductive sorcery. He had to look away as the Inspector stammered and yet tried to answer.

"He just –" the man began. "There wasn't a way for him to win his fight against my senior after he took it as far as he did. He waited too long to make his escape from the rite," Wserkaf cast his eyes down, unable to look at the young woman's face. "My senior saw to that. He knows men's hearts well. It was your Marai's *own* pride, too. Had he humbled himself –" the Inspector suggested.

"The sons of Ahu are stubborn men," Naibe spoke in Kina, but her thoughts told the Inspector exactly what words she had said. Her shoulders sagged as if she really wanted to weep again but had no energy left.

"So often, men are proud and might prefer death to disgrace," Wserkaf added. "What I know now is my senior was testing both of us. He thought to win me back from a faltering faith by showing our way as the correct one. Now, he knows that he has *lost* me as surely as we have both lost a great one," the man's eyes moistened with guilt and regret at the sacrilege he had committed.

Chapter 15: A Priest at your Altar

Somewhere in the witness of the dream, which unfolded as a blending of Marai's memory from the tomb and what he saw now when he held Naibe's veil, he felt himself ache in frustration when he sensed her eyes welling up with tears. He saw Wserkaf wipe them tenderly, then gather her into his arms to touch and kiss the fresh tears away. When he sensed that moment, Marai remembered how he had cried out in the tomb, when he *knew* it was the end, and how he hoped Wserkaf would care for Naibe's aching heart.

Sher-Ellit, he whispered at the sight of her in the Inspector's arms. *Strong as my goddess should be, but she'll want to avenge all the wrongs done me. Maybe Wserkaf – Well it explains why he lied, at least.*

Marai knew Wserkaf was about to succumb to Naibe's charms in the same way that he himself had once fallen deep in love. Her image, born from his *own* dreams and fantasies of a goddess, had overwhelmed all the priestly discipline the Inspector possessed.

In the vision, he gently lifted her and carried her to the pretty guest room where he had slept last night. At that time, long ago, the room had been filled with soft pillows and finely woven cushions. Now it was bare, stripped of all the memories.

I felt nothing of her there. Someone must have done a cleansing ritual to rid it of her energy.

Though Marai knew it was right for them to be together if he was thought to be dead, his heart still ached until he wept over having ever been lost. Solemnly, the sojourner allowed the vision of the past to roll through him.

Wserkaf sensed Naibe's vibrant spirit-voice. It swept through him, gaining a song-like strength as it did.

"Your touch is sweet and gentle; heartfelt," she sighed. "I believe you truly sorry for my Marai's —" her voice caught and couldn't continue, weeping again.

"Shh. Shh, young Naibe, rest." He smoothed her hair, noticing how soft it felt as the loosened curls slipped through his fingers. He placed her on the edge of the guest bed and sat beside her, holding her briefly before assisting her in lying down. That done, he lay beside her and cuddled her.

"It hurts my heart and every part of my soul, so much," she sighed.

The Inspector wanted to console her; to stop the weeping and get the fleeting and magical smile he saw when he spoke about the water wheel to return.

"I know now, my poor Marai came to trust you in the end. Now we heal the hurts in each other, it seems, but know this one thing:" She reached to smooth the wrinkles in his brow. He saw the corner of her mouth twitch in what might have been an understanding smile. Her layered voice deepened the sorcery as they lay together.

Marai is the plow to my earth,
His seed is in my fertile place.
I am his evening star woman.
My flesh is fire
My eyes are smoke
My hands long to touch and be consumed by him
Whose loin longs to fill me with its burning.

He felt her thoughts whisper through him one last time. They spoke like a prayer that said no one could ever take his place, but her words didn't matter to the Inspector because at that moment, her softness and sweet caress had already lifted him into a quiet, spellbound universe.

"Then I would be *your* priest. To lie beneath; to submit to your altar." As Wserkaf lay beside her, he felt the magic begin as he stared into the golden star shimmers that rose in her eyes. "I would worship you as woman, sweet one with golden goddess-eyes, true daughter of Hethara. I cannot replace a god, nor do I wish to. We can only be truth in all we are," his lips gently took hers.

He would later remember that what followed was sweet and tender, more than mighty and passionate. Her radiance flowed and rippled through everything in the world he knew the moment she touched it. It was her kind of magic, her spell.

Though it hadn't been intended, the magic swept across Wserkaf's estate, ripping through the calm, restful energies of the night. Princess Khentie woke. She sensed a change in her silent household, like the odd sensation in the air that comes just before a storm. She sat and saw that young Mya was still asleep in her small frame bed beside her. Still bothered by something, she looked around her darkened room for the random signature of a spiritual presence.

We can only be truth; in all we are.

"Wse?" she whispered because the presence sounded like his gentle voice. She laughed, sighed, closed her eyes, and then stood beside her bed with her arms open and palms up, emptying her thoughts briefly.

"Wse?" she asked the empty air in front of her because there hadn't been an answer. "Beloved? Are you ill?" she tiptoed from her stateroom out into the breezy upper walk, rushing quickly by the potted plants lining the tiled path that separated their rooms to check his bedchamber.

Empty? she frowned, straining to hear sounds of him taking a stroll in the plaza to take in some cooler night air. Then stunned, she realized as the whispers sounded in her heart that she felt the sound of shared passion.

Khentie knew, without any deep contemplation, exactly what she would witness if she went down the stairs and passed by the doorway of the guest room.

Oh, Goddess of bliss, how – could – this happen? No, it just can't. Her silent thoughts rioted because Wserkaf had agreed to protect and console the youngest of the sojourner's widows. *I thought this might happen, but he assured me it would not. And Father asked it of us, too! Now everything's changed — and it's wrong.*

Khentie couldn't understand why she was bothered. The lovemaking struck her first as divisive and rude. *She should find our care of her a humbling honor*, Khentie sulked. This first thought was quickly followed by another: *She and the other two are damned lucky they weren't turned into the alleyways to beg.*

That emotion was quickly replaced by horror of Wserkaf's behavior. *This isn't like him, to take advantage of someone gone mad with grief. And I asked what his plans for her were, but he said none. He's never lied or held back truth from me.*

Khentie turned around and went back to her room, shaken. *I must figure out what to do*, she thought, knowing she needed to meditate and reflect on this unpredicted turn of events.

He lied. That's the worst part. She paced outside her stateroom so that Mya wouldn't wake. *We pledged often to one another that we didn't require other lovers, particularly after my poor sister and that monster, Maatkare fell together. Dalliance is normal, healthy, and expected in those of god-blood, but the two of us set ourselves above that even after I went barren. He refused to take another even to check if the flaw was his seed and not my womb. Then, too, we were busy with our duties.*

When she had paced enough, Khentie returned to her couch confused.

I could accept and forgive some random carrying-on with a servant, but to lie about his needs or his intent — that's different.

Wserkaf was aware by morning that his wife knew everything that had taken place between he and Naibe. He attempted to explain how it had happened. The young woman lay peacefully asleep after so many restless and weepy nights. Khentie shrugged him away with a sarcastic *'well I know what you did last night, instead of sleeping'* giggle. Frustrated, he tried again later in the morning, when they were both in the upper hall between their bedrooms.

"I love you dearly, Khen, I just —" His voice faltered and then he hung his head, unable to explain anything further.

"Just?" she pursed her lips and lowered her eyes. "It is what it is but *do* keep it in its place and fully respectful." She turned and walked away from him, this time with an air of forced indifference surrounding her.

He knew he had hurt her and knew it was over his breaking his word more than over the act itself. He also knew she wasn't angry with him, just annoyed at the situation and would likely speak her pleasure with her father the King if he didn't manage to smooth the situation over. For now, a stony silence reigned as they both tried to move forward, acting as if nothing had happened.

That day he noticed that Naibe smiled a little more but remained humble whenever she was in the same area as the Princess. Although she rarely spoke, he urged her to be brave and to speak to Khentie sweetly and graciously. On his urging she told Khentie how the date candy she made for the market was made and then showed the Princess how to "couch rope into the edge of a veil."

He felt life was going well when the Princess told Naibe how she made incenses and scents from hard boiled palm wine. For a very few days, all seemed well, but by the end of the week "keeping it in its place" had become impossible. Wserkaf didn't understand why he had become so quickly besotted with Naibe.

"She's cast a spell on you, and you can't see it," Khentie whispered. It's so easy for *me* to see that," the Princess worried aloud as they walked together one evening after dinner. Sometimes they would swim and even make love like they were newly mated in their private shed near the water's edge. That had been a long-standing tradition with them and just this evening he had thought of it as a chore, not blessed moments together.

The Inspector remembered he hadn't known what to answer. Part of him wanted to object and part of him wanted to either agree or to defend Naibe from the accusation. At the edge of the water, under a romantic moonlight, any sentimental mood he had managed to stir up was shattered.

"Beloved. This is not –" She spoke slowly and deliberately, but stopped when she heard him sigh, exasperated.

GOING FORTH BY DAY

Silently, he turned her toward him, embraced her, sensed her disquiet as much as she sensed his confusion, threw up his hands, and walked away. He had lost all will and power to make a rational decision or to even discuss an irrational one.

The following day, when he was at home, he asked Naibe to sit with him in his chart room while he worked on his calculations and geometric theories.

"You are, and have been, as the sun in my darkest night." She whispered, gently laying her head on his shoulder.

Wserkaf knew his heart should have floated up to heaven except he realized that even when they were very young and burning with desire for each other he had never asked the Princess to sit by him while he worked. That revelation said only one thing to him.

"This can't last. This burns too hot and will burn out and because I love my wife unceasingly."

"I know," Naibe had whispered softly, taking his hand in hers and then placing it on her breast. He felt her heart beating gently and wanted to stop his work and place his head there too. He knew another thing.

It's no secret. Everyone in the house has noticed us. Whispers. Khen has been staying away more at the temple of Hethara to give us the room we need. But I've become a child in Naibe's arms; finding more ways to work from my table here so that I can be with her whenever the moment strikes us. I've even been late – I was never late years ago when it was new with my dear Khentie. She's right. It is a spell, and a cruel one at that.

Naibe drew his head to her so their lips touched tentatively then hungrily. In moments he swept her into his arms, his work not finished or notations put away, and carried her to the guest room.

Marai roused himself slightly to contemplate all he had seen. He sighed, disheartened but fully aware of all that had happened in this house and even in the room where he sat.

Answers why Wserkaf never checked on me until yesterday. I'm guessing he journeyed in spirit, at the old man's request, to sense life signs from me on the third day. I must have been too weak for him to read.

He wondered if the Children of Stone had done something to the Inspector's perception that made the man think his body was cold and hard – that the will of the Gods had been carried out before he came to collect the women and the box of stones.

He envisioned a very upset-but-guarded Wserkaf stating that perhaps his heart was smitten with a terror he could not overcome. Marai knew Wserkaf either didn't believe it and lied to himself so that he would be convinced. Later that was because he'd lost his soul over young Naibe-Ellit.

Marai slipped back into his midday reverie and stared at the somewhat rumpled linen scarf in his hand.

You've told me much, he addressed the cloth. *But how did you get lost from her?* As if it was a fortune-telling device, a scenario formed in his thoughts of a mild confrontation between Naibe and the Princess that indicated how quickly things had begun to deteriorate.

He saw Khentie, Naibe, and the handmaid Mya doing needlework together on a sunny, but tense afternoon toward the close of the week. Naibe continued the lesson to the Princess on twisting fine gold wire with colored thread couched onto the cloth.

"Know first, Lady Naibe, that you are well appreciated as a good woman in our household," the Princess spoke suddenly; out of nowhere. "And that we understand you bear us no evil intent. You cannot hope, though, that Prince Wserkaf will ever call you more than a concubine simply because you are in our house and he has taken special interest in your care."

Marai saw how polite, through the teeth, and firm Khentie was and knew she was about to scream like an irritated cat.

" –nor shall I give any child of yours a title. It will just never happen," she explained, setting down her needlework. "Not if both of my sons *and* my brother were struck down in the same hour and my husband, on some whim of the Goddess, was to himself ascend to the seat of God could he be free to do so either without my request and consent of it." Silent, Khentie waited for the girl's response to what had been a variant of a '*know your place in our household*' speech which one might give a wayward or overly ambitious servant.

When Marai's vision showed her sigh and cast her eyes down, he ached and wished he had been beside her.

If I had been there, though, none of this would have come to pass.

In humble tones, she replied. "He is a good man to me and he is ever kind, but I still grieve so much for another whom I cannot forget… This he *also* knows, Your Great Highness."

The sojourner felt darkness cross the Princess' face when she heard Naibe's words. It was a beautiful explanation that Wserkaf had never lusted for her but had fallen so naturally in love with her by trying to not only heal her sorrow but to absolve himself of his own wrongdoing. Naibe knew he wouldn't be able to explain it to her any more than she would be able to explain that she had no motive for bedding him. That they had been intimate was simply her way – as a goddess of love, and –

"You are a prophet?" Khentie suddenly asked. "Have you come into my house to show me what will be? – that there will be rifts in the house? Is that why?"

She knew, then. She knew what was coming soon, the deaths and the separations. She thinks Naibe coming into her house and seducing Wserkaf activated the curse. Goddess – Marai shook his head inside the vision, knowing that the Princess had all but predicted the death of her father and even more. *That's why the Princess worried. She knew her lecture about Naibe's place in the house had no effect and it scared her witless. She was losing control. But…* Marai contemplated.

"Great Lady –" Naibe protested. "I prophesy nothing, I –"

"It is well," Khentie paused and Marai sensed she was genuinely sympathetic even though her words came through as conniving, "but your gifts might be of better use in the healing of my father's heart as it was originally intended. He *was* touched by you and has asked if you are ready to come to his house. Should I say you are?"

Naibe's face crumpled. She dropped the veil and ran from the open plaza to the guest room. There she lay, weeping until Wserkaf returned from the temple. A gentle breeze wafted it deep into the stand of papyrus where Marai had found it.

GOING FORTH BY DAY

CHAPTER 16: AWAY FROM HERE, TO WHERE?

When the Inspector received a message the next morning that King Menkaure and Great Wife Khamerenebty would dine with him that evening, he wasn't entirely surprised. He knew the King craved departures from the daily official business of his rule and enjoyed seeing members of his extended family casually after the day of duty and work at his own palace or temples was done. Later in the day, as everyone cleaned and prepared, Wserkaf's youngest son, Kakai, arrived from Per-A-At with another reminder.

Oh, blessed truth, the Inspector moaned inwardly because he'd completely forgotten another reason why the King had decided to visit. Tonight, his son's cousin and future wife would attend with her parents. The youth's days of childhood were ending.

In a few months, he would build a house and establish a household with the girl as his chief wife. This dinner was to be one of many "formal meetings" between them even though they had known and liked each other most of their years on earth. The King and his wife enjoy witnessing these pairings. *And another thing*, the Inspector realized with a greater degree of anxiety: *Naibe. She was intended for Our Father. Now that has all become difficult.* Wserkaf knew the liaison with the young woman was becoming far more strained than it needed to be. Khentie fully accepted that as a royal. Her alignment with the Goddess of pleasure engrained in her that other men and women might come through a household from time to time. Some might even stay on, particularly if more children were sought.

She understands this but remains distant as if I have abandoned her. Why? he kept repeating to himself and answered: b*ecause neither of us thought it was in our nature and neither of us saw it coming. She thinks it's dangerous heka – a spell on me, not true lust or even a need. Maybe it is. I felt something weeks ago from all three women – native skills. I warned Great One, but the fool man dismissed it and then had the gall to agree to the King asking me to heal her. Maybe Marai, may the gods ease his journey, was right. Maybe Hordjedtef is testing my own loyalty. Maybe he sees me floundering like a youth over her sweetness. But, she is so much more than a seductress. What can I do but let it play out as it will?*

GOING FORTH BY DAY

Wserkaf placed Naibe on his left and his wife Khentie at his right at the table. No one said a thing about the seating arrangement but their expressions, though muted, said enough. The young foreign woman had assumed the position of favored concubine or second wife as they reclined.

After the pleasantries, meal, and the light entertainment, when the King was waiting for his bearers to assemble in order to carry him and his wife back to their separate residences, King Menkaure pulled Wserkaf aside.

Here it is, the Inspector sighed inwardly dispatching both Khentie and Naibe to their separate rooms. The King ordered the Inspector to follow him to a place just outside the walls, then told his guards to stand where they could see him but not hear his words.

"My son," the aging but still statuesque man began.

"Great Majesty," Wserkaf bowed, then kept his eyes down, hoping the great man wouldn't be too condescending.

"The young woman, the sojourner, has become *more* to you than a servant?" he stated. "Tell me about how this has happened, as I thought the outcome might differ from what I saw at supper," the King glanced to see if the royal chaise was ready.

Wserkaf knew the King didn't truly want to speak to him. He felt a slight tremble in his heart. *I'm not ready to speak about her. I can't even explain these feelings to Khentie, who has been my solace every single day until these past few days. How spurned she must feel.* "She has improved, your Majesty, and – I – have become more than fond of her."

"I see," the King paced a few steps then turned on his heel and returned. His own instincts had told him how uncomfortable and embarrassed Wserkaf had become.

"My child approves, then?" he asked.

Wserkaf felt the air rush out of his lungs as he gave the King his expected answer. "I will respect her wishes; protect and yet obey her desires," his words were sad and dull.

"My loins all but created you. Speak to Khentkawes and speak to me through her," the King paused in his pacing. His men were ready. They bowed in position so he would know to mount his chair. His wife had already departed.

"Majesty," Wserkaf offered. "In some days I will prepare for my duty weeks in Khmenu. I just want Lady Naibe to be safe from the pain she has endured and to continue to heal her heart. I want happiness for her again. There are things –" the priest caught himself but felt instantly relieved that the thoughts of the King had apparently moved on. Menkaure had turned to get into his chair. His men and guards were lifting him. As if he had become the statue of a god, the King looked straight ahead. He spoke once more without looking at his Inspector.

"Take care of your heart that it may not break. Too many hearts in my household go forth with knives run through them. I know this young woman can see into your soul and she will drink up the bitter parts. Be safe, my son, on your journey."

Naibe worried about her future. She didn't want to say anything to Wserkaf about it because she knew he was as upset as she was over everything that had happened.

He's been my everything since you died. She stared at her hands and visualized them touching Marai's face the night by the well in the wadi when she encouraged his passion to explode. *That I could bring you to love changed everything about me.* Sadly, she saw the vision of his calm and loving face fade and saw her hands become weak and transparent as she tried to bring him back from the death he had certainly endured at the hands of the priests. The waking vision made her want to weep again. It was the same one she saw the evening just over a week earlier. That was the night when Wserkaf's face formed in her hands and they became whole again. *These hands I have – Is it my gift that I will heal the broken hearts? I wanted to curse you, W'se, because I thought you were part of my beloved's destruction. Something about you told me that you were a friend at the end of his days walking in Earth. Then, you healed me as much as I could ever be healed. It can't last. Nothing ever does, I guess. I am what I have become, and you are what you will be. That we met in*

GOING FORTH BY DAY

desperate moments – is it fate or chance? A blessing or a curse?

The thoughts woke her. At first, she hadn't realized she was dreaming. She was still holding the inspector-priest in her arms. They had loved splendidly earlier, but the ecstasy in her heart was dimmed by the thought: *he cannot replace Marai, and I know now more than ever that he loves Princess Khentie*. It was as simple and as difficult as that.

After that night, young Kakai remained there. He had met with his betrothed in the "eye of the King", then shortly after that he took and passed his oral examination with the local priests of Ra. After another week at home, he would return to his grandfather's school in Per-A-At to complete more studies.

One day following the dinner, Naibe reclined by the pond. She wasn't thinking about the boy. She thought about the water and Marai and tried to conjure some of his essence to gaze upon her from the afterlife.

Hand in the water of the great river when I glide to meet the news of your death, beloved. I wanted to drown, not dance for the men. I wanted to drown, but each time the water saved me. What is it with water anyway? And the sun and moon that strengthen me? Am I as you said a goddess of the elements? She slipped out of her skirt and stepped into the shallow pool to swim. She remembered how the water always comforted her. Then, she glanced toward Wse's open cubicle where he sat to do his calculations when he was at home. *Wse is in his study room this morning. Perhaps I will charm him again – show him my strength; how I've become more whole despite your dying my ever love.*

Naibe swam near the edge of the pool by the papyrus pots, then rose from the water unaware that the boy watched her. She twirled, lost in her own world of sun and water. The beauty of the moment was shattered by a youthful catcall.

"Aha! Hethara at the river's edge, awaiting a divine mounting, I see," the boy called aloud. He laughed and sauntered toward the pool as if curious.

"Why thank you," Naibe giggled in a lighthearted innocent tease, then lifted her breasts in the classic Ashera pose. Caught up in the moment, she wandered around the edge of the pool with an extra kick in her rump, dimly recalling the way she used to dance before the changes – a "come hither" that was more a joke than anything else.

When she looked up to see the effect, the youth was gone.

Odd. Well, no harm there. Remembering. Wonder where he went so fast. Shrugging her shoulders, she slipped back into the pool and ducked underwater, no longer mournful.

Wserkaf was in his chart room transcribing a worn notation onto new hide in preparation for its being handed over to the newly initiated sesh candidates in Khmenu the following week. When his son approached, he briefly looked past him and saw Naibe re-entering the pool. He smirked, distracted by the shimmering quality of her sunlit but wet body.

"Father," the boy chortled in his new, but still squeaky, lower voice. "I have an idea."

"Regarding what?" the Inspector looked up, distracted from the vision of loveliness. *What does he want? I'm tired. Know why. I've slept as little as a bridegroom.*

"I was just watching your fine new ka't playing in the water," the boy grinned and quickly glanced back over his shoulder as if he was about to tell a dirty joke.

Wserkaf felt the blood drain from his face, then rush back in barely controlled rage at the youth's disrespect. His eyes narrowed, but he controlled his response.

What is he —? A ka't? Rude!

"That wasn't kind, boy. Lady Naibe is a guest in this house and should be treated with better manners, not words used over women of no value."

"Oh," the boy answered sounding flippant and continued his former thought as if Wserkaf's admonishment had never been made. "I didn't know."

"And?" Wse tried to control his rage. He felt the disrespect an instant before his son's words formed.

"When you go on duty, I think I should like to climb aboard it a few times until I sail back to school. We wouldn't want it to be without that daily shot for too long," the boy beamed expectantly.

It. He called her a ka't, the Inspector's world turned crimson, then black. His son's form shifted into that of some grunting young monster who needed to be defeated.

"It?" his mouth shaped the word in horrified speechlessness. He stood quietly and in one movement which he never recalled later closed his hand around his walking stick and with the grace of a young lion, flung aside his lap board, leapt up, and cracked the youth so hard across the face with his walking stick that it bloodied the boy's nose and blacked one of his eyes.

"No! Stop! Don't hurt me! I didn't mean it!" Kakai shrieked, ran out to the pool, tripped on a bench, and then tumbled flat. The Inspector towered over him and was about to rain some more blows down on the him when he felt arms seize him and drag him away. Men held him until he stopped struggling.

"What? He called her – No. Let me teach him. He will not speak of her like that!" he gasped, out of breath and still feeling the need to visit the boy with more blows. One of the men took the staff away.

"Highness, stop. That is your son. You've hurt him," one of them urged while the other grabbed his neck and pulled him down into a seated position. It was the sesh and his attendant, who had come from Hordjedtef's estate to receive the translation.

Wserkaf sat, dismayed, eyes fastened on the bleeding and sobbing youth and some servants helping him up. In the background he heard the clamor of feet and shrieks of horror.

"No son of mine! He would not!" Wserkaf struggled once more, but as his thoughts cleared, he saw Naibe standing frozen at the pool's edge and staring at both the bruised and bleeding boy who cowered on the tiles and him. As if she had suddenly become ashamed, she huddled, arms crossed over her breasts as if she attempted to hide them, her eyes turning away.

He sat gasping and still stunned at the chaos, not believing what had taken place. "Blessed Truth, settle me," he murmured a broken prayer, wanting to go to the boy who was being led away. The men relaxed their grip on him and helped him to rise.

He couldn't see Naibe in the water now and wondered where she had gone.

What have I done? Goddess truth! I can't. I never hit him so before.

Princess Khentie, fetched by Mya when the scuffle started stood calm-faced, with her arms folded and an imperious look on her face.

"This stops," her voice was barely above a whisper, "by my divine order. Today." All motion in the sunny open plaza froze at those words, as if everything had become a block of stone or a statue. "My divine brother, Shepseskaf, has need of another handmaiden. I have already discussed it at length with him, that it is past time for her to leave us. There will be *no argument* or discussion on this." With that, she went to assist Kakai. The men holding Wserkaf fully released him and went to help her with the boy as well.

"He's mad, Mother. It was just a joke. I didn't know."

Immeasurable pain and sadness filled the Inspector then because on one hand Naibe had been almost guiltless and on the other hand he had humiliated himself and nearly beaten his own son senseless. He recalled his words to the King; that he would not question his wife's decisions on the matter. There was absolutely *nothing* he could do other than respect and honor Khentie's wishes when she invoked her right as Daughter of the God. Silently, he went back to the chart room, picking up the scattered lapboard and writing utensils as he went.

Marai sighed as he came back from his vision.

I should feel rage at him for taking my Naibe, but I don't. I was dead after all and for some reason the link between our stones was muddied and still is. I can't see where they are, and I would guess they can't know I am alive. He ruined himself over her in trying to help mend her heart. Who could have seen that a man so disciplined would have cracked and been broken so easily? Marai keenly understood the misery in the priest's heart as he stared down at the veil and remembered the Inspector and his beloved Naibe's entire time together as if he had been with her himself.

GOING FORTH BY DAY

The gentle voices of the Children of Stone whispered the stories to him, as if they were narrating a legend.

The decision of one to comfort
And yet now needs comfort.
So frail the will
The need

He knew they had begun to understand a little more about the emotion of such intense love.

It was right for them
to be together,
if you were thought to be dead,
but your heart still aches.
You weep now, man of Ai,
that you were ever lost.

But where is she? Did she go to this Shepseskaf's house? Where are Ari and Deka? Marai felt weighed down with the fatigue of all he had realized and returned to his room to lie on the straw and wicker bed, knowing Naibe had slept there for so many days. He clutched the little veil sadly and wished it was the woman who had sewn it instead.

I must do better than this. I must think of a way to get around the spell that divides us. Maybe I could send thoughts to the palace and make one of the statues come alive, speak with the voice of the King and demand where my ladies are. They are safe for now, Wserkaf told me. Can I trust him, though?

Marai felt weak again, the lasting effect of however long he had lain in the tomb not entirely gone. Studying the veil and stroking the stitches that created the red and golden bulls on the border as if they were her gold-skinned shoulder, he decided: *I'll stay for now, but nothing will stop me from searching the very universe and all time itself until I find how I can go to them and take them in my arms again.*

<blockquote>Meekness of will is an enemy to pride,
Man of Ai you taught us.
Be that and learn more than we can see
through you or through them.
One step further.</blockquote>

It'll at least show me who the greater enemy is and the right target for my vengeance if it is not Hordjedtef. First, I'll hear Wserkaf's version when he returns to check on me tonight. He's skilled and he can block his thoughts from me, but he doesn't know what I have already seen. If his story differs, there will be a reckoning.

Then, Marai thought sadly about Naibe and everything that might have happened to her. She wasn't weak, though she pretended to be. Her apparent naivete was part of her charm. That she was drawn to give love to any in need without restraint was the problem. Marai still didn't know how much time had passed since the events that he saw had taken place.

Not years; Wse looks the same, but long enough so that you truly knew I would not return. You couldn't help yourself, could you, sweet goddess. It's your gift to take a man and own all that he is until he exists no more outside you. Marai caressed the veil in his hands, dotting tears from his own eyes at the aching sweet-sad memory of their time together he felt from it. He saw, in his heightened thoughts through the touch of the white cloth, that Wserkaf had given her a lovely loin belt. It had hundreds of little jingly, coiled serpents that rang like tiny singing bells on the chains that composed it. They made such sweet music whenever she walked. Her magic, the placing of heka by goddess-given instinct, was the reason why. Lying on the little bed she and the Inspector had shared, he held the veil up one more time. *Is that her scent, like warm honey and buttery spice?* Yes, it's still there, Marai relaxed in the scent of his love and the sound of the jingling in his memory as he waited for the evening to come.

GOING FORTH BY DAY

Chapter 17: No Ordinary Man

When Marai opened his eyes again, he noticed the low reflected light of an oil lamp as it flickered on the wall. Someone, perhaps the servant who had assisted him, must have brought it into the guest room while he slept. Through the undraped door, he saw that the plaza also blazed with dozens of strategically placed lamps. At first, the sojourner didn't notice the Inspector of the Ways sitting in the corner of the little room. The moment he did, Marai knew the man must have come to check on him, then stayed to watch him rest and to reflect on everything that had happened to him. Tonight, the Inspector wore a formal long shendyt and his dark cloak; he had recently arrived from the King's palace. A bright yellow-gold sash of mourning, that symbolized the soul rising like the sun, crossed his chest and was tied at his waist.

"About three months," the Inspector shook his bowed head, but quickly continued. "I don't see *how*, by all the gods, unless you *are* a god already. There is just *no* magic or sorcery that can bring someone back after such a long time without air, food, or drink." Wserkaf's eyes cast down and then up slowly, almost reverently. "I was *certain* you had died; that your visitation to me that first night was your winging away forever, with all the poison you took. But you *didn't* die, or else your unprepared corpse would have festered. You *must* be a god! Asarmaat, true Asar," he sighed, then leaned his head back against the wall. "Gods. What has my family done to itself now?" his laugh bore a sickened but quiet tone. "And Hordjedtef, proud old fool that he is, just couldn't see it."

Marai scanned through the Inspector's solemn face and let all the emotion play through it. He fiercely guarded his own reaction of shock at the passage of time even though the Inspector apparently didn't guard his own thoughts.

Three months, *not days, have passed. I wasn't even under the protection of the sleep pod in the Children's ship. Now all this? Far too much has happened.*

"I – I can't study with him anymore," the Inspector's whisper grew dismal. "I spoke to my father again; made amends after over half my life of not speaking to him except through my sons. But now this: *All* of this is going away," Wserkaf made a sweeping gesture with his hand that indicated everything in his home was included. "This life, all that I've built of it or ever known!" his eyes closed. "As soon as we have mourned and buried our Father Menkaure, I will go to Per-A-At on a regular tour but then seek asylum there when I arrive. It's where I belong. Old Dede won't suspect a thing until after it's done." The priest announced and then grew silent.

Marai read his clear thought.

You haven't asked me about them tonight; the women, your sweet Naibe. I don't know if I can even answer. He ignored it, wanting to hear more about the changes all this had brought on the house of Menkaure.

The King is dead, Marai realized he was still stroking Naibe's veil as if it was now a pet cat. *He acts as if what happened has now set more in motion.*

"You don't seek glory in any of this, do you?" Wserkaf's hand went to his head, almost in a salute. "You've said to me and even to my senior that there's no skill, nothing that makes you a god, yet here you sit wonderful and strong. You speak on the wind. You've touched magic and you whisper to the heart and *now* you've overcome death!" the Inspector rambled in breathless astonishment. "My senior forced enough sweet horizon into you to fell two bull elephants out of dark and wretched Kush in mid-charge. It should have hurled you at the pylons of Amenti before we finished ten of the more than two hundred divine utterances! Then there is this matter of the three months, when the required three *days* without the medicine or a guide have killed even those who have prepared for years."

"So that's what he gave me to drink? Sweet Horizon? I thought it was 'Ben', the 'What then is it'?" Marai sat back and shivered. He still felt weak and out of focus. He wondered why he couldn't keep his thoughts on his wives or any other subject for more than an instant. Across the room from him was a man who had begun as a foe and who in the last minute had become a friend. Now he was a rival over Naibe, but Marai sensed that even *that* relationship had changed. She was gone. The Inspector of the Ways didn't covet the young woman; he had simply become awe-struck and now his astonishment verged on worship of them both.

An ordinary man would curse you, Wse, Marai mused. *Or maybe you'd understand me better if I leapt forward and beat you into the earth. I just know there's more and I need to guard myself as I did when Ari would taunt me with other men before we loved. It hurt, but I never let her know. You, I need to speak about everything even though my feet want me to stride forth to find them – unless I stop time itself.*

"It *was* 'Ben'. Great One just mixed it with the sweet horizon. That's much stronger and can be varied according to need. Purple cone flower seeds, Nefer Nebty, and Hul Gil fruit," Wserkaf sighed bitterly. "A very small amount put in the drink quiets fear and eases pain. Change the mixture's proportions and death can be either swift and painless or prolonged and filled with suffering. It's his choice. Still, I've never seen so much dumped into a cup. I truly thought it would murder you before you drank it all."

Marai shrugged. He'd heard of Hul Gil. These plants had red flowers with black centers that dropped their petals to grow a deadly seed-filled fruit. His journeys into the future while he slept were part of his deep memory but somehow he knew more about the Hul Gil than he had been taught: *Kingdoms will be built and wars fought over that stuff, in the name of needful bliss. Beautiful Lady. It flushes the face, brightens the eye, but too much gives haunted visions and then purple cone: wolf-bane.* He shuddered to think his poor body had been wracked with such a dreadful potion. Nothing about the ingredients could be construed as a mistake or an accident. The elder's sole intent was his death. "But, why kill me? Because of what is locked inside? Why not leave it locked and send me on my way, not a bit wiser?" he shook his still-aching head.

"I asked him that myself," the Inspector sighed once more, the stricken look on his face evolving into one of disgust. "Great One explained to me that you're not as locked as you want us to think. It's the thing placed in your head at the site of your inner eye: the Ta-Ntr crystal or Kernel of Wisdom he calls it. You call it your Child Stone. Every hour you're alive, it whispers more and more to your heart. You grow, you change, you evolve, and you learn. We saw that when you were writing for us. It wasn't *what* you wrote that worried and offended him, it was your capacity to write too many truths – to reveal too much! We've seen that your wives learned as eagerly too. In so many years, nothing would be able to touch any of you or hold you back. You say you are no god, but I say I am witnessing the birth of one from a man. I think he wanted to stop all four of you while the power to do so was still in his grasp."

Marai felt Wserkaf's words again, and savored the deeper meaning:

'You say you are no god, but I am witnessing the birth of one from a man.'

Listening to Wserkaf speak, Marai knew the man was spilling plenty of truth, but that it was going to be increasingly hard to bear.

"Great Hordjedtef felt he was pruning the garden of knowledge; protecting it," the Inspector continued. "One nips the odd growth between the strong shoots before it saps the whole of the plant so that nothing bears fruit. Can I fault him either, for trying to save our way of life from being overtaken, stolen, or polluted by the outsider?" he shook his head again, then looked beseechingly into the sojourner's eyes. "It's all changed now, though. With the King dead, my wife now becomes the matriarch of the new king's house. Everything we have built here is lost. I had thought I would be so much older, perhaps dead myself, when the gods called her to fulfill her sacred agreement."

Marai frowned. "Her half-brother, Shepseskaf, is now king, isn't he? She must marry him?"

"Exactly," the Inspector lamented. "It's something you wouldn't understand; a fidelity marriage and often it's nothing more than that. His chief wife and other wives usually bear the children of his body, unless the gods dictate otherwise. Even so, it's well known by all physicians she is barren nearly ten years. It didn't matter to us with our line made firm buy two healthy sons and soon a grandchild."

Wserkaf was now on his feet in the little room; he paced in agitation. "Shepseskaf is up against it, though, so he might ask it of her if he cannot find a likely concubine. It would be a wasted effort. He has but one child, already promised to the rising priest of Ptah, a cousin of ours. On top of it, he has so many enemies *including* Prince Hordjedtef. My senior never liked him being the chosen one because he is only fully royal by his marriage to Khentie. His mother is a commoner, so he was also considered one. There were other more royal choices, but the wise women and queens dictated this pairing after the curse was laid."

"So, she has *divorced* you?" Marai drank in the Inspector's absolute misery. He had just seen, in the memories pulled from the veil, how the woman shunned him as she left that early morning.

"No. She is my wife. We will simply share husbandship, but his is divine and mine of Earth and the heart." Wserkaf stared into the lamp-lit but empty plaza from the window in the guest room. "She will live in her brother's house. I will not. After the Grand Mourning of so many months, when he is elevated, I will petition that we might be together again; that she returns to live at my house."

Marai fell silent for a long time at this. After what he had sensed from Naibe's veil, he knew Khentie might *not* want her husband to return if sweet Brown Eyes was in the same city. He was almost afraid to ask about his other wives. It would be too much salt in either of their wounds.

When the Inspector turned and made eye contact with him again, Marai did not have to ask about his wives. He had a vision of the priest's last moments with Naibe as he moved her to Shepseskaf's house. They clung to each other like lost children, then let go and turned away from each other. The Children of Stone had etched the sorrow both felt in their crystalline souls.

"Your place is not with us; not yet, but maybe one day." Naibe had sighed sweetly, gently bringing his head down to kiss his lips and then his eyes.

"She was so lovely, Marai. I just —" the inspector-priest stopped mid-sentence, too overwhelmed to continue. "Couldn't refuse her a thing, and she missed you so, even to the last day with me. She was sent to try to bear a child for Shepseskaf and Bunefer because it was feared the Wife of the Body could not." Then, the Inspector remembered something else. "There's more, you can guess. You know she cursed us for what happened to you at first," Wse sighed.

A distraught Naibe's words when she first arrived played through Marai's eyes. As he sensed the moment it was as familiar; he had seen that moment in one of the random visions that assaulted him when he lay suffering.

"A curse is on all of you!" Naibe snarled. *"You knew it was wrong, but you did nothing to save my beloved... Death is in your house!"*

Forcing the Inspector talk to him had created a link between the men. The only thing Marai considered then was how much would he learn, given the limited time they had before the Inspector would be missed.

"Death is in your house –" the sojourner repeated. "She said that, but I don't think she meant the King's death, do you?"

"I *did* have that thought for an instant today as did Khentie, but I dissuaded her of the notion. She would have lifted such an utterance considering what came between us later."

But she could have, Marai thought. He knew Naibe was impulsive and often dangerously so: her darting away in a storm, the risks she took in reading Deka's thoughts, and then playing as if she was ignorant. *Did Naibe pull the secret of the King's death into the light? Was it merely that, or did she bring his death on him for his indifference?*

Marai knew Naibe was powerful. He'd seen the strange flash of fire and dark under her innocent golden eyes and told himself it was a joke. She was beauty and love. The dark or destructive aspects of Inanna and Ashera missed her. Her temper was even and she cried like a child when she was afraid. He sensed that any rage she had would be slow and deliberate, nearly invisible. It still made him wonder if anyone else noticed.

"Great One mentioned it to me," Wserkaf added after a moment's silence. "It was at the first viewing."

Marai's brow raised in a 'go on, say the rest' expression. He balanced his foot on the edge of the couch where he rested and embraced his knee then quietly contemplated everything that Wserkaf said, then sent the Inspector a thought to see if his ability to do so had been harmed by the poison.

Tell the rest before dawn is on us and you are missed.

"True. But let me tell you as much as I might," Wserkaf answered as if he had heard the sojourner's thoughts aloud. "I knew I was due to leave Ineb Hedj for Khmenu temple for two circuits of Iah. I knew I needed to end it with Naibe or come up against the King as well as my wife," he fidgeted, not entirely comfortable with looking the sojourner in the eye. "Khentie is completely disciplined in these matters of state. She crafted young Naibe's future for her and told her that, should she bear a child for her brother, she would then be allowed to suckle it and indeed be a part of her child's upbringing, as perhaps a nurse. It wouldn't have been a bad life, all told. She was even going to have the company of your other wife Ariennu who was already in that house as a concubine."

"But what madness was it to put Ari in a royal house as one of those?" Marai frowned. He looked for something to drink. The residual burning thirst had become an issue again.

Wserkaf looked out of the guest window and signaled one of his idling bearers to go to the storeroom and pull out a jar of beer for them.

"Ari takes sport in men. I think she used to pride herself in that," Marai cautioned, almost amused by the witless decision to put her in a house and expect *her* to be a brood cow. He remembered in a flash all the mocking and teasing the tall woman with the russet colored hair had given him throughout their time together. He thought of her skulking around in alleys for a quick one with any number of men, and laughingly erasing her face and form from their memory. "When she was changed, she re-formed herself barren, but appearing ripe because she had tired of being unable to raise any child she brought forth. She isn't a woman to be tethered, not even by a prince."

"Princess – *Wife of the God* Bunefer is a seer and a prophetess in the house of Hethara," the Inspector went on. "She is intensely gifted. It didn't take her long to know Lady Ariennu's truth, but rather than ask for her dishonesty to be punished, she sent her to the King's harem. He already has his heirs, but had recently needed a healer, so it was." He shaded his eyes again as if he was about to weep as the jar of beer was brought. "No one knew he was that sick."

Marai nodded politely. He took the jar from the man when he brought it in, tipped it to his parched lips, then handed it to the Prince.

"I had no choice but to let Naibe go. Maybe something was trying to tell me you weren't really gone. Something told me I was losing my wits over her and poised on the brink of madness. I just wanted more than anything for her to somehow be safe.

Being in another royal house would give her safety, or so I thought," Wserkaf's head was in one hand. "But then –"

"Damn," Marai felt a different coldness creep through his chest. "Stop," he whispered to the priest. "I know you're holding something back. Just *stop* and *look* at me. Look at my eyes." Marai seized the Inspector's hand and sought his eyes despite the Inspector's struggle. Then, Marai heard the memory of Naibe's last words to Wserkaf sounding in his thoughts.

> *You must stay but be in Per-A-at.*
> *There, you will ascend like the sun.*
> *We will be together again*
> *when your work is done*
> *and this priesthood purified*
> *of the wrongs in it.*

"No," the Inspector protested.

"Don't be too hard on yourself," Marai grasped the Inspector's arm, sending a powerful sweep of energy up his arm and into his heart.

> *Talk to me this way.*

"Gods. What's happened? Dream talks. You want that? I –" the man stammered as Marai's touch lifted him into a trance state as sublime as if he had prepared and meditated for hours. He nodded drowsily, then spoke the proper utterance that would make him a conduit for everything ethereal Marai wanted to examine.

"You must trust me," the sojourner whispered then realized he was asking the same thing of the Inspector that had been asked as he went through his ritual.

Wserkaf spoke just above a whisper. "I did not see what you will see. I do not know what we will now learn. I temper my will and open my thoughts to the ghosts of their memory. I place and I submit to the god Ma-at. I will speak the truth as it comes forth through me."

Releasing himself to the heightened trance, Wserkaf thought of everything that had happened. He remembered the way the women were taken from their apartment in Little Kina Ahna and of all the misery he helped cause. Then, he silently thought of the good times; the way Naibe sent tender thoughts into his heart through her golden-starred brown eyes. She had been so sweet to him each early morning when he lay resting in her arms. As he sank deeper into the trance, he sensed a white flash beyond his consciousness.

Her veil. He put it on my neck to read her. His neck too. He sank deeper. The last sensation the Inspector felt was Marai's huge hand resting on his shoulder.

First, the priest remembered the way he fell asleep cuddling Naibe the week they had been intimate. Her graceful fingers smoothed his brow.

Because Marai had touched and kissed her hands so tenderly, the touch of the sojourner's hand on his own reopened the sweetest memories of her sitting at his pool, arms raised up to the sun in an attitude of worship. The light had blurred her face as she looked up into its light. The brightness shaped and bounced off her breasts, implanting itself again and again. It woke new memory, an image hidden in Marai's own heart and sent to him instead of shared by them. Time moved so slowly now. There had been wondrous glimmers of hope in the Inspector's heart when he held the woman of the evening star in his arms. Through him, he remembered all the sighs and the pleasure growing through each other until they wanted to die. She was his star of mercy in a hopeless life.

Oh Wseriri! Help me forget the aching my soul has. Touch me until you heal the tears in my heart for my Marai.

She had begged that of him that first night they were together, and he had caressed her with every gentle healing touch he knew. She had kissed his hands and made them glow with the glimmers in her own eyes. For her, he had pulled all the stars in the sky down to heal and touch her glowing goddess body. He disappeared into those eyes and into every pore of her flesh until for so many moments that stretched into hours, he was no longer himself but part of her.

Those nights, too, became ghosts as he released them. From that point, even though the priest knew nothing of the events, the link between the men Naibe had loved and the stones in hers and the sojourner's heads became a window into the world of Sweet Naibe-Ellit, Marai's Ashera.

Chapter 18: The Sacred Cow

As Wserkaf let his last tender moments with Naibe flow out into the universe, Marai relived them. He saw Wse standing beside the litter in which his porters had carried them both to Shepseskaf's palace. They both clung to each other like souls lost in a swarm of emotion. At first, Naibe didn't appear greatly changed. To him she appeared ever tender and sweet, but a deeper sense revealed she was sad beyond telling. He wanted to reach months into the past to console her and let her know he lived, but he knew even if he could slow time, he could never reverse it so that none of her pain would take place.

Naibe wondered how she could ever bring herself to accept the loss of *two* men so close together. The only comfort for her, she knew, was that Ari would be there.

But, Marai mused apart from the vision, *Wse said that wasn't so either.*

No, sweet Irimaat Wser, my ever-strong truth seeker, she whispered those words to the Inspector. Her lips trembled, making Marai's vision of the memory even more painful. She spoke with the power of her Ashera voice, yet because of her desperate fear of the future, there was little strength in the enchantment which would give the Inspector the strength to leave her. *Your place is not with us, not yet.* She sighed sweetly and gently brought his head down so she could kiss his lips and then his eyes. *You must stay but be in Per-A-At soon and not in Ineb Hedj. It is there you will ascend like the sun. We will be together one day when your work is done, and this priesthood has been purified of the wrongs in it.* She turned away then, unable to look at him any longer.

In Naibe's already dismal moment, she looked up and saw Ariennu standing at the back entrance to the women's quarters.

"Wise MaMa!" she rushed to embrace and kiss her, but then realized the elder woman seemed tired and slightly irritated. Beside her were her things, packed in a basket.

"You are doing well enough?" Ari embraced her back, ignoring Naibe's questioning look about the baskets.

"No. I'm not," Naibe mumbled then asked plainly: "What's all this? Your things are here."

Ari pushed away from her, as if the heart to heart conversation was suddenly awkward.

"Good Morning, Your Highness," Ari softly bowed as if she had been trained for years in the art of courtesy. "I have prepared myself."

"Prepared? Ari?" Naibe whimpered, her eyes seeking Wserkaf's. His face had grown stony as he gestured men to bear Ariennu's baskets and eased her into the sedan. Without any change of expression and a small, fake smile stuck on her face, Ari answered:

"You didn't know? It's a trade. I'm off to the King's and you're here."

"No. I –"

Marai saw the tears spring to Naibe's eyes and shared her thought to run away or fight rise to the surface then fail.

"Shush, Baby. It'll be alright." Ari breathed out, suddenly showing her own feelings of depression. "I'm lucky princess mittens didn't have my head when they found out I can't have a baby for them."

"No," Naibe gasped, looking as if she was about to have another fit of fainting. "No child by me. I can't."

Ari grabbed the young woman by both shoulders and pulled her close enough to whisper in her ear. "Just do what they tell you to do and keep a good smile on it. I'm still working on something to get us all back together, even bring Deka back. Swear I am." Ari sat quietly in the sedan and waited for Wserkaf to sit with her. Soon, Marai saw the sedan borne away down the winding, walled alleys.

Once Wserkaf and Ariennu began to move, Naibe bowed her head, refusing to watch. At any moment, she knew she might lose control and chase after them both.

But you were not mine – you never were, she sobbed internally. *You were just good to me when no one else was and for that you were nearly ruined by us together. But, my true love is still dead. Where's the fairness in that? You love your wife and your family. If I really wanted to cast a spell, I could own you. I could seduce you and hold you captive, but it wouldn't be right. I don't want to make you my slave, but to come to me cleanly, as I needed my beautiful Marai to be free of his Ilara whom he mourned so long. I release you. I release you. I release you.*

Marai wanted to stop everything in the story that came so effortlessly through the Inspector. He felt as if he should cry aloud for her and send death on the wind to everyone who made them fall apart, but he needed to know more. She was doing what was best – letting him walk away no matter how much it hurt.

Has everything I dreamed of been destroyed? Is there nothing but this shade of memory because I died? the sojourner blinked sadly. *This is too much. Little one in my thoughts, show me Ariennu for a little longer while. Poor Naibe I can't bear to watch when there is nothing I can do about these long-ago things.*

Obediently, the black-metal stone in his brow switched visions to follow the Inspector and Ari. The woman who now sat beside Wserkaf and craned slightly to see if Naibe was waving goodbye was beautiful and elegant. He always felt she was a beauty. She had been pretty, but more of a pleasant and warm creature after she had been changed by the Children of Stone. The woman he saw now had changed from being the witty prankster who loved to laugh and play away lazy afternoon rest times, or the naughty evenings on the roof or in the alleyways of Little Kina-Ahna. If Naibe had been heartbroken, Ari had become hard and cold as the woman in the band of thieves, but without the failed health. Her eyes reflected little of the sorrow Naibe exhibited. Those dark eyes seemed almost animal – as if they had now seen far too much to ever be joyous again. Her lids were fiercely lined with kohl green paint and her lips reddened. She was resplendent and proud, as if she was truly the goddess of pleasure merged with the image of a wise elder, but she was not *his* Ariennu. He only hoped that when he saw her again, she would be.

GOING FORTH BY DAY

Marai's thought of sending her a message to brighten her dour mood as they traveled, but decided against it. She remained silent and stone-faced through the trip to the palace; even he could not dig into her thoughts.

At the last moment, just as she and Wserkaf arrived at the rear entrance to the women's villa, her fingertips crept to his hand as if she was reassuring him.

When the litter was set down he helped Ari stand, then stayed with her. They waited for the guards to pass word into the room that she had arrived. Marai saw through the Inspector's memories that even though the sun was bright that morning, the air seemed sad and gray.

"She *got* to you, didn't she?" the woman spoke almost shyly.

The Inspector startled as if a closely guarded secret had slipped.

"I can't believe it," she giggled, amused, but stopped.

Marai knew she had felt the emanations of sadness from the look in his eyes.

"Love?" she asked.

The Inspector didn't answer her.

"Nah, don't tell me that!" she teased. "Bewitched loins, maybe," she turned to face him gently, as if she felt suddenly sorry for him. "Awww. You sure?" she asked, but apparently didn't need his answer. She touched his sad face and felt the memory of every moment of their togetherness just as Marai himself had seen. "Yeh, I guess you *must* be one of us too. You don't have a Child Stone yet, but in time you may as well. Maybe one day when this is all sorted out, like she said, you'll come to us." She embraced him then, kissing his eyes and lips just the way Naibe had kissed him; the way Marai had kissed her some weeks before. "All this because Marai's gone. I *still* can't believe it, I just still *can't*," she sighed.

Wserkaf returned her firm embrace impulsively, as if he tried to hold on to the memory of Naibe through her.

"Oh, now don't get me started with you. I'm too *old*," she mocked, knowing fully that age no longer meant a thing to her. When his silence became too painful, she broke it again. "You *know* Princess Dainty Mittens and her little priestesses just *had* to tease the damn secrets out of me. They want a child just that bad."

Marai knew Ari was stalling and knew Naibe would be even more miserable in this house than she had been in the Inspector's home. His heart fell through the memories, relieved for Ari that she had gotten out of one situation without someone trying to behead her but sick at heart that Naibe now faced the same fate after losing the only friend she had on that side of the river.

Ari shook her head, muttering her discontent to the Inspector as they moved along. "Felt like a cow in a goddess-cursed breeding pen. At least *here* that's not going to be the main thing I do. Majesty's got plenty of girls, I hear. He just needs wise talk and tea from me. It'll be a relief for a change if he allows me any sort of liberty later. Maybe too much to hope for."

"I have to go to Khmenu," Wserkaf's voice told Marai he hadn't heard a thing Ari said but remained focused on his own plight. "Can you somehow see she'll be alright?" he asked.

"Mmmm. She got you bad," Ariennu clucked, half in pity, half in fun. "I guess your wife didn't like the competition much, did she? Now she sends her to another?"

Marai knew such an idea would have made the russet-haired woman beside herself with delight in the possibility of Naibe casting love spells and destroying the royal family from the inside.

Ari, he started to send a thought then stopped, reminding himself that what he was seeing had happened in the past and that he could only watch it unfold at this point. He saw her expression sober and knew she realized Wserkaf had done something far more manly and brave than most men would do by setting Naibe aside in order to return to his beloved.

"Two circuits of Iah away from Ineb Hedj with constant cleansing and fasting can heal many needs," the Inspector mused. "I just want to know you'll make certain she's safe somehow."

GOING FORTH BY DAY

A blink of light almost broke Marai's concentration. Rainbow shimmers became stars that sparkled around their edges. He felt faint from the after-effects of the long sleep and thought he would collapse as he sat with the inspector-priest. Then, he felt the warm summery rush of Ariennu's presence as if she still searched for him and had not given up.

Ari, he whispered. *Woman, I am with you. I'm not a ghost. Just say where you are, and I'll come to you.* There was no response. When he shrugged to clear his thoughts and returned his gaze to Wserkaf he realized very little time had passed.

I'm doing this. Time is *slowing so that I can learn everything.* He firmed his hand on Wserkaf's shoulder and realized he was looking in on Naibe again.

Naibe followed the maids in stunned silence. She had seen them gathering at the rear gate when she bid Wserkaf and Ari goodbye.

I'm not going to cry again. I cry too much. I must stop, or I will go madder than I already am. She stopped and gasped slightly when the procession of women arrived in a large room with six beds. The small and roundish young woman who had followed them suddenly pushed ahead and stood facing Naibe with her arms folded. When she did, the other women took Naibe's few possessions and placed them by one of the sleeping couches.

This is so much bigger than Wserkaf's house. She felt panic rising at the way she had suddenly been thrust among strange women and the way her things had been taken from her as if they were no longer hers. *Princess Khentie had only the one maid, Mya, who slept in her room. The other servants stayed in a row by the garden. Oh –*

Naibe raised her gaze to the young woman who now stood in front of her. *Who? A chief of maids?* she wondered.

Look up. See my face, new one.

Naibe felt the woman speak to her thoughts. Her eyes widened and the woman silently projected one more thought, testing her. *I hear you read thoughts. I was checking.*

Goddess! It's the new princess. The one who's supposed to be a prophetess. Naibe wavered, unable to smile.

The woman took a step forward then eyed her up and down inspecting her differently now that the probe of her thoughts was complete.

"Oh! Look at you!" her voice chimed as if she was a young girl who had just been given a wonderful present. "You *are* what they say. You look just like a little Kina-Ahna goddess doll." The woman walked around Naibe, eying her up and down. You're a dark ivory and ebony hair with such sad golden eyes. You will make a *fine-*looking child for us." Then, she paused and looked closer at Naibe's dance belt. "Ah, little serpents on your belt, too! It's as if you even live the stories of your land," the woman's linen-mitted fingers reached forward to bat and jingle one of the snakes on the belt Wserkaf had given her.

Marai, living the vision of those moments in the past through his link with the Inspector, ached inside. He knew Naibe had wanted to wear the belt as a magical totem, not to Wserkaf but to the goddess to help gather her flagging energy.

She'll protect you, Sher-Ellit, he hoped his thought would pierce time and travel backward to comfort her. Instead, the Princess frowned as if she had sensed something instead, then gave Naibe a sign for her to sway her hips and make the serpent-belt sing.

Marai settled back in the present moment with Wserkaf as the channel and watched. Through his stone and the veil, he shifted into Naibe's thoughts as if he had become Naibe herself.

"Yes... I... My Lady," Naibe twirled nervously, her hips twitching with a tight shimmy. *I don't know her name. I think I heard it, but I can't be sure.*

"Oh. I've been rude. We will grow closer and come to trust if the stars ordain it, but call me Your Highness for now," the woman giggled at the sound of Naibe's belt as it jingled. "And you have such a pretty speaking voice. I understand you dance exquisitely. Let me see some of it," she phrased a gentle command, but she could not hide her breathless anticipation.

"Uh…" Naibe cast her eyes down, shyly. "Wh – what part? I don't – There are no –" she tried to say she had never been taught dance. She just moved about on instinct and exuberance of spirit.

Marai knew the Princess was attempting to sound friendly just as she had when he saw her with Ariennu in a dream. This time, however, she was anxious, and it wasn't setting Naibe at ease. As Marai's identity merged with Naibe's thoughts through their stones, he spoke one last thing to her through time hoping the Children would adapt it and it might comfort her.

See her thoughts.

She has heard of your strength

Naibe sighed, knowing it was indeed the Children who spoke.

I am strong enough. Marai said it. Wse said it. If it's so, then why do I feel afraid for my life, but not truly care now if it ends at the same time? She stared at the Princess' mitten covered hands, but the young woman sensed Naibe's thought and adapted.

"Put out your hands then, I feel I must show you I intend no harm," she ordered in a gentle yet firm voice.

Naibe put out her upturned palms in an almost convulsive gesture. In return, the Princess removed one mitt, but did not touch her. She stared as the Princess continued to visually examine and sense any energy.

She's looking for marks or tattoos of my power, like Deka has on her breasts. She won't see any though. Naibe felt slight mirth until a chill in the air caught the Princess' attention.

"No marks. Nothing says you are schooled to worship, but I feel the heka flowing through you. Will you try to use it here to seduce my king and husband?" her eyes seemed so very earnest and absent of hostility. It was as if she thought any of Naibe's attempts might come across as feeble in *this* magically protected household.

"I –" Naibe started then went silent. *Wserkaf's Princess Khentie knows her and has told her I cast a spell. That's what this is about.* "I never sought to cause harm, Your Highness. I only wished to return the love I was given. It was nothing more." She bowed her head, then sagged to her knees. *This is going to be horrible*, Naibe gasped inwardly as an image formed in her thoughts. She turned away, shielding her eyes.

"No, don't do this to me," she begged as she saw the vision of herself bathed, perfumed, stretched out on a couch with her legs wide to receive the Prince's seed. She was only treated with a little more respect once her belly filled with his child. It was to be an emotionless arrangement where love or any connection other than being of compliant service was forbidden.

"You seem healthy, and younger than the one with red tinted hair. A child from your womb will have fairer skin than I would like, but good form and shape," she commented as she continued her circular walk around Naibe. The woman stopped and stepped back, suddenly. "Forgive me for continuing rudeness," the corner of the Princess' mouth twitched. "Your name is?"

"Naibe-Ellit," her voice came out in a whisper. She shook with doubt as she looked up at the Princess. The woman stopped, folded her arms beneath her breasts, and stared narrowly.

"Speaking with My Lady?" she translated roughly. "Who named you this?" she said indignantly. "This is a Goddess name, a name reserved for those of royal blood. Are you Kina-Ahna nobility then? Whose house?"

"I – I –" Naibe stammered. She tried to think of an answer but knew she hadn't *had* a name. "No house. No. I – Brown Eyes was my name before, or Little One. Your Highness…" Naibe didn't know how she would safely communicate that she had been all but an imbecile until she was given her gifts. She knew of words like 'stink kuna', 'pop-eyed she-devil', 'howling monkey-girl' and a host of others. *Used to think those were good names until the Children whispered the name Naibe-Ellit to me as I went to sleep in Marai's arms on the vessel in the sand. They taught me what it meant, too.* "I don't know, Highness," she mumbled, her heart in her throat. "Women in a temple far away nursed me. Hazor I think. I did not know my mother. She birthed me in the year after she did her ritual. They say my sire was a God, but I never knew him either."

"A God?" the Princess paused in her circuit of tiny steps around the kneeling woman. "So, you have a sacred bloodline, but were not trained? How did that ever happen?" the Princess continued her scrutiny.

Naibe didn't want to be there. She wanted to tell the woman that she simply called on the great Goddess once long ago and was gifted for it but then she realized just in time the folly of telling the woman of such a revelation. Added to that came the realization of her own life at this moment. *Marai is gone and now sweet Wserkaf can have no part of me either.* Once again, even though she fought it, tears and trembling sobs came from her. She sat on her heels with her face in her hands, unable to say anything more. The Princess stepped back in a combination of stunned and puzzled silence. The interview ended. Some of the serving girls helped Naibe up, cooing and attempting to hug her as they coaxed her to rest on her little bed.

For a long time that night, Naibe lay awake. Even though the night was hot and there was little breeze, she shivered when she tried to comfort herself.

I don't like it here, she realized even after she had been allowed to remain resting in the women's apartments. From time to time she knew someone looked in on her. *I'm a thing to them – new female to breed. I can't do this. I won't. I need to find MaMa and get away.*

The Princess returned later in the afternoon to help her get ready for a formal introduction to Prince Shepseskaf.

Great Lady Bunefer – I think I upset her so much she never gave her name to me, but I heard the other women and maids say it. Naibe reflected as the woman seated herself on a stool and motioned for an attending handmaiden to wave a short-handled nefet over them. Other attendants provided soft linen for Naibe to begin arranging into a shoulder drape in the fashion of the Princess' garment.

"I know you thought I was rude this morning," the Princess stated almost apologetically, even though her tone remained matter of fact. "You'll forgive me, but the other woman who was brought here betrayed my beloved with her heka. She insulted my gift of prophesy stating even that my beloved husband was not whole and could not bring a child to me when he had sired our daughter. I knew right away that her young look and form was *indeed* some kind of sorcery, thus I needed to discover its source. Then, when I heard of the intrigue at my dear sister's house, I needed to draw *you* out to see if there would be *more* trickery."

Naibe finger-combed her hair with perfumed oil gel and stared at her reflection in a shiny bronze mirror.

I hear her talking, but I don't want to listen. Princess Khentie told her I knew charms and heka and now this princess boasts of it and dares me to use it when anything I do is of the heart and not plotted out. Can she not see what I truly want, or does she just not care? And MaMa's gone to the King for what reason? Another trick, or just his amusement when I know he has a Great Wife still alive and a house of handmaidens for his pleasure? Naibe gasped. *Oh, sorry,* she thought she spoke aloud.

Great Lady Bunefer's mittened hands crossed each other in a brief dispelling gesture as if she was trying clear the air for Naibe before she asked:

"I *do* need either of your spells and it is why I forgave her trick as one of desperation."

Desperation? Naibe quietly thought, almost amused. *More likely locating the treasury through later couch talk.*

"If your heka could awaken my womb from its slumber, I would ask for you to use it on me," her voice quieted into a whisper but still sounded like a nasal sing-song meow.

Knew that from Wse and from MaMa. So many of these royal women do not come with many children or if they do the little ones do not come to birth or live to grow tall. It was suspected that for too many generations the attempt to purify the "god-blood" by counting as royal only kings' sons and daughters paired near birth. Prince Shepseskaf's daughter wasn't royal enough, thus paired with a candidate for high priest. Now that his birth had been legitimized by Menkaure, they needed new heirs.

Maybe why they let me live back in Hazor. They expected me to die, but when I did not fail, they looked to see if I would prophesy. When I didn't – and my thoughts were dim – Naibe shuddered, wondering if her own situation had been similar. *And then I was taken, traded, and lost.* She sighed, saddened again. *It always comes back to you, my sweet man who sang the goddess' praise. You found me, but for what now, I ask? And not so certain I might bear one either. They should see to Raawa, the woman under me in Little Kina-Ahna with four babes in five years. What could I say?*

Truth

Naibe heard another gentle and inner voice, then nodded.

"I – I ask you for nothing but safety and shelter, Your Highness," Naibe shifted on her bed, determined not to weep again over words that seemed like accusations. "I had thought I would be with my Ari again, yet she is gone too, as is anything which has *ever* brought me joy. I do *not steal men*," she sighed. Naibe wanted to get up, run out of the entire estate, and vanish into the unknown parts of royal Ineb Hedj.

I don't, though. I don't even take them for a few moments pleasure as Ari does. Men come to me. Even when I was ugly they did – she started thinking, but then realized that after she had been changed by the Children of Stone and either modeled on or assumed the goddess of love and fertility, being with a man had become a much more powerful and commanding thing. Men were inexplicably drawn to her as if they had indeed been captured by some spell she had woven about them. Once she took them in her arms, they were powerless to live without her.

Truth.

Naibe recognized the voice. It was the thought voice of the prophetess Bunefer. To Naibe, it seemed as if the woman had felt enough of her thoughts about stealing men that it humbled and even worried her about the coming liaison with her husband. She withdrew her steady gaze and stared at her mittens.

As the Princess stared, a thought as pure as the whiteness of a dry dawn suddenly came to Naibe. "You'll bear a child for your king yourself," she stated without even thinking about her words.

"And you just saw this?" the Princess' eyes widened and the corner of her mouth twitched in suspicion, as if she thought Naibe was playing a game to save herself from a desperate situation.

"Just now, Your Highness – the thought came to me. I – " Naibe answered quickly, but then paled as the shadow of the stormy dark lurked to one side of her thoughts and began to grow in size. A familiar, dreaded thing was hiding near her and watching. Something else was with it – a smaller, slim creature regarded her. The worst part of the new vision was that both the figure as large as the sky and the smaller one were advancing. The afternoon Wserkaf had come and had unleashed the terror on her soul, she had sensed the same two beings but thought the second one was Deka. "No," she whimpered. "Not this, not now," Naibe dropped the mirror in her lap and gripped her arms to ward off the sense of horror that suddenly enveloped her.

"What?" the young prophetess bent forward, concerned. "Do you see something else? Is it a *bad* thing about the child I'll have?" she started to remove her glove in order to send some protective energy but paused as Naibe shook her head.

"No Highness. No touch –" She warned that the Princess needed to protect *herself* instead. "A storm; I see a storm in my thoughts. I had thought it was about my Marai and his death, but it's back again, when I tried to see your future." Naibe looked up at Great Lady Bunefer and understood what had happened.

It's your storm. It's you, not me. The instant before she mentally fled from the image she saw; she recognized the young woman in front of her clad in shining golden clothing and wearing the vulture crown. She was performing some sort of ceremony and weeping bitterly. Nearby stood two young children about the same age, perhaps five years old – a boy and a girl holding hands. A brother and a sister. Also present was a girl about fourteen years old standing beside a grown man of middle years. At that moment, the storm image obscured everything in black and red rolling clouds of dust. "I saw two children near you – one boy, one girl." Naibe pretended the anxiety had passed, and hoped the news of two children born would be so thrilling that the young seer wouldn't notice her own terror. She knew the boy. He turned as if he knew someone was peering into his world. His eyes blazed gold fire and his dark, nimbus-shrouded head became part of the storm. He rose into the air with a murderous scream as he stared at her. The scream sounded like: "Mother! I live again!"

I must get away. None of this is over. Her breath came in gasps. *She will bear only one and I will birth the other to look like me for this prince. A divine pair born close in days.* The same storm that had worried her across the sands of the wilderness as she, Ari, and Deka had journeyed with Marai to Ineb Hedj haunted her once more. Now the image had strengthened with Marai gone. Only the reason for the winded dark and its focus had changed.

Just when Naibe thought her head would explode, she felt a sense of calm creep tentatively through her. Bunefer was smiling and touching Naibe's arm with her bare hand, as if she suddenly trusted her enough for skin contact.

"What just happened?" the Princess asked, a new sympathetic tone filled her voice.

"A spirit vision, your Highness," Naibe answered as she sighed and rubbed her eyes with one of her hands. "It's an old one, though I can't say why it has come back."

Bunefer took her hand away and shook it away from them both, whispering a light prayer. Naibe mouthed it with her to dispel the evil energy that may have invaded their presence. Then, the woman put her glove back on her hand.

"Perhaps I should let you rest some more," Bunefer rose and beckoned to her retinue of handmaidens who had given them room to speak privately. "Until the evening meal, then." She looked over her left shoulder as she departed, but Naibe didn't notice.

I can't really tell her what I saw. The child. A pretty and tawny skinned boy, not a brown one like the girl. He cried out "Mother". He does look like me, but if the child isn't going to be Marai's son, I don't want it. I don't care if having one for the future king, who might be chosen as king himself, means a safe life and glory to go with it. I have to make a run for it, tonight if I must.

Naibe lay on her bed again, desperate for inspiration on how she would get away, but nothing came as the day ticked on toward evening. As she waited for the evening meal and the introduction to the Prince, she quickly fell into an exhausted sleep.

Chapter 19: Lilitu

At the evening meal, Naibe was reintroduced to Prince Shepseskaf. She barely remembered his face from the evening when she and the other women had been separated. As she picked at her delicious food, hardly interested in eating it, she couldn't stop thinking of her predicament and the way everything had changed in just under a month.

I was happy – so happy, Marai… She spoke through her stone, hoping the message would reach him in the spirit world. *…and then you were taken from me by these men. Wanted to make you a child, but now this man orders I try to make one for him. Will I? Will I show that I am mad, so they cast me out and then what? Go on my own? I don't know.* She felt herself drifting, oblivious to the movement of others in the dining plaza until the women got up.

One pulled on her arm and whispered.

"Time to dance, now."

Naibe shook herself, stood, and danced with the other women, but her heart wasn't in her movement. She turned her glance away from the Prince: *I don't want to look at him or I'll feel his admiration and begin to make a connection because I am who I am. Why can't I fly away like Bone Woman or wall up my soul like MaMa. Dance, be over soon.*

When the entertainment for the evening finished, Naibe went with the other handmaidens to the women's bedchamber but lay awake long after the rest had settled and the lamp in the Princess' room had dimmed.

By the middle of the night, she felt she had tossed and turned enough. She sat up and looked around the silent room.

I hope the guards are asleep. I just need to see if there's a way out. I think if I can get past where the servant families sleep, I might get out. I remember plants in the back of the plaza where I could hide a few moments if someone hears me. Then, I might have a chance.

Naibe pulled her yellow shawl around her shoulders, lamenting that she'd lost her pretty white one at Wserkaf's house. She gathered gold and glass beads to trade if she needed food or a boat journey, but then paused, realizing she hadn't made complete plans. Thinking through things a little more, she asked herself: *If I leave, where will I go? Wse can't take me to his duty when he goes to the temple at Khmenu. Maybe it doesn't matter. I know I have the power of binding him or almost any man now. I'll just get to the royal docks, find his boat, hide in it, and then compel him to order his men to turn around and take him to Per-A-At. I know he doesn't want to serve under the Great One anymore. I know Wse's father is there. He could make amends to the man, swear his fealty to the cult of Ra, and we could start over.*

Then, she shook her head at her own folly. *I'm grown, but because I had not two wits to set next to each other for so long I think I act as a child! He loves his wife. What we had together shocked him. Even now I hear whispers of a spell I cast, but I don't* want *to steal him. I want him to choose me and I know there are too many reasons why he can't.*

First thing, she sighed. *Out of here at least. Just that far — Maybe I'll cross the river and get back to little Kina-Ahna. Maybe Etum-Addi hasn't gone yet.* She strained her thoughts, then sighed as the vision of the merchant's family hurrying and bidding farewell came to her. *Too late! Maybe find Raawa and her family to shelter me until I can think of a way to get MaMa and Deka back with us.*

Naibe crept down the brick steps to the plaza level and then looked out toward the reflection pool. This one reminded her of Wse's pool and the one where she wanted to drown herself at Great One's estate.

The sesen flowers were closed and resting just below the surface of the water, waiting for a new day. *Wish I could hide beneath the surface like you do,* she approached the water and pushed her toe into it, just to see if someone might be watching her. It was still quite warm from the heat of the day. Its seductive warmth beckoned.

Stay.

A whisper of child voices wove among the reeds and potted shrubs.

No. I mustn't, she shook away the thought that she had allowed herself to be so distracted by these lovely surroundings. *No guards. They walk the perimeter in these big places, I'm told, and that means they'll be back soon. If they find me, they'll send me back to the women's area and make someone watch me until I sleep. If I'm going, I'd better do it.* She stood at the edge of the pool, but thought of one more thing keeping her here: she promised to help Princess Bunefer.

If I go now I insult her kindness, but maybe save myself from being unable to give her the magic she needs. Naibe kept watch for movement of any guards as she considered the last thing that oddly still held her here.

Use your magic to waken my womb, she says. I don't know what she thinks I could do. She's a Hethara prophet, and a high ranking one too. She stole past a large potted tree, scanning for a yet unseen exit. *Don't they have dances for that? For fertility? I hear they can even cause a child to begin its growth without the seed of a man by dancing and jumping an open flame. Something else must be binding her up.*

Marai opened his eyes slightly. He kept his hand on the Inspector, to preserve the channel and link he, his stone, and the veil in his hand had created. Looking up, he noticed something outside the window.

The moon. It hasn't moved much. Sick as I am, I still have some power in my poor thoughts. Wse seems no worse either. He's a trance master, but letting this much flow through him should have caused him to at least shift or struggle. Then, he thought about Naibe and the fact that he was totally unable to alter her past. He could see it, and perhaps whisper a layer of soothing thoughts over that which had already happened, but it was all he could do.

Thank you little one within me for at least letting me see her. Marai sent a comforting thought back through his own silvery stone. *I only wish I could comfort my beloved in some way. If I could speak back through time somehow; if she could speak to me,* he thought.

As he sank back into the level of visualization again, he saw that a lovely full moon had risen high into the sky early on that evening months ago. Its light bathed the plaza in silver shimmers. He watched as Naibe stepped back from the pool and leaned against the wall by the stairs that led to the sleeping areas for the royal family.

At that point, Marai drifted into the vision of the past once more.

GOING FORTH BY DAY

See how sad I am, Naibe felt the warm night air surrounding her. As it did, she tried to remember Marai's tender arms holding her. *He was such a big man, you'd think he would hold too hard or be clumsy or smelly, but oh! Those fierce muscles of his would get so soft and gentle, as if he thought a hard hug might break me. I felt so secure. Oh, Goddess in me. What am I to do?* she begged her own soul for peace. *Maybe I'll just dance my way out of these gates; fly up over the wall and into the gates of the Underworld.* She unfastened her shift and let it fall, whimsically re-donning her cloak for reasons she didn't understand, since she had planned to escape but now was changing her thoughts on the matter. She stepped to one side, with a silent sway. She hadn't worn her bangles or her belt because she hadn't wanted to make noise in her escape, but now she wished she had them with her. *If I go back and get the belt – no, it calls me to stay. No. I can't.*

Beloved One, the whispers rose through her heart.

Is that your voice Wse? Is it a memory of my Marai? She pleaded, but when the answer came, it puzzled her.

> *Don't be afraid, my sweet one*
> *Of what you become*
> *Never be afraid of what you already are.*
> *Take great joy in all you do.*

She decided it was the voices of the Children of Stone that had stirred within her heart. They tried to console her again.

'I just want to leave, but my heart and these voices say not to. She realized one more thing: *Marai must have wanted to leave this place too, but they told him to stay. Why?* she sighed, turning her face up to feel the full light of the moon. Imagining the moon was Iah, the Kemet moon in his gentle form, she reveled in its reflected warm evening light. The silver-gold light transformed into a vision that reminded her of the way Marai's hair used to shimmer in the increasing dark when they were together. The ache in her heart had returned. Her walk outside tonight hadn't helped her feel better; it had only taught

her she was not to escape.

I just don't want this kind of life anymore – not with the Prince or anyone else. Not like this, her shoulders slumped. The Child Stone in her brow remained silent. She knew the Children, who gloried in the human and even animal sense of love and lust-sharing, could not understand why she'd be reluctant to use her gift of a loving nature.

Naibe knew Wserkaf would never hear her plea tonight. The only response had been the little verse that sounded like Marai. She looked up at the moon again.

Talk to the children his way. She smiled as she remembered her first words to Wserkaf the evening he took her into his arms: *the Children are all we have without Marai, but now I don't even know what's become of the rest of them.* Only the silence comforted her as she talked to the sky.

Sweet one, Naibe, hear me.

A different voice answered.

Marai! Naibe sighed as a zephyr of happiness rippled through her soul.

She knew the words were his and that somehow they were tearing into the world of the living from the land of the dead to reach her.

Is it you, my love? she asked the air between herself and the moonlight. *Oh, please be you!* The voice didn't heed her; it sounded undirected like an announcement in a great hall.

Be as you were to me. The answer drifted, now broken and hard to hear as if it came over a great distance. *Don't be afraid. I will find a way for us to be together in both worlds,* the voice faded.

The thought of Marai watching over her, even in spirit, saddened her, but when she shook off her doubts and thought of leaving, the small voice inside her repeated quite plainly:

Stay

GOING FORTH BY DAY

Why? she asked back in silence.

Steps. We guide you in one or two choices

The answer came.

Naibe blinked, confused that the message asked her to do something that made no sense at all to her – to stay.

In secure hope you stay,
You rise in greatness and in love
Run now and gain naught
Stay and bring all together.

Oh. It's about getting MaMa and Deka back together and breaking away from here together. She blinked, disgusted that her plans were ultimately rejected by her own inner thoughts. *Maybe one more night to think about this. His Highness didn't ask for me tonight. Maybe he doesn't favor me. Still, the moonlight's so lovely out here.* She innocently stretched out her arms to encompass the light of the moon the way she embraced the sun on those lovely mornings in Wserkaf's home.

Ah see me. How good you feel tonight my sweetest Lady. I embrace the light of you picking me out, her thoughts whispered and she unpinned her cloak so it fell off back as the fire of dance and joy rose through her breasts. The world could have fallen away as she breathed in and out, feeling rapture and ecstasy descending and ascending through her body so strongly that everything faded away and she floated up from the plaza, turning slowly.

Flying! Not so high, just off the ground. Can I go over the wall?

It made even less sense to her that everything in her thoughts told her to dance sweetly to an audience of no one. Tonight, the fire was a gentle, abiding one that moved through every part of her body. The starlight became ropes of pearls that she imagined herself wearing. They flowed down from her hair, over her shoulders, and draped the length of her body. More stars channeled down around and through her, then rose, entering her and evoking. She twirled and then laughed. In the rapture she felt, Naibe understood who and what she was.

Marai called me his "goddess", but men sometimes cry that word when they are enraptured by lust. Am I to prove it? I could not save even a scrap of Marai other than his sweet memory. That's the only spell I'm called to cast. Yet, everything I am asks me to do more and do it tonight.

"Pretty lady —"

Her ecstasy was interrupted by a whisper just behind her and to her right. Startled, she looked in the direction of the man's voice because it seemed to be the answer to the question of why she was out in this plaza dancing naked in the moonlight. She lowered her head, suddenly shy, because she knew who it was.

The Prince. Him? Tonight, after all? Naibe-Ellit asked herself, then turned away as if she hadn't noticed him and danced a little longer to see what would happen.

Her hands drew down so much of the moonlight that it burst up her arms, circled her head and brow, bounced on her breasts, and erupted from her mount as she continued her ecstatic dance.

Prince Shepseskaf stood frozen near the bottom of the steps that came down from his stateroom. He thought he had heard something in the middle of his restless night and when the guards didn't respond, he got up, grabbed his blade, and crept down his steps to see who was wandering in his plaza.

Lady Naibe. Dancing. He paused; his breath momentarily taken because she moved gracefully, oblivious to him watching her. He recalled Bunefer telling him earlier that evening: 'The stars are in the correct position for a momentous conception!' she had started. 'The merits of this grouping will last for only a few days. We should try again. I have seen a vision of the ancestors smiling on us this time, and this new concubine is gifted too. She has seen there will be two children in our home soon! If you cannot make one with me, you must go to her quickly, before the spirits tire of waiting.'

That had stung, but she spoke the truth. He didn't want to admit it, but her obsession had become his own lack of desire. He loved her more than his own life, but couldn't call her to his arms at night. Now, as he watched this young woman dance, he felt puzzled that he had become so aroused. His heart melted for her in a feeling much more like love than lust. The Prince took a step forward as Naibe turned and drifted blissfully back to the ground to stand beside him. Their fingers touched tip to tip and when they did and he felt a slight spark of energy.

Beautiful! his thoughts whispered. She looked up and reacted as if she heard those thoughts. She swayed gently in front of him with fathomless eyes that gave no indication she truly saw him. They were no longer light brown; they had become wells of flashing golden fire. Together with her eyes, the spark from her fingertips drew him like oddly pleasant static as she pulled him gently out into the light. Her fingers locked over the top of his fingertips and she began to dance with him as if they had practiced all the steps.

Fire, he thought briefly before he let it consume him, j*ust like my lady said.* He swayed with Naibe, moving among the urns of potted trees and flowering shrubs.

No guards! No one hears us. It has got to be an enchantment… he smiled, happy to drift away.

Much later, he remembered very little. The world he knew fell away from his feet and he let her sweet sorcery sweep him into her fantasy. Her sighs seemed like his heart singing to her. Their lips touched, mouths open and wanting, but all he recalled was seeing shining and stars issuing from her brow and the curious little place that glimmered like lapis with perfect golden veining in it. That part burned with its own fire and the more he thought of it, he remembered hearing children laughing, sighing, and singing.

Then, in a flash of light as if lightning had struck near them both, he saw her lying and moving passionately beneath him on his sumptuously cushioned couch.

Lady, his thoughts cried. *How?* he asked, because he had no memory of the moments between her first touch and kiss and this one. Like a dream-vision, the image shimmered and faded. He felt he was with a woman, enjoying and craving her touch, but he couldn't see her face. *Beloved one, my goddess!* he whispered into her hair. As his eyes cleared, he saw his wife where he had assumed the new concubine lay. Lady Naibe wasn't there at all. *Did I dream?* he later asked himself, but then remembered there had been *true* lightning outside. *No. I saw this tonight. She saw it too. We were standing on my porch. I was comforting her before I carried her to my couch, because she hesitated as if she was a virgin.* When the lightning streaked across the heavens, it touched the tips of the three pyr-akhs and arched down them. The temple statue of his great-grandmother, Hetepheres as the lion-woman, leapt to life and roared triumphantly.

Shepseskaf had bowed his head to Naibe's breasts, spent and exhausted. The errant question: *How?* remained unanswered. *Why can't I remember?* he kissed her closed eyes. *I was only watching her dance. Why does it feel like a dream?* The shimmering intensified. Confused, he pressed her to him and was about to say her name when he realized he was with his wife, and still deep in the throes of passion. Her ecstatic calling swept through him like a wildfire. In another flash of light, he saw Naibe holding his head to her breasts, one of her legs clasped over his back. Then it was Bunefer again, with her legs wrapped around him.

Shepseskaf's reality spiraled away between the visions of the two women. Darkness and numb oblivion took him.

Chapter 20: Another Departure

Naibe woke from a particularly vivid dream, wondering why she felt more upset and tired than she had when she went to bed. At first, she thought the Prince hadn't called for her and that she merely dreamt she had been with him. Then, memories of pleasure, of their bodies tangled and enthusiastic, crept back.

No, it *did* happen. *Too real to be a dream*, she thought. *I need to freshen, too,* she struggled to sit, then twitched in discomfort. *And here's more proof: my shift is gone. I took it off to dance before the moon. If it's still at the sesen pool, then it's certain.*

Wait. I was running away. I was dressed and looking for a way out of the gates and the little voices told me to stay. I didn't want to, and then the Prince saw me. She frowned, understanding that somehow she had been with the Prince and they had enjoyed each other. She couldn't remember anything about it except some enveloping shadow which wrapped itself around her and then departed. As she had been instructed, she had risen after the Prince slept and made her way to the women's quarters, but now realized the entire evening had become a fading and almost entirely blank space.

She rose as soon as the rest of the women did, but said nothing. Those were the rules: no gossip. After the women ate and went about their various duties, Naibe took up her needlework and went to sit with the other maids who were stringing beads for collars. Shyly, she joined the conversation about which beads and glasses were good and how to put them on a circular loom so that when they were added they would not bite or pinch the skin. The Princess had hurriedly dressed and journeyed to her sacred temple duties and the Prince was already gone for the morning, so there was no way for Naibe to read his expression to see if his memory was better than hers. Later, the Princess returned, but stared at her without saying anything before going to her own room.

Naibe thought the woman would say something or project a thought, but all she received was a mystified stare. That alone toyed with her until she made excuses to be near the Princess and some temple companions to see if she could overhear them without being noticed. Naibe knew the Princess had experienced something she hadn't expected.

Odd woman, the Shinar, she thought she heard. *Not sure I favor her.* Then there were more whispers, some sounding sympathetic and consoling, after which Naibe heard: *Did her duty, I think, but Shepsisi was with me and claimed she was not with him. Some strange heka that will need to be watched.*

Naibe-Ellit listened to their voices fade into the distance. *So, he doesn't remember me? Did I do that? Heka? She said heka? Me? I guess I did, then. Only because she wants a child enough to have a second woman brought in and not wife her as most of these men would. I guess he can't since I own no royal blood, whether it's true a god sired me or not. I don't know if my mother was royal or just a priestess. I don't even know how it works in Shinar lands.*

I was with him. I was just talking to him the way I talked to Marai at the well, hearing his sad story – the way I listened to Wserkaf telling me his story of service to that wicked man and how it tore his family apart. I know his ways, but somehow I know the Princess was there with him and yet not all three of us at once, as some men like. She lowered her head again, averting her eyes from the humbling truth. *He didn't really want a consort. He and Wse both love their wives and don't need handmaidens except now to have a child. I don't want that, though. I had to do something.*

Naibe felt a twitch in her brow as if the blue stone there was sorting her feelings and blending new as well as old information. She *had* been with the Prince. It hadn't been any other man. But what did the Prince remember? Did he remember being with her, or that a goddess very much like Hethara and Divine Raet had kissed and danced with him in the moonlight and that his own sweet princess-wife, a prophetess, had called her down inside of her to make the spark of a child in her womb.

What will he remember of me? she mistily smiled. *Maybe only that I was there?* Naibe lay back on her bed in the now empty women's quarters and replayed the fading memories to herself as she slowly tried to recover from the night.

Marai remained seated across from the inspector-priest, stunned at the clarity of the memory of these events. He knew Wserkaf could not have heard more than vague rumors of the images now projected through Naibe's veil.

But I'm seeing, somehow, things that happened to Naibe after she lost the veil – things that befell Ari, who never touched the veil. Perhaps they truly need to tell the story.

He felt so profoundly disturbed that he wanted to break the link of veil and touch. Wserkaf sat in a deep meditative trance with his face turned up. His eyelids twitched slightly, as one dreaming. Frustrated, Marai sighed out once again and re-joined the "dream" as it continued to spill its hidden truths.

The next thing he sensed was night of the same day. The household had settled. Naibe turned over on her bed and then sat when she heard a rustle of less-than-dainty steps outside the women's room door.

His Highness. Naibe's shoulders slumped, because she wondered what he would say about the previous night. During the day, he'd looked confused whenever his glance had drifted in her direction. In response, she had feigned expectant delight, but the expressions and feelings exchanged masked their true thoughts and she knew it.

"Lady. Come to me," he whispered.

At first Naibe worried he was masking some sort of anger, but when she exited the room, he caught her arm with a gentle touch. She looked into his eyes, smiled tentatively, and then demurely looked down.

"Are you well?" he asked.

"Oh – Well – Oh, Your Highness! Her thoughts about motive made her stammer when she first spoke. Her heart skipped, but the moment she looked up into his eyes she felt more confident. "Nothing that passed between us was against my will. You are too kind, and ever gentle," she teased with a layer of childlike innocence.

"Then it's true? It *was* you in my bed, and not my beloved?" He frowned, less comfortable with the agreed-upon sex now that sorcery, heka, and dream visions were involved. He drew back, one hand forming a symbol Naibe recognized as one for self-protection. As if to break that spell, she touched his arm and sent a silent thought:

GOING FORTH BY DAY

No need. I would never harm you, my Prince.

"But, you saw that you were with your wife and not me?" Naibe asked as she felt a surge of energy rise in her chest; a desire to charm the man before her. "You *were* with your wife. You wanted to be. So, I wished you would see her. That's what happened."

Shepseskaf pulled away, annoyed. "But even now you lie, pretty one. Do you not worry over the crime of untruths to one such as myself or my beloved?"

"Lie? No, Highness! I spoke truth!"

"There is more you didn't say. My beloved whispered to me of something blessed that was no dream." He paused in thought, then snapped at her: "More lies?" He raised his hand, about to slap her, but when she simply smiled he couldn't. "If I was with you, did you send some demon to visit my wife?"

Naibe gasped. The thought of demonic intervention had never occurred to her.

"I sent nothing to her! Believe that, Highness. I know what you wanted so dearly — that it has worried you that you have no desire to simply *take* flesh offerings as other royal men do. You have wondered if that is why you have not yet had a son, since your father and other kin have wifed more than one and bedded so many more." She realized her hand was still grasping his arm, but she couldn't move it.

"You — and I," he mused, glancing at her hand. "And now you tremble?"

Naibe knew her apparent vulnerability was arousing the Prince.

"Because of the power over my life you have; when I had only wished to do the duty, your mercy granted. I don't want to disappoint you." She sighed and followed him as he beckoned her through his pale linen draped doorway. *Little ones,* she thought internally. *Don't do this for me this time. Let me see what happens so I can know my own strength. This time, I'll pay attention — see how this happens.*

She and the Prince kissed, and he walked her backward toward his couch. As she shed her drape and crawled up beside him, caressing his chest and shoulders, she silently thought: *If you wish, see her, not me. Let us become as one: her heart and spirit, my fertile womb, even though I regret what I do.* She sighed out and felt as if her spirit had blinked.

When she opened her eyes she sat, not in the Prince's bed or in her own bed, but in Bunefer's bed. Sleeping handmaidens had not stirred.

What? How? she giggled. *I did it, I think.* But then, another odd feeling of helplessness came over her. It wanted to send her back to the Prince as if her flight had been a misbehavior. *No. Let me do it!* she struggled to keep the illusion, but it exhausted her.

Naibe-Ellit. Lady of the Sea and Star
Know you do what you must,

The children are warning me, but why? She wondered, but the Prince's passionate words distracted her.

"Your eyes. They *are* the gold of stars. It *is* you gentle Lady Naibe," he whispered tenderly and she knew she was still with Shepseskaf. Nothing had changed.

"Ohh…" she sighed but it came out as a groan of pleasure and then everything in her thoughts became blurred and dreamlike as her passion increased. She saw herself with the Prince and the lovemaking, but then she felt an odd separation as if she had left her body on a spirit journey. She hovered near the ceiling of the lamplit room, observing the scene of the Prince making love to his wife.

But he just said – he knew it was me. I knew it was an instant ago I feel him touching me, entering me – his thrusts and how pleasant they are. She remained aloft, then considered: *Where is Lady Bunefer?* Her spirit body shot through the palace to the women's quarters, wondering if the Princess was there, but found herself lying fitfully on the Princess' bed. She quickly sank into her form as the dream deepened and her sense of story vanished into deeper sleep.

Two more nights passed in such a fashion. Each late night began with Naibe going to the Prince and making the wish sent aloft:

Come to us. Be me and I will be you. Each night she remembered the Prince and his ways in his bed and seeing Bunefer. Each morning her confusion deepened added to one more fact – the Princess' attitude was misty and girlish. Her interactions with

Shepseskaf were more intimate as they passed each other. They often paused with knowing glances before they went their separate ways.

Toward her, the Prince seemed relaxed and familiar, but reserved and somewhat awe-struck.

By the eighth evening, Naibe had almost settled into the routine of washing and anointing herself with the same scent the Princess wore, because it helped set the transition. As they began lovemaking she whispered into his ear:

"Know you are so loved – that love bears fruit." Then, the gasping and giddiness of all arousal's peaks and valleys took her, but she faded into a different feeling as the fog of passion overwhelmed her. She saw herself, not the Princess with Shepseskaf. Almost distracted, her thoughts rioted. *We haven't switched.* Her spirit form barreled through to the Princess' room and found her asleep, but mumbling.

"I can't. I'm so very tired, Shepsisi, not tonight."

No, you must, Highness! She urged and then Bunefer sat up, blinked, and gasped.

"You?" she squinted, poked at Naibe's essence, and gasped when her hand went through.

Quickly. Take my place. Hurry and – she summoned what had become Ariennu's classic trick of forgetfulness. Naibe reached forward and touched the Princess at her heart, drawing out her spirit and rushing locked arm in ghostly arm with her. They entered the room like a gust of midnight cooling air, but Naibe paused, because Bunefer was already there enjoying her husband and her spirit joyously rejoined.

But – who's in the Princess bed? What? And in the next instant, she found herself in the bed, shivering and frustrated as her own spirit reentered her body. The voices lulled, their whispers sounding like chanting as she calmed herself and drifted.

As it should be.
Joy to you in the passage of days
And for the one you serve
As the sun rises.
Know all things change
A different petal in the flower
A new life.

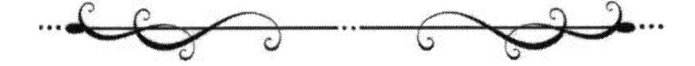

Chapter 21: Intermission

Before he saw the man move, Marai sensed the disturbance. Opening his eyes slightly, he saw Wserkaf purse his lips and twist his face into a grim expression. He broke contact with Marai's hand, indicating with the gesture that he needed to catch his breath.

"Are you well?" Marai asked, amazed that his own weakness had made him truly ache after he had shared memories through physical touch and Naibe's veil. *Wonder if the old bastard damaged my stone permanently. I thought I was going to be harder to kill than this, and he almost had me. I should be shaking this off.*

"Let me get Anre to fetch beer for us. I'm a little achy, but I'll be well if I stand up and stretch. I also need to see what hour it is," Wserkaf eased into standing. "I said earlier, Great One let me come back under the ruse of getting my own purification tools. If I am back by sunrise he won't suspect, given all that's taking place now. Still, you must be hidden by then. If he knows you are alive, it'll be bad."

Marai watched as the Inspector moved through a very brief stretching and breathing routine, then trotted outside to look at the sky. He returned quickly and sat again.

"Still early. Like you *did* get time to slow down," Wserkaf frowned. "Not even Hordjedtef can do *that.*"

Marai stared back, then sighed and relaxed. *And if I could stop time until the tales are told, I would. I know there's more and not a bit of it is good news.* He took a deep breath, mostly to calm himself, because he had a great urge to strike out in any direction, weak as he was. All he had seen was that Naibe was being treated little better than a cow in a pen and that even with her sorcery there were too many ways for everything to go terribly wrong. Ari had escaped that work, but had been sent to the King who had now died. Deka? Of the Ta-Seti woman, he sensed even less. It would be up to him to slow down and then attempt to pull all the ends together. "Do you know what thoughts came through your heart?"

"Some of them," Wserkaf continued extending his arms over his head and stretching with a yawn. "It was about what became of pretty Naibe after I went on my duty." He nodded thanks when the manservant brought cups of beer.

Both men sipped and reflected on everything they had seen. Marai shook his head. Part of him wanted to get up and go to Prince Hordjedtef with murder in his heart, because the man had spellbound the women somehow but again, he knew he needed to stay and listen.

"What parts *do* you know as fact from strong rumor from those you trust?"

"I can tell you that within days, despite the idea that Naibe had 'settled-in' with her role as a fertile second, Bunefer began to feel ill and presumed she had become with child, far earlier than even gifted women ought to know. Without me there to intervene, since she was no longer needed, Naibe was then sent to the King to join Lady ArreNu."

"Was she with child?" Marai asked.

"My lady wife mentioned only once that sometimes things are less certain than others, but Bunefer insists there is a child. I didn't press her about it. In time, we will see what we will see," the Inspector paused. "Another thing, though, which leads me to think the gods have in some minor ways assisted us."

Wserkaf's eyes brightened his thoughts came together.

"What?" the sojourner asked.

"Great One is pointing at the ladies as being workers of vengeance for you. He didn't like that Lady Ariennu and Naibe were both attending His Majesty, though Our Father was taken with them. He states to all who care to listen, and to most who don't, that he tried to protect the King by sending them away, but may have been too late. He's more than implied it could be *their fault* he died so unexpectedly."

Marai gasped at the revelation. "No… what? He actually *said* that?" The big man pushed up from the couch with singular thought: to go all the way to the royal palace to pull the old man's head from its stump with his bare hands and murder anyone who got in his way, until the gentle voices of the Child Stone in his brow admonished him.

In truth revealed

Decide the wiser course.

Wserkaf gasped with a start, his eyes growing wide. "Your little voices. I think I heard…"

Marai raised one eyebrow. *Maybe he can hear them. He'd be more open to the stories coming through tonight. But can I trust that? Could Great One know and be able to read him at a distance?*

"So. You heard?" The stone in Marai's brow lulled and then paused with a gentle tweak.

Listen to the Truth

In the passage of moments

all things are possible

to a peaceful heart,

even if it wants to break

"Mmm. Beautiful," Wserkaf settled in his chair again.

Marai groaned, tapping his forehead, "*this* I know. Their talk is always beautiful and peaceful, imploring me to go against my rage when all I want to do is just murder that old man in front of his fellow priests. The first and only time they allowed me that rage, thirty men died."

"You might," Wserkaf observed, unruffled. "My senior told me that story, but you have since learned that while you have strength enough, you'd only get yourself killed in an unspeakable manner. Even if you wore his body down, you'd find yourself battling dozens of his allied priests with combined hundreds of years of experience and in your half-killed condition I daresay it wouldn't go well for you, regardless of how glorious the death would seem at the start. Perhaps there is more to witness."

"Well, one day, even with all this peaceful talk, the children will find I won't listen to them so readily," Marai grumbled. "Tonight, because the poison still makes me ache, I will." He put his cup down when the Inspector had centered himself, then he drifted to the quiet place in his thoughts. "I know she's not connected through this veil the way Naibe was, but I need to know about Ari. Can you show me her story?" Marai clutched the veil again, concentrated, and created her symbol – an arc of rainbow light – beneath the palm of his hand as he placed it on the Inspector's shoulder.

Instantly, as if the Children of Stone had been waiting for the link to re-establish, a jolt of energy that left both men giddy and nearly senseless with bliss, began to form.

Chapter 22: Ariennu and the King

In his forming vision, Marai saw Ariennu standing in a large open-air room. When he looked down, he saw that the floor was composed of fine inlaid tiles. Following her view up and seeing things as she had, he noticed a ceiling painted with golden stars. A slight breeze issued from the window facing her through to the doorway behind her, rustling the sheer linen drapes that covered it. Glass-bead ropes draped over the linen tinkled gently. She worked what he assumed was a wonderful scented oil into the shoulders of a man who sat in a fine ebony and gold chair in front of her. Her low hum mimicked the melody a distant harpist played. In the center of the room, a large raised brazier smoldered with lumps of incense. At first Marai could think of nothing other than how much he wanted to be the man in the chair.

Goddess, she is so beautiful! Marai studied the way the image of her dark hair glimmered red in the lamplight. Knowing she might sense his intrusion through her stone, he took extra care as he merged his thoughts with hers, walling off his own feelings. He experienced all her actions back through time as if they were happening once again in his present moment.

This is so simple! he thought. *I can speak through the Children this way and old Hordjedtef can't block the thoughts or keep me from it. But, to see any of them make mistakes and doom themselves — knowing I can't change a thing without dooming the moments I have now — that's agony. If it's too much, I'll have to break the link. This is just Ari giving comfort to a very alive king; not one who had died suddenly in the night. Is this why she and Naibe are now accused of murder? I never got to see the King; Hordjedtef wouldn't let me do that.*

In the sojourner's vision, King Menkaure appeared as a big, dark-copper-skinned man with black-eyes and close trimmed, graying hair. The monarch of the Two Lands was heavier than his youthful statuary depicted him, but he still seemed physically fit. Ariennu now gently urged him to his wide bed and sat with him as if there was nothing unusual about her being in his bedchamber.

Marai sensed she was at ease, the way he would imagine a seasoned wife might behave.

Hmm. She's been with him, if I'm guessing right, not too much more than a half moon. That's her skill. No guards nearby? He trusts her touch? Marai mused, quietly recalling her tale that when she had been a very young thief in the cities near Tyre, her skill had been one of picking out wealthy men to seduce quickly so that her companions could plunder any estate she entered. *Always had them – even before the Children made the changes. Now she's just so much better at it.*

Even though the sojourner had heard *this* king was much more approachable than his predecessors, most people had never seen him, or any other high ranking noble, bare-headed as a peasant. That this king allowed Ariennu to not only touch him, but to see his real hair, meant they had been more than intimate.

She has him in her spell, then. That's my Ari... good girl! Marai sighed, missing Ari as much at that moment as he had longed for Naibe earlier. *Want to be with both of you, so much it hurts.* He bowed his head, aching in spirit that seeing through time was all he could do. *Three months... but something awful happened after this night – some trap set by the Great One. That much I feel.* Marai thought as he settled into receiving the sequence of events through his Child Stone.

From there, the vision unfolded before him as Ariennu saw and felt it.

Ariennu quickly settled into the routine at the new palace, joining a dozen other women who were either handmaidens or who had advanced to the role of full concubine. The King had no minor wives at this time, but Ari knew already from the gossip that His Majesty might be reviewing the chosen women and once the sixth year since the wicked prophecy had passed might choose one.

It will be me, of course. If my poor Marai is no longer of the living, may his soul see that I am doing well.

As it had been in Shepseskaf's home, a large open plaza and a narrow tube-like alcove from the nearby common area separated the women's living quarters from the King's guarded sleeping and lounging area. The Great Wife, whom the King affectionately knew as "Sister Khammie", lived on her own estate with her mother and grandmother. She seldom visited, even though there was no animosity between them. Despite that, an elegantly furnished stateroom stayed prepared for her in case she should come to spend a late evening visiting her king.

Doesn't hurt for women, though. Not like Shepseskaf, who'd rather have only his wife. He's different though. He has his pick of these pretty young things, and isn't really interested in any beyond the sex or how charming they look at the functions his wife misses.

Ari knew the tale of her being infertile preceded her, so she stated she was merely an entertainer and a healer. Her honesty without eagerness had stirred his interest.

When each of the women had arrived at the palace, Ari learned the King spent time with them for a day or two. He was gentle with them, but reserved. Once he was satisfied with each new addition, he would dispatch them to the women's rooms. When he wanted company, he would pick one or two of them. He was such a fair man that he tried *not* to show favorites, because he knew doing so could cause fighting or discord in the women's area. As in the other palace, gossip was forbidden. That rule was constantly broken, even if in whispers.

Still, Ari wasn't surprised to hear instant whispers about herself.

This foreign woman, they whispered, *Majesty wishes to see her again.*

This is four evenings now.

I hear she cast a spell on His Highness Prince Shepseskaf and his wife.

Look how tall like a man she is, and what bony pale-skinned shoulders she has!

Such a wretched, unhealthy color and hair the color of dry blood too!

You can tell she is older; some sorcery makes her look young.

She must be from a sojourner's camp. She's not one of us.

The Great Uncle has said we should watch…

Ari heard the catcalls and saw the girls hush each other as she walked by. She wanted to answer back, even get in a fight or two, but knew this wasn't part of the wise and calm image she was presenting. *And the Great Uncle fed them with lies?* she thought.

I should go ahead and cast a spell on the bastard. He's got some skills though. For now, she would bide her time.

She returned her thoughts to the King, continuing to massage the King's shoulders and back, gently turning him and lovingly rubbing his chest the way she used to soothe her Marai's stiff shoulders and neck after a hot and dusty day of work in the market.

Ari quietly and obediently listened to the King as she provided him comfort, then she boldly gave a little sign – an open palm in front of her mouth – indicating that she wanted to speak. The King nodded to allow this.

"There, your Majesty should sleep well now. I have managed the worst of the knots."

"Oh, not too long. Just a little while. You will lie down beside your King and hold him. Then, go. My man will see that I rise before day…"

Ari gasped inwardly. *He's exhausted though. He almost fell into a deep sleep while I worked on him. He needs to sleep all night and maybe the rest of tomorrow.* Obediently, she shut her eyes and settled on the couch with her back to him. He gripped her with his heavy but tightly-muscled arms. Although it was only the fourth night the King had asked for her to come to his bedchamber, he relaxed enough to speak candidly.

"It's nothing a sojourner as you would understand. I rise in the middle of the night to do a devotion to the sun, to Horus before his birth. Perhaps I might rest again before my other work begins, dear lady. I've been so weary," he sighed into her hair. "It's as if this feeling descends from another realm. I've consulted oracles and some of my best interpreters as to the cause, but they have given me nothing to understand," he sighed.

Ariennu smiled inwardly, knowing her skilled hands had opened his thoughts and gained his trust. She knew, by all accounts, that the King was *considered* elderly. He was in his early fifties, but he appeared healthy and in excellent physical condition. His only lament was that despite his mighty physical training and prowess in battle when needed, he had begun to put on a little weight around the middle. His body may have been well, but his mind and will were shrouded in feelings of despair and exhaustion. In just the short time she had been there, that mood worsened. She wanted to say something, to tell him she understood that he had to appear strong for his people when he was falling apart inside. *I can feel the tired man hiding inside you like your own secret,* she snickered to herself. *Look at hard old me acting like I care, but that's what Marai did for me: got me to care again.* She gently stroked the King's fingers as they locked around hers. *I used men before I met him. Now, even with him gone, it's different. And you drink too much. I remember trying to drown the demon. Never works. Someone sees you.*

Testing her influence, Ariennu had servants bring a warm and salty duck broth followed by some warm honeyed milk for His Majesty before he slept instead of the fortified wine Great One recommended. He accepted it from her on a whim, but the following day remarked that his sleep was better and she must have it brought every night, rub his shoulders, and lie with him in comfort. All seemed well until he woke quite suddenly in a shouting panic, after what had been a sound sleep. Ari had been making her way down the steps to go to the women's apartments when she heard him shriek in horror. He called out to his manservant, jabbering a frantic question about the lamps.

Ari turned and headed back up the steps, but the guards prevented her from re-entering the royal bedchamber. As she stood outside on the landing with the on-duty officials and physicians pushing past her to enter and tend to him, she heard the poor man ordering an immediate inspection of *all* quarters to see if any of the lamps in the other rooms of the palace had begun to sputter or go out.

What? Screeching like a child in a terror? She recalled at once Naibe, before and after the changes, wailing in horror at some night demon. *No, that's not what this is. This is something much worse.*

From that night on, Ariennu became more and more worried about him. Each night he needed her to hold him tightly and soothe him as he sweated from something like a fever, then shivered with chills. He whispered for her to "take away the pain" and told her that it was "too much for him to bear his sadness another hour". She began to think about death. *Is he dying? Is it possible?*

He told her the legends of his people and of how magnificent he had been as a young warrior and a statesman, with so many campaigns into the Tjemehu lands and even to the Copper Road and down to the Sin-Ai. He was dearly loved by his people rather than dreaded the way his father and grandfather had been. Above all, he had loved his children and loved to have other nobles visit just to bring their children to play and study. They had all left him now, even his wife because sadness had cursed the palace.

When she held him, she waited patiently for him to tell her why he was so anxious, but he never did. He merely said he would defeat the curse this year and then peace and joy would reign in the land once more. She settled into being a wise elder concubine, there to bring him relaxation and temporary joy. Other than that, he fasted and prayed for strength to make it through the year.

The King woke himself at night or had orders for a manservant to wake him so he could tend to some bit of reading or planning by lamplight.

Devotion to god Horus? It's a brief incantation and a blessing. It doesn't take that long, Ari realized, wondering why the man put himself through so much when, as a god, he could simply command things done.

At dawn, exhausted but content that his household had stirred enough to manage life there without his constant care, he slept fitfully for a few hours. Later each day, he would conduct meetings, pray more, make offerings at various temples, and entertain nobility – especially those with young children. Their presence reminded him of when all *his* children had been young and playing with their friends in his beautiful palace gardens and orchards.

"Have I been a good king? I know you have been here just over a year, but beyond that. You can see it, can you not? I'm told you are a seer, a prophetess, or an enchantress in your home country," King Menkaure asked Ariennu on the tenth evening she came to him.

Nothing she had tried cheered him. She knew he sensed her uneasiness, but she tried to mask her frustration. If it had been any other man, she might have made a quick and uncharitable comment, but this was the King. It was a continuing strain for Ariennu to calm her own inner fire and her tongue enough so that she would still seem caring and nurturing. After just these few days, she began to think the King *should* have taken Naibe-Ellit instead. She bowed her head and let the tiniest bit of her dismay show.

He saw it and reached forward almost paternally.

Don't worry. So little fetches my interest lately; I will still call for you, his thoughts spoke as he continued aloud. "One of your kind, in Buto, has told me I have not been forceful or watchful; not godly enough! My devotions and protections are too kindly and not seeking to enforce right and truth. What do you think? See the mighty works I have made grow to the sky? How is that not like unto the work of a god? Why do you think my brother gods try me?"

"I never heard of anyone who dreaded your rule while I worked in the market across the river," Ariennu smiled again, understanding that the King had taken her into a rare confidence that showed her an altogether human side of his divine nature. "I've heard you are so greatly loved by your people that they feel you are truly their father in all ways but your seed creating them."

He smiled as if that comforted him, but an odd expression filtered over his face that showed her he didn't know if being loved more than feared was a good or bad thing.

"You remind me of my sweetest sister, Khammie, when she was young; gentle like that."

Daughter of the God Khammie, Ariennu laughed a little inwardly, *must have been a lioness for him.* She'd seen the statues of them together and thought of the woman dragging him around this pretty bedchamber, completely done in.

The King sighed, his thoughts far-away. Ari rubbed his shoulders again, working her fingers up under the band that fastened his plain, casual nemes to his head. He nodded and she gently lifted it from his head. Ariennu felt him shudder in delight as she worked that area at the base of his skull.

"There. I know you must wear that, but maybe you might command a different kind, like a soft head wrap that wouldn't pinch like that." She laughed, but realized his

GOING FORTH BY DAY

thoughts had shifted.

"The little dancer, is she recovering?"

Ariennu didn't know *what* Naibe was doing. She had learned from the quick glance through the eight child stones weeks ago that the King had truly been sympathetic the night they had been distributed to the households. She was whisked away early by Prince Shepseskaf. Of Deka, she heard that she had simply vanished. Ari knew that she had been chosen by the brutally delicious piece of decorated meat, Prince Maatkare Raemkai, but nothing more. The woman of Ta-Seti was never close to any of them once the Children of Stone made the transformations. Ari couldn't even *sense* her anymore.

"I can't say, Your Majesty," Ari smoothed the King's deep copper colored shoulders. "I haven't seen her since…" she started to answer, but sensed the King growing increasingly tired. He'd had the broth, but after that he had taken in the spiced wine his "Wise Uncle" had insisted on him taking to cure the sweats and tremors that visited him at night.

And that's someone who needs to go away as far as Deka or Naibe, but I'm not so lucky! Ari lay back, cuddling the King a little as he drifted. *Great One is enough to bring night demons, that's for sure.*

Count Prince Hordjedtef came to speak with the King every other day. Ari did not witness or understand what the visits were about until she had been living at the palace for the better part of two weeks. She despised him, despite his attempts to charm her.

"Oh, Lady Ariennu –" he called in a sing-song tone whenever he saw her. "Good to see you are well." Many times, he sat beside her at the common pool, took her hand in his own bony hand and stroked it affectionately as if he was suddenly fifty years younger. *This beast is a flirt,* she decided, *and quite a charmer when he wants to be – like a pretty serpent or a painted frog. Marai said that about him – back when he could still send thoughts to us – when he was alive. He's a man with two hearts, just like Marai said.*

One heart was that of a doting old man and grandfather, and the other belonged to a ruthless wizard and an incredibly skilled manipulator of people. She shuddered to think of what life in Kemet would have been like if he *had* been chosen as king.

Great Goddess Hetepheres, I worship your wise shadow as you pass, Ariennu saluted the air. It had been Hordjedtef's sister, Queen Hetty, now quite infirm but cared for by her daughters, who had chosen the count's half-brother as king instead. That choice had forever dashed Hordjedtef's hopes of reigning over the two lands.

The morning of her eleventh day at the palace, the Count arrived as usual. She sensed him standing for several moments at the perimeter of the plaza. Today, she sat with her lap loom at the greater pool working on a pretty red sash with yellow-gold bees in the border. It was going to be a gift for the King.

After a few moments Ari felt the stab of his staring eyes decrease and heard Hordjedtef order his servant to set up a stool beside her. He invited himself to sit. This was followed by the hand grasp, the hand-rub, and the compliment which left Ari wanting to kneel by the pool and drag her hand through the water to clean it.

"So, not doing this weaving in your apartment plaza today?" he blinked.

Snake eyes, Ari thought. *Bastard needs a forked tongue slithering in and out of his dry old lips. I know he's trying to work something out of me, though.* She took an imperceptible breath and drew the sparkle of a rainbow through her thoughts to make them seem purposeless, the answered.

"I don't like the company there. The others are constantly looking at my work and talking about it. It distracts me."

"I see," his lips pursed.

Ari knew the man could tell she was shielding her thoughts and hoped he wouldn't drill at her. She shifted uncomfortably.

"Tell me then, Lady Ariennu, about this broth of bird you have served His Majesty, *without* his required herbal tonics."

Ari sighed and set her loom aside. She stared at her hands. "It helped him have better sleep. I consulted his physic and he allowed it." She then sent him a very clear thought. *Trying to start with me? He was tired and worn out! And you're* not *his physic.*

GOING FORTH BY DAY

"And yet, within two days his agitation returns? Perhaps not the wisest of choices, then," his voice grew condescending. "I humored you, but now you see the truth in the matter. My prescription was, after all, the superior one. However, it is harmless. His Majesty has told me he *does* like the broth and perhaps warm cream as he retires, but that the herbed wine I've long employed might also be imbibed afterwards, Mmmm? – For perhaps a keener rest so that he might be able to defeat the taunting of Apep within his heart. I have heard he tried this last night and slept without issue. Without inner anguish, he could strengthen his resolve to be truly mighty as the oracle at Buto had once advised him. I know he has spoken with you of this, yet your insistence on your own way is coming close to the mocking of a god."

Ariennu relented. Her shoulders sagged in defeat. She wasn't going to break the old man's influence over the King by using simple motherly charm and didn't like the idea that his wine was drugged. *Maybe it's best to have him take both if he has such ungodly shouting fits in the middle of his dreams. I'll think of something else. Baby and Bone woman will eventually turn up. Maybe they're working miracles in their own households. Maybe this new mission was what the Children wished to be our lives now Marai's gone.*

Just starting to almost like it here, though. It makes me feel young again, and powerful. Not sure I'd want to give that up in the name of freedom. She shrugged and nodded, then picked up her loom. After she had tamped down the next few rows and straightened the borders of the belt, she noticed the old man had realized he was being ignored and had left.

Ariennu decided to see what kind of herbal mixture was in the wine the next evening the King called for her, but it wasn't *that* night. One of the more beautiful ladies, Netjirah, went to King Menkaure instead. As she prepared herself for her evening, the young woman couldn't resist a barb in Ari's direction. Even though she kept her lips sealed, Ariennu easily read her thoughts.

Your days of influence are over, you old, used-up, Set-haired ka't! Majesty wants me *tonight. He has had a vision that you aim to overwhelm him… to steal his sacred seed like your sister is doing at the Prince's house! Irika told me you were a thief once, and now you both cast spells on men. But he is strong and wise – a god! You are powerless before him!* The woman flashed a snarling glance, then fled to the waiting guard for her escort to the King.

Ariennu shrugged, knowing at least three of the younger concubines had been conspiring against her. *Oh! That one he tempts me to give her a weeping sore on her kuna, so His Majesty sees it and turns her away, but that's Deka's style.* Storming to her own little bed, she sat heavily. *Oh Marai, why did you get yourself killed! None of this!* she shook her head. *Now that bastard Hordjedtef is talking up our life before this. You knew me well. I was never ashamed of anything I ever did, but now these little jabs force me to speak so they don't turn into a pack of lies bigger than a swarm of locusts!* She sensed more whispers – someone had sensed her mood.

Ari smoothed her hair and with a tired sigh went out into the open plaza to listen to the musicians playing for the monarch and his choice of woman for the evening. She would come back to bed after the young woman returned from her duty and had gone to bed. Cloaking herself in shadow, she sulked; mulling over new thoughts to escape and an increased desire to gain some advantage over the Great One. In a gentle breeze, she thought she heard Marai's soothing whisper in her thoughts.

Know I have not left you, sweet Ari wife…

Might as well have left us, though, she thought, then paused because she hadn't heard Marai whisper *anything* to her in the last two days before he took his final test. *And now you speak to my thoughts as a ghost? Perfect.*

Ari, listen to your heart. It will make you even wiser, MaMa. So much.

She shook her head, almost hoping the voice from beyond death would stop.

And if you were *alive, you'd see what I see. The old man is controlling Majesty with these mixtures he puts in the wine,* Ariennu thought partly to herself and partly to the "ghost" of Marai. *I will find out exactly what that buzzard is slipping him.*

Marai's memory of his own poisoning left him feeling ill. When he sensed the vignette of the past moments through his link with Wserkaf and his child stone, he wanted to shout '*Yes!*' to her through time. Of *course,* old Hordjedtef was controlling the King. Instead, he shut his eyes again and sighed quietly, seeking another image. He saw Ariennu return to the King's bedchamber the following night; a new arrogance on her face as she breezed by the now somber-faced Netjirah who had entertained him the night before.

Nasty, Ari? Did you curse that girl after all? Marai wondered, but he knew intuitively that Ariennu's presence was like Naibe's residence at Shepseskaf's house. Because of their beauty and self-confidence, they had filled every nearby female with self-doubt. No spell was even needed.

Marai wanted to shriek through time that he was alive, knowing at that moment he lay struggling and trapped in a tomb. He hoped later visions wouldn't reveal she did anything too foolish, but he had an ominous feeling she was about to commit an outrage of some sort. It was just her nature. If he remained calm and merely observed – if Wserkaf continued to help – he would find how to get to all of them.

If he couldn't contain himself, he knew he would reach out too strongly and change the lotus petals of choice on which she stepped, altering her future as well as the destiny of everyone around her, if not the entire universe. For a little while longer the women needed to believe he was dead. He needed to keep watchful and silent or run the risk of making everything that lay before him much, much worse.

The day had been particularly draining for King Menkaure. He didn't tell Ariennu why this evening, and she knew not to ask. Ari rubbed his shoulders with hot oil the way she did every night, but once he relaxed, she bent forward to whisper quite seductively in his ear:

"Your Great Majesty… What is it His Highness, the Great One of Five, places in your wine to calm you in the evening?"

The King raised one brow, pausing at her audacity in questioning his trusted uncle, but then reflected on her words. His hand reached up to pat her hand, affectionately. "You worry for your King," his expression, at first paternal, grew distant.

Ari sensed something in the tone of his voice at that moment, but didn't truly understand the nature of his thoughts. He seemed detached. The words *'my death'* formed in her heart. She wondered if the King was thinking of the curse on him and perhaps if he really *would* die soon.

The only "king" she had ever considered at that point was Marai. She thought of the luxury in which she had lived these past few days, but also thought of the dreadful emptiness in her life as she lived in the service of these two different godly men.

Quiet, yet gentle and reassuring words that seemed to be part of a spell or a prayer filtered through her thoughts. The words reminded her of Marai, carried on the memory of his voice. Her instincts told her to repeat them, that they would comfort the man in her care. She whispered them in Menkaure's ear as they played in her heart: "If emptiness flourishes, my King cannot take his food… If my King flourishes, emptiness cannot take its food."

The thrill of her words raced through both men's hearts; one struggling in the depth of a deathlike dream, the other dreaming of death in a candle-lit room.

"The words…" Menkaure paused. What seemed to be a tear caught in the corner of one of his eyes. His lower lip dimpled slightly. "How is it that a woman such as yourself, a sojourner, knows them? They are taught to the sacred only," the King blinked, then moved his lips to her ear. "Do you know the rest?" he asked. "Gladden my sad heart, woman of the fire. Speak *her* words to me so I can hear them again."

Ariennu felt her own heart skip as a quiet spirit drifted through her. She suddenly felt as young as a new woman who was still learning about life and all its joyous mysteries. At first, she thought it was Naibe's essence, but then she knew it was a different young woman who had died. *Goddess. A goddess… he loved a young goddess, but she was taken from him. He did not protect her!* All at once, her heart thrilled to the sound of the King's words. She had never heard these words before. She couldn't explain to him how she knew them, or why, other than because of her own temptation to use heka, she felt compelled to repeat them.

"Take me with you, beloved, that I may eat of what you eat," she spoke calmly but realized that such a spoken devotion asked for love beyond the tomb. She could never give anyone but Marai that kind of devotion.

The King rose from his couch to fetch the onyx cup which was sitting near the edge of the coals in the brazier. He poured a little more from an ewer into the cup to cool the warmed contents, then sat on his couch, crossed his legs, and faced her. "Close your eyes, woman," he gently commanded her.

Ariennu closed her eyes obediently. Menkaure reached up and sweetly touched her closed eyelids, blessing them, then spoke the companion piece to her words: "That I may eat of what you eat… that I may drink of what you drink, that I may be strong…" his voice broke here and Ariennu almost opened her eyes when she heard him pause. "That whereby you are strong…" Then, he tipped the vessel to her lips. She sipped a quarter of the draught. "Open your eyes to me, woman of wisdom, yours…" he started, but stopped himself.

Ariennu knew he had been about to say: *Your servant begs you.*

When she opened her eyes, he had finished the cup and lay back on his soft couch beside her. She sang the soft and low words to some sweet silly song she had learned from the other women. As she lulled him to sleep in her arms, she noticed a strange, unearthly calm steal over her. It made her feel hot and drowsy at the same time. Wine had never been this strong for her.

Perhaps strong drink doesn't go well with the changes the Children of Stone have created in me, she thought at first. She noticed the haloing around the candle-lights and the rainbow shadows grow so large they overlapped as she drifted. When she woke she felt nauseous, but shook it off, got up, and returned to the women's quarters determined to ask the priest exactly *what* spices and herbs he had put in the wine and *why* he felt it was necessary to dose his King so heavily.

Chapter 23: Naibe Brown Eyes

When Ari woke in the morning, she still felt queasy from Menkaure's wine concoction. She lay quietly hoping the swimming head and bright sunlight in her aching line of vision would cease. She noticed the other handmaidens had risen and were moving about the room. No one spoke to her. They were avoiding her and that worried her. Dressing quickly, she made her way from the women's area, across the wide plaza, and toward the stair that ascended to the King's stateroom.

"Where do you expect to go, woman?" She encountered the first group of guards. One dropped his staff across the steps, preventing her from going up.

He knows me. He knows I'm not going to try anything. Why this? She grumbled inwardly, but quickly feigned a respectful bow and added a face of genuine concern when she looked up at the guard.

"My pardon. I had a feeling –" she covered for her impulse, but knew it wasn't proper for anyone, especially a commoner, to just visit the King without his invitation. Even his grooms had to be invited to dress him. They knew what times he expected things done and knew to be nearby, but never violated the sanctity of the royal stateroom while he was inside.

"A vision –" Ari continued her lie. She had slept as if she was dead, but wanted to make certain the King was well after such an emotionally draining evening of sensing his thoughts. "I feel he is being poisoned by someone he trusts. I would like to taste the food brought to him."

One guard looked at the one posted nearby, puzzled, and then both men looked back at her. The first guard went up the stair but remained outside in a location where he could not see into the room. "Your Great and wondrous Majesty, the Lady Sojourner is here with a vision about your morning meal. She feels it may have been poisoned."

Ariennu heard the King's voice, then saw the guard beckon for her to come up. The porters, who had just brought two trays of food overheard the exchange and balked. She knew they worried that they would be blamed if something went wrong. Pushing by them to go up the steps, she turned and whispered: "Don't worry. Just follow me in."

As she parted the bead drape to go in, the guard cautioned her.

"You can't stay this morning. Taste the food and leave, but don't speak. The Crown Prince will be here soon for his meetings."

"Oh," Ariennu mopped her head with the back of her hand as if another wave of revelation had just come to her, "and the Crown Prince in the same meal. Dear Goddess!"

Losing my touch. That wasn't even a good lie, but at least I got in.

King Menkaure appeared dull-eyed, but calm. He nodded to Ariennu affectionately as his grooms quickly dressed him in a simple kaftan and thoughtfully adjusted his nemes before they touched up the kohl lines on his eyes.

She went through the motions of sampling the broth, the minced pie, and warm sweet cakes the Prince and his father would share. After she sniffed at the pickled fish sauce, she left the room. She had accomplished her real goal: satisfying herself that the King was in full possession of his wits.

Ari hurried to the women's apartment to get food that may have been brought there for the women and their maids to share, hoping her detour by the royal bedchamber and office hadn't caused her to miss any of the honey-pepper loaf she'd smelled earlier. As she crossed the wide, sunny plaza, she saw the Prince approaching in the distance. She waited for him to arrive at the steps, and then lowered her gaze with a bow and a sigh as he grew near, pretending she didn't know him. Ariennu contemplated breaking decorum to ask him about Naibe, but at that moment she saw the young woman trailing through the gates some distance behind him. Porters brought her basket of things in and called nearby servants to fetch the guards to the women's rooms so she could be led there. Prince Shepseskaf had turned to acknowledge her deep bow and looked as if he was about to tell her what she already saw. Forgetting all about the food and the Prince, Ari broke into a run to hold and caress Naibe-Ellit.

"Brown Eyes!" she cried out. Ari would have wept happy tears if she had been the crying kind. "I have so much to tell you! Are you here now? For good?"

Naibe's quiet nod told Ari she was exhausted from her short trip between the two estates. With her arms slung around her sister-in-fate, Ariennu led her to the women's bedrooms. The two women sat on Ari's bed while the maids to set up another.

"What happened?" Ari held and rubbed Naibe's arm.

"I'm sent here to be a maid, I think." Naibe's voice sounded relieved, but as drained as it had almost two weeks earlier when they had seen each other outside Shepseskaf's palace.

Hmmm. That's not good. Ariennu considered, then cuddled the young woman with the thought: *Talk to me like this then.*

Nobody wants me Ari. The Prince and his wife were good enough to me, but they've sent me away now. She said she is with child. She was thankful, but I know there isn't a single way even with her gifts that she would know that so soon unless she's had – no, not her –

Ari knew the one way might be for the Princess to entertain one of the many young guards in her and the Prince's employ. *No. Not her,* Ariennu agreed and smoothed Naibe's dark wavy hair tenderly.

"You know –" she whispered, pausing. "It's just not fair that they made you into his goddess. Oh, baby, I could just crush you and take you away from all this, but for what?" Ari felt a surge of protectiveness laid over the need to caress and touch the young woman the way they had shared pleasure sometimes when one of the men had been too rough with her.

She would be a 'gentle' man for her, holding her until she stopped shaking; caressing her until she found the bliss and understanding all she had missed. Before she had known Marai's love, she had denied it was 'love' and called it all pleasure and the easing of lust.

The young woman looked up.

It's alright MaMa. Her thoughts purred and her hand reached to Ari's throat. They kissed lightly. She knew their affection had caused some of the maids to stare.

He's been asking about you, baby… the King has. Ariennu continued passing her thoughts to Naibe. *He tells me he was really worried for you that night when we were all chosen, but* I'm *worried about His Majesty, Babe.*

The King? Why? Naibe instantly understood that every ear in the room waited on some chatter-worthy morsel to come from either woman.

You'll see. Just – well, everyone here is always –

You've been with him, Ari? Like that? Already? her young face grew wide-eyed with amazement. *Doesn't he have other maids? I thought –*

I need to slap you, Ariennu laughed inwardly. *I knew my way around men before you drew your first breath and he's just a man, not a bit a god – and he's so tired of these spoiled little girls. He had me on him my first night here to check me, but after the business part he just wanted me to stay; to just be someone to talk to. He misses confiding in the women in his life. The girls he can* use, *if the mood comes to him. I keep secrets. He knows he can* talk *to me.*

The King… Naibe's thoughts repeated and she grew reflective, watching the women finish her bed.

For only an instant, Ariennu wondered if Naibe would be relegated to the corps of pretty girls the King invited to his couch, but then her instincts told her Naibe would be much more to him.

He just needs people around him to count on. I don't mean the old high priest, either.

Naibe paled at the thought of Hordjedtef from Ariennu. *He's here?* she scooted closer, certain one of the girls had sensed what they were communicating.

Far too often! Ari continued; *hovers over him like a damned tent! Talks to him about matters of state when the vizier is off on a task or a journey. Stays at him until the poor man breaks a sweat and needs to drink his special herbed wine and take a rest.*

Can't he just order him away? Naibe wondered.

Ari moved to look as if she was whispering to Naibe, then shook her head. *I wish he would. I wish Majesty would order that old man straight to the bottom of the river, I do. You wouldn't know the Count is doing anything wrong, though. King Menkaure trusts everything he tells him about people; almost. He didn't listen to too much about us I guess, or we wouldn't even be here — especially at the same time. I bet that chokes the old man's neck.* Continuing aloud and in Kemet, Ari tossed out a scrap for the benefit of the women making up Naibe's area. "Hey, I have to tell you though, the Great One's been nice to me."

"How so?" Naibe tugged her basket of clothing closer to herself so her bed could be finished.

"He's being sweet as a dim-witted grandfather, advising me on proper etiquette and behavior." She spoke and then added in thought, *trying to work his way into my heart, as if I didn't know what he was doing. Last night, I asked Majesty if I could share his evening wine and he let me drink it with him, Brown Eyes. I could swear the old fart is poisoning him. You know I used to be able to drink strong men to the ground when you first came to us in the sand wastes before I got sick. Quarter a cup of that wine he was drinking knocked me silly last night. I think the old man's made Majesty needful of it, too. We must watch out for him, Naibe. I don't like him at all,"* she paused, realizing how tired Naibe was. The young woman sat staring at her hands.

"Really, MaMa, I don't know how much more of this I can bear. I wish my wits would just leave me and I could keep being pretty but go back to being a thing men desire. I just know the princesses must hate me. What's next? An uprising against me from these girls we stay with?"

"No one hates you, girl. And maybe, just maybe, the Princess did get a child in her. You'll just have to tell me all that you did." Ari continued in Kina, certain none of the others understood by the blank looks on their faces.

Ari remembered just a week and a half earlier the way a very sad and dejected Wserkaf brought Naibe to Shepseskaf's palace. They hadn't spoken that day, and the link between them still seemed muddled. Half the time Ari thought it was the Children's doing, so that she, Naibe, and Deka wouldn't depend on each other too much until they understood the next steps.

Naibe turned to Ari and answered quietly, guarding the expression on her face from eavesdropping maids.

"I didn't think it could happen so soon after I knew Marai was gone, Ari, but Wse and I —" she struggled to assemble her thoughts. "It didn't make any sense. I wanted to hate him for what he did, but the more he spoke to me, the more I knew he meant no harm to Marai. He knew the Count lied to him about us, too." Naibe shook her head dismally. "I know you'll think I'm stupid and that I was just desperate and scared, but…" she shed a little tear. "Now I've lost them both, Ari. My heart dies a little more each time. I don't know how much more I can take."

"Nah," Ariennu hugged the young woman tightly to console her. "I came out to this place in the Inspector's chair. We talked about it. I think he loved you, alright. He was pretty torn up about having to send you away, but you know the man is nothing more than his duty with trimmings. Those loyal royals are just that from birth," Ariennu shook her head. "And then there's you and men. I think even when you were in the camps, they would get all get so stupid and silly around you. I should be so lucky. Imagine me lying about all day and night, men on me making my womb's thunder roll without ceasing."

Naibe frowned and swatted at her. "If that's what you think I'm like, you go ahead, Ari; you take that power from me then." Naibe glanced at the bed the maids had finished, nodded her thanks, and remained silent until they left. Rising, she bent to test if it had been roped and pegged securely.

"Hey, I didn't mean —" Ari wondered if her quip had been more of an insult than she intended. "Come here —" she extended her arms. Naibe's glance back was at once hurt, but forgiving — a red flash in golden amber eyes.

"I know. It's just wearing me down. I feel their pain now, when I go to them. Marai was the first and I wish he had been the only. The Children want all of us to heal others when all I wanted was to be his wife and mother of his children — to be the goddess in his life. What did you honestly want from them?"

Ari hugged Naibe. She didn't really know more than being healthy and able to go her way. Thief? Raider? Endless adventures?

"I didn't want to think about it too much. Guess I just wanted to keep moving — you know, like Bone Woman wanting to get to Ta Seti. Now let's not over think this.

You need some rest. I could use a moment too."

The young woman lay down, pouting. She wriggled her shoulders in the bedding and checked the padding on the headrest first, but soon drifted to sleep.

Ari watched her sleep and then sighed in her own dismay; *I sometime wish her wits weren't there. She stirs up my own questions that can't be answered – like why I didn't scan everything, take a few goods, and hit the shore of the river first chance I got. Staying, especially now that Marai's a ghost, isn't who I am.* Then, she thought again. *I think you lied to me, didn't you?* she addressed the stone in her brow. *About changing our bodies but not our hearts. Look at me, staying here as if I think this king needs me when he's got dozens of others to count on. All I do is make one mistake and I'll be having to get off quick.*

> *Things unseen,*
> *but taking form*
> *Wise MaMa your name once*
> *Wisdom needed.*

Came the answer. Baby and Deka. Once together because we needed it. Now, even though we are healed, maybe we need it more. Is that it? I still work to change their hearts.

> *Long ago in your present form,*
> *you saved the sister of this Marai and her family*
> *from worse shame and death.*

I just didn't want N'ahab cutting me loose, I wanted to win – maybe to kill him before he could kill me. I cut the competition loose. There wasn't any pity or charity. I held her squalling pups down while the men did them. I beat the man and broke his jaw – made him watch.

Ariennu saw the images again and heard the boys screams – the ones that had all but faded from her memory. *I was wicked then. Maybe I still am.* She thought, turned, and tried to blot out the thoughts. *Maybe I'm here for vengeance on Marai, seeing he was the one good thing that ever happened to me. But who? Not the King. Not the lackey Inspector. Not the Prince with all his problems that has nothing whatever to do with Marai.* She paused, smiling and turned on her back again. *Old man Hordjedtef, damn his hobbled, bony rump...* Ari started. *Him — But how? He's damned smart.*

Ari lay on her own bed for a few moments. She wondered what anyone who had seen them today might be whispering now. *Wonder what the old man's plan is* now, *to let two she-wolves at his majesty. Maybe I can get her to see His Majesty before the old man comes. If I'm lucky, maybe the old man is away on his own duty or in bed with some old man ailment. If King Menkaure could know we're both here...* Ari quickly decided that as soon as Naibe had rested, she would take her to see the King in his bedchamber. If it was just after the middle of the day, when it was hottest, she knew the King would have eaten a light soup and bread for his midday meal.

Hmmm. He didn't call for me to rub his neck, she thought. *Breakfasted and had business with Prince Shepsisi. Maybe it was pleasant. Still, he* should *know Naibe is here. He should have sent for her as he did for me when I came.* Thinking again, Ariennu realized that it was *indeed* odd that the King might not know they were both here, given how there were so few secrets within the palace walls.

As if she heard Ari's thoughts, Naibe opened her eyes. Ariennu was already preparing a scented wash pan for her and had stolen some of the flowers from the plaza to put in her hair. Soon, both women went to the bottom of the grand stair up to the King's open and breezy stateroom that overlooked *everything*. Instead of seeing the guards on the stairs, the women saw them coming out; worry on their faces.

"Majesty is..." One of the men waved the two women away. His expression indicated his thoughts. The King was ill, and physician had been fetched.

"Dammit!" Ariennu cursed herself for having spent so long getting Naibe settled and wondered if her ruse of the poisoned morning meal had been somehow made real. The Crown Prince wasn't there or suffering. She got a quick nod from the other guard, but towed Naibe-Ellit past the beaded entry curtain and into the stateroom before either of the men could object. A new woman being brought in to meet the King when he was in less than godly condition was strictly forbidden.

"No! Not you..." one of them started to grab for her, but Naibe's head snapped around so she faced him.

Hide this! Ariennu cast a shadow over both herself and Naibe. *Null face? Now? Are you mad?* She knew by the energy signature that the young woman had just shown the guard what she named a '*null*' face; a dark, but beautiful face that had the power to paralyze anyone who approached her. She'd tried it at the market once when Marai had been up and walking about and a man saw that as a great opportunity to make his move. The poor bastard froze in the spot and as soon as Marai returned no wiser, the illusion faded. If either hers or Naibe's illusions failed to hold the guards, she knew they would be slaughtered on the spot.

Suddenly the guards stepped back, somewhat confused because they had heard their monarch's quiet command.

"It is good for me to receive these lovelies. Lady Ariennu may have even saved me this day." A silence and then a pained gasp followed by: "Put away your weapons and allow them to come."

When they entered, Ari saw the King lying sprawled and limp on his couch. His head tilted backward on his padded neck rest and his mouth gaped as if he had been seized by some misery that made him gasp and suffer to the point of fainting.

"Oh no!" Moved with pity, Naibe-Ellit darted further into the room and dropped to her knees by the right side of Menkaure's couch. "Ari, I knew the night I first saw him that he suffered, but now *look* at him," she touched the King's lips tentatively.

The guards moved behind her, roused from the temporary dazzling effect of her enchantment. They waited for the King's next command, but paused when they saw his fingertips rise slightly in a gesture for them to stop.

"I didn't think it was *this* bad, Ari," Naibe-Ellit beckoned Ariennu to come closer. "Was he so this morning?" she looked up into her elder friend's face.

Ariennu knelt on the other side of the King's couch to check his breath sounds. She frowned, puzzled, wondering if her charade about the poison might have been a *real* premonition. He had been groggy this morning, but rested. His grooms had been changing his clothing from his official starched and pleated temple shendyt and golden regalia designed for sunrise offerings to Ra to the casual sheer, loose linen tunic and informal nemes for breakfast meetings. He hadn't seemed ill. She shook her head.

GOING FORTH BY DAY

"We have to do something," Naibe glanced quickly at her older companion. She took the King's hand in hers for a moment, remarking, "it's so cold."

Ariennu took the King's other hand and blew her warm breath on it, until she saw his eyelids flutter and a look of very slight relaxation overtake him.

"There, Majesty," her throaty voice soothed him. "Your Lady Ariennu has come to help you now."

King Menkaure stirred a little and then tensed, realizing he had lapsed. "Is it time?" he whispered. "Is it time?" he repeated and gasped a little. Raising his head, he noticed Naibe, then startled again. He scooted up on his couch, but a strange weakness made him fall back again. He looked around, motionless, seeking his gold cup of spiced wine.

Ariennu knew he was drunk, and it was shockingly early for inebriation, but she also knew he had taken in more than just wine.

"Here," Ariennu jumped up to fetch a bowl of lukewarm duck broth which had been put on the edge of the smoldering coals. "Naibe, give him *this,* not that wine he's wanting."

Naibe eased her hand under the King's neck and lifted his head. The guards paced restlessly, waiting for the order to discipline the women.

"Here, Your Majesty, this is better for you," she spoke breathily. She was unaware that her compelling voice of power had blossomed again.

She's gotten stronger, Ari noticed. *First the null face and now this voice.* The multi-layered, charming voice had grown into an instinct with her. It seduced, the way a cat calls its prey. That voice, combined with its natural dusky-sweet and ecstatically vibrant sound, compelled every listener. Ariennu poked Naibe, urging her to be careful.

The King pushed himself up and sat, rubbing the pressure mark on his left temple with his fingertips. He seemed only dimly aware that his nemes wasn't on his head, but drank the broth like an obedient, sick child. When he looked up, first into Ariennu's face, then Naibe's eyes, he recognized the younger woman smiled weakly.

"Ah. You're better now, my sweet girl? You've finally come to stay in my house?" his voice sounded winded and drained. "I need – I need – Pretty one, do you see a little white bottle?" he began to fret, looking for the onyx bottle that contained the powder to mix into the wine he drank. The thought that it was gone agitated him.

"Shhh. Shhh. We'll find it for you, Your Majesty," Naibe's fingers went to his heaving upper chest, followed by her head, so she could listen. She beckoned Ariennu to listen.

The elder of the two women nodded, her thoughts whispered:

His heart isn't strong... just quiet and quick. See how his hands tremble? See the yellow cast in his eyes? I had this illness once, girl, you know I did.

"Your Majesty, you're using the wine too much. You need to eat more; some meat and then sip some more broth," she urged. When she looked around the room, Ariennu didn't see the bottle or anything else for him to eat. He had already finished what was left of the broth.

She knew he needed to rest more than anything else. He needed to stop his worries about the welfare of his people and he needed to stop drinking wine to calm his spirit. Ari understood that too well. The memory of using wine to stop the pain, or even end her existence, was never lost on her. The King needed friends and seemed to have only fearful servants or consumers.

"I saw the cooks putting up some pickled rinds in the lower kitchen. I can get some of those and some fresh pressed nectar. You stay here, Baby One," Ariennu stood and went to the door, very much like the chief wife of the house, leaving the King in Naibe's care.

"Help me bring the food for him," she ordered the first guard in the doorway as she passed through it. "He'll need a stew and some juice... and fresh baked bread as quick as it can be made up for him." She and the guard trotted up the exterior stairs to the great kitchen on the roof. She almost giggled at the ease of getting the guard to follow but didn't have time to think about how it had happened.

Naibe stood up quietly then circled to a spot behind the King, to smooth his shoulders and play her fingers over his aching brow to soothe it.

Menkaure's eyes turned up to quietly stare into Naibe's face. At first, his pitiful expression pleaded, but then it occurred to him that he needed a much more composed demeanor. He looked down once, then up, took her hand from his forehead and gently kissed the inside of it, placing it over his heart.

"I am grateful for your care, young beauty, and glad you have learned to take more joy into your heart. You must tell me your secret of this joy, so that when I am stronger and have defeated this cruel spell placed on me, I may come to you as a god. I have grown so tired of this helpless thing that I have become."

On impulse, Naibe bent her head over his and kissed him, amazed that he returned the kiss and sat up to pull her into his arms.

At that moment, Ariennu and the guard returned down the stairs with the food but found Elder Prince Hordjedtef standing at the beaded entry in the alcove and staring into the royal stateroom.

Damn! Ari's thoughts raced as she hid her expression of disgust with a smile. *Is he the physic the guards fetched? Is there no escape?* she saw he held the small white onyx vial in his hands. With a silent snarl, she pushed past him and entered the room, but stopped when she saw Naibe in the King's arms and that he seemed to be recovering quickly. They shared a deep and passionate kiss, despite the presence of others in the room.

Careful, baby, the old man... Her thoughts went to Naibe but were unheard.

Ari turned to the high priest to block his view of the King, but he had already seen enough. His brow crinkled in distaste.

"See how much better he is already!" Ari quipped. "His man didn't need to call for you to come all this way after all," she indicated the vial of medicine. "*We* didn't even have to give him his wine today, just more soup and a little tenderness," her voice filled with delighted sarcasm.

"Which will be fine, dear lady, until his dreams return. What then?" Hordjedtef responded. "Then, will you answer for your neglect, my dear? Does a kiss cure shaking and fever? Sometimes, but not for long!" his eyes turned inward in a scoff, dismissing her words. He started to move toward the King and Naibe, but Ariennu stopped him in the doorway, and bent to his ear to whisper. "I know what you're doing, you bastard! I know you killed our Marai, too!" she hissed. "Just know that if I am anywhere near you on the day you die, I will dance on your corpse until your *ka* won't recognize it and will cast itself on the wind in despair. So, you just watch out for me!" she moved ahead of the high priest with the bowl of stew and set it down beside the embracing couple.

"Majesty…" she greeted him and knelt by the bed with the extended bowl, "His Highness the Great One has arrived with your medicine, but *do* have some of this nice stew first so that it does not sour your stomach."

King Menkaure looked up and then saw Hordjedtef standing disappointed in the doorway. He looked back down at Naibe's winsome smile and smelled the stew Ariennu set down. At once, she offered it to him to sip, drink, and scoop up the pieces with the fresh flat bread. As they teased, giggled, and fed him, his mood brightened. Soon, he touched and kissed both of their heads.

"Both of you are such gifts to me. Such joy," he smiled.

Hordjedtef milled about in the anteroom at the top of the steps. He stared in at the women. Ariennu knew by the look on his face that he was carefully framing everything he planned to say.

The King rose from his couch and beckoned for his attendant to put a loose robe on him. The man lifted the plain nemes to place on the King's head, but Menkaure waved him away. Naibe waited until he sat in his folding ebony and gold chair. She found a brush with short boar bristles on the fine wooden chest by his bed and then tenderly brushed his hair once he was seated. Ariennu rubbed his shoulders and the back of his neck again.

"I feel so much better," were the first words out of his mouth after he drank the last of the soup. "This suits me, excellently! I believe I will *not* take the wine for now!" he almost laughed, but noticed Prince Hordjedtef had become even more impatient and irritated. He paused and asked: "do you wish to speak to me, Uncle?"

"Majesty," the high priest of Djehuti began, his voice filled with false deference. "Do take caution among these. I would have you remember they are *storied* women," he reminded him. "I was merely startled that you had come to embrace them so closely and so quickly, recalling they are widows of a would-be usurper. I would think you would want to be wary of their energy, given the present frail health of your most glorious body. It would be a tragic day indeed, should any true motive they might have emerge," Hordjedtef glanced once at Ariennu through shielded eyes.

"And I was not *fetched*, good Lady Ariennu," he beckoned to the scribe and a porter who were still standing in the alcove at the top of the stairs. They brought in the afternoon list of business for their King and Vizier to place into record as soon as the other elderly gentleman arrived. "I was due to arrive and was being borne through these holy gates when I sensed the commotion and came to assist," Hordjedtef continued. He turned again to the King, bowed, and added courteously: "Perhaps it is a healthy thing after all that you enjoy them, but take care not to draw them into your kind heart as beloveds," he turned his face away as if the women did not exist.

Nebemakhet, the Vizier, entered with a public official and *his* servant. The meetings were about to begin. The King put down his cup, worry darkening his face.

Ariennu and Naibe stared at each other in openmouthed shock. Neither of them could believe the audacity of the priest when he spoke of their supposed hidden need for vengeance while they were still in the room. The guard advanced and moved behind the two women to gently usher them toward the beaded drape.

Motive? Motive. You goddess-cursed bastard! Speak about us like pets, Ariennu glared, but felt the venom of her thought instantly turn back on her. She winced a little in discomfort before she touched her own temple to create a barrier of protection against the high priest.

"Your Highness, Great One," Naibe turned around at the door but lowered her eyes seductively. She walked back toward the high priest, brazenly positioning herself directly in front of him. Standing close to his body and looking directly into his eyes, she smiled, cryptically. "If you have *truly* listened to tales of me, you would know that it is the *women* who fear what I am, not the men," her voice vibrated slightly in the gentle whispering tones of her Ashera voice. "I would never harm His Majesty, *never*. I would only wish to heal him, as does she," Naibe indicated Ariennu, then went back to the King. Going to one knee, she looked up. Her eyes implored but riveted the King's eyes.

King Menkaure pulled the young woman close one more time and lightly kissed her brow. He whispered in her ear: "oh yes, my little love. Don't let my uncle worry you," he chuckled. "I will take you when I am strong, and you will find me splendid."

Naibe bowed her head, blushed, and giggled a little. The two women gathered the soup bowls and left the bedchamber with the rest of the personal servants, hearing the high priest speak as they left: "We have word, your kind and wise Majesty, that Prince Maatkare Raemkai will be sending forth to Ta-Seti in a few days."

"It is *known* to me Uncle. I have just this morning approved the goods and troops for his excursion there to see tribute is good, that the mines are being handled properly, and that the governors remain content. Do send word to his household that I have decided to *personally* host his good departure this year as a mark of goodwill in this sixth year since the declaration at Buto."

Ta-Seti? Ariennu thought as she headed back to the women's rooms with Naibe. *Deka will be there. Deka*, her eyes silvered a little because now this was all going to get *very* interesting.

GOING FORTH BY DAY

Chapter 24: Bakha Montu

Marai sighed, haunted by the sheer volume of all he had relived when he touched the Inspector's shoulder. He shuddered, closed his eyes, and hung his head in contemplation. He knew not much time had passed because of the instant transfer of all the memories through his child stone, but it gave the illusion he had slowed time.

Wserkaf sighed, stretched, and stood, breathing and posing to fully rouse himself. When he finished, he lifted a beaker of beer from the table beside his seat and poured it into a cup. Sipping it, he offered some to Marai, who finished the cup.

"You saw everything you wondered about?" the Inspector asked, looking as if he still heard echoes of something. Marai didn't quite understand why, but he knew the children were still speaking to the Inspector. He nodded, but added:

"I know there's more though, isn't there? A lot more! I just need you to be truthful so that you in your heart know you are clean of the wrongs done to us," Marai shook his head again, dismayed. "If you are guilty and you can't say it all, I'll just take my leave of you. I won't hurt you because you helped me go forth."

"I've told you what I can bear to tell you, but if you need more, here are my thoughts." Wserkaf sat wearily, searching the position of the moon, a puzzled look on his face. "Once I understood Great One's plan, I moved away from supporting his actions. Fortunately for me, most of the truth came to me while I was in deep contemplation of the god while I was away on duty," he stood again and moved toward the doorway. "I think Hordjedtef must have continued to spread the rumor that both Naibe and Lady Ariennu were using heka on our families, because neither ended up staying at the palace of the King." Wserkaf came forward to pour more flat beer from the beaker. He sipped again, offering more to the former shepherd. "By the time I returned from Khmenu, they were no longer in Ineb Hedj."

Marai felt his head start to spin realization of the deepening mystery settled in his heart. "So —" he spoke slowly and deliberately. "It wasn't enough for Hordjedtef to try to end *me*, he had to tread upon and shame my ladies? He ran Etum Addi and his entire family – his life's business – out of town too, so my ladies would have no other bloodless course of action? He caused them to go with his people as if he owned their bodies?" Marai focused on the thought that the women were no longer in town when everything in his visions while he lay entombed underscored that they were still in Ineb Hedj, living in *someone's* palace. *Wserkaf said earlier 'because it wasn't safe'*, he remembered. "Wserkaf, wait," he started. "Where are they?" he leaned forward, elbows on his knees.

"On the way to Ta-Seti with Great One's grandson, Prince and Grand General Maatkare Raemkai, if they aren't already there," the air rushed out of the Inspector in defeat. "It has been over a cycle of the moon since the 'Sending Forth' celebration you saw Hordjedtef mentioning in our vision. You also need to know that the Ta-Seti woman who was your wife is now his chosen concubine for the journey. She asked that the others be allowed to come with her as her companions, according to my teacher, and he saw fit to make that happen. He has always blindly doted on that young man; despite all the havoc and chaos he has caused in our household. My Khentie will not even be in the same room unless she so ordered and that only by her father," Wserkaf continued. "Prince Maatkare hunts lions at this time of year and carries on a diplomatic relation with the Ta-Seti peoples. Prince Akaru-Sef serves as a sepat Governor there so that the lands of Buhen, Ta-Seti, and Kush do not rise up."

"What?!" Marai felt his consciousness fading as if he was about to faint, his rage was blackening and growing unchecked. An awful lowing formed throughout his chest and up into his head, then cackled like a demon of the underworld. He reviewed the Inspector's last statement.

"You also need to know that the Ta-Seti woman who was your wife is now his chosen concubine for the journey. She asked that the others be allowed to come with her as her companions, according to my teacher, and he saw fit to make that happen."

The words echoed and turned over in the shepherd's thoughts. The violent trembling and the shrieking spirit continued to well up inside him until its darkness threatened to leap out of his skin. He stood and advanced to the window that looked out onto the plaza, his hands gripping the high sill. He paled as the answers to all his questions emerged: the tentative and remote voices of the Children; the old man bragging he had a way to control them.

"The Children. Does the old man have *them, too?*" His hands went to his ears and he gripped the sides of his head to stop the flow of thoughts racing behind his Child Stone. *Ari was supposed to have kept them safe. If she's been made a captive – How could that even happen? She's a power to reckon with. She'd kill anyone trying to capture her, I know she would. She's taken life before and would again. Even Naibe could use her own sorcery to keep herself from harm if she was threatened. Why didn't they defend themselves? Is it true? Can the old man control them as he said? And he says Deka is helping? Why? There should be death and destruction blazing through all of Kemet, unless – Unless –*

Marai felt black lightning roaring inside him with renewed strength. It flashed along his arms the same way it had moved when N'ahab-Atal and his men met their deaths at his hands so many years ago. Something wasn't being told. Wserkaf, or maybe even Ari herself was blocking the rest of the truth. *Ari, why? Why hide truth? I can't. I won't.* He couldn't control his rage an instant longer. *I want that Great bastard dead! I want to get inside his rotten soul, so he suffers!*

At that moment, however, he could only rage. The sojourner seized the bed behind him. With a roar, he hurled it against the opposite wall and it shattered to bits, but that gesture of rage only fueled more.

"Enough! All in this place. All of your wicked hearts!" he shrieked, rushing from the room toward the plaza gate. He gripped his ears. "You can't trap me here. No more stories!" With an animal bellow, he hurled himself at the metal-sheathed cedar doors. Damage unseen, Marai felt the gates crumble and give way. "Free! Now they die." He pictured himself, now in the form of a giant bull running and roaring into the alleyways between the white walled estates, bursting into each estate to destroy all inside, but something froze him at the cracked door frame in an agony that was even too great for the rage and too loud to be heard by human ears. Blind, he continued to grow until he had become a blind bull that towered over battle and would know no rest until all had been destroyed and all wrongs had been avenged. Freeing himself again, he rammed the thick wall with his shoulders and head.

Then, like a whisper, another frantic thought entered in the middle of his ranting.

"Damn you Marai! Get control! Hordjedtef will hear!"

GOING FORTH BY DAY

Wserkaf. No. Don't stop me. He must die. Marai didn't fight the thought that he had become a maddened bull. It was entirely rational. In the instant before he lost human consciousness, he pictured the faces of Deka, Ariennu, and Naibe cast with emptiness and fading. His thoughts turned his face black and slavering but lit with an eerie silver-white shimmer shrouding him like a magical skin as his horns launched themselves. His manlike chest grew, filled with a low of mournful despair fueling even greater rage. In the background a small creature who might have been the Inspector had begun a chant. The words were inaudible whispers playing into his anger like icy needles.

Don't! No! Don't stop me.

And the words became clearer, the voices of the Children of Stone joining the verse.

Cease – cease – cease!

Cease and calm

Rise above it.

No vengeance upon the righteous.

Holy Ra and true Djehuti

Rein in the Daughter of the sun,

Sweet Bastet!

spit flame upon the evil intent within you

Beneath those words, he sent a thought:

Cease

Do not let him feel you!

Do not let him win this way.

Do not give him the food of victory!

Marai heard and understood the spell, but he shrieked silently once more. With a mournful lowing sound, the big sojourner hurled himself against the thick wall again and again. Part of the support structure crumbled into a pile of brick and white-limed dust. The small creature behind him was thrown backward but out of the corner of his eye he saw it scramble and right itself, then spring behind him.

Something black and blood red rode the sojourner's back and merged with him, but this time he welcomed the demon, allowing it to sink in and become part of his glowing flesh to emerge as the Bull of War. It wanted to send death throughout the entire kingdom. He was ready, but another voice rose in the distance, carried on the wind.

Him. Hordjedtef. Die, bastard! Marai's heart felt like shattering as he cried, but then grew silent as he heard the elder's distant words followed by the solemn ringing of a deep gong, once, twice, and on.

"The great bull has died. His death cry has gone out*,"* the voice halted and broke with emotion, then continued. "Dear ones, let us mourn Our Father..." It was part of an invocation, captured and sent on the wind. That voice brought a flood of peace to the bull spirit in Marai, stopping his witless battery of the wall. Then, he felt a firm hand leveling him at his shoulder and dagger-like fingers digging into his throat. He knew the touch. Somewhere in his thoughts, he remembered that touch as being able to shock a man and even make him faint. He was too angry for the Inspector's skilled fingers to have that effect, even though it paused his rage.

Marai fell to his knees by the splintered door, then looked up through eyes of a bull knowing its slaughter was imminent. He felt another touch behind his ears and dimly noticed calm sweeping over him. Fingers crept around his face to spots beneath his eyes.

"Marai. Stop this! Don't curse in anger, it comes back threefold – arrow into spear into army. *I'm* in that household! It curses *me* too! Not *all* of us are your enemies. Dear gods above and below, has not sweet Naibe already cursed us through and through? Our Father is *dead!*" The priest commanded, then released him and moved in front of him, pacing back and forth.

"I *know* Hordjedtef heard your cry, but for now he thinks he heard the cry of the bull-spirit of Our Father Menkaure moving another level further from this world. He will know the truth soon enough and come for both of us. If you go on like this, I'm *sure* he will know you live. The *dead* could feel your wrath."

Marai stopped, letting the priest work his calming touch into his hard-corded shoulders and neck.

"I can't stay here," the sojourner gasped, breathless from rage and exertion. He felt the rage and the dark leave him in a rush, but then he sank into profound depression as Wserkaf worked calming touches on his lotus points. "I have to go to them. I must get them back. I know my rage is – I just wish I could bring you with me, so you could keep me from killing many along the way," he panted, retching and heaving in anguish, but sensed the Inspector studying his features as the specter of the bull-spirit faded. He gradually felt his color return to normal except for the menacing dark ness of his aura.

"And you *know* I would go with you, with every beat of my heart, if any part of my life was even mine to chart," Wserkaf whispered dully, despair in his tone. "This. This right now is too much. Our King is *dead,* and I am trapped here in Ineb Hedj because as the sun of Menkaure sets, so does the reign of Hordjedtef. It is *I* who am now destined to replace him. Yet, even as I do and as he still breathes, it creates a life of even more danger for me whether I stay *or* go." He shook his hands several times, ridding them of wretched cramps, then moved behind Marai. When he massaged the sojourner's temples, both men began to sway back and forth. The feeling of the Inspector's fingers made Marai shudder in chilled pleasure as the malignant energy faded.

Wserkaf's fingers cooled the stone in Marai's brow.

"Hmph. Then there's *that* – which tells me I have no business whatsoever running about in your world or in hers."

After several moments, the Inspector faced Marai whose head was bowed as he shamelessly wept. The Inspector sat on his heels, between Marai and the battered gate wall.

"I know *she* had a pretty blue stone in her head. Hordjedtef told me you each had been given one and without it none of you would ever be a threat to us; that one just needed to find ways around the energy they transmitted that made you four like gods. He was certain he would learn how to do that one way or another. The ancient Djedi had known some methods of control or reversal and taught them to him."

Marai nodded solemnly, observing the damage he had done to the gate, doors, and the wall. He mopped his eyes with the back of his hand. He ached, body and soul, but knew he needed to level himself. *Wserkaf isn't going to be able to cover what I've done.* Marai didn't turn his head, but knew the few servants in the back who hadn't gone to assist the new royal family had certainly rushed out during his now simmering outburst. They had returned to their preparations of foods which would be delivered to the palace. *Someone will talk, even if Wserkaf threatens them with beatings, and he's a gentle sire for his workers. Silence? Secrets? Soon nothing will be hidden. It's begun. Wserkaf knows. His wife knows something has changed.* The sojourner had seen through his shared vision. *First pretty Naibe came here, then I came on the night Father Menkaure passed into the Field of Reeds. Hordjedtef knows something; he must. He's just waiting for Wse to step into a hole, so he'll have him.* Marai sighed, feeling the overwhelming urge to murder strengthening in the back of his thoughts. *He knows it's unbelievable, even to him in his long life of deep and far-reaching study. He learned early I wasn't some piece of wilderness trash to be used and discarded. He knew his awaited 'Ta-Ntr' people were what we called the 'Children of Stone'.*

"Marai the Shepherd of the Sin-Ai wastes, you're so much more than that," Wserkaf looked into the sojourner's eyes, enchanted. "I get it now. You *are* the 'no ordinary man' old Lector-prince Djedi once mentioned to great-grandfather Khufu, aren't you? You're a man made of the stuff of dreams, the one who can unlock the secrets which have been left to us." Wserkaf paused long enough to take a breath and continue. "That you're an outsider, and an unschooled wanderer, makes you so much more dangerous to us as priests because we're tasked to keep the secret learnings pure."

The Inspector shook his head, dismayed and almost amused. "Once I ally myself with you, I'm no longer just a hapless fool bewitched by a charming Lilitu – I become as much of a problem as you. But what do I do about this now, Marai; what to do?" Wserkaf reached forward to examine the scrapes and wounds on Marai's shoulders and head where he had repeatedly rammed into the wall. "See? You should have beaten your head and body to a pulp, but now you've all but healed."

Marai nodded, half-wondering where the Inspector was going with this line of thinking.

"I know you call these stones 'Children'. Great One told me this and he told me what his own teacher had said – that they are not of this world. He said their kind visited the world of men long ago when the gods walked as men and *are* these gods in another form. My mentor was truly amazed that they would take the form of pretty stones that depended on men to bear them. I don't think he really understood how they worked, though he pretended to have full knowledge."

"Well," Marai answered. *I know what he's doing. He's getting me to talk and draw off my rage.* Marai turned away from the gate, but continued to pace away the desire to visit his wrath on the Great One. "They *do* come from beyond the stars," he continued, "but maybe they even come from a different *kind* of world; one where time itself doesn't have rulership."

"Beyond the laws of Djehut and Ma-at?" Wserkaf lowered his head. "How is it possible that there are such lawless worlds and god-beings? Are they as stones in their own country?" he reached up to examine the place on Marai's brow again. The Inspector felt the slight tug of energy being drawn from his fingertips, and felt like he was being examined by discerning eyes for a moment. A mild purr of approval followed. "Hmmm. They purr when they like you," he suggested.

"I don't think so," Marai answered, the touch of the priest's fingers continuing to calm him. "They haven't shown me more than a vision of them being made of light, so very tall and bright. They come and go as if they have bright wings like the sun, yet they can take whatever shape they need at any given time. They are like *djin*, or old ones called Anunna, but they did not ever come to our world to enslave us or be our overlords. I asked them to show me, but they said I would go mad to see them." Marai tilted his head backward as the Inspector continued his "touch" treatment, realizing he'd left out mention of the peculiar dark entity which seemed to be just as much one of the "Children" as the others, albeit wayward and with a different, conquering agenda. The sojourner's rage continued to transform into desperate fatigue. "They told me they have come back to teach some more of us. This time, they imbed themselves in the head at what they call the *star eye*. Within the stone, smaller than any eye can see, they are composed of bits of spirit and memory, tiniest sparks and essences. You might call it ka. The stones become part of us until the moment when our body dies; and it will do that *one* day, they said, but not too soon. So, now you know. They teach, they change us, and they make us grow."

"They make you into a god," Wserkaf repeated, then added "– explains why Great One lusts for them. He's old and never ruled when he believed a conspiracy by his sister kept him from it. It's the invincibility, a regained youth and power – or to at least be able to command his own mortality.

"I think not. Not really," Marai glanced over his shoulder at the sesen pool, briefly recalling the image of Naibe soothing herself with her feet in the water the night Wserkaf took her into his arms. He wanted to feel the same cooling water on his feet and to somehow bring her forward to this moment in time so he could feel her softest skin as she held him in her arms. "I haven't felt like a god, especially lately. This Child Stone… " he tapped his brow "…transformed my body and wakened me to my truer self, but I'm still just an ordinary poor man, just a shepherd. All I wanted was peace for myself and my family. I'm no king, god, or warrior. I'm no wizard either. I just want to get my wives back and then to go look for a little piece of land to work, with some sheep or maybe cows this time. I didn't really want any of this."

Wserkaf, noticed and followed him as the sojourner continued:

"Doesn't matter what I want though. He's beaten me, your Hordjedtef has, and now your king has died. You are here destined to take his place, and he is free of duty. He can try to lay his hands on the Children of Stone as he has always wanted to, as long as he still draws breath – another reason why I should just slip into his lodging in the form of a shadow and strangle him quick." Marai shook his head in dismay, knowing that a man like the Great One likely had spiritual guardians to battle long before he reached the old man. "Are your physicians certain he didn't murder the King?" Marai asked. "Great One knew you were drawing away from him. I could sense that the last day before the ritual. He knew you'd have to stay close to him if a disaster struck your household."

"If I even think of considering that –" the Inspector's face grew pale as he sorted the idea. "No. Majesty's *been* having fevers and fits of despair for years since the great tragedy befell him. I think his thoughts finally wore him down and broke his noble heart," Wserkaf affirmed, but Marai read the look in the Inspector's eyes and knew the idea the King *might* have been murdered suddenly wouldn't leave him.

"Poisons or traps set in battle are all too common when any position of power is disputed. But Our Father loved his strong drink and festivities as a Prince. As years moved forth, he drank more and on so many occasions would be senseless in public," the Inspector mused. "He played it as speaking with Horus and Ra, but we knew. Even later, when drink was denied him, he got in a state. Great One dosed him with a calmative potion – just a small amount of his famous Sweet Horizon. No one considered he'd have the audacity."

Marai shuddered that he might have been right, but Wserkaf added: "It *is* an unsettling point. When I return to the palace, I shall privately ask my brother become King Shepseskaf to allow me to join the lector in the 'Tent of Purifying', when the first cutting is done. If there is something unclean about the humors in him, I will see it and I will report it to him," his face darkened again. "For now, though – You do need to leave Ineb Hedj as soon as possible. Hordjedtef will retire to Nekhen as Shepseskaf ascends the golden throne."

Marai visualized the image of the younger and fit Hordjedtef in possession of a Child Stone and wreaking havoc across the Two Lands. It was an image from a dream he'd had long ago, perhaps as he was sleeping on the Children's vessel of stars.

Unless he somehow gets his hands on the Children Ari hid for me. In a perfect world, they would burn him for even thinking about it.

The Inspector sat beside Marai at the end of the pool. From time to time, he checked the big man's vital signs and energy as he worked his shoulders and brow to make sure the big man continued to calm himself properly.

Marai remained quiet now, sorting through all he had learned and dreading what he would learn next.

"How did you come to be in the chamber the other day? Was it to save me? If I had truly died, you could have quit your post and taken Naibe-Ellit to another kingdom."

"Oh… that. I almost thought about it, you know – running away – but Khentie and I are bound and beloved of each other and there's never been ill between us." The Inspector hesitated, still unsure about telling the sojourner of his feelings for the woman they had loved. He breathed out and continued. "Naibe and I sensed it one night when it had been so splendid between us that all the stars watched us, and it seemed like even the gods wept too. Even that night I knew, inside my heart, that it was just *not my path* to take her, even convinced you had died." His eyes widened in grief that wanted to weep but did not dare.

"I obeyed. I thought if she might have a child for the Crown Prince, that a new birth might ease her pain. Every woman I have seen, unless deeply troubled, rejoices at a new birth despite her misery – a royal one – I had no idea that Princess Bunefer would feel threatened by her. I didn't know she was getting so much more powerful. I had not thought *at all* that the Ta-Seti woman would ask for the others to come with her when Maatkare Raemkai took her up the river. When I returned and found Naibe had left us, I was devastated, but I knew there was nothing I could do at that point but wait for the general to come home with them. Then, the bond between my wife and I grew a little sweeter. My Khentie knows me well, I guess, and dismissed the lie I told her. A few days later, she opened her heart to me again," the priest smiled about his wife.

Marai couldn't see his face, but knew the man had resolved the last of their difficulties together and that he had been able to reclaim her trust.

"That night, we retired early and reaffirmed our sacredness to each other. I begged her to stay with me through the night rather than go to her own bedchamber."

Marai felt a pang of jealousy then. *I should be with mine, not listening to how they were mistreated.* He kept his forced evenness of temper and continued listening to the Inspector.

"We slept in each other's arms like newly wedded ones, but then she waked from a horrid dream about a man trapped in a tomb. The man had the face of the King, she told me, but then the face turned green and showed a most horrible agony as he tried to break free of that tomb. He could not yet go forth by day. It was Asar, she told me, but wondered what the dream could mean and why it formed in her night journey.

GOING FORTH BY DAY

The thought that you had somehow not died came to me at once, but I could not accept it as truth. Then, the thoughts became so strong, that by next evening, just after nightfall, I took a man with me to conduct an inspection over a matter in the chambers and asked that she not mention it should anyone ask. When we came down the secret stair, we saw the lid of the trial sarcophagus cracked apart with the bottom part tumbled to the floor as if a thief had pounded it apart," he continued his tale. "I have seen death and I know how an unprepared corpse should feel as it rots, wet or dry. When I reached into the broken part and touched your leg, I knew that something of the gods had taken place. I had to help you go forth. I'm sure you know the rest from there."

Marai shook his head in disbelief of what he had heard.

Wserkaf, you're just too honorable not *to be telling the truth. Were you able to let Naibe go? Even I wouldn't have let a woman like her get away from me.* Then, he realized he did. *I let them all go because I was too proud to run back to them when Hordjedtef offered me an escape. Now, they're all with this prince who's spirited them away to a life not much better than the one they knew in the wilderness. All three women against one prince and they didn't defend themselves? Something's not right*, Marai puzzled. Though it was true that his wives had just begun to learn their strengths when he crossed the river to meet the priests, it shouldn't have mattered. *All three women with one mere mortal prince? He should have been dead in a hurry! Deka, a concubine? Deka? The man should have been dead before he even thought about taking the other two. Who is Maatkare? What is he? Could he be more than a simple mortal as he seems? Some unknown force is still piloting this mystery. I just hope I can find out what it is. No, I will find out what it is.*

Part 3: Sending Forth

GOING FORTH BY DAY

Chapter 25: The Wdjat

Prince Wserkaf knew that as Lord Inspector of the Ways, he would have to return to the palace before the sun rose. He sat with the sojourner Marai to make certain the big man had recovered, but knew the vigil and the First Rite of Passing, with all the attendant chanting and invocations, was being spoken over the deceased King at this very moment. All the priesthood in Ineb Hedj and any visiting priests from surrounding sepats were expected to take part in this first crying out over Menkaure's earthly shell. After that, early in the morning and under heavy guard, his body would be taken to the *ibu*. Then, the creating of his *Akh* for the afterlife would begin. The Inspector knew he was already missed. Wserkaf hadn't, at least, felt Count Prince Hordjedtef reaching out to him. The only reason the elder *hadn't* done this was likely due to scramble of his own official duties.

That, and I was truly convincing in my "spiritual illness" during the initial ceremonies in the King's bedroom earlier. I need to get Marai out of here and down to the river as soon as we eat. Where he goes can't be any of my concern or Hordjedtef will discover the truth. It's just futile, even with his powers, because Great One has powers that worry even me and my friends throughout the priesthoods. Then added to this is Prince and Grand General Maatkare Raemkai and all His *loyal troops, who would favor commands of his Grandfather over the new King. Madness. Marai'd need high and very dishonorable sorcery on top of his calling in all favors owed by any gods he worshipped. As for chaos heka, the general is familiar enough with those arts. Even if Marai was to gain on him in battle, he would likely decide the women weren't worth the trouble and have them slaughtered. At that point, if the sojourner so much as blinked, he would be defeated as well.*

The only hope of this coming adventure having a good outcome is its unpredictability and its seeming resistance to fate.

I thought Marai was dead at one time. I believed Naibe would never appeal to me. I knew the King would live to be very old and that I and Khentie would age gracefully in this beautiful garden estate, greeting our grandchildren when they visited and watching them grow. I believed Hordjedtef was truly wise and truthful in his teachings and writings — that they reflected the way the elder lived his own life. After so many errors in perception of the way things were, I wonder if I'll be wrong about Marai's chances when my heart is screaming. And, here it is, then.

"I should at least feed you once more before we go," Wserkaf attempted to distract himself from the grim thoughts. He rose from his seat and tiptoed to the larder near the servants' row to see if anything could be gathered. He didn't want to rouse any of the cooks. They had worked all day and through the early evening to prepare what they could in advance for the mourning guests, who would begin to arrive by the following evening.

"Lord," a tired voice issued from the closed pantry.

"Oh, is that Rephtet?" the Inspector startled when the chief cook moved into the dim light of the moon. When he saw the man wearily nod, he continued. "If there is a platter of yet unsalted meat and some bread not crumbled, my guest and I would wish for some," he requested, but almost regretted it as soon as the words left him. *I know he's really worked hard today. I should give him an extra day and portion to be with his family in town during this time of sorrow.* "I'll take it if you can fetch it for me," he continued. "Then, you go get some rest. Tomorrow will be hard enough for us all."

While the Inspector waited for the cook to get some meat from the light salt, he thought of the way his life had changed in so little time. Four months ago, he now recalled, he'd felt an odd sensation in his chest. At first it was a thrill-like feeling. Then, it became gnawing doubt of the journey toward wisdom he was undertaking. Ever since the day after the Sailing of Bast, when he had been sent to investigate the rumor of a strange sojourner who had brought immeasurable success to the Kina-Ahna market, he had become increasingly suspicious of his teacher Count Prince Hordjedtef. That doubt ate at his soul and slowly changed him.

As a youth, in awe of his teacher's knowledge, he had heard the old man's stories of the Ta-Ntr. Wserkaf had always thought the tales of these beings were metaphors or legends; a remnant of stories from the "First Time" when the gods were here on Earth. His teacher and he hadn't dwelt on the stories until a week or two before he went to check on the people at the market. At first, Wserkaf didn't think there would be any connection between the people he met and the legend his teacher liked to repeat; but that changed almost instantly.

He eased an old woman's suffering with the touch of his hand. That would have been stunning enough, but the essence that surrounded the man made him at once fearsome, yet irresistible to behold. His sunny and cheerful manner and the grace of the women he called his wives spoke of another world. When Marai had come to them to study, Wserkaf saw him "put down for his own good" by the teacher he had always trusted. The man had *died* but had come through his death to go forth by day. This led the Inspector to question all he had been taught.

Gods of legend, not men, defeat death. The Divine Bull Asar returned from death to mark the change of the seasons. If I believe that Marai is Asar walking in flesh again, it means Hordjedtef is as Seth, who strove to defeat him. The priest shuddered, remembering the dinner party that celebrated the former shepherd's demise, and the way he had been locked up in a box. All events in his recent life imitated the very same legend.

What does this mean? Is Marai the god walking? Am I the one to stop all the evil set in motion by Hordjedtef and whatever forces he truly serves? he asked himself. *So much of the future is unknown. It's pointless to guess. I need to focus on all that is in the physical dimension, not this. I am now to be the Great One, and I'm blood royal, too. It's my duty to stay close to my new King and our wife, lest harm finds them, too. Right now, I can only go with the body of poor Menkaure to the ibu. There, I'll make certain there was no murder.* He felt heart-deep dread the more he thought about the possibility that the old man's medicine had been used to kill the King. If poison *had* been used, it would leave a mark or an odor on his holy organs that could be noticed as the body was prepared. *What's the use?* he continued to contemplate. *If I see something, who will I tell? Shepseskaf? Khentie? Hordjedtef is too well respected. He's one of the most beloved priests in all of Kemet — more loved than my brother who now wears the sacred pschent. Only one thing to do: watch and keep record.*

Dismissing the cook, he carried two platters of food out to the pool. When he set them down, he darted to his chart room for "a few more things" and then returned to enjoy a somewhat cooled meal of roast duck, fruit, beer, and flat bread with his friend. It was a quickly-thrown-together feast.

"I believe we can go on the river a short way tonight. The water is still of a fair enough height that we might not get trapped in the silt." He handed Marai a plate, then sat by the sesen pool with him again. "I can get boatmen to take The Sun's Wisdom up the river just far enough tonight, then turn around to ferry me back to the dock at the Royal Palace, the priest decided. "Those people in the Poors, that young stonecutter and his family; would they hide you for a few days? I could get word to you when it's safe." Wserkaf knew the words he said were just hollow promises and wishes. If he had been able to keep a promise in the past, he would have fetched Marai three days after he had been entombed, cleansed him of the poison, implicated his senior to the King, and proven Marai's right to pursue further training perhaps in the House of Ra along with him. "I still wish I was free to go with you. You'll need someone who knows the governors along the way, or you'll be challenged by warriors at every step." He watched Marai tear into the roast duck with much more energy than he had possessed earlier.

"Don't even *wish* to go, Wse," Marai spoke with his mouth full. "I have to do this on my own. I don't even know if Djerah and his family will accept me. I *do* know I'll just push on if that happens. You must stay here and keep Hordjedtef off me. If he tries anything else, I *will* kill him. So, don't stand too close," Marai paused, then added: "maybe I'll do it anyway, if my wives have suffered as much as I think they have. The balls on him, bending them into common servants of the body *and* learning how to thwart all that had become strong in them through the Children!"

Suffered? Wserkaf thought, *then Great One is already dead.* He poured the last of the beer into the two cups.

"We have to go, *soon*." Wserkaf reminded Marai as they continued eating the meal. The sojourner knew the Inspector's thoughts rioted in frustration. "The worst of it is that I need to tell you more, even what I only heard in tales and rumors. I need to stop time, to master it like Lord Djehuti who walks through it and around it. If this was any other night, I could hide you myself and then get a writ from Shepsisi so I could go to Ta-Seti with you. With Our Father dead, there's no way in the heavens or on earth I can escape the mourning or the preparations. I'm not going to be able to keep the fact that you live a secret much longer either. If he guesses, I'll tell Hordjedtef someone stole your body. It's a weak excuse. He'll know my hand in it, punish me, and then not rest until he either controls or kills you."

"Damn him," Marai pressed his lips into a flat line. "I wish I had it in my power to stay and take care of this too. I can't, though. I *must* get my ladies back and into safety before I do anything else," he started, but then thought of something that hadn't occurred to him before. "How does your elder know things of you? I know the man has his powers and wisdom, but you're no weak acolyte. Certainly –"

"The trances," Wserkaf quickly replied. "It was always my special gift. I had powerful dream-visions, even as a child. When I came to study with him, we made a fealty pact that I would always be open to him."

"And you've never shirked that duty? Protected even a *small* secret? You seemed quite good at hiding them from *me* when we met. Only young Naibe –" Marai thought of Ariennu and her ability to hide *everything* from the light of wisdom and knowledge. He also thought of the loving way Naibe could open them up and could see into anyone's dark corners.

"Naibe," Wserkaf began, saddened again. "Yes, I know she could do that, but when we were together it was good for her to see me. She knew my truth right away and knew I wasn't playing with her heart. Unfortunately, as you know by now, Great One can open me too. During your training, when we argued, I tried to close my thoughts. Each time, he used the control he had instilled in me when I was new in his tutelage. I haven't found a way to close my thoughts from him completely. I just have to be careful of what I think when I'm around him."

Marai remembered the silent syllable under a word Hordjedtef had used and the way it gave him a blinding headache when he first visited the elder's estate. The same thing had happened when the Ta-Seti sesh found him and the women in the market. Now Marai remembered the sesh *had* acted as if he thought he was being watched. Either the sesh knew the control, or he had allowed Hordjedtef access to his thoughts in the same way Wserkaf allowed it as he wandered the booths that morning.

"The tall dark sesh who works for you; he has a fealty pact to Hordjedtef too?"

Wserkaf froze, his cup half-tilted to his lips, then nodded. "Young Aped'meketep? We all do, or at least those of higher skill." Worried, he drew closer to Marai as if he thought old Hordjedtef might suddenly hear his thoughts. "I just – It makes more sense to me now, given what I'm learning about his hand being in so many things,"

Wserkaf shook his head and shifted, the necessary passage of time bothering him.

"Like the southern armies?" Marai asked the Inspector to continue. "Tell me about this general – his grandson. I thought I knew the names of the princes who were close enough to the King to command anything." Marai drained the rest of the beer and stood, stretching his arms tall to the sky. He took a deep breath, held it, and then gently let it out. He silently gestured that time had not been passing then watched the Inspector take note and try to hide his wonder that the stars seemed different and the moon had migrated to an earlier post.

Marai went to inspect the gate frame where he, in the half-form of a bull, had run against it. New brick would have to be laid in and it would have to be plastered and painted. It would never be ready for the security of guests by the following night.

Only temporarily mystified, he returned his thoughts to the character of the general and the idea of Deka becoming a concubine. "Is he a decent man?" Marai asked of the general, even though everything he sensed told him the man was not.

He thought of Deka. When he first met a bony, spider-like woman, she had been one of three women living in what was once his cousin Sheb's hut. She had offered her body to him as a reward for *saving* them from the men who had held them. She had been devoid of any emotion in the offer. Embarrassed, he had refused.

Later, when they had been transformed in the glowing pod filled with the crystalline forms of the Children of Stone, she came to him again. That time, he had been shy. After that, she withdrew from him and even from the companionship of Naibe and Ariennu. She never approached him or any other man again.

"Will he treat them well?" the sojourner asked, but before the phrase was out of his mouth, he felt the answer come to him.

"He might – if it suits him," Wserkaf quipped. "Walk with me though, before you decide to send his death through the sky also. You should know he's not so easily killed, just as *I* would not be so easily overtaken by you. All princes have a degree of native as well as trained skills, and *he* has been a chaotician since youth. You may not easily predict his true feelings or actions on any matter." Wserkaf walked with Marai to the servants' row with the platters, put them down quietly, and left. This time, no servant stirred.

The Inspector handed him a worn, dark brown cloak to wear. When he put it on, he saw that it was miserably short on him, but generous enough to hide his silvery hair from any late-night passers-by. Marai quelled the second rising of rage at the situation. The more he learned, the less inclined he was to hear the rest. *If this "general" is hurting my ladies in any way, he is doomed.*

"It's not good, Wse. I still can't feel them. I should be able to." He tried to sense the women again by bowing his head and casting out a silent cry for them, only to realize he still couldn't sense them through his own Child Stone. The "One Heart" link he had forged between the Children of Stone, the women, and himself had been mysteriously severed. "I feel other resistance at work in addition to Great One, so you'd best tell me about this general before I start making things up.

"Well, Prince Maatkare Raemkai has a nasty temper to him and a strange, cruel manner," the Inspector had gathered up a few random items to put in a basket that could be slung over his friend's shoulder, "but he's a bright tactician, and an excellent hunter and warrior. No man of Kemet looks finer, but sometimes things happen that can get in the way of the finest ambitions."

Soon, the two men had gone down the steps and headed into the path outside the walls of the Inspector's estate. One of Wserkaf's servants walked ahead of them, lighting their path but distant enough to miss the conversation.

"Seven years ago, the King even declared him his son, but he soon fell out of favor."

"Declared him son, but he's not his son?" Marai paused, one eyebrow raised in wonder. "If the King declared him his son, then why am I just now learning of him? What did this man do?"

"As children, all of us played in Our Father's yard and studied with our teachers in his plaza, but Maatkare Raemkai was about ten years younger and seldom with us. Soon, his father began to train him to one day take over the southern campaign and after that we didn't see him as much. Still, I heard Our Father Menkaure loved him and would deny him nothing. This young prince became a consort of the widow of

Menkaure's son Kuenre, who had no child. Our Father adopted him and allowed her to claim him as consort. Meryt pushed to give him the title of Crown Prince after that," Wserkaf shuddered, the recitation of the story wakening painful memories. "I always knew Great One was behind bringing him to Ineb Hedj to re-introduce him to her."

"Goddess, wait," Marai halted them. "Why did I just hear of this? A princess named Meryt?" he looked down at the Inspector in disbelief.

"Princess Merytites was Our Father's daughter, older than Khentie by only a year. From birth, she was the joyous one and Khentie the more studious. She was the first one designated 'Daughter of the God' and 'Mistress of the Sycamore'. She and the General Maatkare Raemkai desired each other from the instant they met, but theirs was a stormy and passion filled bed, so much so that it became unsavory and embarrassing to the rest of the royal family. It ended badly less than two years later. Great Menkaure has been keeping Maatkare on distant missions and distracted with women, since his daughter –" Wserkaf's voice trailed, bringing up the next unpleasant memory "– killed herself. She put her breast bands about her throat and leapt from their upper porch one afternoon. It was thought she may have been drunk."

Marai stood in stunned silence, sorting what he'd been told. "If that young princess *did* commit suicide, then there was truly no one to blame. That this young prince was sent away means he was at least suspected of more. It doesn't make sense. "If he had in any way *caused* her death, with her being the daughter of the King, justice would have been instant, unquestioning, and fatal." The sojourner knew that no excuse or reason would have had time to come to his lips. "You'll have to explain to me why this man is still breathing then," the sojourner almost laughed but stifled his reaction.

"One word," Wserkaf replied as he urged his companion to continue walking. "Hordjedtef. And there's no peace between Khentie and Maatkare either. She and her sister were close all their lives; as children and as young women in the temple of Hethara, as sisters of womb blood and the divine arts. She will, even now, resist attending events where Prince Maatkare is present. It is also why Great Wife Khammie remains in her own estate caring for her own mother and not remaining with Our Father."

Marai paused. A thought had struck him. With a sharp intake of air, he faced South to send a prayer composed of the women's names. At first, nothing returned, but then a memory of something the old man had said: *You are so full of passion no one could resist you or contain you – my own heir.*

And that's who the bastard is. Marai now realized that Hordjedtef had almost spoken about Maatkare that day, but had stopped himself at the word 'heir'. He remembered the sensation of a snuffling hound at the elder's side. Out of the corner of his eye, he had seen the vaguely formed image of a medium-sized but muscular black hunting dog with a grey, brushy wolf tail and glowing green eyes. He had thought it was a spirit animal or familiar. That watching sensation came to him with a quiet and powerful snarl tonight.

"Your wife never believed her sister would kill herself, did she – not even on accident?" Marai turned his attention back to Wserkaf.

"Not at all," the Inspector urged Marai down the path again. "There was talk for a while of it, but Princess Meryt never suffered from that kind of despair, and she was quite disciplined even in a drunken state." The Inspector continued as the two men walked. "She had miscarried twice in a short while during her intimacy with this young prince, but she, like our Great Father, liked drowning her regrets or any other harsh emotion in strong drink. Then too, Princess Mereyt and Maatkare would rage and fight as if they despised each other, often coming to blows. This was always followed by a disgusting show of weeping apologies and blistering passion. It was said this happened quite a bit by their servants."

"Miscarried from his bad behavior?" Marai felt a grumble of disgust at the unknown man rising.

"No. Other factors I think, but it soured things. She wanted to cast blame on him and there was a strong rumor they fought over it. Her last day he had been drunk, cursing and threatening. She ran out of the bedchamber and a strap of her gown caught on her neck. Maatkare said she had jumped from the stone rail at their porch – that he tried to get to her but could not grasp or reach her without further strangling her neck. The rumors were darker – spoken by a servant – that his young highness had pushed her from his porch and the straps had been on her neck like a lead for a cow.

The King had been nearby and ran in to help when he heard the servants calling out. The Prince was halfway over the rail sawing at the straps by that time, but when she had been cut down, she lived only long enough to die in her father's arms. Poor Father Menkaure was never the same after that. His heart broke. Maatkare was banished for a short time, but has since proven himself as a model leader and indispensable to the militia he leads. Hordjedtef urged the King, over time, to believe that young Maatkare was the thwarted hero; that he tried but could not save her."

Marai continued strolling and listening to Wserkaf as he contemplated the dark story of strife in the royal houses. He sensed that the servant who bore the tale vanished and then he visualized someone hastening the man to crocodiles at the river's edge. The Inspector continued:

"He married his concubine and remanded himself to the temples of Wepwawet for a short while, but even there he was judged worrisome and more fit to lead a living militia than to guide the souls of the dead. Now he has three strapping and pretty children, but the woman he married has come to despise him and her children are only interested in what plunder or riches he brings them when he returns from his campaigns. It's said he is in a constant state of thirst for varieties of women almost as much as he craves the hunt, drink, and the prospects of battle. It's really a miserable household. Servants are constantly begging to come out of their service."

Wserkaf paused and stood still as if he wanted to say more but didn't dare.

"And?" Marai turned and stared him down. "Go on. There's something else, isn't there?"

"Indeed," Wserkaf sighed, defeated. "That box containing your Ntr stones? Because he took the women and their things, Maatkare has those, and worse for me he managed to get his hands on my leftward wdjat."

Marai tensed, considering once again the idea of bringing death up the river to wherever the young general was camped in distant Ta-Seti, but then chuckled and shaded his eyes in his hand.

"That *is* something else then, isn't it? Another thing on top of ten, I see," he whispered and at the same moment realized the lasting effects of his "death" of three months still toyed with his physical form. "I'm not worried about the Children of Stone. I've witnessed them self-protect. It just," he shook his head, "doesn't make sense. I don't *even* know why this prince isn't lying crisp on the sands of Ta-Seti or, even better yet, face down in the river in front of us." He continued to follow the Inspector as the priest resumed walking, but stayed out of the light of the lamp the man held out in front of them as he led the way.

"Hordjedtef told me once that he had learned many of the words of the language the Ntr speak from his old master, Djedi. I was taught the phrases about calmness and peace, so that I could alleviate your fears if they arose – and yes, at first I was ordered to befriend you by him, but he didn't understand that I would develop true trust and fealty to you. Be that as it may be, I'm convinced there's another word, spell, or device at play here that one combines in a whispered or wished utterance. The word *nau* seems to resonate to me."

Marai paused, uncomfortable. The child stone in his brow tingled.

That, he thought. *If it is one of the words of a spell the old man knows, the rest of the words, if he knows them, might have been the way he slowed me down, blocked me from the women, and gained control of the stones they possess. Not good. That he's teaching it to his subordinates is even worse. When the young Ta-Seti sesh showed up and said what he did, I thought the stone would grind itself out of my head. Why Hordjedtef would have taught a scribe-trainee the stronger phases and yet not teach them W'se, his closest protégé, makes no sense. Maybe he knew before I even met him that one close to him would betray him and so he never told him. Wonder if W'se understands it was about control, not readiness for wisdom.* A different whisper sounded below his thoughts; intended to answer.

Not words,

yet alliances and energies

used by the one sought.

"Wait," Marai interrupted, putting his hand on the priest's shoulder. "The Children don't speak in words or use spells among themselves. They communicate in 'knowings' – instant knowledge. Any language they create is just for us poor humans who cannot speak to them this way. It was another reason they came to me. I 'talked' to my sheep. It was just a bleat here and there – different tones."

"Well, whatever the truth is, he taught *some* words to me and has doubtlessly taught others to Prince Maatkare to aid in his control of the women. If you go to him, you should expect he will use the same utterances on you. And because he has *all* the women, my wdjat, and the box of ntr stones, he's bound to try them as well," Wserkaf sighed dismally.

The men stood on the path within sight of the lagoon. In the light of the quarter-moon, the boats tethered there showed as dark shapes on a still, flat surface. A few men were seated near the dock playing senet for beads. Most boatmen wouldn't work at night for fear of the river demons, but with the King's death, a few decided to stay attentive for early boating needs. Dawn would be arriving in a few hours to drive away the evil spirits that lurked on the water at night.

Stepping quickly for a moment, Wserkaf saw his own boatmen among them and told the man carrying their light to go ahead and inform the men at the dock that they would need a boat.

"It was my fault the wdjat got away from me, but I wasn't thinking clearly that day," the Inspector continued. "The Lady Ariennu took it from me when I brought Naibe to Shepseskaf's house. I knew, but I *let* her take it because I was beginning to suspect something worse than Great One's solution for you was in the works. It was as if a spirit was telling me it wasn't going to be safe in my house or even on my neck anymore, and I never took it on my duty. Great One had always wanted control of it, and lately I'd caught him staring at it as if he coveted it once again."

The Inspector glanced at the sky and urged Marai to pick up his pace.

"The sky should soon begin to get' lighter behind us. At dawn they start with the purification. I don't know if I'll have time to get back.

Marai placed his hand upon the Inspector's shoulder and breathed out again to calm himself.

"Are you well?" Wserkaf asked.

"I just —" the sojourner found a low wall that ran along the opposite side of the lagoon path. He stumbled dizzily and sat, head in his hands and worried about the lasting effect of the spells and poisons. "We came so far, the ladies and I did. We *trusted* the Children, but I wonder now. Are they abandoning us before we even complete the task?"

"The lotus petals sometimes fall unbidden," Wserkaf consoled his friend and sat with him. "Those you choose to step out on sometimes dislodge the petal nearby."

See, my sweet man. See the hidden thing.

It was Ari's voice. He knew Wserkaf sensed it too.

"Lady Ariennu's voice; here in my heart," the Inspector gasped.

"Ari. Where are you? Call to me so I can hear and come to you," Marai's aching voice spoke just above a whisper. He closed his eyes, not even realizing he had drifted into a semi-conscious state.

A thing hidden, because —

She sounded quiet to both men, but her spirit-voice had a bloodless and different tone to it as if she was sleeping and had come to him in a dream. Both Wserkaf and Marai sensed the day the wdjat was taken. It was when he had brought Naibe to Shepseskaf's house.

"She'll be stronger soon. No, Highness, don't worry so much. Naibe's stronger than the rest of us. She just doesn't know it yet. It's not so bad here with Prince Shepseskaf. At least it won't be if they think she can have a child for him. I know she wanted Marai's child, but with him gone I've told her maybe this will be the best answer; bear a young prince for the family." Ariennu said and pressed Wserkaf in her arms again.

Marai envisioned her hand slipping to the Inspector's throat to take the wdjat, but there was something else. At the last instant, when she kissed his eyes, she pushed a small leather purse into his hands.

Take this, until we can all be together. Think of it as a trade. These are the eight my Marai told me to keep safe, so use them wisely.

Marai realized that was the reason Wserkaf hadn't worried about the wdjat; he had hostages. She was asking him without words to keep the eight safe. At least, if he could hide them, they would be out of Hordjedtef's hands.

"Will you want me to keep these still?" Wserkaf showed Marai the narrow leather purse in his palm, then handed it to him.

"You had –" Marai suddenly understood why he had been able to see Ariennu's adventures of the past few months. He had seen Naibe because of the veil, but the bag contained the eight child stones that Ariennu had set aside. She had handled them for a few days before giving them to the Inspector to take on his duty instead of the wdjat. It also explained why he had felt nothing from Deka. Marai wanted to kiss the priest, because it was a way in; past the blocking spells. Now that the women had been whisked away to Ta-Seti, these stones were all that was left of their essence in Ineb Hedj.

Wserkaf looked at the stars and the position of the moon, then glanced narrowly at Marai again.

"Is this your doing?" he pointed at the sky. "You slowing time again? We've taken long. Feels like it should be near day."

"And yet, it isn't." Marai admitted, understanding exactly what had happened this time. "Perhaps time isn't slower, but the stream of the tale telling is faster than starlight."

He saw the Inspector mouth '*but how*' – and then asked another favor.

"Once more, friend, while they prepare the boat" he lay the closed bag on his right thigh and took Wserkaf's hand to place it on the unopened bag. "There are still so many things I must know, such as how my women were beguiled, who did it, and how in the goddess name they were spirited away from the King's household. You already told me you were on your duty, so unless someone told you the tale, this is the only way to know."

"You're too weak. Another trance could unhinge you," the Inspector protested. "Working time's illusion like this and then seeing through it into the past and into another's life is madness; pure madness," Wserkaf started to pull his hand away.

Marai reached to touch the Inspector's temple and replaced the man's hand on the bag.

The trance-like feeling swam through both men at once, enveloping them.

Wserkaf settled into his calmness and emptied his thoughts, believing he heard Marai's voice in the distance.

If I die tonight,
I care not.
This knowing is for both of us.
If I do not wake tonight,
you will know what to do.

Marai slowly breathed out again. He saw it was afternoon in a wide room with a few beds. Ari was there, looking in a mirror.

GOING FORTH BY DAY

Chapter 26: Preparations and Discoveries

Ariennu put a shine on the bronze mirror with a scrap of linen. Naa, the youngest of the concubines, had given it to her. The still water in the central pool had always given Ari *some* idea of her reflection, but a shiny mirror would reveal less noticeable imperfections. She wanted to be sure her face was perfect.

The big "send-away" for that General Maatkare who took Deka is tonight. Almost all the dignitaries in Ineb Hedj and their families are coming. Maybe he'll bring her and then we can see why she's been so quiet when the two of us are all but screaming these past weeks.

She'd heard enough fragments of juicy gossip about the general to make her think Deka had gone silent because she was guarding her interest. She learned the first night that he was Count Hordjedtef's grandson even though there was little more than passing resemblance between them. As much as she disliked the old man, she was only mildly concerned over any similarity between the two men.

Today, she overheard enough snickers about him to make her want to hide behind one of the drapes between the rooms so she could listen much more carefully.

"Ooh! Go with Highness Maatkare if I am not chosen by our Great Majesty tonight? I know he would take me, but I think not, sister!" Ari had heard one of the women speak in low secretive tones. "I like being able to walk to my room later, not lie in the floor like a dirty rag!"

"Ha!" Ari heard another. "The man is a demon – on and off his couch! He's trouble and it goes much worse for a woman if she begs for mercy – you know that. You could die with a stupid grin frozen on your head and knees that forgot each other's names before the bitter end! You know I've heard he even…" the women moved out of range, laughing and teasing to Ari's great disappointment. She didn't really *need* to hear more. She already had enough of a case of thigh sweats over the Prince.

GOING FORTH BY DAY

Mmm. I wonder what that meant, she thought. *Maybe time for me to see about him, then. I could use a good and forceful one now and again among all these respectful men. A challenge.*

Moments later, Ariennu cornered young Naa as she left the privy, grabbed her arm, and casually whirled her back around to a more private area behind the enclosed benches over the clay-lined cistern for a "sisterly" chat.

"So, tell me about this pretty man who comes here tonight," she asked the young concubine – in case he should come to me. Is that even allowed?"

Ari didn't care if it was allowed. There were storage rooms and back halls, chases through estate gardens in the middle of any celebration that might not be so guarded.

The girl's eyes popped open. She glanced around as if she had become worried someone would hear, then moved closer. "Oh, don't let Our Father hear you call him pretty," she cautioned. "It's – well he's –" she stalled.

"Hmm?" Ari knew the news had to be excellent if the girl was blushing *this* heartily. "What do *you* know about him?"

"He lived in this house until his own was built; before I was here. It was before the bad things started."

"So, are you going to tell me about it? I'm getting tired of you ladies hushing it up around Little One and me as if we still don't belong here," Ari folded her arms and tapped her foot, irritated.

The girl hesitated, looked around, and once she was certain no one else could hear her speak, she began.

"Father Menkaure-kha had another daughter once who was the *true* divine one, they said. Everything she did, her songs, her dances, her celebrations, and even her lovemaking was magical. She *was* a young Hethara, they said, and he loved her so very much."

Another woman approached. Naa led Ariennu out to the garden and as far away from others as she could go without the guards coming to question them.

"Her divine brother, Prince Kuenre, died and she had no child by him. Not long after that, she discovered Prince Maatkare Raemkai and told Our Majesty she liked him so much that she wished for him to take the *pschent* crown next. He *was* blood royal as Great One's grandson, through his daughter, so it was allowed. Our Father adopted him as son and named him Princess Meryt's brother by decree. They had a palace built nearby, right away, but then she lost two babies by him and then one day she suddenly died. After that, Prince Maatkare was sent away far to the south. No one would speak of how she died, but I heard some say she hanged herself."

Ariennu frowned, feeling an odd sensation of foreboding in her belly and upper back. *Happy? Merry? No one like that kills themselves. And that man was sent away afterwards? Did he kill her?* she wondered. *Nah. No one kills a princess and lives to come back in* any *kind of favor. I wonder, though. Maybe it's a secret to keep for now, but maybe a later one to be shouted from the roof.*

Ariennu had never heard the story of this princess spoken in the palace. Naibe had said something about feeling the spirit of a goddess whose presence made the King sad when she first arrived, and one night Ari had sensed another feminine entity but hadn't thought much about it until now.

"We're not supposed to talk about it, *at all*," Naa urged, "and *do* never ask Majesty about it. It really upsets him so," she emphasized, suddenly worried the tale would be spread and she would be named as the source.

"Hmmm. Well, I could be persuaded to keep a secret like that. But, why should I after the way most of you treat us?" Ariennu turned to go back to the sleeping rooms, but as she did she heard the girl grumble in frustration.

"Come with me, then," Naa caught up with Ari and led her by the hand.

Well, something *bad happened*, Ariennu sensed, following the girl to see what she would offer for her silence. *Damn me. I can live in a royal palace, pet the King, and still be a thief! I should make these deals more often.*

"Everyone I talk to says Majesty changed," Naa explained. "He buried her in a beautiful wooden casket in the shape of the divine cow and had it covered with gold. Every year he marks the feasts and anniversaries with hundreds of garlands of flowers in her temple." She took Ariennu to her bed and handed her the bronze mirror.

Ari decided she wasn't going to ask the King anything and she would warn Naibe not to ask either, but this made the contract sweeter. It was a good mirror. Although Naa had been nice to them recently, it was quite possible she was setting a fine trap at someone's request. All the conversation might have been a fiction fed to them so they would ask forbidden questions and cause the King to banish them. The mirror, if the girl wanted it back, would keep her honest.

"So, he's changed?" Ari insisted on continuing. "How so?"

"This party. In times past, he would never have hosted the party for his Highness *here*. He has always been sad when they are together. He thinks of his daughter when he sees him," the young woman looked around fearfully. "Now, no more, please," she begged pointedly.

Ariennu dimly remembered the King the night she went with Prince Shepseskaf. He'd been almost too drunk to sit upright. His back had been turned ever so slightly away from the young general as though he didn't want to look directly at him. It confirmed what the girl had said. He *didn't* enjoy the man's company. This party represented a drastic change because the King had invited him to have his party at the palace and apparently had even looked forward to the celebration.

"A word, Lady ArreNu," Ariennu was distracted from remembering her afternoon conversation with the girl by a man's elderly warble. He was calling into the entrance of the women's apartments from the tunnel that led to the adjacent sunlit courtyard.

Ah, Count Prince Hordjedtef again. The man is relentless! she grumbled. Prince Hordjedtef being here this early in the afternoon truly annoyed her. Soon, the women's rooms would be bustling with visiting female guests and their servants; there would be no rest or privacy once that began. Visiting women always came into the women's common to refresh themselves and exchange gossip before they joined the other guests in the main plaza.

At first, she pretended she didn't hear the Great One call her name. There were so many other things she preferred to think about, such as the man's grandson. She remembered a delicious and tempting thought-statement he sent to her as he left with Deka; that there would still be plenty of him left for her.

Since that night weeks earlier, neither she nor Naibe had sensed anything from their former sister. Deka, Ariennu decided, would have to answer for her silence. She wasn't dead, sick, or injured because Ari knew her Child Stone would certainly have informed them of that. Only stillness and serene peace returned when either she or Naibe spoke Deka's name into the universe.

It was time to provoke a response. She would openly *compete* with her for the Prince. His roving eye and complete faithlessness was legendary from what she had heard. For that, she needed to look flawless and stunning enough to attract him and fine enough to irritate her old companion into taking a stand.

Ah, but everyone loves a good cat fight! she thought, remembering the fights they used to enjoy in the wilderness camp. *Like old times. Her beautiful man might even...*

The old man's voice sounded again, irritated. "Lady ArreNu! Do you hear me speak?"

This time, she tensed at the sharpness of his voice, let out a miserable sigh, and turned her head to the distant entryway where the old man stood.

Men aren't supposed to come back here, she thought to herself. In just this short time living here, however, Ari had learned that the Great One went wherever he wanted and would probably follow a woman into the privy outside the large sleeping room unless specifically asked *not* to do so.

"*What* do you want?" she snapped, then decided she knew what he wanted. *He's coming to complain about our healing on Our Father. No matter except for that one bad day he's gotten better. No matter he's taken to us as sisters — I've heard him warning him plenty. 'You are allowing too much familiarity with these. It's not safe. It's unheard of. You tempt the closing of the prophecy now and to not defy it? Only women of our own blood or family must enjoy such easy treatment. These ka't of a scoundrel have settled in far too quickly. The tall one should have been thrashed for her impudence in bringing the younger one to you while you suffered in your head and heart. Instead, you welcome them?' Pah!*

The old man was right. It wasn't without notice that King Menkaure found it so easy to relax in their presence.

They think heka. I've heard the whispers — especially after we went walking with him arm in arm about the city with no royal guards around him — just one or two — and over to the place where his Eternal Pyr rises from the ground. So lovely it is! Not so tall as the others, but he showed us the plans for the colored bands on it. It'll be special.

Continuing to ignore the elder, she dreamily thought of the jealousy of the other concubines and had threatened the one who started a rumor that she and Naibe were chanting over him.

Speaking Kinacht, the ignorant slug. And Our Father wanted us to speak it to him so he could learn it better. Old man probably started that one himself since he can't speak it.

The best part of their stay was that just the previous night, the King enjoyed a full night of peaceful sleep without his usual spiced wine. He officially claimed he was no longer worried about outwitting the gods by staying awake. He proclaimed that if the gods were truly wise, they would understand what he had been doing for the past six years and should have already come to take him. He was ready to battle them for his life if he needed to. That was the *real* reason he had invited Prince Hordjedtef's grandson to celebrate his send-away at the palace, Ariennu realized. He felt safe from the curse.

That's on us and he knows it. He's lost the grip he has on the King in just a few weeks.

Outside the women's quarters, the old man beckoned at Ariennu from a distance. When she finally acknowledged him, a silly smirk filled his ancient face. "Oh, I *do* apologize, Lady Ariennu, but I need you to come with me for a moment," he motioned for her to follow him to the main courtyard by the large reflection pool. She knew he had more in his thoughts than the enjoyment of the tranquil blue sesen blossoms floating there.

Ariennu put down the mirror, smoothed her hair, and quickly tied a ribbon around it before she followed the high priest. As she trailed him, she absent-mindedly looked around the pool for Naibe-Ellit. She spied her, laughing and singing a child's song, then engaging in a hand clap game with a group of the youngest serving girls, much like a little girl herself.

The priest indicated the elder woman should sit beside him. When they had seated themselves, the able-bodied groom who had followed him placed a wooden chest near the old man's seat cushion. He dismissed the man, then reached to tug the chest closer to them.

Ariennu's eyes narrowed even further.

Oh, goddess bless it, I see you didn't come on any chance visit. Remembering her manners with annoyance she didn't even try to hide, she spoke:

"I see the day is a good one for this celebration. But are you not early, Your Great Highness?"

"I trust you are *truly* enjoying your time and your new tasks here?" he began. She knew he'd read her resentment and had ignored it.

"I think His Majesty is feeling better, yes. You see his color is good now," she answered, knowing it had been *her* skill in healing touch, equal to that of his physicians, that was stimulating his interest in healthy food and proper rest.

"Perhaps this is true, but do not confuse this temporary rally as his complete cure," Hordjedtef's lips pursed in a vain but mildly offended expression. "His Majesty is strong as the bull of his name, Lord Kha-Ket denotes, and his will to appear mighty is even more so. Only those truly close to him understand the *weight* on him that is at the root of his suffering," he remarked. *For instance, a good and mighty warrior for a son; one who inspires growth and fertility in his land.*

Ari knew she heard the old man's thoughts correctly and that led to ire coiling in her guts. She understood now that this evening's party was likely his idea about presenting the infamous grandson in a favorable light once again.

You manipulating bastard. Everything about this old man's motive was suddenly clear to her.

GOING FORTH BY DAY

Though ancient, the high priest was still very much the power behind the golden throne. She knew the legends. He had never been king, though he should have been. Failing that, he had been an invincible force for many kings before he had attached himself to the ailing monarch she and Naibe currently tended.

You would have been too cruel as a king. Maybe your sister knew that, Ari mused, hoping he read her thoughts. *No one means anything more to you than senet pieces moved around life's playing board. You work people so they will always look fondly on you and no one else. For that, you had to kill Marai before the Children of Stone had finished making us strong as him. If you'd let him be opened, that would have brought us along. You wouldn't have been able to control us. Still, if you think you can control me, old man, you've made a mistake,* Ari's thoughts whispered. She made no attempt to hide that portion of them. *Marai never controlled me, he celebrated me – it was his way.* She wanted to wish Hordjedtef out of the seat into which he was settling when she thought of the third thing that she missed the most, next to the warmth of Marai's love and the openness of his heart. The difference between the two men was intolerable to her.

I see you; her thoughts rang. *Just say something else, anything else. I will slap you into some worse regret of me.*

"Weight? You mean the *wait* on Our Majesty, as in '*wait* on him to die'," she whispered under her breath. "Murdering bastard," she inspected her nails, suddenly unable to look him in the eye. "You had something to tell me, Your Highness? If not, I would rather visit a ripe privy than sit with you this morning!" She shuffled, positioning herself to leap from the pillow cushion by the pool and storm back to the privacy of her own room.

Hordjedtef's eyes transformed into reddened, bird-like slits. "Still a vile little temper and a wicked tongue?" he reached for the chest, "and still blaming *me* for your former consort's comeuppance, I see. You *do* know it was *I* who had Our Majesty's ear about bringing you and your sisters' aid. It was *I* who asked that he not cast you three into the alley, as *your* manners alone to me say he *should* have decreed." He lifted the lid of the box slowly. "I understand the Ta-Seti woman who came with you has truly charmed our young Prince Maatkare Raemkai, and only unfortunate situations have prevented the young Kina-Ahna dancer the status she deserves. And look at yourself;

almost as respected as any of our wise women. Why do you complain against me so?" he asked, a sing-song but petulant tone in his voice.

Ariennu bowed her head, almost ashamed. *He's right. I don't need to do this. Not now. Things are good. I just wish he wasn't here.* If the King recovered and totally defeated the prophecy he had received at Buto six years ago, perhaps she and Naibe might become more to him than gentle healers. For most women, especially former commoners, a life as part of a royal family like this was a dream come true.

When she thought of Marai, however, and saw him in her various memories of their journey together, everything she knew now was still too painful. He filled her thoughts far too often. Her first image of him as she groveled in the wadi hut long ago haunted her dreams so strongly that she woke at night weeping, even though she had vowed to be hard enough never to cry over him. The gentle image of the way he held her the day she sought to conquer him, and the way he encouraged her heart to open, was still too much to bear now that all of it was gone. On so many nights she saw him. He would be so real in her dreams that she almost felt he was still alive. Every instinct in her heart *told* her he was alive, but somehow trapped and unable to move or come home.

No! that image shouted and screamed her name. *It's* not *over.* She knew her life with him had so much more story that needed to be written before the stars all over the world fell from the sky.

The priest cleared his throat, severing Ari from her thoughts of Marai. The carved box that housed the Children of Stone was in his hands.

"Oh, you damned, you…" Ariennu hissed. She wanted to seize the box from him, even if the Children scattered everywhere. Instead, she looked away from him, but the familiar purr of the stones in the box beckoned her. Slowly, she turned her head again. "I see. You want me to help you *use* them," she mocked, a slight smile at the edge of her mouth. "Well, I can't. Seems like you got rid of the wrong person a *little too soon*, then, didn't you?" Ari knew the younger priest had railed against his senior on the day she, Naibe, and Deka had been collected. They hadn't been able to use the Children of Stone *that* day. She wanted to mock him and remind him of that now, but felt it would only make an increasingly bad situation worse.

"So, you claim to know *nothing?*" Hordjedtef re-stated, his voice rose in a doubt-filled question. "Yet, here you are working your healings as well as any skilled and trained physic?" the count sniveled. "You seem to be able to identify tinctures and herbs better than *many* who have studied for years. What was it you did for a livelihood, dear, that gave you the knowledge of a prophetess? What exactly did you learn to prophesy through those several devotees you encountered in the road at night?"

"Now you insult me!" Ariennu snapped. "I listen and hear well enough these days. I know it is your wise women who have always taught men in exchange for their protection. I know, too, that *some* of these men in times past and even *now* have learned to abuse this knowledge. We have greater untapped knowledge to share. As a Great One of Djehuti, *you* should…" she snarled and faced the priest, then closed her eyes. She was too angry to speak. She wanted to keep shouting that men of his ilk stole knowledge of the woman ancestors and would, in time, claim to have invented it. She didn't have the chance to say it before the old priest continued.

"Preventing the growth of an unwanted child in the womb, or ceasing it entirely, and other savory, gentle arts, my dear? How appropriate for a woman such as yourself who claims to ally with the creator of all life yet attempts to manipulate what life comes?" the priest continued, honey dripping in his voice.

Give me strength, Ashera mine, give me strength… Ariennu gasped silently, wanting to jump up and kick the elder priest until either he fell silent or tried to cast a spell on her. She would cheerily twist it on him, then roll his suffering body into the sesen pool and… "Marai was going to teach us even *more* things when he returned, after you priests were supposed to teach *him* how to use them himself, but you ordered he be destroyed and don't deny you did. So, *you lose!*" a chortle formed in her throat instead. "I *should* laugh."

The high priest simmered at her sharp remark.

"Bites like a bad dog, doesn't it," she felt victorious laughter rise inside her soul. "Seems like your dear Prince Wserkaf was…" She was about to say 'right', but the high priest grabbed her hand and stuck it on top of the mass of stones in the carved box. They shimmered beneath her hand.

Touching them, Ariennu sucked in a shocked breath of air. *He has me do it for him. I must make him touch them.* She thought of the boy Salim, whose hands had horribly burned when he tried to steal the Child Stones the night Marai and Naibe first shared their love. *Strong! How is he this strong, to hold me faster than a young warrior in an arm-wrestling match?*

Hordjedtef carefully mouthed an utterance, commanding the Children of Stone to a quiet and watchful rest.

Ariennu almost saw it. At first, she wasn't sure what she was looking at because her eyes swept past it whenever she tried to clear them and to focus on a dark thing riding on the old man's hand. Each time, a vortex of energy drew her thoughts down like water draining through a bung hole. *There. A ring, or something on his middle finger. Nasty black thing like a twist of black hide. Awww… can't look at it!* When she tried to stare at it, the sight of it turned her stomach and made her tear her gaze away. Her eyes couldn't send the image to her thoughts. She felt its cramping, cold energy as his hand rested on hers, like snow from the northern hills beyond her homeland had lodged under her hand and seized her fingers.

She heard the Great One's thoughts: *Calm, calm. Blessing of the first time's sweetness of light to you. Do no harm. Gently rest, in Her abiding name.*

Ariennu felt the rush of ecstasy that flooded from the Children going through her hand and up into her arm. The light from the stones grew stronger as they recognized her touch and a dizzy feeling floated through her entire body. Marai and everything he had ever been to her held and touched her once again. All the joy of being lost in his strong arms that incredible afternoon when she embraced his pure joy came back to her in an utterly sensual rush. She fought the pleasure, keenly understanding that the Children would want to communicate to her through sensuality. Passion was the emotion that drew them to Earth eons ago. It was the way they *spoke* to each of their hosts now. Her eyes silvered. She wanted to cry out in the intense pleasure of the feel of Marai inside her, but she remained quiet as the Children of Stone lifted her thoughts and carried them to a strange dark box lost deep in the blackness of a forgotten chamber. Everything was still, silent, and lifeless. Marai's body had become pale, cold, and very hard like stone itself as he lay there.

Oh damn, Ari cried out internally. She tried to fight her way back from the dark and keep her pleasure hidden because the old man desired to control her with it. *He knows about the pleasure aspect, dammit! I wanted to see where he lay dead, and this is it. I know it! I know it now. Lose me in the silence. Lose me now!* she cried, but suddenly realized: *Wait, you told me there was no body to see; that my Marai had been burnt to dust in the light of ultimate knowledge. If that's so, why am I seeing this? Goddess, you can't know what I see!* Ariennu refocused her energy into blurring all that she saw with rainbow prisms. She sighed heavily in joy so Hordjedtef would think it was merely the growing thunder through the depth of her womb. Then, she relaxed and let the vision come.

Her shadow stretched out along the surface of a black polished stone tomb. She ached in pleasure, but sobbed like a child. The top of the place where he lay dissolved in the steam of the memory of their passion. For those moments, he was alive again. *Aset. Oh Great Goddess I am Aset to bring and nurture life out of my dead womb to revive his seed in me.* She felt faint with ecstasy and saw nothing but blurs. *It's too late to go to him, too late to revive him, too late to bring Asar back from his untimely death.* Her free hand touched her brow. She noticed the Child Stone had risen.

Hordjedtef saw it too. "But they *do* speak to you, and they will *continue* to speak to you as they have just let me see," he said. "I can *see* when a vision has formed behind someone's eyes, even yours," the confidence in his voice increased. "At first, I thought you were nothing, some tired wastrel of a ka't as you would have most think. I didn't know your duty, your sacred gift, but now I do," his eyes thinned a little more.

Goddess, he can't know what I saw. If this isn't a fantasy, Divine Aset, please open my eyes to the truth but blind him to what you showed me, Ariennu blinked. The servants moved about, as they cleaned for the party. The only thing she had managed to keep private was the spiritual struggle between the two of them, which the Count was coming close to winning. She sensed that the others in the open plaza merely thought the two of them were sitting calmly, deep in reflection. Instead, her struggle against the show of pleasure left her trembling in more ecstasy.

The presence of the water bird overtook the visage of the elder gentleman. She had not seen it before, but sensed when it happened. Now, she saw it clearly: the down-curved dark beak and shiny black eyes. The sight of his speckled feathers horrified her so greatly that her concentration frayed, even though such a bird in real life would only annoy her before she kicked it out of her path.

"*You're* the secret keeper now, aren't you, dear?" Hordjedtef seemed so satisfied at his discovery that he rocked backward but continued to hold her hand firmly in the box.

The sensations of pleasure continued to ripple through her body. Her nipples stiffened. Everything from her kuna-gate to the depths of her womb ached in joy. Between her clenched thighs, all had melted into throbbing, helpless waves of pleasure. He was winning.

"Oh," he quipped, "you may *wish* to keep your secrets from me." He continued, boyishly entertained as he studied her physical response. "And maybe you will try just that, but at some point, these ones in the box will whisper to you where the other eight I seek are and they will link your thoughts to them. At that time, I will learn it from you, if I but simply speak their name again."

For a moment, Ariennu perceived the roaring dark sound of a word: *'Auuuuu.'* *No, it wasn't right, 'Nauuuuu'*. The darkest sound she had ever sensed flooded up from the pit of some hidden abyss in her heart. *Nauuuuuu*. "Eight?" Ari gasped, open-mouthed in a combination of passion, terror, and anger. "Eight what? I don't know of eight," she tried to free her hand in vain. The ecstasy and whatever had come into her hand through the dark ring-like thing on the high priest's middle finger stunned her with the memory of so much pleasure that all her strength to resist fled. The priest's words hammered inside her ears.

"Oh, but you *do* know very well. We *both* know there were seventy-eight that fell to earth, and that there are four of them now hosted within once mortal flesh, which should leave us seventy-four. I have somehow counted only sixty-six little stones," Hordjedtef's expression became at once calm and bland in satisfaction. "You knew how many there were when you came out of your house to see us. You are not a stupid woman despite your origin in the alleyways of Tyre. I have read your heart, in unguarded moments, and know of your life as a thief. Counting, cyphering, and even ways and numbers are not beyond your grasp. You indeed brought all remaining seventy-four of them but managed to hide eight from us. One was lost in the death of your sire, but soon enough the others will turn up with a reapplied and diligent search when we have divined how the others call out to it."

She felt his nails dig into her hand. The pain gave her a brief surge of freedom from his spell. She pressed his wrist once with her free hand that had an instant before touched the opalescent stone in her brow. Hordjedtef's hand bent in a spasm of pain. Ariennu quickly drew her own hand away and off the Child Stones. "And now you are lying to me most fiercely," she smirked..

The old man nursed his hand, amazed that she had broken free of his spell and the power of the ring on his finger.

"Perhaps everything you've said, even about my Marai, is a lie." Ariennu stated and then shook her head to clear it. She forced herself to her feet, still wobble-kneed from the fading sensations. "Now if there's nothing more you need to explain to me, I would like to check on His Majesty to see if he feels rested enough for this evening." She turned her back to him, still shuddering inwardly in horror at her inability to overcome the heka the elder priest had used when he questioned her. "You claim I know things; I tell you I *don't*. Maybe I'm lying to you too. But," she turned to look at him as he closed the box of stones and tucked it into the chest he'd brought, "you'll have to explain to me why it is you even *think* you have the right to ask me about the Ta-Ntr as you call them, other than greediness. You never explained to me or any of us why you need to lay hold of the Children of Stone. Can you answer that?" She smoothed her shift and went to the stair, then headed up to the King's guards to seek entry into his room.

The priest's eyes widened at the audacity of her question and at her leaving their exchange without being dismissed, but he didn't answer.

Something he wears on his finger. That's how he does it. I wonder what it is. Little ones? she asked her inner thoughts. A slight whisper returned. Ariennu glanced briefly, but saw the priest was preparing to leave. He had beckoned for his groom to help him rise.

Worry not.
It is hidden and forbidden

You will overcome it

Remove it from the fear

that gives it power

Another thought distracted her, as if the Child-Stone wanted her to stop thinking about the dark thing on Hordjedtef's finger.

Deka, a concubine? Incredible. And this priest's grandson is taken *with her, is he? Still no excuse for not sending so much as a* thought *to either of us after all we've been through.* She knows what we were and that we've gone back to it but with just less sickness and starving. To think of her not sharing something that juicy. I'll get her tonight, and then I'll use her pretty pet to get at the old man, too! She'll just have to step back while I work him. She *owes* us for her silence!

Ariennu turned at the top of the stairs, staring quietly back at the priest as he moved away from the pool. Her lips curled into a quiet sneer before she cleared to a cheerier expression and asked to see her King. When she heard talking from the King's chamber, she found he was deep in a conversation with his vizier "Neb".

He glanced up and saw Ari standing at full height so she could see above the guards. Winking and nodding at her, he acknowledged her and told her he was too busy to talk at the same time.

After she saw he was well, she turned and allowed the guards to escort her back to the women's area. She did like to check on the King, but in truth it had been a simple diversion to increase the distance between her and that horrid old priest. As she walked with the men, the Great One, who was apparently leaving the palace for a short while, passed beside her. The chest containing the box of Child Stones was tucked tightly under his servant's arm. She could not believe how smug he was and how innocently he walked away after what he had done to her.

Ari shielded her thoughts and made no direct eye-contact with Hordjedtef. In the comfort of her prismatic mask, she cursed him. *That man will die begging for mercy! First, he kills Marai, now he came to* me *with questions about the eight? And him gloating like some dung-eating keleb holding me down and cramming it to me! I need to speak into dear King Menkaure's heart. I need to tell him what happened today, but how could I even do that without seeming like a whining little child?* she grumbled to herself.

The encounter with Hordjedtef left Ariennu emotionally drained, which gave way to fatigue. *I should nap too,* she thought, then wearily trailed to her bed amid the fussing of the other concubines over the status of each other's hair and wigs. Completely uninterested in their banter, she sat hard on her frame bed, stretched out, and fell asleep.

Chapter 27: Arrivals

Ariennu woke with a start when the crowd of women and children in the room suddenly thickened. During the time she had slept a solid and dreamless nap, it had become late afternoon. As she returned from the privy, she stood for a short while by the doorway to the orchard and watched the noble children as they played. When their parents released them, they darted off to amuse themselves with the monkeys and hounds in the large yard. Some had little toys they had brought, others engaged in a stickball game and games of chase. Later in the evening, as the celebration wore on, the children would fall asleep in the women's area until the festivities ended. Naibe watched at the edge of the yard, too.

Oh, Little One, she laughed at the sight of Naibe watching the children so intently, but the sight saddened her. *How different would it have been for you if you had always been pretty and loved by men instead of used. Would you have married and had ten babies before your life was done? Would you have grown old in his arms? Would it have somehow been Marai?*

Once again, those other thoughts returned. *Marai should be here to see her laugh and play like this. This isn't right. None of this is right. Instead, he's gone. He's just a ghost now*, she shook her head and stared into the wide, green orchard of olive trees, fig bushes, and date trees.

When she broke away from that distraction, Ari saw Naibe had found a new little friend. A slim, light-brown-skinned boy who seemed about six or seven years old stood looking up at her. His head was closely shaved with a single braid looped and fastened to the side of his head with a single band in the fashion of little boys of Kemet. To Ari's surprise the child suddenly dropped forward from his waist as if he was about to do a handspring, but then began to walk on his hands instead. He wobbled as he righted himself and Naibe reached to catch him, but then as the child stayed in her embrace, he gained a smoky hue before he darted off behind a tree. He was gone like a dream.

As Ari watched, curious about the child, Naibe sauntered wearily to the rear entrance of the women's rooms. She paused for an instant, looked up, smiled at someone on one of the many balconies in the distance, and then came in to sit on her own bed for a last-minute rest.

"I hope you didn't wear yourself out playing like that, Baby One. It's going to be a long, hot night." Ariennu followed the young woman back to her bed, noticing Naibe's uncomprehending stare. Her quiet sigh turned suddenly reflective and sad.

"Oh, I'm fine. I was just walking and seeing the little ones play – wishing I'd had Marai's child. Mama, I miss him so much."

Ari bowed her head, "me too. I'm going to *get* that old high priest though, swear I will, even if I die doing it."

Naibe looked up at Ari, the edge of her light brown eyes turned golden in an indication of quiet ire. Her hands pressed into her lap. "I saw him sitting with you. Did something happen earlier?"

"Bastard is trying to make me tell him something about the Children," Ariennu stopped short of telling the young woman about his desire to know the location of the eight stones. "I fought him off for now, though," Ari bent closer to the younger woman to whisper. "Take a warning though. He wears this black thing on his hand that comes into a ring, Baby. It keeps the Child Stones from hurting him and makes it easy for him to get into our thoughts. Just stay away from him and don't try to look at the thing on his hand if he comes up to you or asks you something. Maybe if you don't look at it or try to block it out, it won't have the power to take you," Ari stopped. Her voice trailed off because she saw Naibe had stopped listening.

Both women lay back, oddly distracted by other thoughts. Ari wished for that small space of time that there were no eyes in the room because she would have kissed, caressed, and embraced the woman until they were both lost in sighs and comfort. Those thoughts hadn't come to her – to be with a woman – since the days when they were in the thieves' camp and the three would often pleasure each other to ease the mistreatment the men had made them endure.

Getting too lonely, though there's no shortage of 'el' in this place. Different hunger, I guess.

In a very short while, the celebration would commence. Ari knew she wanted to be free of everything but the essence of joy tonight. She didn't want Naibe's misty loneliness to make its usual inroads in that plan.

"Did you see Majesty looking at the children playing too?" Naibe asked her. "He was watching me a little from his rear porch. I think he might ask for me to come to him soon, now that he feels better."

"You and your little friend who walks on his hands, eh? Whose son was that?"

Naibe paused, a look of bewildered confusion on her face.

"Friend? How do you mean, Ari?" the young woman shivered. "I was by myself. There weren't any children who wanted to play with me. I was just watching them."

Ariennu frowned. She knew what she had seen and couldn't understand why Naibe would want to lie about a new young playmate.

"You saw a little boy? About how old?" Naibe mulled over what Ari said, mystified.

Ari rose and sorted out a carved bone comb from the girl's basket. She sat beside Naibe and began to pull her braids loose.

"Six or seven. You telling me I was seeing things?" Ari yanked at the young woman's hair gently.

"Oh. Him. I dreamed him up, MaMa." Naibe looked up, her large light-brown eyes rimmed with moisture that wanted to be tears again. "I was looking at the children play, and it made me sad again because I wanted to have a baby, a little boy, for Marai so very much. I used to talk to this little boy in my dreams when we were all living across the river. I knew back then he was waiting for my womb to make him. Sometimes, I even used to hear his voice back when Marai…" Her face fell. One tear drooled down her plump cheek.

Ariennu sat beside Naibe-Ellit to console her with an embrace. "Funny you said that. That man even had *me* wanting to make a baby for him before he left. *Me!* So, you're saying I saw into your secret the way you do with others? *I* gave that child a shape made of air?" she combed the girl's long wavy tresses and re-braided them tightly so they wouldn't come loose.

"Oh, not so tight, Ari," Naibe held her hand up to stop her. "I just want it done with one braid on the top. The rest of it just tie back with one ribbon so I can take it loose in case I decide to do a dance tonight," she reflected while Ari combed her long black hair out.. "About the boy, though. He *was* there, I guess, I just didn't think anyone else could see him. I told him I wouldn't be able to give him life anymore, but he tried to tell me not to be sad; that he would still come into me one day. You think it could mean he has chosen another to sire him, and not Marai?"

"Maybe," Ariennu shook her head, "and it's bound to happen sooner or later unless you're as barren as I am. Do you have the heart seeds I gave you?" Ariennu remembered the vision of the boy more clearly.

Naibe didn't answer.

Ari knew this meant Naibe hadn't eaten them, and probably wouldn't use anything stronger in the way of solving an unwanted pregnancy than the mild Acacia and honey pessary. To her, *any* child would be a gift of the goddess, even if it came about under dreadful circumstances.

"The boy I saw looked a little light-skinned to be made out of *these* men's seeds."

"Marai was lighter than them," she mumbled so quietly that only Ari would hear her. "Anyway, he came up to me and did this trick on his hands as well as a dancer might. Then, he saw I was sad and he came to hug me and told me not to cry any more. He told me that everything would be alright, that he would give me magic tonight."

More women came into the common area to inspect each other's clothing. Any hope of a private conversation was gone. It would be rude to speak in Kina and one never knew who might know enough of that language to understand what they were saying.

"We'll talk later," Ari smiled stiffly at the newcomers and then finished with Naibe's hair before checking her own again.

The afternoon wore on into earliest evening. The two women overheard that the men were refreshing themselves in a secondary plaza complete with their own attendants and butlers to wash their feet, oil their bodies, and give them massages. An entire area was set aside, one of the visiting women laughed, for cosmetics, and another area had mats set out to create a fan-cooled retreat. They saw a few more children go into the yard to play. More women and their servants bustled toward the lower area of the women's apartments. They gossiped, adjusted flower garlands and scent cones, and then rested with the ladies who had arrived earlier.

Bored, Ariennu quit the sleep area to help the servants who brought the garlands for everyone's necks. Some tidbits of food had been brought out and placed in little clay dishes along the edge of the water, in case anyone wished for a little to eat before the festivities picked up. Ari saw puffy little sweet cakes, melon slices, and little cups of a light syrupy beer. Wives, dancers, children, and concubines in twos and threes flowed in and out of the gathering rooms, taking some of the food from the table. Ari wasn't hungry. She busied herself with other tasks around the common area.

Party better start soon. I might be trouble, she thought, then felt a chill and a voice under a nuanced phrase.

Pretty. You can have some too —

Her thoughts shot back to the night the three of them were sorted out to the various households. *Watching me? Sorcerer!* she snorted, but Naibe darted out to point out that the two princesses Khentkawes and Bunefer had entered the women's area with their handmaidens.

"There they go," she whispered. "From the looks on their faces, they don't want to be here either."

Ari saw them walking proudly together, like parading sisters joined at the arms and whispering in low tones. They spoke to only a few of the guests. None of that mattered. The feeling that someone was watching her was hard to shake. The chill of a man's touch on her arm when no man was present made a shudder of need pass through her.

GOING FORTH BY DAY

One of the serving girls beckoned to her. Ari welcomed the disruption of that thought. If that was the psyche of the mysterious grandson reaching out to her and not the delusion of sexual need, the result was uncomfortably the same. She gestured to Naibe that she would be right back and to see if the princesses wanted for anything.

Naibe watched Ari pause and bow to Princess Bunefer. The tiny woman greeted her with a mittened hand wave and a coy smile. Encouraged, she turned, but instantly felt ill at ease when they all but ignored her and quickly turned to go meet privately with the King for a few moments. When they returned, their handmaidens had arranged two portable boat-styled beds of woven rushes filled with great puffy pillows. The two princesses reclined to rest without any further conversation.

Naibe ambled dreamily around the room, frustration becoming irritation that the princesses and even the concubines weren't interested in speaking to her.

And MaMa walked off – left me here. She blinked, then nodded pleasantly. *Yes, my sweet highnesses. So kind of you to ask about my life here in the palace!* Naibe imagined she was speaking to the sleeping princesses and their maids. *Oh yes, things are so much better for me now. And you? How is your life?* she pretended to speak to Khentie first. *So, his Highness is on duty now and young prince Kakai is back at school? Has your grandchild been born? Will you sail down to be with your son at Per-A-At to help his wife? Here, the strap on this scent cone is a little crooked. Let me get that for you.* And then to Princess Bunefer, she imagined saying: *oh yes, my lady, I have been asked to dance later. Oh yes, indeed, you'll like the dance I'm going to do!* Naibe bowed again, then moved off in her own world to think about a ghostly boy. *Safe now. You can see. She wasn't supposed to see you. So Shh, my little Asteri Asar.*

Ariennu moved up to the roof kitchen where cooks were hastily preparing the large trays of food which would be brought down the steps to the waiting crowds of guests reclined around the pool and in the main plaza. She thought about helping until she remembered she was wearing her best bright yellow kalasiris with the hip sash of patterned red and Tyre purple stripes. She had carried a few things before, but knew she needed to avoid the potentially messy food trays.

Feeling suddenly useless, she watched some of the dark, oiled, and beautifully muscled young men milling downstairs. In a rush of temptation, she came down to visit them, hoping to strike up a conversation before singling out one or two of them for an evening of delicious entertainment.

Ari bumped into one of the concubines, Irika, who until now had been far too haughty to speak to either her or Naibe.

The girl saw her ogling the men and made a point of teasing. "Well look at you coming down from the kitchen," she grinned. "In your party clothing? Whatever have you been doing *there*?"

Ari ignored her, but the girl continued goading.

"*I have* been chosen to be with Our Father this evening. I will sit with him and so will Suenma, not *you*," Irika quipped. "So, don't you be anywhere *near* him doing your pale-skinned pretend-heka tricks; you or your little dove-girl with the big golden eyes, either."

Ariennu whirled around, blazing. The haughty banter was finally enough. *Dove Girl?* she silently repeated. Ari knew the term was meant as an insult, even though woman to woman love was not too unusual in the women's rooms. That the thought of comforting Naibe had already wormed its way into her heart earlier shocked her and made her wonder if their affection toward each other wasn't as private as they thought. Dove Girl or Lizard woman implied that a woman favored the embracing arms and kisses of her own companions to the King's godly manhood. *That* was punishable. Normally, the accusation would have made her burst with laughter. Tonight, it was too much.

"Excuse me? Dove Girl?" Ariennu reached out and grabbed the young woman by the arm so hard that she almost jerked her off her feet.

"Ow! Let me –" the girl rose on tip-toe to stop the twisting and pain. "I was just –" she protested.

"What? Saying you were sorry? Is that what you were going to say to me?" Ariennu twisted the girl's arm behind her and dragged her closer again. "I can break it for you, you know, or twist it so hard you'll be making a sore and sad face when Our Father touches you tonight."

A guard at the bottom step that ascended to the King's quarters saw the rising scuffle and moved toward the two women with a stern look spreading over his face.

"What's this?" he asked.

In a frantic and very angry moment, Ariennu sent a thought into his heart. *The King. Take me to see the King!* She saw the man take a step backward up the stair, and knew he had sensed the thought, but couldn't allow himself to acknowledge it. His hand stroked a scarab amulet imbedded in his collar as his head snapped back and up over his shoulder. The guard at the top of the stair shook his head. "Ladies. Our Father rests. He also speaks with his divine son. Do not bring a petty trouble his way."

"You don't understand. I had a *feeling* again, another vision. I wanted to see if he —" Ariennu called out as she released the girl in her grasp.

Irika scrambled through the crowd, pausing some distance away to shake out her arm and turn a wicked snarl in the elder woman's direction.

"Is that Lady Ariennu?" a familiar voice called down the stair.

Prince Shepseskaf emerged from the grand bedchamber and made his way down the steps to face Ari as she refastened a stray curl of her ruddy hair.

Ari tapped her lower lip with her finger, proud that her outburst had roused someone who might make a difference, but shuddered inwardly because her efforts had worked.

"Yes Highness," she quickly composed herself. "The princesses are resting well in the back suites. Shall I get them?"

"No, no don't bother," he remarked. "My sweet sister Princess Khentie didn't wish to come at all, but Our Mother Khamer has sent word she is ill this evening and cannot attend. Princess Khentie is with my beloved wife, who had no interest in this gathering either, but we do what we must."

Ari looked up just past the crown prince's shoulder to the beaded opening of the King's bedchamber. "Then he will need –" she started, but Shepseskaf stayed her bare shoulder. She knew he understood that she was trying to sit with the King, but other arrangements had been made.

"He is well, as can be expected, but he rests now and should be fit to begin the evening soon. Just so you understand us, my beloved wife has advised him to take the company of ones who will be simple of heart yet be bred to more of our formal ways."

"Like that righteous little kuna I just turned loose, eh?" she chuckled and turned with an added sidelong glance.

"Perhaps" the Prince remarked, "but you should know the King *does* value you and the Lady Naibe very much. He agrees to this not out of anger or disappointment over either of you. It's just expected for his attendants during these major celebrations to be more –" Shepseskaf seemed at a slight loss for words.

"Ah!" Ari smirked, turning again. Her hands mocked the gesture of an elegant coif and large buttocks. "More ornamental, I see it now."

"Enjoy yourself tonight, then," the Prince bowed his head to hers, then turned but paused for a moment. "But not too much" he added and went out to the plaza to move among some of the other important men of the Two Lands.

Ari thought he would kiss her head before he left, but he didn't. In that moment, she understood the King, the Prince, and the other members of the royal family were still uncomfortable with this party. The odd and almost unfriendly airs she sensed were about the greater mystery of the King's elder daughter who died, and this delicious looking Prince of many naughty rumors who seemed to be in the middle of all of it.

Oh tonight, you sly and pretty one, she chuckled to herself. *If Bone Woman can't keep you gripped between her thighs, you're mine!* The thought of her own legs wrapping around his hard and eager body made her heart beat furiously with all sorts of delightful and sweaty imaginings.

Amused by the idea, Ariennu shrugged it away and moved back into the thick of the crowd which was starting to mass in the outer plaza. She gawked at all the finery as each new family arrived, then trailed the myriad of servants as they directed the women back to the private areas to rest and rejuvenate themselves. Unable to resist an old instinct that surfaced, she evaluated their fine clothing and jewelry.

It's been a long time since I tried to lift something other than the Inspector's eye jewel. Wonder if my Child Stone, and how good I've gotten with making rainbow blurred memory, would make it easier. She snickered, knowing she could strip the entire women's apartments, bag the items, and take off running. *But where would I go?* A peculiar thought of her running with a boy in her arms in the middle of the night came to her. *Naibe's little friend? Why? When is this?*

Ari grimaced silently, distracted, as Hordjedtef's countesses arrived. *Them. I should get something off them.* She watched as they situated themselves on poolside couches and asked for their handmaidens to attend to them. Once settled, the women chatted with the princesses. Her study of the women was interrupted by the grumbling of the stewards.

"His men are already here, waiting in the common," one man called to the two men in the storeroom where the huge storage jars of beer and wine were housed. "They've already finished down two. Take out four more and get up the steps to see if His Majesty is ready. This needs to start before the food is cold and everyone out there is falling down drunk."

Ari hadn't been to a celebration this large, but all day long she had heard the concubines, handmaidens, and the servants rehearsing the schedule of events as they prepared.

The King would be notified just as the guest's entourage approached the outer gates. He would then come out, extend his blessing, allow the Prince to enter, speak another blessing about the coming mission, and then declare the feast officially started. At this point, everyone waited for some sign that Menkaure was ready to start.

As the sun sank lower, however, the guest of honor had *not* arrived, and the King had *not* emerged from his upper suite. More tams and cushions were added and adjusted all around the pools. Musicians played, but everything and everyone simply waited.

Just at sunset, a cheer rippled from the area of the gates and a press of men moved toward the guarded gold and cedar doors. When a horn blast sounded from outside the walls, the guards at the top of the stair to the royal bedroom ducked into the room. As if he had been waiting for this moment, a wiry but muscular, dark-skinned attendant clad in a shining white shendyt and gold pectoral emerged from the King's outer balcony with a large wooden striker in his hands. The assembly hushed expectantly as the man took a swing at the large bronze gong mounted on the King's outer rail. King Menkaure appeared then, hands inclining his body slightly so that he looked down into the plaza below. The echoes of the gong radiated through the air and down to the distant river. All the guests in attendance froze and bent low with averted eyes until the King trotted down the steps to sit in his polished pink marble throne. His pleased, almost amused expression grew both regal and paternal as if he had personally fathered each of those gathered before him. A corps of butlers followed him, stuffing wonderfully sumptuous dark blue pillows behind him in the chair. He clapped his hands twice, and then settled in his cushions. His right hand braced his ceremonially bearded chin for a few moments as he surveyed all his assembled subjects. When the sound of the gong finally faded, he nodded, and the crowd eased a little.

Look at him! Ari's heart quickened because even though she had been told he would be miserable tonight, he looked magnificent – regal and magnificent.

Breaking protocol, because she knew she could get away with it, Ari pushed her way toward the throne. One of the butlers handed her a slim gold beaker of calming flower and basil tea to test. She knelt, gazing seductively at the King as she took a sip and sent him the thought: *Anything you need Your Majesty? Find me ready!* Then, she offered him the beaker over her head. The King's eyes met hers, and by his expression she knew he read that thought.

"I bless you, Lady Ariennu," his voice spoke just a little above the rabble coming from the gates. "But –"

The gong sounded again. A murmur ran through the crowd and a cheer went up

GOING FORTH BY DAY

in greeting. The crowd praised and prayed for both Maatkare and the King's long life at the same moment.

Ariennu paused, suddenly awestruck at the honor she and Naibe had received over these past few weeks.

And here I am, right by the King, a living god walking as a man, and he's ignoring those girls he picked out. The old man said it earlier. I wasn't born or raised here. I just never understood how far we've come because of these little ones within us.

The attention of the crowd and even Menkaure's attention had shifted to the entering group, but Ari thought more deeply.

Maybe it was because we saw him sick first, not like a god. Never has, really, until tonight — Would a god walk arm in arm with me and Naibe as if we were his daughters? He's just a lonely and tired man who needs so much more than a god would expect his subjects to know about.

Tonight, King Menkaure seemed almost happy. He joked, but most of the time he sat pensively in his throne. Occasionally, he reached down to caress Suenma's head or touch Irika's shoulder while they were seated adoringly at his feet. He didn't notice Irika's forced-but-charming smile when he touched her arm. He merely sipped his tea and called for more of it instead of calling for the imported spiced quince wine. Two acrobats performed amazing feats of flexibility and balance with hoops and ribbons before him. He nodded approvingly as serving girls bore trays of bread stuffed with meat or honeyed fruit delights that had been baked into fancy shapes. After the King and the assembled guests finished taking portions of each new dish, dancers and singers entertained until the next course was brought out. All the while, other servants meandered among the reclining guests with smaller jars and urns, ready to refresh any extended cups.

Just after dark, a combined gasp and a light cheer from the entrance on the King's left side announced the entry of Prince Maatkare's entourage. He hadn't bothered to come into the wide plaza through the gates in the front. Instead, he opted for a showier entrance on the King's left.

Ariennu looked around, desperate to find Naibe so her young companion could see the moving display as the family arrived. She found her standing almost timidly at the entry to the women's area, far out of sight of the King. Ari beckoned wildly, but soon gave up and went to the entry herself. It was still a good vantage point for seeing both the main and the women's plazas.

Deka's going to be with them. Ariennu knew that, but she still wondered: *nothing from her, even though I'm sure she's heard we're living here.*

The Prince's servants led a heavy set and solemn-faced woman clad in a tasteful but unflattering red and gold kalasiris. Even though it was highly fashionable, it clung to her body as if it was wet and it made her look like a vulgar imitation of a noblewoman. Behind her walked her three children wearing gold belts, fancy bracelets, and apron skirts, followed by a handmaiden and the children's nurse. *This* group, but not the Prince or Deka, was led to pay homage to King Menkaure, then ushered into the area to the right of the throne. The handmaiden quickly schooled the little ones to keep silent while the heavy woman scanned the plaza for a place to sit.

His wife? His children? There's trouble topped with a bad joke, Ariennu snorted. *And he's not even at her side? She fell from grace and lost the charm to get him back beyond making his brood for him. If she's the one Naa told me was his concubine, he must have married her out of guilt when the Princess died. She's a commoner, though, like me. I don't think I'd put up with a man who would shame me like that in front of all others; I don't care what the riches were. I'd just be gone... leave him with his wealth* and *his ungrateful little bastards,* her thoughts flashed. *Wealth and title though, and a monster in the bedroom I hear? Hmmm...* That thought brought her to Deka's silence over the past weeks and to the thought of luring the Prince away from both women again. *I could handle him,* she laughed. *I'd have him on all fours and begging for a treat from* me.

Curious again, Ariennu's eyes focused on the little family as they pushed past her and went into the women's area. They were tired and already plagued by the celebration. Ari sensed some heavy and screaming argument had made them late. They didn't want to come, even though the party was going to be a great one. The little girl had begun to whine, the older boy and his mother looked as if they wanted to be anywhere else, and the youngest child, another boy, was already being carried in the nurse's arms.

When they brushed by her again as if she wasn't there and came back out to the great plaza again, Ari waded through the crowd and grabbed Naibe by the hand. She decided to trail the Prince's family part of the way, then she found them looking around for empty cushions by the low tables. Eventually, they found a place to sit near Hordjedtef and his countesses.

"Little one —" Ariennu pointed out the alleged "wife" and children as she pulled Naibe closer, "notice something funny about them?"

Naibe's big-eyed and wonder-filled expression told the older woman she *didn't* understand, but then the young woman was so very innocent of any social norms. Naibe looked harder and then sensed the answer Ariennu wanted.

"A place wasn't set for them?" she asked. "Did they not send word they were coming?"

"Right! If this man is such a high-ranking prince, why is his family being ignored? I was wondering about that myself. This whole evening's funny. Something's not right."

The two women gazed across the pool to the low tables where the elder wife of Great One sat. They saw her annoyed expression as she called for more seat cushions to be placed near her and then ordered the noble families nearby to scoot over and give the woman and her family some room to sit and eat.

"Eh, Baby — did you see that? They just sat over by Great One's family but there's no room for this prince and Deka."

Naibe nodded as if she agreed they would sit separately.

"Maybe not so strange, MaMa," she suggested. "His majesty changes who is with him from night to night. Maybe this is like that."

"Maybe," Ari nodded, her voice and attention trailing. "Funny, though —"

After everyone had settled again, Ari and Naibe remained to one side to watch the festivities proceed. The Prince still hadn't appeared, and Deka hadn't arrived either. Naibe moved into the entryway, shying back into the women's area for some unannounced reason. Some of the women and servants who were tending the smaller children were eating back in that area; food was being brought to them there.

Ariennu shrugged, abandoned again.

Go then. I'm not hiding in the back. Too much going on out here and I want to see what's keeping this prince. Time for me to get out among the people and make a friend or two.

Just then, a thick swell of the crowd built up in the direction of the entry. A herald cried out the long-overdue arrival of the Prince.

"Great Majesty and Father God. Lord of the Two Lands, His Highness, Prince Maatkare Raemkai Grand General of the Upper Lands comes, grateful of your mercy and your blessing in this Divine host!"

"Wa…" Ariennu began. She darted into the women's area to grab Naibe so she could see. Ari felt like a young girl again, excited at the appearance of a hero in a parade. She bobbed up and down in joy.

"Ooh look, look, look – it's them look!" as she saw the flash of a deep blue nemes with two single gold bands pass by her within an arm's reach. It was the Prince, and even though she had met many princes, the sight of the passing blue head-cloth elicited in her a fury of passionate torment. Beside him walked a woman in a hooded black cloak. Her cinnamon-colored hand held it closed. Even though her skin color was common among women from Kemet, Ari knew it was Deka.

Both walked forward in even strides as if they had practiced parade steps. Deka held her head high and looked straight ahead, not adoringly at her prince and not respectfully toward the King. Tonight, it seemed, she had reclaimed the role about which she had once whispered and dreamed – Deka had become the reigning goddess. The announcement of praise had been for the young prince, but the Ta-Seti woman acted as if every bit of the glory had been for her.

Naibe gestured to Ariennu. *Why is she…?*

Ariennu sensed Naibe start to ask why Deka was cloaked and appeared to not recognize them, but didn't answer. She stared with an even harder gaze than her open-mouthed younger companion. "I know, I know…" Ari stilled Naibe's question.

GOING FORTH BY DAY

"Come in here with me. The night's hot and she's going to have to store her cloak somewhere. We'll just get there first and get her to talk then. I want to hear all about that scrumptious thing who paid for her. I've heard all the stories and so have you! I want to know what he's really like on his couch!" the elder woman towed Naibe back to the women's plaza to wait for their old friend to enter.

"Well, we've had some times with men too, Ari. I just hope she's happy now," Naibe shrugged as they walked. Ariennu knew the girl was still thinking about their tragedies: about Marai being gone, Wserkaf being apart from her, Shepseskaf's family being wary enough of her to possibly tell lies about the Princess' pregnancy to get her out of their house, and now their being reviled by the other concubines here.

Deka didn't come in. Long moments passed. In the distance they heard announcements of the accomplishments of the man being honored.

"Maybe she's attending while they speak of him, Ari," Naibe sighed, bored. She loosened her hair absent-mindedly.

"You're not going to lie down, are you?" Ariennu stopped her.

"No, I know there will be dancing later. I thought I might dance for the King, too. I want to see him smile, like the story of Old Ra's daughter dancing to make her father smile."

"Oh," Ari shrugged again. "If the prophetesses don't stop you, you should. It better be a *special* dance too."

"It will be," Naibe's smile was misty.

"Will it?" Ariennu worried about that. Ever since she saw the spirit child this afternoon, Naibe had been in a strange and almost detached mood. Ari feared it might be an early sign of madness taking her. She touched her brow briefly, making certain Naibe didn't feel any message that was transmitted

What is this with my girl?

Thoughts whispered in her own voice answered.

It is as it should be
She rises high and is of the moon and star
Be watchful.
Something hidden waits.

Ari sighed and frowned, but decided to temporarily reject the message. *Like a bunch of mothers. And Shepseskaf telling me not to have too much fun either. I doubt they know the meaning of the word*, she laughed to herself.

Ariennu paced the floor in the women's area. The food and feasting continued outside with only a few morsels being brought to the back. From time to time, she went to the tube entrance to the main courtyard and looked out to see if she could find Deka. Soon, tired of waiting, Ari decided to go back into the outer plaza. As she emerged from the women's room and moved through the covered passageway, the Ta-Seti woman passed her, but drew her cloak tighter as if she didn't want to be seen.

Ariennu leapt for her. "Oh. Deka, oh goddess, *at last*," the elder woman embraced her old friend.

Deka tensed and then hissed in defense before shaking herself free of the woman's grasp. Head high, she moved into the women's sleeping area and then stood between Ari's and Naibe's cots. She stared down quietly at Naibe's upturned, astonished face. The Ta-Seti woman growled softly like a strange cat that no longer recognized its old litter mates.

"Whoa, what?" Ariennu turned, realizing she had been pushed away. "You didn't just push off from me, raisin crotch." She would have grabbed Deka and slapped her instantly, but the Ta-Seti woman held up a gentle hand as a signal she was about to explain. A zephyr-like wind issued from her palm.

This night will be hard for us, Wise Mama. Do not make it harder now that our eyes meet again, her thoughts came through Naibe and Ari's hearts in her low, musical thought-voice.

That part of Deka hadn't changed. She possessed the same regal aloofness the princesses demonstrated. No one had ever been able to humiliate that demeanor out of her, even when Chibale, the failed Kush conjurer, hauled her into N'ahab-Atal's camp in the wilderness eons ago. She had been no different. It didn't matter that Ari had beaten her into a kind of complacency. Bone Woman, as Ari had called her, had come to stay in the thieves' camp. She wouldn't be traded out to other owners for a price. Ari had watched as the dark woman had bedded the men in the camp with a silent enthusiasm that seemed artificial. In those old days, she seldom smiled and never spoke. It had not been until young Naibe arrived two years later that Ari and the Ta-Seti woman began to tolerate each other. It was a harsh testimony to the reversals of their fortunes.

"Ah back to the old shrivel pus, I see. All Marai's changes gone now because he died for these bastards," Ariennu snapped in guttural Kina.

Every bit of Deka's cold, imperious nature had returned. The woman put down her raised hand. One of the handmaidens for the room, struck by Deka's goddess-like beauty, rushed up to her with a mirror so she could see herself in it. Deka quietly let her hood fall and then removed her dark cloak, placing it over Ari's bedside basket.

Tonight, she was dressed in dramatic finery: a slim red kalasiris with gold metal beads and red cloth ribbons interwoven to form the breast straps. A little circlet on her head bore a golden disc that reached down over her forehead, almost covering the place where her stone lay.

"Deka. It's me, Little One. Don't you know us anymore?" Naibe's voice wound up, sounding as if she had suffered one heartbreak too many. Ari came to her, sat on her cot, and held her, a snarl for Deka edging her lips.

"She's too good for us now, Baby. If Marai could see this," Ariennu began.

"I know well enough who both of you are," Deka continued quietly in the Kina tongue she had learned in the thieves' camp. Her eyes were lowered and not making contact with them. "How have you been?" she asked, along with more questions, but she was clearly uninterested in the answers she would receive or in any pleasantries of conversation. Moments later, she returned the mirror to the handmaiden, bowed gracefully to give Naibe a little hug, and then edged out of the women's area. When

Deka stepped into the plaza with a forced, bright smile, her eyes danced again. The look behind them was colder than the snow of a wilderness winter.

"Damn her," Ariennu cursed dejectedly, "something's bad wrong there. You see that? Like she doesn't even *remember* us now. I don't know how she did it, but she broke the Children's link between us." The elder woman stood, rubbed her brow, and sensed only a void that followed Deka as she left. "That does it. I'll make that piece of maggoty fish stink pay for that. Put on that manner around me? Lost her wits, she has!" Ari once again became the hardened slave-trainer in N'ahab-Atal's camp, ready to punch and kick the Ta-Seti woman into submission.

Naibe-Ellit shook her sad head. *It's her new way, Mama Ari. It's something she does to keep the madness away. I can feel it inside her like a fire burning. Just let her go for now,* the young woman shrugged, once again preoccupied with her loosening hair.

"Know what?" Ari pushed her lips around, got the mirror Naa had loaned her, then checked her eye and lip paint. Tossing the mirror onto her bed, she straightened her wide shoulders and moved to the tunnel entrance to the main plaza. "I think I'm going to get a drink, several maybe. Let's just see how many this useless rock in my head will let me suck down. After that, well we'll just see what happens!" she turned quickly in a huff and left Naibe-Ellit alone in the sleep area.

GOING FORTH BY DAY

Chapter 28: The Dance

Naibe didn't hear the rest of Ari's sullenly-muttered rant as the woman left the room. To her, at that moment, the dance garment she was putting together was far more important than threats and promises the older woman made about getting into trouble. They fell on purposely deaf ears.

Irika and Suenma will sit with His Majesty tonight. The prophetesses are going to dance praises for him, and then I will dance. I saw him looking down at me from his rear porch all happy while the noble children played in the yard. He needs to have another son even though at his age he might not live to see the child become a man. He smiled at me, and I posed, but maybe his smile wasn't for me. Maybe it was for the children after all. Tonight, I'll do a better dance to leave him feeling happy and renewed enough to enjoy the attentions of the girls he's chosen.

Her thoughts crashed as the memory of Marai entered them. *Goddess I miss you, my sweetest song of a man. I was on the mend almost, but then the little child came to me. Even Ari saw him,* she silently laughed. *I thought of him so much I made him appear. Even he tried to make me feel better.*

Since she had been at the palace, she had become more confident and almost happy. She guessed the reason the King had not asked her to entertain him was because he sensed she was still grieving, even though she covered her pain with much greater skill. *Ari is with him plenty, but her heart is different when she's with a man. She can play. Me? It's like I start reading the man and I see his trouble and want to fix it. Maybe he thinks some things can't be fixed or maybe shouldn't be. She says he's gentle and sweet, but even she's seen that awful sadness he carries.* Those thoughts brought her back to her own vale of tears as she fastened the pins in her hair just so.

My Asteri Asar, little star, my sweet child, where are you now? She cried out for the vision of the shadowy child she had seen in the garden then sat on the edge of her bed, feeling oddly weak. *My sweet son who will never be, my life that is forever gone. I wish there was a miracle I could call down so you could bring me the shade of my Marai to lie with me once more and give you life.* Tonight, even with all the exciting festivities going on, she felt only rising tears.

Mother, don't cry, a little voice spoke and the touch of a hand met her arm. *I said I would always be with you. I am with you now. I will help you dance tonight. I will help you bring greatest joy to another who is sorrowing.*

Naibe reached for the little hand but touched her own naked shoulder. The child wasn't there. *Maybe he hasn't been here at all*, she thought. Maybe he was a symptom of madness; a little dream voice that came to console her.

Naibe knew through the intelligence she gained from the Children of Stone that the women of her birth land danced for Ashera in tribute of her descent into the underworld. It was a darker and dustier place than Kemet's "Land that Loves Silence" but otherwise not too different. It would be the completion of the spirit dance she had begun at Shepseskaf's house on that moonlit night. Tonight, her dance would be so much more beautiful, she felt. In part it would salute Marai's memory, and in doing so she would mark the end of her mourning time. Her heart would say: 'It has to be enough, now. I am becoming my own. Tonight is my first night alive since my heart of hearts died.' She would draw the energy down and combine it with the goddess spirit burning inside her and the spirit of the impossible child beside her. Her dance would be a gift for the King, because he had been compassionate.

Naibe fastened the belt of serpents Wserkaf had given her over seven pinned and draped linen wraps. These she had wrapped loosely so that the belt could tinkle and chime beneath the fabric when she danced. She re-fixed the flower garlands on her shoulders and her arms, loosened her hair, and combed the melted perfumed oils from the last bit of the scent-cone through it. Pressing a simple circlet on her head, she unfastened her hair so it flowed loosely to the top of her hips. The task of dressing complete, she slipped quietly back out to the plaza.

Ariennu wandered through the crowd, watching the assembled populace enjoy the feast set before them. The encounter with Deka had made her too angry to eat.

Ass sucking kuna! And Baby One trying to defend. Gone haughty is what it is. Haughtiness isn't the same thing as grief.

The guests reclined on cushions around the pool and throughout the large open plaza. Woven wicker platforms had been set on brick risers in front of them. The wealthiest guests, who sat closer to the throne area, had polished wooden table boards placed on carved marble blocks. People didn't rise to get their food. Instead, servants wandered amid the lounging groups, tending them like bees tended flowers. From time to time a face turned up to notice her as she ambled by.

Now where to sit? Maybe next to her so I can say more to her about her manners, but there she sits by old Count Hordjedtef. She recalled her morning encounter. Ari didn't want to get that close to the old sorcerer. *If we started something, the old man will just have me taken out of the party and that'd make me mad enough, the way I'm feeling, to start a riot. No, the old man Hordjedtef is the one who really needs a killing, but his death I want to save for later. I want to see that bastard suffer.*

"Ssst! Here! You can sit with us," a woman in a light, leaf-green kala tugged on Ari's hem. It was the first sign of true friendliness she'd seen in the palace. Usually, the kindness she had experienced was civil, artificial, and polite.

"Thank you" crept out of her mouth even though she tried in vain to see what Deka was saying. The old man was speaking to her. She was nodding, but didn't look pleased to hear what he said. The people tugged Ariennu's skirt again and she eased down beside them. The woman shoved a plate of sweetmeats in front of her that sizzled with honey and crackling fat. *Chicken? And Honey pepper?* she dipped her fingers in the flower-water bowl and pressed them into a common linen towel that was near the tray. This far away, she couldn't tell *what* was going on.

Unable to hold on to the venom that had caused her to lose her appetite, Ariennu ate, realizing quickly that she had been hungrier than she thought. She sat and listened to the people tell her of their good fortune to have been invited to this celebration. They owed it to their son who was moving up in the ranks of the army. Their words gushed and yet droned. Hot buns were served and fat-honey locusts that had been baked crisp were put out next. Ari made a face until a servant popped the head and legs off, leaving a juicy carapace that tasted slightly fishy. She ate one, but decided she didn't like that delicacy too much. She thought of the destruction the hordes of them could bring, the beady eyes and feelers, the barbed legs, the crepe-like wings, and shuddered inwardly.

Ariennu glanced around, increasingly bored. She didn't want to be rude because this family was feeding her, but the temptation to drop her prisms of silence and secrecy on some good-looking young man just long enough to ease her loneliness and the irked feeling toward Deka surfaced as soon as she stopped eating.

Hordjedtef stared at her from his place in his family group. His beady eyes bored holes in her as he attempted to read her hostile thoughts from such a distance. Her spot at this feast in his line of sight was becoming more uncomfortable by the minute. That he had been able to impose himself into her thoughts enough to discover some of the talents the Children of Stone were helping her develop embarrassed her. Now, every time she caught him looking at her, she wanted to turn away. She quickly obscured herself from his glance and in a moment, pretended she saw an old friend. Excusing herself, she got up from the young soldier's family and ducked into a crowd to watch some of the jugglers. Thankfully, this allowed her to avoid Great One's staring bird eyes for the next few moments. From time to time, she caught a glimpse of Deka sitting with the countesses and the wife of this celebrated young general.

Wonder if he plans to marry her? Is that why she's gone all cold to us again? She playing the part? Then we will see what we will see about that. I'll wager some gold I can get him in my arms this very night, Ariennu smirked, eager for mischief. Her eyes sought out the man being honored tonight.

The Prince was roaming through the crowd like a stray dog. It became very quickly evident to Ari that he was focused on celebrating the event with his assembled ranks of men rather than devoting his attention to Deka or the woman who had given him children. He stayed away from the King and the families near the throne, including his own family. She saw him move among clusters of his men to other groups. He would sit and joke for a while, then move to another group to quaff some wine. Occasionally, he would grope or pester a serving girl.

Seeing the man in his normal behavior, Ariennu suddenly realized she wasn't really that interested in him. *Look at that. I can feel the vanity on him! Thinks he's hotter than fire itself. What an animal. And those girls let him feel them, too, like it's the best thing they could dream of to have his hands on them. I like a man who's a force in bed, but I think his bed is always going to be too crowded. Maybe Deka already sips her bitter herbs with that one. Maybe he makes her watch him part other kuna lips. Maybe I —*

A murmur rose, building up in the crowd near the throne where the King sat. Drawn from her thoughts, Ariennu turned her attention towards the area. A nearby musician struck a different chord on his harp and his companions, glanced at one another then listened to find the new harmonies.

Naibe had entered to begin her dance.

As if they had been told what to expect, some of the servants moved the torches around the back of the throne so that the area darkened. Combined with the distant moonlight high in the sky, they formed a softer light in the plaza. The crowd opened slightly so that the King and even Prince Maatkare Raemkai, who found he had drifted closer to Menkaure absent-mindedly, could see.

Some of the young men nearest Ariennu stopped chatting and stared in awe at Naibe's body-covering garments.

Ariennu knew exactly what dance would be performed, though she had left before Naibe had told her. She knew it would be Ashera's journey into the Underworld. Like Inanna, Ashera sought her slain lover Dumuzi and traveled into the land of death to retrieve him. It was a haunting and poignant dance if done properly. Considering the magic she already felt emanating from her sister wife, she knew it would be.

"Is that a peasant's burial shroud she's wearing?" one of the men asked. "Is she supposed to be a ghost?"

"No, I hear bells. A ghost wouldn't have bells. Hear the tinkling? She's tawny-skinned like a Shinar servant. Maybe it's a Shinar dance," another replied.

Musicians situated themselves so the young woman would have more room in which to move. Princess Bunefer and her assistants imposed themselves at the edges of the crowd to get a better look, in case anything sacrilegious might be shown as part of the dance. As soon as the crowd stilled, Naibe spoke quietly, but beautifully, as if she had already begun to drift into a trance.

"A dance is what it is," she said, "but more importantly, it is about whom it celebrates. I salute Ashera of my own land and ask that her greatness comes unto me to honor those who have lost all as I have," she spoke in perfect Kemet.

"Let me tell you a beautiful story."

Her Ashera voice compelled every ear and every soul. All eyes focused on her.

"My truest love lies sleeping…
In the Land that Loves Silence.
I cannot live another day in the waking world.
I will go to speak to she who reigns there,

yet

I dance as a woman rejoicing in the pleasure her body feels
As it goes to be with him in his death.
I desire his hands touching my breasts,
stroking the wettest lips of my
honey lotus as it opens, until I cry aloud
his lips and tongue on all of me,
his plow to my earth deep inside my womb."

Then, almost under her breath, she whispered in her native tongue:

"She knows she would go to him,
but he has become a god and
she must leave the things of living on earth,
all her fear —
behind her

as she goes on her way."

Hordjedtef tensed at her words. Ariennu bowed her head as more bitterness rose in her heart. She thought of the way their journey had brought Naibe's soul to this deepest onslaught of mourning. The King blinked too, troubled and sad, understanding the true and deeper meaning of her words. Some of the prophetesses quickly translated the last words she spoke back and forth among themselves, then pressed intently forward to pay close attention to what she would do next.

The music began slowly at first. Naibe raised her arms to the sky. Her pose symbolically sought the energy of the goddess. The almost mystical light that had been formed by the radiance from the torches in the open courtyard caught her arms as she began to draw the sense of magic quietly down. Throwing her hands up in supplication then quickly down again, her body drank in the glowing of the torchlight and the waning moonlight. This time, she did not try to hide the glow she exuded when the spirit took her or hide any of her sensuality. No one could speak. All sounds stilled except the shake of the sistrum, the pluck of the harp, and the pat-a-pat of the small drums, along with the tiny shimmering sounds of her belt of little brass serpents.

Ariennu distracted herself in a renewed search for Deka across the open court. When she found her again, Ariennu noticed softness in the dark woman's expression.

Ah. Now her humility shows as our sister dances for our departed king, Ari's bitter thought soared to Deka.

Deka's head bowed. She put her hand over her mouth to hide its expression.

Ari knew Deka heard her thought, but she wanted to keep pummeling her with more bitterness. She saw the Prince's wife glance at Deka once, obviously unaccustomed to seeing the new concubine's demeanor change. Ariennu silently growled. *I see you looking and then hiding your face, damn you. She's dancing it for* all *of* us, *you fool! At least you could have shown just once that Marai meant something to you before you pranced off with Prince Happy El like he was some room full of rubies!* the elder woman's thoughts shrieked. She didn't care if what she felt came through as words for the entire assembly. Her jaw set, she felt the blush of anger lining her upper cheeks.

GOING FORTH BY DAY

Deka took a deep breath and gave the appearance of shifting in her cross-legged position on the floor. Now, she sat on her heels and watched her former sister move, turning her attention away from Ari.

Ari noticed Prince Maatkare standing nearer to the throne than to his own family. With a glance up as if he had sensed the impact of Ariennu's thoughts, he began to snicker. About to burst into a riot of laughter, he tottered in a circle and bit his own hand to stifle a loud cackling guffaw at her epithet. Somehow, although no one else but Deka gave an indication they heard her, Ari knew the Prince had sensed the thought and most of the anger behind it. Maatkare moved behind the throne and then disappeared into the assembled crowd.

Naibe danced, circling gracefully. She seemed to rise from the ground in total ecstasy and abandonment, as if she was being lifted by moonlight. Some of the people who saw her would later swear that she had been glowing, and that webs and trails of stars swirled in her wake as the veils and garlands of flowers she carried trailed behind her. From time to time, she let a veil waft to the floor. The first one fell near the edge of the assembled crowd. She picked it up, teased with it, slithered in a snake-like fashion with a sigh and a shoulder roll, and then dropped it a little closer to the throne. She faded into the edge of the crowd, almost vanishing like a girl playing hide-and-seek, then re-appeared, whirling and leaping, settling and swaying.

When she drifted into the group of prophetesses, she drew them out into the plaza with her. Soon, these holy women began to sway, as if the immense spirit of sensuality in the air had entered them too. This foreign dancer had called so much of the goddess' passion that it could not be contained in one mere human form. Following her, they danced in a wonderful serpentine that wound about the plaza. If a veil came loose, they revered it, passed it back, and graced the floor near the throne with it. The King was almost on his feet by that time, beaming in joy, his heart melting. His eyes misted with the thought that the women, his prophetesses and truth-sayers, could show him so much love after he had brought such a sense of quiet-but-troubled sterility during these last six years of his reign.

Naibe felt the rolling surf of a distant sea inside of her body as she moved. She became part of the ocean and felt the memory of Marai, come to her as if his ghost was transformed into the strong surf that crashed down on her, briefly owned her, and then drew back out of her. That was her last clear thought before the ecstasy overwhelmed her. The faces blurred, her mouth gaped joyously, and she knew nothing more. The dancing continued, though, more intense than before. Some of the women wept in ecstasy as they danced a little more slowly and reverently. The men's faces were chalk. They wanted to be with her too, but knew oblivion waited in her sweet arms. This was a woman's prayer to the spirit inside all that is a woman in her passion.

Ari grinned ear to ear, like a silly imp, but continued to watch Deka out of the corner of her eye. *Deka, what's happened to you? You're not Bone Woman in the wilderness, you're not our quiet sister who lived with us in Little Kina-Ahna.* Ari knew she was looking at a queen re-born. *Did sleeping with him do this to you? Is it more than that?*

Deka gave no indication she felt the thought.

As Ari glowered at Deka, the dance finally rushed to a peak. Then, it paused. And Ari heard Naibe's sultry, but child-like thought voice.

Oh Marai, for you,

my first true love.

Would that you had lived.

If my dancing could wake you.

To return you from death

would be my delight.

Burn through me.

Consume me.

Take all of me so that I cannot exist apart from you.

Naibe bowed her head. Her chest heaved slightly as she panted and sighed. She genuflected near the throne, just short of King Menkaure's foot. He bid her rise, his hand grasping hers and he lifted her so her dance could continue.

Ari felt her own emotion and grief over the loss of Marai rise at that moment.

Oh, little one. You are so lovely. Know he hears you. He does, I swear he must.

Ariennu took a step backward, but as she did, she sensed someone standing behind her. Gentle fingers touched her waist and then crept around it. Ari saw an immaculately manicured dark hand and felt its controlled strength. It was a man's hand. Ariennu sensed who the man was without fully looking at him: Prince Maatkare.

Chapter 29: The Competition

"I would prefer if you did *not* touch me," she tersely whispered under her breath to the male behind her.

A slight, throaty chuckle, like a deeper version of a hyena's titter, responded. Something about that sound chilled her heart, but the thought didn't last.

"That so?" the Prince tugged her backward against him then brushed his hips and cedar hardness in a semi-gentle grind against her rump.

"Whew! Dance got you on a rut, Highness? I can *feel* that!" she smirked, a little more wide-eyed.

Sits my king with a cedar rising in his lap.

Ari felt a verse to the Ashera poem she had known since her childhood in Tyre drift through her heart. *And here comes this one with the biggest tree in the whole damned forest. I think I will want to see that tonight, after all,* she cackled to herself but fought back the instant delight that wanted to turn her kuna-gate into running honey and her knees into jelly. Everything about him felt good to her; too good. Even worse, she knew he could read her excitement like an inscription on a monument.

"Uh, Highness," she said as she tried to hide her regret at needing to turn down his silent offer, "seems like the women you need are all over there." She vaguely pointed to Deka and the plump, sour-faced wife with her maid, trying not to visibly shudder in delight.

Maatkare ignored every word she said and nibbled the back of her neck insistently. The edge of what she believed was his double-striped nemes tickled her bare upper back.

"Damn you! Stop it," she whirled, then realized she had been rude to a man who could have her destroyed in the blink of an eye. She hesitated with a sharp intake of air and dropped her gaze in false deference to the Prince. Ari felt his hand firmly grasp her chin and raise her eyes to him. She knew he had instantly read her complete lack of reverence.

As he released her, she stared directly into his smoldering green and gold eyes that didn't quite match his dark, rich brown skin. *Like a dog* she thought, then caught herself. *Whoa. That's Deka's eye-color; her cat self. Some animal magic going on here?*

"True. They are over there," he admitted, moving in to insistently nuzzle, nip, and lick the side of her neck. "But, I'd rather have *you* tonight. You have a question or two about how this will be, so come walk with me. Taste this new wine they just brought out. At least do that," a sly, self-assured smirk curled one corner of his sensuous mouth. The Prince tugged Ari out of the crowd that was straining to watch Naibe's dance.

Like he pulled Deka to old Hordjedtef's gate on our first night this side of the river. Something else about the touch of this man's hand struck a familiar note. As he held her hand, she felt his thumb suggestively caress her palm. The gentle and incredibly sensual feeling compelled her to stay with him, even though moments ago, her anger spent, she had begun to think her mission of taunting Deka was a foolish one. Then, she saw something.

A black leather x-strap like the one the old man had on his hand this morning! He's got one of those damned rings on his finger! Ari glanced at the Prince's hand as it lay over hers, but grew too dizzy to focus on his elegant-but-powerful hands. In a sidelong glance, she made out the twisted leathery ring at the base of his middle finger. *Ummmmh... Goddess, he's gorgeous. So why does he think he needs to compel me?* she averted her eyes, a fake shy expression on her face. *I'll grab some wall for him, he just needs to point me to a good place away from all this commotion and we'll get some.* She giggled, *I was thinking of getting something tonight anyway. Why does he want to do it this way? Proud fool,* her thoughts trailed as she stumbled through the crowd, towed by the man who had been her hottest of fantasies until the moment she was confronted by him. She didn't *like* being the hunted one, especially when it had been *her* idea to hunt and conquer *him*.

The Prince half-dragged her to the wine room where the large, painted ceramic urns and barrels were kept. Servants, directed by the stewards, came in one after another to refill pitchers for the crowd. One huge red jar stood in the corner. The

Prince filled its dipping ladle and with a comical bow, he offered it to her.

Ariennu didn't want to seem *too* easy to conquer, if the evening was going to go the way she expected it might go. Being coy would only heighten her pleasure and his, when she finally let him take her. "I said no," she pretended some resistance. "Now you want to make me drunk enough to fall down and let you crawl up on this?" her voice lifted in mockery as she indicated her mount through her kalasiris. "I know you take me as eager, but I can see your game. Your grandfather has already showed me how your kind charm your prey before you pounce."

"Just plain good wine is what I'm offering. No trick," he stared past her, as if he was disinterested in her comment. He quaffed the wine himself.

Supposed to show me it's not drugged, eh? she thought to herself. She quickly regretted not guarding herself as the green-eyed twinkle Maatkare possessed reminded her that he could sense her thoughts.

He re-filled the ladle and offered the wine to her again.

Ari sighed, sipped the ladle first, and then gulped the rest. The drink was smooth and rich; just what she needed. This day of misery had begun when the count toyed with her and had grown worse when Deka shunned her. When Naibe began her wondrous dance for Marai and Ari felt all the young woman's sadness at his death, her own wounds re-opened. Naibe had filled the plaza with so much magic. She must have still been weaving dreams around the throne. That she would miss the dance because she had planned to humiliate Deka seemed so childish now, but it wasn't something she could stop. Ari knew her plan to mock the woman for her coldness and her Prince's eagerness to wander were about to meet head on.

Yeah, Naibe, you go dance your dance. I'll drink with this one and then go do what I've been wanting to do for a while with him. Ari stared over the ladle at the Prince's confident smile and saw the flash of his dog teeth as he laughed at his ability to know her thoughts. *Pride,* she thought. *So proud you are. Make me just a little sick. Would have been nice, but now any pleasure I might feel is just going to feel like work.* She didn't care if he heard her thoughts; he had demonstrated that skill often enough. She sent him the conscious message: *What you don't know is how much I can drink and still walk around to talk about it.*

GOING FORTH BY DAY

Maybe I don't really want *you to crawl up and hunch my leg anymore. Did you ever think of that?*

The situation wasn't at all what she had hoped for. *Make me want to get at both of you and the old man too! You watch,* she protected one thought from exposure. *I'll just drink you down until you're too drunk to be of any use to me or any other woman here. About to leave for months and want a different kuna? You cold young bastard, I should wish your el soft just so I can laugh at it. Have me in your dreams.*

She knew if he had any regrets, he could blame the wine, even though he didn't seem to be the apologizing sort. This irked her even more. Keeping herself in that huff, she walked with him silently as they headed back out to the main plaza.

Maybe I was hungry enough once to give my body up for food or a soft place to sleep, but that was in the alleys and gutters of Tyre. I was just a girl then. Now I'm not so fast, Your Highness, her thoughts went to the Prince as he continued to move with her to another urn of wine in another part of the plaza. He looked at her out of the corner of one eye as he walked, so she continued her slightly disgusted but silent rant. *I know how you think this is going to go. You'll try to get me drunk, then drag me off somewhere, take me, and then leave me to sober up alone and sick as death while you sail off to Ta-Seti with your Deka.* Ari paused and faced him for the last part: *won't happen that way though. It's you who'll be loaded on your boat while I'm on to my next good day and it's Deka who will nurse your abandoned aches from the wine.*

She watched him fill the new ladle and offer her another drink, as if none of her deliberate message had made its mark or affected him in any way. "Hmmm… It's good," she grinned.

The Prince silently took another drink and gave her a matching one from the ladle. *So you want a game, then?* his thoughts spoke after moments of silent drinking. *It's your turn, so have another one.* He offered her the filled ladle again: *You're going to lose, you know.* Each time she finished one and returned the ladle, he grabbed at her and tried to close her in his grasp.

Oh Goddess, would you look at those arms! Those wonderfully muscled and oiled arms, Ari found herself taken for a moment.

He surrounded her and embraced her; his hands cupped her breasts. He tucked his fingers inside her kalasiris straps to stroke her nipples.

Hmm. Not bad at all, she thought, realizing with each passing moment that she really didn't want to play the game of resistance. Every move he made felt so good that she thought she might have to start screaming just to distract herself if he continued. His skill in the art of pleasure clearly matched his beauty. *I need to slow him down! This is happening way too fast. In a moment he'll have me on my knees and going for a taste right in front of his men.*

The Prince tittered, but responded with a thought. *You slow yourself down, woman. You know what you started and why. Maybe no one ever told you if you poke a wild animal with a stick, it will come at you fierce like this! But that's what you like, isn't it? Fierce?*

Ari pulled away, leading him. *I could do this, let my nature have the better of me, but there'd be no sport*, she sobered herself.

Ari wove the Prince around the perimeter of the courtyard. They each drank from various vessels, teasing each other and joking as they wandered back and forth through the crowd. *Odd, he's not getting that drunk*, she noticed. He moved casually among his men, bending stiffly toward them in his tightly laced and woven rib armor. From time to time he turned to include Ari in his conversation, but she remained a distant ornament most of the time. Any time the conversation paused, he touched, held, and stroked every part of her his hands could reach, but only as a tease. It was, as he intimated earlier, a fine game of hunt and chase. She listened to him gossip about some of the guests below as they made the rounds of the upper levels, then he would turn to her to share filthy but hilarious bits as if she was one of his men.

Harmless! she thought. *Can't believe the stories I've heard so far. He's just a strange rich young man. And yet, they treat him like a young warrior-god*, she giggled, suddenly beyond thrilled. *Oh, you've got wealth, Highness, and I've been with wealthy men before. But you think you're a god, or nearly so, I bet. Beat you there, too. Been with a god, and he liked me a lot... helped me become what I am t'day*, she smiled as she sipped from the ladle again. *Add a little sorcery, a little craft*, she pulled him closer at one point then exhaled rapturously into his face. *Like reading your thoughts, just as much as you like seeing into me. Maybe you're even casting your heka on me to get me to loosen up, eh? Is that what you did to Deka? Hmmm?*

Ariennu meandered through the party, arm in arm with the Prince, laughing and drinking as if they had become dearest friends. Despite her thoughts to remain somewhat distant from this prince – to relate to him on a physical level only – his natural seductiveness had begun to overtake her. She kept glancing at the ring and the hand strap that matched his grandfather's device or maybe was the same thing, waiting for some spark or emanation to come from it, but nothing happened.

Hmm. Feel really drunk. Doesn't do this to me most times. Makes me want him again; bad. Is that from the charm he's wearing? No. The Children then? she grinned, but then sighed. *And I'm going to get him drunk, and then what? Maybe Deka fell for him so hard she didn't* want *us to know about it,* Ariennu continued musing. *Maybe she's a little ashamed that all Marai's gentle, shepherd-y charm was never able to get to her that way.*

She realized the Prince had finished some random chatter with one of his officers and that he had turned his attention back to her.

And the bad part? I must watch myself with this fool. He reads thoughts! Worse yet, he lets me read him and see he can make any woman feel like a goddess on his couch the first night, and desperate for more of him every night after – until he gets bored and goes on the hunt again. It's easy for him – so tempting for me to tease and turn him. *I'll get the pleasure I want from you soon enough, Highness, but it's you who'll be begging for me to come back for more, not me gasping for you.* She chuckled, but noticed he had sensed her last thought anyway, by the sly and quizzical look on his face and the way his tongue slid over his lips in a tease back at her.

The Prince nudged her toward the steps and up to the private carved stone balcony areas outside the vacant royal bedchamber meant for the King's Great Wife, but Ari knew he had no intention of laying her out on the woman's couch. It was in good view of the chamber for the King across the covered walkway that joined them. Both rooms overlooked the main plaza. Nearby, in the center of the two rooms, another narrower flight of brick step led up to the kitchens so the servants could bring informal meals to the royal bedrooms.

"This is strapped on a little tight," he spoke aloud, interrupting her study of the way the rooms were laid out. It was an old instinct from the thieving days. She saw he fumbled with the tie-straps on his rib armor; his fingers slow from the wine he'd been drinking. "You can help me."

At last, she thought. *Now he'll want me to help him take this off and soon – just better not be up here after all.*

The crowd of men below looked up expectantly, as if they knew he was about to do something showy. Ari knew then that he brought her up with him as part of a stunt for the entire assembly of guests even though she thought she still heard the passionate music of Naibe dancing her heart out for Marai in the distance.

Two of his men had followed them with his big war bow and arrows and now fixed tethers and leather straps to the rail. Ari tensed and shook off the vision of a long-ago princess involved in a similar stunt.

"Planned to get a little drunk and put on a show with the bow for us," she mocked under her breath. "That you're good even half-drunk? Good enough to lead your men? Only a fool – here – I'll help you." She didn't like being used as an accessory so he could make a point, but the night was still young.

When the Prince's rib brace had been removed, Ariennu paused, eyes glued to the brutal-looking double row of muscle that had been hidden by the woven reinforcement. Tight bulges extended from his chest into the gold-clad belt around his small and nipped-in waist.

Mercy on me, she shook her head, her fingers extending forward to touch and inspect his belly.

He nodded in approval, rolled the armor, and then set it out of the way. Then, the Prince turned with a little yawn and overhead stretch designed to show off every part of his exposed physique as she ran her hand down to his waist and then smoothed the decorated brocade apron flap over his shendyt.

"Mmm?" she cooed, arms surrounding him in an embrace. She gently but suggestively thrust her hips against him, then stroked him to arouse him even more. Her head sank to his chest and her knees slowly bent as she kissed and lowered herself to his tight belly, then lapped at his naval. In the background she heard cheers of admiration from his men.

"Show? I'll give them a show right here –" she mumbled as he stumbled backward before regaining his balance.

"You think I'm drunk, don't you," he plucked her hand from his groin and dragged her up by the chin, then pushed her back against the balcony wall. "We'll get to that part later, Red Sister, but this show's still *mine* for now." Another wave of intoxication visibly passed over him. He staggered, but recovered quickly. "Um... not... drunk. This is how I can tell," he slurred.

Red Sister. Charming. Say you're not drunk, but you're so damned drunk you can't even remember my name. Oh – she giggled, *you never asked it.*

Ari felt tightness in her cheeks, a sure sign that the wine was having more effect on her than it should. She instinctively tapped the space above her brows where her Child Stone lay, but then sensed its comforting purr rise to greet her fingertips. *You in there,* she started, *you going to help me out tonight like you did when I was new or just get in the way?* She remembered the night she sampled the King's medicine and the way she had felt drunk that time. *Didn't help me then, did you? Well, oh well then. I guess I'll have to watch myself,* she sighed, but knew now that she'd started drinking, the old instincts to self-obliterate had begun to whisper. She watched the Prince sit on the rail, take the other ends of the leather straps in his hands then loop them over his ankles. *What is he* – she sidled closer and reached to stroke his arms. *A trick on this rail?*

"Watch," the Prince ordered her, then beckoned for her to hand him the bow and take one arrow from the quiver for him. When she did, he nocked it perfectly.

"See the tight little piece of ka't that just went downstairs with the tray of bread on her head? Middle loaf, dead center, keep watching." The Prince studied the girl's movement, turned his back to the plaza, sat on the rail, and raised himself until he was squatting balanced on it. He sprang up to clear it, then dropped backward over the rail so he swung slightly, suspended by the straps. With his body arched magnificently, he took aim and fired the overhead shot into the crowd. The arrow made its mark, but not without causing the serving girl who held the tray over her head to yelp and drop everything. The clot of people nearest her pointed and looked up while a roar and a cheer erupted from many of Prince Maatkare's men who noticed what he had done. The cheer continued to rise and ripple through the entire assembly while some of the people found the loaf he shot, lifted it by the arrow that pierced it, and waved it overhead to even louder cheers.

Tight little piece? Is that what he called her? Ari leveled a dirty look over the rail at the dangling Prince, then gasped in delight as he crossed his arms in a funeral position, put the bow in his teeth, then with a deep breath, slowly crunched his belly until he curled up high enough to grasp the straps. He continued the feat of control and strength until he could grab the uprights, take the bow from his mouth, toss it over, and finally clamber over the stone rail. He stood, breathing heavily at first, then returned a smug stare. Ari licked her lips, then gestured a little "come hither" with the tip of her tongue.

Ignoring all but the adoring crowd of soldiers, the Prince tore the restraining straps loose from his ankles and shoved both his fists, the war bow now clutched in one, into the air, then paraded around in a tight circle on the balcony.

"Yee-oooo… Aoooo…" he cried out like a hound howling loud and long, directing the sound down to his men. They sent up and admiring cheer, some returning the hoots and howling in response. Something in that exchange chilled Ariennu's heart to the point of instant sobriety. It was the cry. It didn't sound like a man imitating a wolf, it sounded like a wolf imitating a man. "Haa… ooooo… Ayoooooo…" he cried again, then dropped his bow to the balcony floor with a clatter. He turned to Ari and swamped her with several frenzied and wild kisses. Another light cheer went up from some of the men on the perimeter. Ari's feet left the ground as he lifted her and devoured her with more passionate kisses. Suddenly, he stopped and set her down, amused at the way she staggered and tried to find her feet beneath her lust-melted knees.

"See? *Not* drunk," he paused before launching another tirade of savage kisses and bites. "Had to do at least one trick for them, though. My men expect it," he panted, suddenly much more inebriated as he wiped a little spit from his lips. "Better not do another one, though. Old man'll be whining. Too many people here. Damn good wine this is," Prince Maatkare tucked Ariennu tightly in one arm and clambered back down the steps to the wine room to get more drink to share with her.

The dance Naibe had been doing crossed the older woman's thoughts. She wondered why the raucous demonstration of archery skills by the Prince hadn't overtaken it. *Is she still dancing? I don't see how anyone could go on through all that noise his*

GOING FORTH BY DAY

Highness and the men just made. Ari strained to see. The music had slowed.

Ariennu thought if she strained far enough, she would be able to see how Naibe performed it. Unfortunately, the Prince pawed at her more insistently than before. His fingers outlined the gentle curve of her belly, moved over the top of her hip sash, and settled far too comfortably between her legs, stroking and insistent. She felt the blinding sensation of the pleasure as his fingers played against the soft fabric of her shift; the heaviness of arousal, followed by her awareness of a spark-like charge from his dark ring. She struggled with him, staggering, and pushing him away as she realized she had all but succumbed to the moment. "I told you I will not be forced by that ring! I felt it that time," she hissed under her breath.

He took a swing at her, mostly to get her attention, but barely clipped her jaw.

In return, he got her fist in his mouth.

He paused, dumbfounded, licked his lip, and tasted blood. "Oooh Red Sister, so fierce you are! I *like* that!" he stood silently again. "You come at me all night, unceasing, then turn on me just as I notice you. Nothing makes me hotter than a good fight and bite," he teased, noticing that some of his men had widened into a circle to watch him. He seized the back of her head by the hair, wrestled her to him and kissed her again, harder; his sharp dog-like teeth stabbing at her lips. "You want a taste of me? You *taste* me, then!" he hissed at her, kissing and groping wildly.

Ariennu only made a half-hearted attempt to stop him. She gasped and laughed, then licked his blood and her own from her lips. He was desperately exciting to her and she was just drunk enough to completely rid herself of her plan to humiliate him. A quick grind in a dark corner might be the perfect cure for such a dismal day, she thought. Ari felt the reddest lust building in her. All night she had felt it build and had suppressed it again and again. *Why is it now that I'm pushing him away?* she wondered. *Is it really the heka ring? No, I'm dreaming it has power over me. I know he's thinking of compelling me and he's getting too drunk to use it. Is it because he belongs to Deka? Oh, blessed be, that's even more of a reason. If there wasn't such a crowd, I'd like to drag this pretty man out to the floor in front of her, mount him, and ride him to madness just for revenge. Make her look at me do it, too; her and his wretch of a grandfather!*

"Dare you!" she darted away from the Prince and into the wine room, then dipped up another cup for him and drank straight from the ladle herself. "You're drunk!" she snickered, but noticed she felt dizzier by the second. How *many dips of this stuff have we had? Ten... a dozen? More? He had a good start before he found me and he's still standing. Damn, the man can drink!*

"Time t' see," the Prince, now much more inebriated after he had hung upside down, staggered badly and lurched into each wall as he followed Ariennu back into the plaza. Once or twice he slipped, cursed, and righted himself. There were fewer party guests near them now. He glanced around the area, then he half-dragged her up to the balcony a second time. Winded and dizzy, both Maatkare and Ariennu stumbled and paused on the stone steps to the upper level.

Has the dancing stopped? Ari wondered, craning her neck to the area near the throne. She and the Prince hadn't gone up high enough to see. Through slightly fuzzy vision, she saw some of the guests starting to point the two of them out to each other, then look around for servants to gather their things. *It must be late. Party breaking up? No big cheering farewell? People leaving?* She decided they must have realized the Prince had become so drunk he wouldn't recall any of their well wishes and farewells. *Where's the King? He's gone too?* Ariennu sighed. *I missed everything following this madman around!* She heard someone mumble about the beauty of the dance, about the wonderful art of the dancer and her incredible beauty, but the guests *were* starting to leave. *The dance must have finished a while ago. The King's taken his girls and has gone up for the evening. Maybe Baby'll tell me all about it once I'm shed of this chunk of meat and gone to bed.*

The Prince pulled Ari to the balcony with him then released her and braced his arms on the rail. Only a short while ago, he had easily vaulted into a squat on it. Now, he could barely stand. He stared into the milling and departing crowd below. "Not so many of them down there now," he paused, then laughed and cursed again under his breath. He pulled Ari to the rail to show her what he saw. "Lookee at that. The Pit of Chaos waits for me right down there; the squealing pig!" He picked up his bow and tried to nock an arrow, but it slipped from his fingers. With an oath he tried again and succeeded.

"You're drunk. You'll kill somebody," Ariennu pulled back on his arm and caused him to stumble against her.

"So? Won't be the first time. It's what I do. I'm Lord o' the Dead, Lord of the Dead by the blood of Aset," he muttered, then spun around so fast that Ari barely had time to shrink out of the way as he aimed and fired the arrow. It bounced and shattered in the tile near his wife's leg. When he saw where it landed, he hollered over the balcony at her horrified and humiliated face. "You waiting for me?" he shrieked.

What was left of the crowd silenced and stared up. Even the few cheering men who remained looked up, amused and awed at the way Ariennu needed to steady the Prince on the rail to keep him from pitching headlong to the floor below.

"Go home! All of you!" he dropped his bow and stood gasping and dizzy, hand to his mouth. "Damn! Why'd I miss that fat cow?" he muttered, then continued in silent, enraged thought. *Would 'a been an accident. Nobody blames a accident. They just want too much of me. Give me nothing but misery, tryn'a put a collar on me!*

Ari's expression wormed between pride in having outlasted the Prince in the drinking and pity that she knew the misery awaiting him when he sobered. She saw Deka looking up at them, expressionless and hard, then understood the Ta-Seti woman had sensed all the ugliness of the Prince's thoughts before he bitterly growled them. They couldn't be heard by others, but Ari and Deka understood the words.

"Even you, Nefira Sekht, your blood's hot enough now to let me run free, but you will want to train me to your lap. They all do. So, you take this good look 'a me with your red sister and take a lesson into your lonesome bed t'night!" He blew a kiss down to her, mouthing more than saying the words aloud: "Go Home!" then turned to engulf Ari in a lascivious embrace.

That he was trying to insult Deka as badly as she had thought of shaming her, made Ari's heart skip. She didn't know whether to snarl at him for using her or welcome him for letting her use him for an evening of excitement. He fell inside the balcony rail and sat, trying to get up once more and failing.

His regulars were milling below, ready to get him moved to his boat before any worse insults were hurled.

Ariennu waved them away, her forced smile explaining that she had everything under control. All her passion suddenly fled as he pulled her to the rail. She knew she had to get him down the steps again before he fell over the rail and took her with him.

"Oh you —" he tittered softly, the sound caught between a growl and the chattery noise of a wild dog, as he looked across the central gap in the plaza between the two balconies. A dim, flickering lamplight came from the King's bedchamber. "Khaket. O big Kingsy MenKhaket. Where'd you go?" Prince Maatkare began to sing-song lightly. "I'm 'a be nasty wi' your cow-daughter. She likes it rough, you know – *craves* it. Not your holy sacrament, all gentle-like. What? You missing it wit her?" he slurred, laughing.

Ari knew that Maatkare was talking about the other wife, not the one he nearly shot tonight or Deka. He was talking about the daughter of Menkaure who died, and of the sacred, god-ordained intimacy she had sensed not long ago when she had consoled the King. He was implying the relationship between God and Daughter of the God had been a purely physical or sexual togetherness. It was heresy, and it was loud. Ariennu knew she needed to get him quiet before the King heard what he said. She embraced him heartily, pulling him back from the rail with all her strength.

"She *was* happy wi' me," Prince Maatkare continued rambling his drunken confession. "Shouldn't 'a tried to *own* me, shouldn't 'a made me mad at her like that. Shouldn't 'a tried to say I couldn't be her King, when I knew she wanted me. Teasing *ka't*, no better than…" he trailed, then continued. "I showed her. Her screaming for it that day – begging. Just a little push 's all it was," he reflected and almost sobbed. "I'm drunk. Not drunk *enough* t' be in this curse-filled house," Maatkare faded, then jumped solidly to his feet and grabbed Ariennu.

She had slipped into a heap beside him, too dizzy to stand up, but straightened nearly pop-eyed, when she heard his words. *Now, after he mocks the King, in a voice loud enough for others to hear.* "Come here, Your Highness," she whispered into his ear. "Let's get you to your men."

"Right," his voice grew quiet and solemn again.

Hauling him down the steps, Ariennu guided the Prince to the common latrine outside the plaza wall, then waited for him to relieve himself, hoping the fresher air would help him gather his wits.

Two men supported a woman who was vomiting from too much wine. Soon, the three party guests filed by with sheepish expressions on their faces, but they made no comment.

As soon as the guests moved away, Ari guided Prince Maatkare back toward the first urn she saw to force a final drink into his mouth. She spied one at the entry to a storage area, just an arm's length or two from the archway that opened to the rear yard. *Maybe one more drink'll knock him flat, then I can get his men to carry him away before he says anything else.* At that moment, the last thing Ari wanted was sex from him, even if he *could* perform.

Prince Maatkare quietly sucked on the edge of the cup she found floating in the urn, pondering his situation. His eyes glimmered slightly as he casually dropped the cup to the floor and wiped his mouth on the back of his hand. "Mmm, could you –" he started, about to lose his balance as he leaned heavily in the doorway.

Ari sighed, dizzy herself but inwardly disgusted. *I have to nursemaid him now. Some wonderful evening this became! You had better not puke on me or I'll kill you, Prince or not,* she thought and then continued aloud: "Not your servant. Just because I brought you out here for some air –" she started, but to her shock, felt him reach for her and pull her up into an embrace so fierce that the cup fell from her grasp. She resisted, but suddenly felt lulled, drowsy, and almost overwhelmed by the return of her own desire.

"No, this is stupid. This is a mistake, I –" she suddenly felt all the humiliation Deka had felt at his behavior tonight. She struggled, thinking Deka would be in front of them and laughing at the way she had disgraced herself when she looked up from her bent over position. "You need to go, now," she broke free of the Prince and began to move past a small cubicle-like room and toward the emptying plaza.

Magically, the Prince rallied and stumbled after her. Despite her half-hearted struggle against him, Maatkare grabbed her solidly, backed her into the cubicle, flattened her against the wall and ripped open the front of her kalasiris with what she thought had been his pearly-painted nails.

Claws? she froze. *What? Changing into a — aww goddess —*

His mouth and teeth licked and bit her neck and shoulders insistently. With a low growl, he moved to her exposed breasts like a desperate animal. His powerful arms gripped her so tightly she couldn't move.

"Damn you. You're too drunk. Even *I'm* too drunk 'n seeing things. Now *stop*," Ariennu hissed under her breath, but the Prince continued to back her into the small room. She struggled some more, even though she knew her attempts were half-hearted at best. The sense of danger and the knowledge of his deadliness had excited her all over again as he sank his teeth into her breasts. They both knew neither of them had any intention of stepping away from each other tonight.

Just a push — The words echoed through Ari's soul like the arrows Maatkare had fired earlier.

Is he saying — Is he saying he killed *the King's daughter?* She felt ill, dizzy, floating, and oddly, more desperate than she had felt in months. *It's the wine and the dance magic, not his damned ring. Nothing is real; none of this is real,* rainbows shimmered through her eyes in self-defense at first that quickly became a strange and erotic welcome. An odd light surrounded Maatkare's head and reflected on a face that had grown intent. *He is changing? No, I'm just drunk — the wine made my Child Stone drunk,* she chortled eagerly.

She knew she was very inebriated, but not enough to miss everything about the Prince that was so good. Her hands sank to the buckle under his shendyt cover and pulled it loose. With that much wine in him, she knew he should have been useless, but the final drink she had given him seemed to increase not only his ability but his desperation and ravenousness.

The Prince paused, unwrapped the loosened loin coverings and, despite his intoxication, twisted it properly so it would fall perfectly pleated when he dressed again. He dropped the bundle to the floor and lunged, half falling against her.

How is he able? Drunk as any score of men might get, but his mighty El as solid and standing as a thick-masted sailing ship? Resist? Why should I, when I need this… oh goddess, this? She wrestled her torn kalasiris up over the top of her head and dropped it, then let him engulf her in his arms as she braced herself against the smooth brick wall in the little room. *I'm just an old kuna made new and pretty by this stone in my head, and him? Oh, he is so delicious...* She sank to the floor with him, laughing, fumbling, stroking, and adoring. "And so *now* you want my sweet honey gate? If you go limp on me now, I'll..." she shuddered in expectation, raising her hand for half a moment to suggest he should at least start gently.

"Never said I didn't. You – you said I *couldn't*, and I won't be challenge..." his fingers dove between her legs, caressing her for a moment to sense her readiness as he guided himself. The pleasure of the feeling as he entered and overwhelmed her swept her into a different world. He growled again, reveling at her instant pleasure. *You feel all of it now. You'll nourish me now,* his thoughts radiated through her body, growing mightier and more forceful with each move. Opening her eyes beyond the first thrill, Ariennu saw his appearance had continued to change.

Animal. Aaa... niii... mulllll! her thoughts cried out, seeing that his eyes had turned a fiery gold-green. Her hands seized, kneaded his buttocks, and welcomed him.

That's true. I am that. See how much so? his spirit voice, unaffected by the wine, answered, followed by his desperate whisper: "You see?"

A feeling like static and lightning briefly spread through Ariennu's Child Stone when his left hand moved from her upper back to her forehead. *The ring... You!* Ariennu objected for only an instant before she faded in another wave of ecstasy.

Does nothing unless I ask it. I know you. You want this hard enough to break your back in two before I'm done with you, don't you?

Ariennu laughed wickedly in joy at the threat in his thoughts. *Animal.* She gasped, craving every thrust and needing more until the sleeping beast in her own heart woke to match his intensity move for move. All the moments blurred and lost touch with any sense of reality. She cursed, cried out, encouraged, and squalled in joy. Amid her wine-filled dizziness and sexual ecstasy, her eyes blurred and her senses showed her a strange haunted vision of the Prince transforming into a black beast-hound with elongated, saber-like upper fangs. The creature had taken his place and mounted her instead. He *was* the creature. Ari, stunned by the idea of a dark furred growling and biting beast riding her, tried to still her racing thoughts.

No, something whispered in her thoughts. *Afraid... no... not afraid of you. I'm afraid of me, what you build inside me... dark... death... sister Ereshkigal goddess... ohhh shhh...* she felt her heart want to stop as she opened her eyes and saw Prince Maatkare Raemkai had now most mysteriously become a green-eyed wolf with dark-furred human arms and legs. He towered above her, relentlessly moving with her and consuming her energy along with all her thoughts. The darkness that issued from his grip, fed by the ring she couldn't see, wrapped itself around her and tightened its grip on her soul. His head bowed once and his fanged jaw sank into the meat of her shoulder, then her throat. What should have been bleeding agony only multiplied her pleasure by what she would later call senseless and wicked hundreds.

At some unknown point, her thoughts went dark with an even deeper delight. One with his rhythm, she was roused only by the burst of his seed and the sudden numb and shuddering tenseness through his body followed by his complete collapse.

Ariennu then lay gasping and windless. She tried to push his upper body to one side so she could breathe more easily. For a lingering moment, she felt the lightning of insatiability spread through her thighs and belly again. Maatkare had been incredible and vicious. He had taken her to a place where her thoughts and her body were equally satisfied and astonished, but she became aware, in her spinning and almost-sickened exhaustion, of an irrational desire for more.

Ari lay in the floor and he lay sprawled over her. The illusion of the wolf was gone and the Prince lay unconscious from wine and exertion. She pushed at him again, but could barely move him. *Dead?* Ari gasped, startled. *No. Dead* drunk *for sure. Beat you down, you nasty cur,* she tittered as she eased from beneath him. Ariennu groped in the dark for her crumpled kalasiris and noticed once again that one of the breast straps had been torn loose and another rip had opened the front of it to her crotch. She remembered being bitten by a wolf, but when she swatted at the places on her shoulders throat and breasts that still stung delightfully, she felt no wound or bleeding.

A dream? her thoughts tried, but scattered as the room spun. *Surely I...* Ari knew she was beyond drunk now. Everything inside her ached and burned from her haunches to mid-back and even as far as her shoulders and neck. Waves of shuddering pleasure still consumed her. She couldn't see in the darkness of the tiny storeroom. A night like this was *so* much like the bad old days in the city *and* in the sand. There would always be drink, riotous sex, and squeezing out from under some man who thought he could bring her down, only to show him up. *It's what I am, dammit – a thieving old fisher's kuna from Tyre, and him, the murderin' Lord o' Death!* She shook her head, still drunk, but now increasingly winded and nauseated.

Just a little push

Maatkare's slurred words echoed in Ari's thoughts again. She sobered a little more, struggling to ease into a sitting position. Her hands swiped and pressed at the stone in her brow, hoping the healing sequence in it would clear her thoughts. It tingled, objecting slightly. *No, he killed his first wife. He admitted it. I must get sober – tell someone.* The tingling grew stronger, but in reaction she felt sicker. At any moment, she thought she would collapse into a helpless and heaving scrap of used flesh. *No, No – no – I need to recover. I'm no wandering easy piece of ka't to be tossed aside when he's done. I can have the King's ear at any time. I need you to fix me,* she thought internally.

The tingling increased. A feeling of well-being surrounded the spot on her brow, but extended no further.

The poisons must be removed from your body.
In the first time as you rested.
You should rest again.

Ariennu breathed easier, her thoughts held together a little better. She panted, salivating and wanting to vomit. *Even if I told the King, I'd be looking over my shoulder for the rest of my life. Maybe I'll have to kill this Maatkare. That would be a damned shame,* she reflected. *Oh, damn, that was fun!* She sat on her heels and stroked the Prince's buttocks with one hand, then rolled his heavy and sated body slightly to one side and chuckled at his flaccid penis. *Mmmm, mmm… fine and righteously beautiful piece of meat you've got there, Highness. Glad I could tear off a piece of it tonight. Think Deka better lock you up or put a muzzle on it, though. Can't let that out too often, even though it gets so very hungry.*

She stood shakily, steadying herself, and found her shift. Ari tried to step into it and, after nearly losing her balance, she straightened up and tried to tie the torn straps of her shift together. Her fingers felt fuzzy. After managing to make a clumsy knot, she noticed the Prince had not moved. Ariennu braced herself against the wall and bent to make sure his head was turned to one side; in case he became as ill as she was in his stupor. She perched his nemes, which had come off his head, over one ear. *Your hat came off, Highness*, she chuckled again, feeling almost proud of herself. *Poor thing. All spent. He had no chance*; she stroked his jaw with the back of her hand then peeled up the front corner of his lip. She remembered something about biting and long, sharp teeth. His "dog" teeth looked a little elongated, but not what she remembered.

Ari bent to kiss his cheek like a mother wishing good night to a sleeping son, then didn't remain beside him any longer. If he woke, he might rally and try for her again, impossible as that seemed. Rising, she tiptoed back into the main area. Everything had darkened in the grand plaza. *Damn. How long were we… And him drunk like that? What demon did he call down? Wepwawet indeed? Have mercy.*

A few vague shadows remained, milling about in the dark of the plaza. Unable to focus on which people were there, Ariennu rubbed her brow gently again, wondering why the Child Stone wasn't working faster. When she did, the nausea rose again. *Damn this. Don't make me sick; just clean.* She looked up the stairs that she and the Prince had traveled up and down all night. An ever-present low light streamed from the King's bedchamber.

Ariennu blearily sighed in relief that the King had retired for the evening with his chosen concubines. She was growing so ill from the wine and exhausted from the evening that she just wanted to go to the privy, rid herself of it, and then go to sleep. *Why does this stone in my head want to punish me? I know it can heal me. 's trying to teach me a lesson.* Shaking, she stumbled again. She sighed, holding the wall near the outdoor privy, but backing away from the reek of the overflowing trough. She felt the wine in her gut start to rise again, but she paused to regain herself, grabbing her head and rubbing it until the warmth of the stone spread again. *I'll find a different place where I won't be stepping in it in the dark,* she turned and decided to find her way to the women's quarters and the separate privy.

She cautioned herself as she reached the stairs to the King's bedchamber and stumbled over the first step. *Goddess though — One part of me's still shaking, for sure,* Ariennu paused, stroking her mount and feeling the chill of pleasure erupt again. *Better not go up there. I'm still drunk; don't even think those things, just walk away from this prince and make him forget. Do the spell with the rainbows. There are enough other men in this world, so who needs* that *man or any man really except for setting off the thunder. Damned beast is good at it though. He thinks that makes him important. Pah!* she spat.

"You, Woman!" Ariennu heard the voice of one of the two guards on patrol near the lower steps outside the King's stateroom as they stopped her.

She paused, trying to steady her step even though she was aware the men had seen her stumbling and probably the direction from which she had come.

"*You* were with his Highness?" he asked.

She saw his mouth flash in mirth and recognition as he reached to paw at her scrambled bright hair and to examine her torn dress. *Ooops — No secret kept* this *time,* her thoughts finished. She almost laughed, but the sick feeling had made her too dizzy to stand upright. "Damn right," she laughed again and stumbled against him and his partner who had closed in to assist. "I think I broke him, though," she cackled and waved one of her arms in the direction of the storage area. It was a good distance away. She didn't remember wandering all the way to the royal bedchamber stairs. Ari felt one guard seize her and pull her upright. He began to move her away from the steps, supporting her.

The other guard trotted in the direction she pointed, then investigated the little room where she and the Prince had been. He went in for a few moments then emerged, shaking his head and chuckling a little. "Lo, He breathes, but his lamp is out!"

"Let's take the woman to her quarters, then come see if we can get his guards to get him onto his boat before too many know how he was brought down," the other grimly ordered, but laughed.

Ari slyly picked up his thought about how he might like to bend her over something because she was too drunk to object. "What?" she sagged between the two men as they half dragged her and walked her to the women's rooms. *You want to whaaaat?* her thoughts echoed. A horrendous giddiness suddenly overcame her. She wanted to be with the Prince again rather irrationally and sensed this was exactly what had happened to Deka. The irrational desire. *Lying bastard.* He did *bind me with a spell.* She remembered, in a flash, that night she saw him through the Child Stones when he said he would have to bind her if she meddled. *Urrrr… daamn him!* "Oh Maaaaaaat – kaaaa – raaaay" her voice trailed. "I wanna good night kiss," she hooted aloud until one of the guards slapped her, then punched her belly. She jumped back, cursed, swung at him, and started to fight, but lost her balance and stumbled to the corner to retch.

After a few moments, one of the guards grabbed her arm and pulled her back.

"Let me…" she protested, but then realized she was being quickly ushered to the women's area and her kalasiris was coming apart again. Ariennu sullenly gripped the sides of the garment like an armor against tempted guards.

It had been quite a party. Everything in her thoughts was going black and sparkly, but she regained herself enough to walk the rest of the way into the sleep area, let the ruined dress fall to the floor, and then collapse on her bed in utter fatigue and drunkenness.

GOING FORTH BY DAY

Chapter 30: Theft and Shadow

Ari became aware of the room spinning. She looked at the shadow patterns the lamplights created on the ceiling, then tried to get control of herself, but the attempt made her want to vomit again. Closing her eyes, she managed to keep her stomach settled and still herself. Calmly, she thought of everything that had just happened while the Child Stone in her brow quietly pulsed.

I know you want me to suffer just a little, don't you? she sighed. *Just help me put everything together. I don't think I want to get this drunk again… can't even think. Nnnn, old girl, you just made things a lot worse for yourself,* she sighed and drifted, feeling the web of warmth start to spread from her brow. For a moment she thought she was going to sleep again, but then the familiar separation and lurch between what the Kemet people called 'ka' and 'ba' rolled over her.

"No…" she mouthed. "Just want to rest…" the same vision she had when the old man put her hand in the box this afternoon returned. *The Children… trying to tell me something?* she contemplated the black rectangular thing that gleamed in the torchlight in her vision. It was a burial box of darkest polished stone. She couldn't see him because the lid was securely on the box, but she knew Marai lay inside it. *I know. The Children are telling me Hordjedtef lied to all of us. They said it before. Marai's body wasn't blasted by flame. They found a way to kill him and then they buried him. But – maybe he's not dead, maybe asleep –* she continued, wanting to struggle until she was fully awake. Unfortunately, she was still unable. *If I could find his body, I could…*

It is as Aset.

The voice of a man that seemed vaguely familiar, but at the same time distant and obscured, spoke in her thoughts. It chanted softly, almost seductively.

Aset to bring and nurture life
out of a dead womb
to revive the life of the bull Asar

GOING FORTH BY DAY

Take his seed from the pieces
Protect. Defend…

She frowned and rose to miserable full consciousness with a wave of nausea. Taking a deep, gasping breath, she sat up. The memory of her vision that morning raced through her aching head. *No,* she shut her eyes in the darkened room. *Stop toying with me. Aset who searches for the body of Asar? Naibe walked into Ashera and Dumuzi with Marai. Me? Aset? I'm just a nobody. The rest of them can be gods and goddesses, but not me. I'm just a stank kuna and a thief who likes a drink and a good hot hunk of a man,* she gasped silently in her own horror again, wiping her mouth. Slowly, she steadied her senses and looked around to see who was asleep in the room.

I've got to find Naibe and tell her. Naibe-Ellit wasn't in her bed. Ariennu froze. The concubines, vain little Irika and lotus pretty Suenma, *were* in their beds. They fidgeted and snored quietly. Ariennu shook her head madly and tried to sober herself some more.

What the? Now where did she go? Ari leaned over and dug into her basket beside the bed. Finding the big shawl she usually wore after any night visits, she wrapped it around her naked body, then stared at her dress, now a crumpled pile of cloth that lay on the floor. *It'll need more than the strap fixed,* she picked up the ragged scrap, then dropped it again. *I was getting out of that like it was on fire. What a beast!*

While she looked for something to wear, a quiet hush, like a gentle soft wind, wove through the open areas of the palace. It was after the middle of the night. She realized she hadn't seen Naibe since the young woman had started to dance for the King. *The King,* Ari gasped. *She's with the King, I bet.* Damn *girl! I thought you might – and over those two 'girls' too. I know you've got some* real *enemies now,* she snickered. Ariennu was half-mumbling to herself as she pulled something simple from her basket, threw it on quickly, and dizzily made her way to the polished brick stair, just to see if she was right. She silently hid just out of sight.

A warm and lovely light emanated from the room at the top of the stair. As soon as the lower guards who had sent her to the women's area earlier had passed by, she began to creep up the stairs. At the top, she saw the King's night-time personal guards dozing. They were seated on the floor on the other side of the landing.

Maybe I can still slip by, she raised her hand in the gesture of secrecy and tried to focus her attention on sending obscurity through the ends of her fingertips. She knew the illusion had every chance of not working because of her drunkenness, the rattling evening with the Prince, and even before that the encounter with the high priest that had taxed her. She knew she heeded to rest so the Child Stone could bring her the healing she needed, but she didn't like the troubling visions they had just provided. *They catch me, I'll just let them know how drunk I am,* she resolved.

Luckily, she felt a little of her illusion wrap into a cloak of faint, but darkened rainbow shimmers. Ari moved by the men like a ghost without touching either of them. Her hand parted the heavy glass beaded ropes in the entry with all the stealth of her thieving past. None of the beads tinkled.

On passing through the door Ariennu saw that the King's bedchamber had been transformed into a place of magical and unearthly beauty. Naibe's dance garlands had been strewn around the room and seemed to have somehow multiplied. *Am I seeing things because I'm this drunk?* she wondered. Flower petals littered the room, from Menkaure's private reflection pool to his royal couch. Dozens upon dozens of candles and low little lamps had been grouped on tables and set about on the floor surrounding his bed. Ariennu saw Naibe sitting up on the King's couch. The young woman was shielded from clear view by the voluminous-yet-sheer linen netting that draped from a round gold ceiling fixture resembling the rays of the sun. She held the King's head quietly on her breasts.

King Menkaure was sleeping. For the first time since she or Naibe-Ellit had arrived, Ari thought his face looked peaceful.

Naibe looked up, sensing the elder woman's presence, then put her finger to her lips. *Shh. I know you are here, MaMa.* Naibe's thoughts whispered. *He's resting now. He's so tired, so very sad. I understand why I could not be with him like this before. We would have destroyed each other with our grieving.*

Did you? Ariennu fell back against the doorframe, almost making a sound before she froze. The secrecy efforts were making her feel worse. She knew she would have to leave quickly before her ability failed. The Child Stone grew hotter in her brow as it redoubled its cleansing efforts – that hurt too.

Uh-huh. Her thought whisper seemed almost shy, like a young girl basking in the afterglow of her first love and still very much wrapped in her "Ashera" trance. *He was good to me, Ari. He lets me use his other name, "Ka-Khet", now.* She smoothed the King's cap-like greying hair, then gently caressed a place near his ear. *You feel drunk, are you?* she asked the elder woman's shadow.

Very... Ariennu nodded. *Still am... beat that crazy man, Prince Maatkare, though. Put him down!* she giggled aloud, licked her lips, and remembered the almost demon-like frenzy with which he took her; how it was followed by his sudden-death like collapse. It made her wonder all over again if a demon *had* been animating him when he was useless. Would he wake and remember nothing because it hadn't been *him* but some demonic wolf spirit instead? *You got romance as usual, and me? It figures,* she drifted, almost visible.

Shh. Naibe reminded her, pointing out that one of the guards was stirring.

Ariennu turned and tiptoed from the upper alcove. She stumbled as she went downstairs, happy to leave Naibe and the King to the rest of their night together. She knew morning would bring so many wonders because she would likely still be in his arms. Her mirage of secrecy faded with each step she took.

Hordjedtef stood at the bottom of the polished stone stair waiting for her. Ari froze, her heart suddenly pounding until rage caught up with the shock of seeing the old man. She realized the old priest had been right behind her spying while she and Naibe shared their thoughts. "Isn't it past your bed-time?" she fired off a sullen remark at him.

The count stood very still, silhouetted by the remaining lamplight from the grand plaza, arms folded across his thin-but-sturdy, ancient chest. An ever-present, self-satisfied smirk wormed over his face.

"Oh, my *dear* Lady Ariennu, it *is* you!" he clucked. "Yes, it is late, but since you've asked me, I'll tell you! I was about to return home some time ago," his all-wise and condescending tone mocked civility.

Ariennu didn't even want to stand up or try to pretend she was more sober than she was. She slumped heavily onto the bottom step and held her head, realizing that even the lamplight had become too bright.

"But, on searching for my dear grandson to bid him farewell and good journey, I found quite the crowd who showed me that he was being rather loudly *entertained,* shall we say, and had been quite bewitched into drinking a great store of wine with a woman." The elder priest grinned like a cat sunning itself. "I grew concerned and decided to stay a bit longer after my dear countesses had gone ahead. When I saw his men take him to his boat more dead than alive, I thought *'what* kind of woman is it who can cripple a healthy young warrior such as he?' My thoughts naturally came to you."

"He started it. I warned him," Ariennu slurred, pouting. She leaned against the wall at the bottom of the stairs, knowing this meeting with the elder priest wasn't going to go well. He stroked the top part of his hand where she remembered seeing the ring. Blurred darkness had formed over his two middle fingers.

"Perhaps it *is* true," his tone became clever. "You *are* El Lilitu? Is that what they call the handmaidens of vengeance in your land?" his smile and voice taunted.

Ariennu felt a horrid vortex forming. Nausea and fever rose through her body. Her Child Stone crackled as if a static spark had leapt through it. The feeling weakened her back and she bent forward, gripping her ribs.

With mocking care, the priest sat beside her on the lower step like he intended to comfort her.

"Bastard," she croaked.

His hands caressed the air.

"Stop!" her world grew dark.

Then, the Great one of Five began his lecture: "A first thing you would learn in any *serious* study is that *excess* creates vulnerability. It is the real reason why you were not retained in the temples of your beloved Tyre, correct?" Hordjedtef quipped. "My own dear heir, young Maatkare Raemkai, has unfortunately not paid attention to this rule and will not reign in his lust either, feeding it where he will. This lack of discipline allows me to now both see and work you both quite easily, to know what you *think* you have learned from the lips of a drunken wastrel tonight," his laughter chittered like the rustle of mice in an empty storeroom. "Good Night, my dear, until we meet again."

Then, blackness. Nothingness came.

After a few moments, Ariennu felt herself being lifted and shuffled in silence. She heard the old man's voice giving instructions to what she perceived to be a crowd of bearers who had begun to carry her somewhere. She couldn't move. She was trapped in his spell, but felt so comfortable that she had no will to even struggle.

"Excellent. You have her things, then?" she heard him ask.

"Yes, Your Great Highness, I have them," a woman's voice answered. She walked with the crowd – it was Deka.

Deka? Deka? Oh Goddess. Deka, what are you? Ariennu's thoughts rallied and yet she couldn't struggle or scream.

"When His Majesty rests again, I've informed the guards to fetch the other one. Do be sweet and see if you can discover the missing eight ones for us, my young Ntr Nefira Sekht."

Nefira Sekht? That name Maatkare called her. Beautiful power? Is that it? What the? Deka – Deka! Ariennu screamed in the dark, frozen and unable to move.

Naibe-Ellit became aware of a pulsing, sliding feeling in the moments before she opened her sleep-caked eyes. At first, she reveled in the sensuality of that feeling and the sensation of water flowing nearby. A gentle chunk, an occasional thump, and a swaying feeling repeated in a rhythmic pattern. Rustling cloth sounded in the wind somewhere in the distance. For an instant, she thought of being in the pod in the Children of Stone's vessel, but it did not last. This was something else and some*where* else. A gentle chanted cadence timed the surging she felt. It was the sound of rowing

— men rowing. The back of her neck ached, right at the base of her head. When she put her hand up to it, she felt a slight, sore lump. She opened her eyes wider and saw that she lay in a tapestry-draped shelter which surrounded goose down cushioning. It smelled of wonderful spices and dried flower blossoms.

Ooohh, pretty… she thought, smoothing the soft, fine-threaded linens, but the fascination lasted only for an instant. Light filtered in at her bare feet, glinting on her ankle bracelets. A coverlet lay out over her nakedness. Near her feet, her dance cloak was neatly folded. Someone had taken great care not to pleat or wrinkle it. Gasping in horror, Naibe realized she was not alone. A feeling of dread rushed through her. She had fallen asleep with one man in her arms and wakened to find herself in the arms of another.

She looked up as her thoughts continued to clear. As she glanced around the draped cabin, she recognized the calm, almost expressionless face looking down at her. She knew who it was. *This* man was Prince Maatkare Raemkai, the same man who had been celebrated last night. He was the one who had greedily spirited Deka away weeks before but had not been above drunken antics with Ariennu at the party. Now, somehow, she and this prince were on a rather large and nicely outfitted boat being swiftly steered somewhere by many men. He was up on one arm, watching her the way an animal might study a bird or small animal it had trapped.

"Where's Majesty? Where's KaKhet?" her first words leapt from her throat before she realized how much talking made her head hurt. The Child Stone in her brow whispered something she couldn't quite understand.

"In his palace, I guess," the Prince's voice steadied her unfocused thoughts.

"Deka?" she tensed, worried. "Ari?" she struggled in fear even though she knew she shouldn't.

"On the boat behind us, but they don't matter to you now. I have you, and you excite me." He seized her hand and began to trace it over his hard, muscled chest down to his flat belly.

Naibe shut her eyes, tired and groaning, then fell back onto the cushioning. "My neck hurts," she shut her eyes again, hoping the complaint would buy her at least enough time to get her bearings. She knew *exactly* what this man wanted of her and could barely contain her horrified astonishment.

Prince Maatkare Raemkai touched the lump at the base of Naibe's neck to see what might have caused her pain.

"Bastards," he whispered under his breath. What seemed to have been a sympathetic comment at first quickly turned into a chuckle of disbelief at his good fortune. "I'll have to speak to them about how it's done. They could have wounded you. Dizzy?" he asked, but didn't wait for her answer. "Come here," he helped her sit with him, then tilted her into one arm, placing her palm over his heart so she could stroke his chest and admire his muscles.

Instead, she bowed her head to his neck. *But why have I been taken away? Why did KaKhet Menkaure let me go? He was so very happy last night. He called me his goddess. He even cried in my arms – so very happy!* her thoughts trailed. She had to have the answer. "But..." she protested, knowing all too painfully where any of the small talk she could muster as a spacer would eventually lead. "Where are you taking me?" she knew the man intended to force her if she didn't comply. She'd heard enough rumors during her stay at the palace. Maybe if she could keep him talking, she might learn what he liked. Maybe a way to escape would present itself if the idea was just too obnoxious.

This was already so terribly disgusting. Someone had knocked her senseless the moment the King slept, dumped her into this pretty cabin and into *this* man's lap. Now that she had *just* come to her senses, he wanted to leap her. Her head was still spinning. She felt how aroused he was – he kept slyly working her hand to accidentally graze or touch him, to worship the size of his erection. Her stomach knotted in nausea.

"Little place called Qustul," a frown spread over his face for just a moment, "but you don't need to know that. You just need to know someone's going to make you feel sooo good inside, just like Nefira, just like your Red Sister," he grinned.

"Qustul? Isn't that almost a month away? You'll be there for several months? That's what the party was about last night?" *The party. The King. KaKhet... KaKhet, how could you let me go? You said you...* Naibe-Ellit sat up and tried to pull away. Her heart hammered in panic as Maatkare's grip on her hand tightened until she gasped. *No, you cannot force me*, she took in a little breath, knowing she was strong enough to overcome a mere man. To her shock, her strength had suddenly abandoned her. A silent sedateness stole through her brow, attempting to soothe her.

No need.

Peaceful be.

To instruct.

To calm.

To learn

Her child stone assured her. The voice inside it sounded wrong though, tentative, as if it was giving her a hint. That, and the fact that she couldn't budge her hand, worried her. *But why?* "You're hurting me!" she pushed at his chest with the heel of her hand in vain.

"You know *why*," he replied quickly, his lips at her brow. "Because you're not supposed to say no… or even *think* it. I can hear your thoughts, you know, every one of them." He wrestled her hand from his chest and brought it to his penis. "See? Nice, eh?"

Naibe fought the little smirk of subconscious pleasure that squirmed around under her lips. He *was* delicious looking, but it didn't make him any more appealing to her. She remembered before she had been changed by the Children of Stone that she would have tried to trip up a man of such excellent form and endowment, then crawl over him, tearing joyously into him like a starving beast. It was different for her now. If there was sex, and often there was not, it was a sharing thing that loved heartily and demanded that love would be returned. If it could *not* be – if there was no warmth – then there was nothing. She knew if she relaxed and didn't resist him, he would certainly take her to a gasping, wicked pleasure, but it would be nothing to her after the sensations faded. The first part of her life before she was changed had been about craving the sex, and she didn't need any more of that.

Through Marai and then through Wserkaf, she had learned that the goddess she *thought* she called down had always been inside of her, even from her birth. It was the goddess of *all* love, not just the physical. Because of the stone in her brow that constantly whispered to her and taught her, she had learned to accept that gift. She sent love out to surround and fill a man like the light of a billion stars; to nourish and heal him with her love. That was the gift she had given Shepseskaf and then King Menkaure.

In just a flash of memory, she remembered her evening with the King:

Naibe-Ellit slowly circled the pink and white throne one more time. Her sheerest gauze veils and garlands lay loosely at her feet. So much joy had come through her during the dance that she could not contain her gasping and gentle sighing, even though the dance had ended. She had planned to fade into the crowd of prophetesses, who had clustered at one side of the onlookers. Among them, she would seek the protection of the women's area, but the thought to go to them wouldn't stay. She quietly sagged, winded, joyous, and gleaming with sweat at the foot of the throne.

Her hands gently caressed her own breasts, offering them in sudden grief remembered. "Oh Marai, Marai my love…" she had quietly mouthed, "come back to me." She remembered feeling herself lifted from the floor, but she was too dazzled to see who picked her up with strong but trembling arms.

Many women's hands touched and blessed her as she was carried past them. They had gently wept in what sounded like joy as if they finally understood her dance and why she had come to Kemet. She had been the beloved of a dead man, but in this dance she came to give herself to a god. They had trembled in awe as she was borne past them and up the stairs.

"Majesty –" she had heard a voice rise in protest. It had been the old priest.

"No, Uncle, not this time," the voice of the King had spoken. Naibe recalled feeling fretful, but the King's attention turned to her. "Shhh. I've got you. Your King has you, sweet one," the sparkly glass-beaded curtain had tinkled past their shoulders as he carried her into his bedchamber.

She had been in that room often during the week, but she had always been with Ariennu. Together they had spoken to him and consoled him in the evening. Sometimes she sang to him. That night, the room seemed strange and different, with the flowers and the little lights everywhere like stars greeting them. It had become part of another world.

Oh, he trembles at the sight and touch of me, she had almost opened her eyes as he set her down. The touch reminded her of *Him*. "Mar…" she began as she was placed, ever so gently, on the King's wide, dark, and soft couch. The last of her veils and garlands had slipped from her body as she was carried.

Menkaure cared for her then as she had once cared for him.

"Ohhh…" she had opened her eyes, fixing them on his gold and indigo nemes, the serpent at his brow, and finally his gentle hazel-brown eyes, which stared back at her in the soft flickering lighting of all of the lamps and candles spread throughout the room.

The weight of a kingdom lined the King's slightly plump face as he had sat there by her. He smoothed her hair with the back of his hand, then reached to remove her ribbon circlet. He soothed the place where her blue stone lay, easily showing her he thought she had hurt herself.

"Sweet goddess," he began.

She sensed his tears forming and knew her dance had opened his oldest and deepest wounds. He had been thinking of those who had gone before, just as she had danced for a man who had gone.

"You have found me in your Underworld of sorrow," he whispered, moving to stretch out on his couch beside her.

When he touched her face, Naibe lifted her hand to offer him the same gesture.

"I said on the day you came into my house that one day I would come to you to give you the honor of my body; that I would come to you as a god." He had removed his nemes.

Naibe saw in her memory reaching up to mark the slight red indentation where it had pressed into his brow. She had blinked her quiet eyes and listened as he continued.

"But my sad heart has now met your sad heart and it begs that you honor me instead, for without worship of you I have no honor."

She had whimpered, as if the thought of lying with an actual king who was a god might be fearsome. Even though she had seen him at his weakest just some days earlier, her lips trembled. Tears had filled her eyes, but his fingertips hushed her. She reveled in his worship.

"You still weep for him, your best beloved. Your dance was for him, too, pretty Kina-Ahn? I can see it was," he lowered his eyes. "Perhaps I will meet such a god of men when I go into the West. We will sail the stars together, brother with brother. I think it will be soon, my goddess."

The corners of Naibe's mouth had twitched, because she knew he was speaking of his own death. She nodded, averting her eyes slightly as he sat and eased her gently onto his lap. He had kissed the surface of her lips then, respecting her entirely as she wrapped her arms around him and looked up into his eyes.

Naibe gently breathed into his mouth, giving him her sweetness as the last act of her dance of love. She had whispered: "we must let our sad hearts touch each other and heal our hurts and sorrows together while we live."

That was why women feared her and men went to their knees and crawled across the burning sand for her. She brought *love* into men and drew it from them again in a way few wives or concubines could ever learn. That was her gift. That was also why none of this day or her being on this boat with this man made any sense.

"Uh-huh," she smiled albeit falsely this time at the haughty creature bending over her. She tried not to feel lost and helpless. Had she been used and abandoned? Had she been harshly stolen? Was there some other reason for her painful separation from yet another man which she could not understand? These questions all swirled in

Naibe's heart. She knew, though, that if she could only get the glimmer in her thoughts started just once more, perhaps she could draw out the real reason *why* she was here. Hoping it would come through and dispel this shadow of confusion, she relaxed enough to deal with whatever she had to in the meantime while she waited for the answer to come.

GOING FORTH BY DAY

Chapter 31: Crossing at Night

Marai breathed out heavily and roused himself. He sat quietly, contemplating everything he had seen in rapid time that evening, marveling at the way the scenes and events had played in his thoughts like a tale told by a seasoned storyteller. His emotions lodged somewhere between personal agony and quiet disgust as he waited for Wserkaf to rise from the low wall where they both sat.

"Are you well? You look…" the Inspector shook out his arms and legs.

"Tired, perhaps ill now, but it doesn't matter. If you saw what I saw, then you know there's only one thing left to do. I'm going to them. Doesn't matter to me anymore if it's foolish or how many will die. Just wish I had time to visit something on Hordjedtef first."

Wserkaf nodded that he understood. As he stretched and drew in his air to fully waken himself, he continued: "You don't bother with him. He's protected. Even if you were to end his body, your victory would be short. His soul is a mighty one, and not so easily undone. You want to get at him, choose Maatkare Raemkai."

If his own vision of the young general was correct, Marai had little doubt he could best him. He was at least a head taller, with mighty chest, arms, and legs. Size alone would give him advantage. Being raised as a shepherd he'd been taught to never rush into a situation. Part of his inner spirit for revenge was constantly poking at him, but haste wasn't called for.

"So, I've listened and picked up the sad misadventures in the wake of my 'death' – learning all the players," he mused aloud. "Time to go though – for both of us."

The Inspector looked up, jaw dropping again. "You did it again, didn't you? Stopped time to get the last story out."

Marai nodded, himself astonished that the servant was only now returning to state that the boat was ready for launch. He'd seen an evening of misadventure and into the following day, but only moments had passed since both interrupted the guard's senet game.

Normally, the Inspector wouldn't have rowed, but the hour was late and so Marai understood he and the Prince would both help. When everyone was seated or standing in position, he heard Wserkaf speak to the men:

"I need your promise that what you see tonight does not leave your lips and, indeed, vanishes from your thoughts. There are unspeakable forces at the bidding of another who would feel no remorse in destroying your lives or those of your wives and children in order to search your heart. I can work a spell of forgetting but if it doesn't hold long enough the task becomes yours," he looked into each man's eyes. "If you wish to go from us now, there's no penalty. If you aid us and do well, I will bless your families as long as I breathe."

The men paused, concerned, but then quickly and grimly accepted their duty.

As the men pushed the boat out, Marai studied the way they tested each glide stroke for depth on three sides of the wooden craft. The crescent moon was higher now, but in the darkness of the low-lit river very little of the water glimmered – the five men were crossing by sound and feel.

Just before he began to row, Marai drew into his thoughts and gently stroked the bag of Child Stones Wserkaf had given him. "Ariennu, sweet Ari –" Marai breathed sadly, grazing the bag with a gentle kiss. He bowed his head, knowing she must have sensed the dire nature of everyone's existence in Ineb Hedj quite early if she had handed off the eight far-seeing stones to Wserkaf. That action had effectively thwarted much of the thought-linking ability of the stones to each other. It assisted the veil of secrecy she cast. Marai wondered if that assistance had been the *real* reason he had been unable to contact the women after he left the tomb instead of some spell from the Great One.

"So, when you let Ari take your wdjat as a trade before you left for your duty, what did your mentor say when he noticed?" Marai asked, absently tapping his forehead with the small bag of stones until he felt a slight squirming thrill issuing from inside. He lay the bag on his lap and took up an oar, trying to keep an even stroke with the men. Because of his size and superior strength, he knew he would easily flip the boat if he didn't restrain himself.

"He was furious with me," Wserkaf answered. "He railed at me it that I had disappointed him once again and that the wdjat was no mere trinket to be palmed off on a *mere sojourned handmaiden* as he called Lady Ariennu. He reminded me that I had *seen* its powers the night before you came to us, when the young acolyte nearly drowned. He scolded me for letting such untrained and unclean hands touch it when my most Holy Mother had only entrusted it to one other than myself."

Marai's attention had drifted. He gently opened the bag that had been in his lap. The sweetest and gentlest of lights shimmered lovingly up into his face. From them, the orbs of light streamed forth, illuminating him with rainbow-filled shimmers. Wserkaf gasped in enchantment but sheltered the light from the other men in the boat.

"So beautiful!" he whispered. "I've never seen – are they weeping? Afraid of what comes?" then "they reach me like her soft touch trapped inside. Is it – ?" but Marai had his own answer.

"I know, little ones, I know. We'll find them," he whispered to them like a father consoling frightened children. "I miss them so much too."

Just as quickly as he had opened it, Marai drew the bag shut and tucked it in his belt. He stared up at the moon sadly, then pulled the hood on his cloak tighter over his head. Soon, just the edge of his silvery beard and hawk-like nose showed. He began to solemnly row with the other men.

As the rudder man eased the boat out onto the open and deeper water of the great river, wavelets lapped at its sides. Marai sensed the wind over the great river stirring as if it, too, marked the somber first night of mourning for the King. Something was there, watching again. The sojourner felt the familiar dark that had entered him when he had raged at the knowledge of all that had transpired while he lay in the tomb. He knew men seldom put boats on the water in the dark, for fear of demons in the form of silt ridges. Now that the flood was retreating, high land could mire or cause a boat to swamp. A trapped boat would then be visited by Sebek's minions and those of Tauret and many other deities of the water who were always ready to overturn the disrespectful sailor.

"Your Highness…" one of the men hesitated, "something's not right about the water."

Marai knew the man sensed the same forbidding darkness that he was feeling. He looked to his left to see if he could catch the Inspector's expression, but discovered the priest gently singing a portion of the Bast Hymn Marai had learned at Hordjedtef's feet. The words rose just above a whisper, so only the men rowing in front would hear.

> *Bast, beloved, when your people call.*
> *Daughter of the sun, with flame and fury*
> *Flashing from the prow upon the foe;*
> *Safely sails the boat with your protection*
> *Passing scatheless where your fires glow.*

Tonight, something about the song caused a pause in the air, as if the dark thing that watched them listened to it.

Marai started to sing with him in support. "Bast beloved…"

"No, not you. Too much force in your voice," Wserkaf gestured for the big man to hush then turned, singing again to encourage the men as they continually probed the depths and pushed back to avoid any silt.

Marai wearily shut his eyes and visualized the water rolling by. "But there really *is* something out there." Marai spoke quietly, hoping the men, who had continued to sing a little of the hymn in the form of a rowing cadence, wouldn't hear them.

"It's pulling you, isn't it?" Wserkaf commented.

That suggestion was all he needed. Marai laid his oar in the hull of the boat and crawled on his hands and knees over the front rowers' bench to the prow. Leaning over the edge of the boat, he let his hand glide in the water that curled by the sides. As he reveled in the feel of the churning water rushing through his fingers, he knew Naibe's hand had done the same thing long ago. He felt the vague link of sensuality, as if his hand had become her young and smooth hand in the water. Tonight, it was faint because so very little of her essence remained.

Marai felt the dark spirit for only an instant before it coalesced into something with more form. *Hunger. I sense it coming closer now. Unnatural hunger – the silt ridge over there. It comes to us, leading others.*

Crocodiles were massing for an anticipated feed. It was their hunger and ravenous nature that had invaded Marai's heart and thoughts a moment earlier. In little Kina-Ahna, his apartment was back far enough from the murky shore and deep in the populated areas. Although he had heard they were a problem in the flood shanties at night, he had never encountered one alive or unbound.

"Do crocodiles normally attack boats?" he asked innocently, still warily swirling the water with his hand.

"Not in a fat year like this," the rudder man called up to Marai, "not unless something tempts them or pesters then."

"Oh," Marai mused, knowing the rudder man hadn't sensed the uneasiness take shape. "I see. Wserkaf, friend," he called just above a whisper, "put your hand in the water and see if you can feel what I do. Now I *know* it's a djin," he turned to the priest, about to say Hordjedtef must have discovered he was alive.

"Damn! Get your hand out of the water! Someone is casting a powerful spell and boosting its power through my wdjat – and it's not Great One; or I hope not." The inspector-priest fell on Marai, grabbing his hand from the river. "Those monsters have become demons! They'll come through the bottom of the boat after us."

Marai's heart leapt as if lightning coursed through it. He sensed the image of someone seated at a still pool of water, touching his finger to the edge of it in a pose of transfer and holding a roundel of crystal carved with a gold and blue eye in his other hand. In a flash, he remembered how the "boost" had nearly wrecked his fledgling family when Wserkaf had sent joy into the air of their apartment and then had simply flipped the crystal disc over. Marai knew both Hordjedtef and the Inspector knew the trick of gliding it on the water. Other priests had at least seen them use it in that manner.

GOING FORTH BY DAY

That meant Hordjedtef *could* have gotten the Wdjat. If that was true, then he knew someone was crossing or knew that Wserkaf was doing something out of his control.

The sojourner excitedly sucked in his breath, shut his eyes, and rocked back and forth on his heels to calm himself. It didn't matter who was steering the animals, part of him wanted to leap from the boat into the water to control the approaching beasts. Every wavelet he saw jiggled and produced a dark and gliding shape that broke the surface.

"Wrath of the Devourer!" Wserkaf grunted and leapt to his feet so violently that he nearly threw himself overboard. He seized Marai's discarded oar like a cudgel.

One of the rowers grabbed the torch which had been fixed in the forward keel and waved it about. He cursed in terror as the light illuminated dozens of eyes perched behind wet, slim snouts.

A larger crocodile moved closer to the boat, its mouth yawning open and inviting any one of the five in the boat to make a foolish move so he could nudge the boat into swamping and begin a feeding frenzy.

Through his own hammering heart, Wserkaf whispered protection spells, but then realized the hisses and growls he thought the great reptiles were making were instead coming from Marai's throat. Looking over his right shoulder, he *saw* the Child Stone shining on the big man's forehead. The normally flat place at Marai's brow had leapt forth into a jewel-like thing the size of an almond. The shape blinked out just as quickly, followed by a shimmering cascade of light down the man's arms that the Inspector could feel more than he could see. For an instant, Marai's copper-skinned face went entirely black and a whitish glow encased him like fine fur; the barest image of the war bull had returned.

Paralyzed in dark fascination as Marai leapt effortlessly from being a man to becoming a bull creature with god-like power over animals, Wserkaf watched Marai edge further forward in the boat to touch the snout of the lead crocodile.

Wserkaf heard the layers of Marai's language, translated into shared silent thought; a remnant of the hours of linking they had shared. He wondered, if he would ever experience this gift again after the big man had gone his way.

You will not eat us

Our flesh is poison to you.

One who has called you to

come to us

Taunts you with hunger

Free us

Show us where the deep and cool water is,

That we may lead you.

to a lame calf and more to eat

on another shoal

More weak things to cull.

The lead crocodile stopped hissing and closed its gaping mouth, puzzled at the being who spoke its own language.

Wserkaf was aghast. He never imagined Marai would have the spiritual discipline to control wild water animals, especially when he suspected they were being compelled by heka. He'd known of only two men in his life who were able to speak to animals in their voice.

Suddenly, the steersman began to point.

"Look Your Highness, little lights!"

Little balls of glimmer that looked like fireflies began to spin and swirl just above the surface of the water, illuminating the ripples just a little more. Then, when the crocodiles had become most threatening, they moved into a strange formation that made an almost diagonal line in the direction of the opposite shore. The sliver of moon showed only eddies of water swirling over the silt-bars to the right and left.

GOING FORTH BY DAY

The Inspector heard Marai's laugh begin low but rise and strengthen as if it was about to transition into the roar of a bull.

"There. You see? Out from under the old man's arm they come back to me!" he cried out, pointing at the lights, but then lowered his voice when he saw the boatmen stare. "Bastard was blocking them with a spell, but how in the goddess name did I not know for certain?" The big sojourner stared narrowly at Wserkaf in sudden distrust.

"Look. You have every reason to suspect me, Marai," the Inspector explained, suddenly defensive. "But would I lead you into a trap that traps me? I only learned it was not a jewel about two seasons ago. It began to wake – to speak below sound to me and he knew it. Everything else – but you – woke it further as if neither of us were fit to own it." Wserkaf bowed his head in saddened realization. "I guess it's why it didn't hurt me that the Lady Ariennu was handling it and then took it."

He watched, enchanted as a child at the circling lights that found the crocodiles who had drawn back and led them out to a deeper channel. As soon as the boat had steered past the threat of the beasts, Marai and Wserkaf sat down again to help with the rowing.

Only Great Djedi could summon a lion, and now Prince Metauthetep the Akaru Sef is said to know the skill. How? the Inspector's thoughts echoed as Marai resumed his normal appearance. The sojourner remained silent; focused on all that lay ahead of him instead of the answer to his friend's unspoken question.

The crossing was finished in absolute and shocked silence. The four astonished men and Marai clambered off the boat at the mooring on the sojourner's shore. Before the three boatmen could shake off the terror enough to lash the keel to a post and before Wserkaf could remind them of their silence about the goings-on, Marai had moved away from them and had begun to stride rapidly in the direction of his old Little Kina-Ahna neighborhood.

"You will wait here. I will return as soon as I can. Be ready to leave," Wserkaf told the men and darted after the tall, cloaked figure that seemed to be increasing in speed with each step he took. As he chased the man he thought: *this heka with the crocodiles was done by someone who knows how to use the wdjat other than myself. Hordjedtef should be the only one who knows the use of it.*

Marai stopped in the middle of the empty market, arms outstretched. Turning around a couple of times, he tried to get a sense of everything that had changed since he left. In a few more moments when the Inspector caught up with him, his energy failed and he sat at the common well in the center of the open area.

The plaza was empty this very early morning. Fewer stationary stalls dotted the edges of the dwellings because many of the regulars had moved back to their dry season homes to work the fields. Marai knew Etum-Addi and his family were gone. The heavy-set, jolly man who liked to break into song almost as much as he did, had essentially been banished just for knowing him. He sensed the family wasn't in ruins; they simply moved their business to the coast earlier than they expected. There, in time, they would finally know a bit of longed-for prosperity.

Although he wanted to see him and Gizzi and their growing generations, to witness them flourish, he knew he could only do it in spirit. His journey with this man was complete. For only a moment, the sojourner thought of his belief in second chances; how they could becalm earlier mistakes. If that was so, perhaps this Sanghir spice merchant had once been the brutal collectioneer named N'ahab-Atal, now spun back into life after his death. He felt it would have been ironic to have killed that thief in self-defense but met him one more time as a struggling merchant with a dozen mouths to feed. Even in poverty, the reborn man still found time to laugh and time to sing in this soul's guise.

As Etum Addi, he had been kindest to some of the very women he had ruined in another life. Perhaps it would be enough to appease. Perhaps the gods would see fit to not challenge him again before he sailed the sky. The former shepherd sighed, knowing he could not dwell on any of this.

Deka his thoughts whispered next as he sat by the well, reflecting on the concept that somehow the woman of Ta-Seti had been inspired to betray everyone. She had met him at this well on a night much like this. It had been the night right before things fell apart. She had almost let him touch her heart.

Now, because of the manipulations of the Great One of Five and his minions, those moments, too, were gone.

The sojourner beckoned for Wserkaf to sit with him to catch his breath before he headed back to his boat. It would be a farewell. Both men knew that and shared a final thought of how the gods must be amused.

Marai looked up with Wserkaf to the single high, large window. He thought of the beautiful but haunted-looking woman of Ta-Seti who sat there during his visit months ago.

Deka. Marai breathed again. *Maybe I could speak to you now – break this prince's spell on you with my devotion, even though we never touched as man and bride. If there's a shred of energy that hasn't forgotten* – he patted the bag of stones. A low lamp burned on the wide ledge in honor of the dead king. *Someone else lives here then. Djerah, maybe? That would be uncommon luck for a change. I thought they would have gone to the worker's village.*

Just then, the two resting men were distracted by whispers. Two lovers met near an alley, then slipped into darkness.

The sojourner laughed. *Ari, I remember us… how you waited to trick me one night out here like this. You were so free and full of joy,* he mused. *Now, who knows? I'll come and set things right for good. We'll be together again. I must think that, or I'll go mad.*

Wserkaf, he knew, was already thinking about what kind of separate future lay ahead for each of them. *Now, after all we have shared, we must go our ways. I hope you will fare well when you return.* It was time. Marai slapped his knee, about to stand. For now, he knew he would have to sneak up the steps and past the door to his old apartment to get to the roof. There, he could sleep for a few hours before trying to find Djerah or slipping up the river alone. The peacekeepers would be alerted before too long, and he still needed to avoid them.

"You know, all of my life, especially since my degrees of initiation, my senior has been afraid of what I know and maybe even of who I am, I think." Wserkaf spoke with a sigh and Marai once again found his plans of rising to leave delayed.

"Maybe this is why you were given your gift of visions so long ago," Marai shook his head. Trying for a last bit of information on a more private level, he gently stroked the purse of stones at his belt.

Little Ones

See your own,

where they are

Inspire them to speak to me

The voices, static filled as if there was an intrusion, answered quietly in a code that sounded as if it was a mixture of the women's whispers, at long last.

Some things have come,

trial needed.

And the suffering

Yet not more than we can bear.

Come,

but not in haste.

Lest destruction.

"Well, I'll have to use these visions to defend my acts now," the Inspector scanned the eastern sky again. The water birds were starting a noise, marking the last hour before dawn. Both men knew the day might break before he finished crossing the river. By that time, no power on earth would distract Hordjedtef from wondering why his protégé was late.

"Don't worry about the time, Highness," Marai looked up once and patted the bag of Child Stones again. The birds fell silent as if they had never begun their morning noises. "Just follow the truth and uncover the secrets while I'm getting my ladies and doing what I fear I'll have to do if this prince Maatkare has other ideas."

"The man's an animal," Wserkaf scoffed under his breath, then followed up with a gasp. "You'll kill yourself if you don't keep *that* in check, the thing you do with time. You have to let yourself heal"

Marai stared into the well, entranced and dizzy from the slow swirling of the black water at the bottom. "Why's it swirl? There's no wind."

See us

The voice of the children whispered behind the big man's brow as he tried to listen, bid a good farewell and solve the puzzle of the ripples in the dark well water.

He must touch us
Before going his way

"Now?" Marai answered aloud, shaking his head.

"Did the stones speak?" the Inspector frowned, his thoughts disturbed.

"They apparently want you to see me work them," Marai nodded. He hadn't mentioned it to Wserkaf, but the Inspector had been right. It was too soon. The trances all evening, the shift to wrath animal and back, and the work with the crocodiles had drained the last of any returning energy. He was horribly exhausted now. The Children knew it. Now they were asking to speak to Wserkaf one last time.

Doing his best to hide it, Marai carefully opened the leather bag and placed the eight stones that had been inside on the wide rim of the well.

The shape was the 'Lady's Star', a simplified variant of the Flower of Life. An arc of light rose above the design as soon as the layout was completed.

"Go on, Your Highness, reach through the light. They want you to see how it feels to you," Marai suggested reassuringly.

Wserkaf passed his hands through the light, then gasped in wonder, giggling almost helplessly as the light leapt eagerly onto his fingers and traveled up over his hands, like a living liquid creature moving up to light his face.

"It feels like her touch," Wserkaf gasped then paused, thinking he'd said too much. Marai knew he felt Naibe's sensual touch pass through him and swell with her sigh of unbearable ecstasy. He tore his gaze away. Marai knew it had been too much. They both missed her.

"I can't look. It's too glorious," he gasped, but made himself look again. He stared in childlike wonder. "And that is why you always seem so joyous except when you feel the rage of the just coming through you."

Fail not.

You are the healer in

A corner of your world

Heed all.

The Lady has wakened your fire

The Messenger has strengthened your will

Know these things

That in the web of time

They will say of you

User-Ka-eve 'Mighty is his Spirit'

Holy Irimaat 'Truth is Accomplished'

Nebhkey 'The Lord Ascends'

Who holds Truth above all?

The prophesied one, the heir

Of Djedi wears the Deseret Red crown

Marai's hand excitedly found Wserkaf's shoulder. "Then you *are* part of this! Whether you want to be part of the legend or not, they said the heir of Djedi just as plain." the sojourner was interrupted by the sight of the images which formed in the middle of the circle of Child Stones.

Watching with Marai, the Inspector saw himself sitting, as an older man, enthroned. The red "deseret" crown was on his head. His image was made of stone in some moments of the images and flesh and blood in others. Even more images depicted him with the white crown of the southern lands. A smaller, pinkish-looking Eternal House with adjacent pink temples in front rose behind his image. Every part of it glittered in the rising sun as if it had been made of prismatic glass.

Wserkaf contemplated the small, glimmering stone nearest his hand in the eight-pointed formation. He looked up, different-faced and somehow more regal, as if the sight and knowledge of what the vision meant allowed him to possess the children's light.

Then, the image blurred and scrambled, hiding itself from something.

Marai frowned, then stroked the stone gently. To the Inspector, it looked as if the big man was petting it.

"What just happened?" he asked, then answered his own question. "The wdjat. I recognize the energy, but it's being tampered with."

"Be at peace little one. I am here," Marai whispered and stared at the image in the middle of the grouping of stones again. Both men saw torchlight burning behind people in the background.

Wserkaf could not decide who the people were at first. He saw a slim, deep brown hand with exquisitely shaped fingers and reddened nails. It guided the edge of the disc as it floated on water somewhere that was many days journey from where he and Marai watched.

Marai sighed out, saddened, because in that moment he saw a reflection in the wdjat as it was pictured through the stones. He knew exactly who it was.

Chapter 32: Image in the Water

Marai and Prince Wserkaf stared into the water in the well. For the sojourner, the night had been less about his recovery and more about the series of Child-Stone-spun memories drawn from a myriad of sources. Most astonishingly, he had learned the legends were true. At some point in time, many years hence and when he was in his dotage, his new friend and savior Wserkaf would be king of all Kemet. None of that mattered in this moment at the well though. What Marai had learned about the mistreatment and betrayal of once strong Ariennu and magically seductive young Naibe *did* matter.

Although his body was slowly recovering from the poisoning, starvation, and suffocation he had experienced in the tomb, Marai's psyche struggled. He wanted badly to send his massed bull-darkness straight to the palace to end the Great One's life in drawn out agony and misery, but the Children of Stone had delayed him again. As if it hadn't been enough of a distraction to witness Wserkaf's future unfolding, he saw one more thing. Someone on the other side of the crystalline wdjat held the amulet gently on the surface of some faraway pond or pool of water, sending the image in reverse to both men. Gradually, the reflected image revealed who was reading the disc.

Wserkaf saw the calm but surreally lovely face of a young man staring back at him. A slight open-mouthed smile revealed oddly deformed but shiny teeth, like dog fangs, at the sides of his full lips. For an instant, his eyes flashed green in his russet skinned face. It was Maatkare.

Marai moved out of the field of vision provided by the stolen amulet. Wserkaf nodded as he noticed Marai obscure himself in shadow. They both knew that even though Maatkare was weeks away, he still might take some action if he learned that Marai lived.

"Ah…" the rich, deep voice behind the russet face breathed, "I can see him now. Excellent, my dear, you have done well." Another face formed in the reflection beside the first face.

GOING FORTH BY DAY

Marai, viewing from the side, felt a hurt coldness when he recognized Deka beside the young prince. Her eyelids were now adorned with gold paint that mirrored the round disc painted just above the place where her blood-red Child Stone had emerged. This wasn't the remote, anxious woman he had embraced at this very well months ago. This was a very different, calm and elegant Deka. Marai didn't dare reveal himself, but even as he made certain she would not recognize him, he sensed a slight tear starting down her cheek. She knew something of his essence was watching her.

The man noticed Deka moan slightly. He raised his hand and beckoned her into a tighter embrace. He scoffed and touched her cheek. "This tear? Of joy, no doubt. Yes. It's because you like me so much, don't you? See, cousin? See what I can take from you; from your world?" His eyes flashed again at Wserkaf. "She needed so very little encouragement to come with me, so very little."

Deka... Marai's thought started. He was unable to hide himself any longer. *See me.*

"Oh, look at this, my dearest creature of the flame. A ghost, I sense," his lips brushed hers and his tongue slithered gently between her gasping lips as if that slight affection had brought her to the limit of ecstasy. One eye opened and looked to check Wserkaf's reaction. "Go you now, back to your Land of the Forgotten. See, she has forgotten you too."

Marai knew the Prince was speaking to his "ghost" and almost betrayed himself at that moment, but Deka reacted.

I see you Man Sun... Her thought came back to him too easily, as if she had felt his presence before he even asked the question.

Should you come?

See us by day?

I cannot say

You are a ghost

And so am I

Farewell...

Her hand gracefully swept over the eye and the image blurred.

Wserkaf and Marai saw nothing further of the two.

After a moment of silent reflection, the Inspector looked up and spoke under his breath. "At least we know Hordjedtef isn't the one who has the wdjat – *and* that Maatkare is charming as always," Wserkaf stared up at the setting moon, shuffled to convince himself to get moving, and complained: "If only I had been there to protect them, to oppose him *and* my mentor this time, and not on my duty."

Deka, Marai wasn't listening to the Inspector's ruminations. He knew what this haughty princeling wanted his supposed ghost and Wserkaf to see. *He knows we were never together like that and he's showing my ghost – strutting his victory over your body; that he's completely and effortlessly jumped in and taken possession of you. No. It must be something else,* Marai thought. That the Prince had seduced her was obvious, but sorrow and torture were still in her eyes. The sojourner couldn't quite fathom the reason for it, if the young general attested to her bliss with him.

"So, he was the one who sent the crocodiles, then?" Marai moved back closer to the well, so that he might see if the Prince or Deka decided to view them again.

"Mmm, indeed – chaos magic," Wserkaf nodded as if he too was distracted by other thoughts.

"What did you say he was doing on his Ta-Seti mission? Hunting lions and touring the mines?" Marai re-asked.

"Yes; out there with the grass, the lions, and the dust. It's where Our Father stationed him before his passing, so that he wouldn't be in Ineb Hedj too long. I think his ill-chosen wife prefers it too! If you're well enough, though, I have to get moving back to the palace." The Inspector turned to go back in the direction of his boat and the men who would pilot it.

"Lions and dust; new slaves and demi-gods." Marai heaved himself to his feet from the lower stone step around the well thunderstruck with a whole new line of thought. "The Children knew all along! Sweet goddess, was this part of the plan too? To stop me cold once I arrived and did their bidding? To divide us like this?" He began to pace by the well as his feelings of shock passed through anxiety, then turned into hurt and disappointed anger.

"Easy. Don't you start doing this to yourself. Your body has recovered, but your spirit is still sorting this out. You'll become ill again," Wserkaf returned and placed his hand on his friend's shoulder, steadying him.

Marai brushed the hand away.

"No. I see what's happened. Deka *knew* the Children's plan all along or part of her soul did. She either kept it from us or kept it buried from herself. It's why Naibe telling her legend months ago enraged her and my becoming her lover caused her to waken her own darkness. It wasn't jealousy. We weren't supposed to know she had been planted among us and maybe she didn't either. I think she almost knew and was trying to tell me, but I thought she was just cold to me. Some part of her directed her to stay away from me and from any man but the one who would tip the scales, like some cursed game!" Marai's shoulders tensed. He rolled them, feeling the hatred build and feeling less able to manage it.

"Might it be that each of you have different dictates written on your hearts? Different tasks in part of a larger plan, as our varied gods do?" Wserkaf frowned, still reluctant to go. "Perhaps she was following a different path to go with my cousin and then to bind pretty Naibe and Ariennu to him as well," the Inspector's faced darkened. "What have I –" he started to say *done* but Marai interrupted him.

"No. I don't accept that. I can't," he shook his silvery-haired head. Inwardly, he knew the Inspector had a point. Hordjedtef had said as much too. As a simple shepherd he was no godling. He was a messenger, a conveyance. *Deka had always said she was not like us and not on the same journey. I thought she meant her journey was about the search for her history and her ancestors. Could it have been a different mission entirely? If Hordjedtef has in any way influenced this…* the irritation in sojourner's thoughts advanced. The specter of the bull increased.

"Wait…" Wserkaf winced. "Just center yourself and breathe. Late as it's getting, even with your time-bending skill, he's bound to feel that." the Inspector touched Marai's cloaked arm. "I felt you start when I said something about lions and dust.

Those were the words our dear departed Majesty used in his pronouncement after that scoundrel came skulking back into the palace to end his banishment two or three years ago. How did *they* almost set you into a fury?"

"The last time the children truly spoke outside of me, they spoke in a riddle that went like this:

'Lions and dust
In the land below foam...'

he shut his eyes, gripping his fists at his sides at the monstrous idea that his entire course had not been his own but had been something charted long ago by the Children of Stone. For a son of Ahu, the Akkad and Shinar drifter such as he was, the idea of someone else controlling him like a bull in a pen stirred much rebellion in his heart.

'Baskets at the gate of the sacrifice.
Stones of the children
In the hand of the grieving bird.
The horizon is split
For a weeping warrior.
Etched in stone
Long in years
Silent in waiting
Walking with us,'

He sighed. "There it is, or most of it, anyway."

Wserkaf stared slack-jawed in confused wonder. Before he could comment on what Marai had said, the glimmering stones spread out on the edge of the well flickered to life again.

"Highness," Marai motioned, "there's more."

GOING FORTH BY DAY

Wserkaf stood in front of Marai to block him from the sight of the Prince as he used the wdjat. In the dim water, they saw an enclosure, like a village, and sensed other people in the area surrounding it.

"I think I see Qustul Amani if they made good time and he pressed his rowers like a murderer."

Marai felt the somewhat menacing but delighted eyes staring at him just as he whirled into a dark blot of silence. An imp-like creature, red with pointy ears or horns and large glowing green eyes atop spear-like downturned tusks crouched in the darkest corner of his thoughts, just out of clear inner vision. *A demon!* he thought. As it rose, it became more man-like, flashing sassiness and youth; like a tiny hunter rising from the brush to hurl its annoying little spear. Marai knew that creature and its doggish familiar spirit. It wasn't a demon but would have delighted in being accepted by a demon clan. "That son out of Apep's bowels knows more heka than just the crocodiles, doesn't he? If that's so why does he need Deka's help when she is only learning what she can do?"

"Oh, rest assured he knows spells and utterances enough to make a nuisance of himself, but he'd be no challenge to you, or even to me, I'm certain." Wserkaf rubbed his eyes, wanting to yawn but forcing himself to regain his composure. "I started to explain a moment ago. His teachers put him out of the discipline of Wepwawet, bright as he was, which is why he commands the whole Southern Division these days," the Inspector reflected. "He's studied as all princes have. It's how we are raised. Some of us continue as priests, others go into governing as ambassadors… still others seem more suited to campaigns as Maatkare is. In *his* case, he's turned banishment into victory. Although, my feeling is he uses most of the time to hunt and then the rest in threats and conditioning his troops. It doesn't require much time to threaten anyone who gets the idea of raising a force to come down to Black Lands. He's too scattered for any depth of the spirit. He might indulge in sorcery from time to time. Even his grandfather says it will one day undo him," his voice trailed.

The light in the stones flickered again in an unseen wind, blotting out the image in the water and showing another image of their own. It was the three women, seated in a small room.

"There they are!" Marai almost fell over Wserkaf as he moved closer to get a better look, but caught himself and stayed off to the side.

They both fixated on the circle of stones. In the latest image, Wserkaf and Marai saw Ariennu, then Naibe. Deka sat to one side, singing the same strange song she had always sung in times of trial.

Ha-go-re!

Akh-go-re

Neter Deka Nefira Sekht

I hear my sacred name.

I waken.

I fly all away –

The song was her way of telling Marai she knew his spirit was there looking in on them. Ariennu was brushing Naibe's hair out as the young woman lay in her elder sister's lap and tried to ignore the cinnamon-skinned woman.

Beneath the notes of her song, Deka's voice spoke to the air in the room, hoping this slight conjuration of Marai's "spirit" had worked. If it didn't, perhaps Ariennu would hear it.

Do you hate me? Please try to understand, ghost of he who was my brief light, she begged. *Is it because of what I am? Am I now one who looks at two from far away, and we are no longer three who look together?*

Ariennu wasn't listening. She continued soothing Naibe-Ellit, combing her hair.

Deka – Marai's thoughts whispered. *Know that I live, and while I live, I will seek you, no matter what arms are holding you now,* his voice tried to caress her. He saw her head lolling along an incline of air as if his hands were reaching through the light of the Child Stones to touch her cheek. *Deka, I miss you. I sit at the well where you touched me, where we kissed so lightly.*

Oh, but you don't understand, her plaintive little girl voice sniveled, eyes looking backward to the veil of finger-woven rope netting in the doorway. *I tried to tell you, but as Wise MaMa says, sometimes you were such a dumb ox.*

Beyond the netting, Marai knew the general lay sleeping alone after a late night of revelry.

Something is awake in me that isn't part of you, never was and never will be. Deka sent a final thought, *and there is nothing you can do.* The arc of light fell dim a last time as she spoke.

With sadness in his heart again over what he had heard, Marai approached the well and gently scooped up the stones, putting them in the little pouch. Bowing his head and rubbing his eyes. He knew he would need to find some place, even an empty vendor's stall, to rest for an hour or two before daybreak. The sojourner pushed aside a careless lock of his hair, but the Inspector noticed the flicker of a silvery metallic stone welling at the big man's brow. It had come forth when they watched the images playing in the stones. "Oh, I really am so tired," the shepherd relaxed again and shut his eyes, hoping to clear his thoughts. When he did, he suddenly lost his balance and started to fall forward, unconscious.

Catching him awkwardly on one shoulder with his other hand reaching up to support Marai's head, Wserkaf accidentally touched the stone in Marai's brow. An instant link formed between the men, flooding Wserkaf with the former shepherd's memory – the past which had been related only in bits. The priest saw Marai's life in the wilderness, the death of his wife in childbirth, his endless songs of reparation to Ashera who never answered his prayer, the night the children arrived, his transformation, the way he had killed the thieves in self-defense, and the women as they had been when he found them so very long ago. Wserkaf shuddered, stunned. In that moment, he understood more about Marai, his mission, and the truth of what was happening in Kemet than the sojourner did.

"Wha? What happened?" Marai woke again and caught himself, then stood.

"And my master didn't care *who* you were or *what* you represented," the Inspector shook his head, dismayed. "His presumption; his foolishness. You have all taken on roles from legend and prophecy, and he didn't desire to know who any of you are becoming. If he had, he would have been on his knees before you instead of challenging or claiming to defeat you. He would have seen you as this messenger of the gods whose goddess did, after all, smile on him. You say you are not a god, but in *our* world what you are *is* a god." the Inspector smiled, oddly comforted.

"Where is this coming from, did you see something from me? I hardly feel like a god right now; just a man half-killed and out of most options."

"Who knows what or how gods truly feel? Perhaps we are both like gods in our own way in that we walk among the legends and prophecies of others. I don't really know whether to hope for this or not. "She told me something, Naibe did," Wserkaf steadied his friend.

"What was that?" the sojourner shook his head again and took a step toward the path indicating he was ready to let the Inspector head back now.

"She said: *'Sometimes things happen that are not part of any prophecy or a legend. Sometimes our feet stray far away from any given path only to find they never left the truest path inside our hearts! We always know inside our souls the way back to the truth on a silent road.'* I don't know," Wserkaf sighed momentarily as the other memories of the night on which Naibe said that filled him with longing. When he looked at Marai again, the Inspector knew something seemed unfinished. It seemed to Wserkaf that at any moment Marai would suddenly transform and leave behind all his earthly fetters to walk among the stars. When they had first met, the priest had found Marai impressive and perhaps a little dangerous. He emerged as a paragon of strength willing to martyr himself to prove a point. The changes had continued. In just the few hours since he had wakened, the stars seemed more his home than the sand or even the white walled estates of Ineb Hedj. "I think I would rather stray from my path for a little longer, and I do not know where yours will lead after you go upriver. I am sure, though, that we will meet each other again – that our silent roads to truth will cross."

"Thank you, Wserkaf, for everything." Marai grabbed his arm reassuringly.

"I'd best get back now, if I'm going to make my move. Maybe I can still help you. King or not, I have sworn to devote myself to truth."

GOING FORTH BY DAY

"I know; one day. Now, though, get you gone." Marai smiled and embraced his friend again, giving the kiss he had ordained as his own clan's form of affectionate greeting: eyes, then brow rather than eyes and lips as the women had kissed him. This time it was truly a farewell.

Wserkaf stood free of the former shepherd, then took a step backward to pronounce an utterance: "Son of earth and starry heaven," Wserkaf raised his hands in the prayerful blessing. "Be well. Be blessed." The Inspector backed away again, folded his arms high, and melted into the early morning sky in a swift and magical retreat to his boat and the challenges that awaited him across the river.

Marai sat again, resting his head wearily in the crook of his elbow on the ledge of the well. His exhaustion showed more rapidly by the second. *I hope he succeeds. Not only for him, but because it would pain that old buzzard too.* Marai yawned, surrendering himself to a well-deserved rest. *I'll just stay here for a few moments, then find some place safer to sleep until the morning.*

MARY R. WOLDERING

Epilogue: The Land of the Bow

You live.
Our efforts weren't for nothing
I sense you coming, wise one, after all this time
Do you send heralds before you?
One among them feels… familiar.
Come to me.
Come to the Land of the Bow.
The Hidden One is coming back
After all this time
It is coming like the cloud of a storm
We have much to discuss
Make haste.

MARY R. WOLDERING

MAP

The Ancient Middle-East

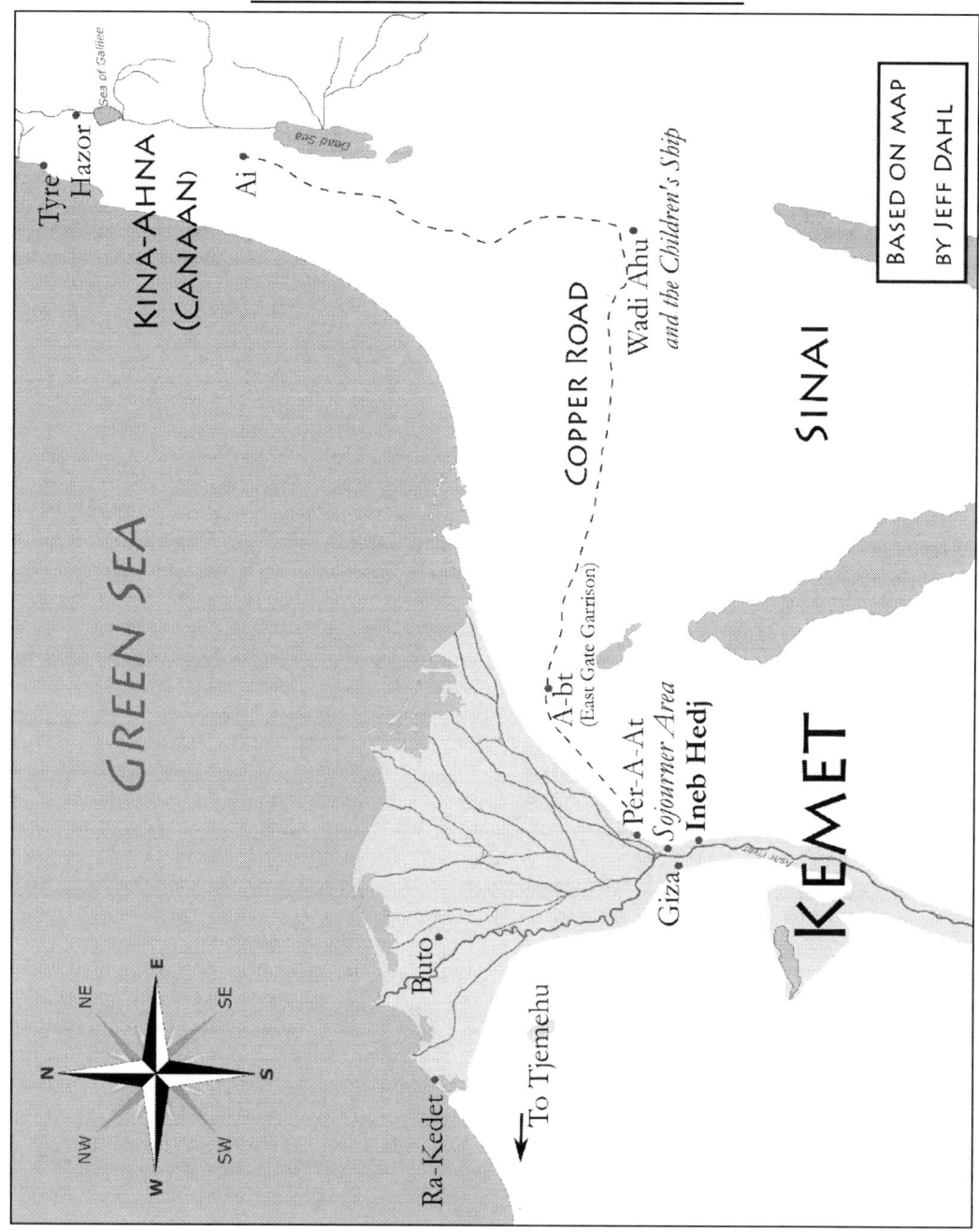

GLOSSARY

Pronunciation note: the pronunciation guides are purely speculative and written in common American English pattern.

Akh (Ahk) – Intelligence after death, memory.

Akkad (Ah-cod) – Ancient name for the area of modern-day Iraq; a person from that region.

Amenti (Ah-men-tea) – The *Hidden*, in Egyptian mythology - the name of the underworld.

Anunna (Ah-noon-ah) – Short for Anunnaki - a group of deities in Sumerian, Akkadian, Assyrian, and Babylonian myths.

Apep (A-pep) – A huge serpent (or crocodile) which lived in the waters of Nun or in the celestial Nile. Each day he attempted to disrupt the passage of the solar barque of Re. In some myths, Apep was an earlier and discarded sun-god himself. Also called Apohis.

Ariennu (Ah-ree-in-oo) – Similar meaning to name Arianna or Ariadne in Greek meaning "most holy".

Asar (Uh-sar) – An Ancient Egyptian deity of the underworld and resurrection. Name of the Nile. Also called Osiris.

Aset (Ah-set) – Old name for Isis, a major goddess in ancient Egyptian religion - one of the main characters of the Osiris myth – she resurrects her slain husband, Osiris, and produces and protects his heir, Horus.

Ashera(h) (Ah-sher-ah) – A mother goddess who appears in a number of ancient sources "Queen of Heaven", consort of the Sumerian god Anu and Ugaritic El (both bull deities) the word 'elat' is used to describe her as "goddess".

Bakha-Montu (Ba-ka-mahn-too) – The meaning of his name was "nomad". The warrior nature of Menthu made him a bull. He would also be represented as a man with the head of a bull. There were at least three great sacred bulls called the Apis of Memphis, Mnevis of Heliopolis and Buchis at Hermonthis (the Bakha).

GOING FORTH BY DAY

Benu (Ben-oo) – Benu Bird – Egyptian phoenix. Both are birds of the sun, both are self-created, both undergo death and become symbols of regeneration.

Buhen (Boo-hen) – Buhen Egyptian settlement and fortress, located on the West bank of the Nile in present-day Sudan. First settled during the Old Kingdom, possibly by Sneferu (the founding Pharaoh of the Fourth Dynasty of Egypt) as a small trading post and copper works until the settlement was abandoned during the 5th Dynasty two centuries later.

Buto (Boo-toe) – Ancient coastal city near Alexandria. The goddess Wadjet was its local goddess, often represented as a cobra. Her oracle was located in her renowned temple in that city. King Menkaure received a tragic prediction there, according to legend.

Deka (Deh-Kuh) – Means "One who pleases".

Djedi (Jed-iy or Jed-eye) – Historical Djedi son of Sneferu. He was the first recorded magician.

Djehuti [Djehut] (Jeh-hoo-tea) – The Egyptian God of mathematics, writing, and scholarship. In some creation myths He is the voice of Ptah (the word or logos that appears in Christian and Jewish creation myths) as Ptah Emerges from the Cosmic Egg. Also called Thoth.

Djin (Jin) – Spirit, often demonic.

Dumizi (Do-moot-see) – Is a shepherd god who represents the harvest season but also became a god of the underworld thanks to the goddess Ishtar (Ashera).

El (Ell) – Canaanite for penis. One of the male deities.

Ereshkigal (ey-resh-kee-gahl) – The Sumerian and Akkadian goddess of death; consort of Nergal.

Heka (Heh-kuh) – Magic, sorcery.

Heru (Hair-oo) – Horus, Hawk deity.

Hordjedtef (Hoar-jeh-tef) – Also seen as Hardaduf or Dedephor in ancient literature. Son of Khufu, Count of Nekhen. Prince, Scholar, Author of the "Wisdom Texts" faded into semi obscurity after his brother Djedephre became king, but name appears as a living person throughout the rule of Menkaure.

Hul Gil (Hul-Gil) – Opium poppy- the "joy plant." The Sumerians from 3400 BC passed it to the Assyrians, who passed it to Egyptians.

Iah (Ee-ah) – A lunar deity in ancient Egyptian religion. means "Moon" transcribed as Yah, Yah(w).

Iaret (Yah-ret) – Rearing cobra part of the king's crown.

Ibu (Ee-boo) – In mummification where the body is "*ibu*" (tent of purification).

Ineb-Hedj (In-eb-Hedge) – Earliest name for Memphis (Men Nefer) later Cairo means White Wall.

Kalasiris (Ka-la-sear-is) – Garment worn by women in ancient Egypt a long linen dress or shift.

K'at (Ka-tea) – Woman, vagina, used as a derogatory term (i.e., "woman good for only one thing") (Egyptian).

Keleb (Kay-leb) – Sexually submissive male or dog position in M/M pairings – a Canaanite term.

Kemet (Kem-et) – Ancient name for Egypt.

Kentake (Ken-tah-kay) – Queen – Queen mother Sudanese tradition.

Kina-ahna (Kina Land – Kee-na Ah-nah) – Canaan (Israel & Palestine).

Kuna (Koo-nah) – Canaanite version of the word Ka't (see above).

Lilitu (Lee-lih-too) – Dark goddess or demon of sensuality, witchcraft.

Maatkare Raemkai (M'yat-kah-ray Ra-em-kiye) – The names mean "Truth in the soul of the sun". It also means "the sun is my life force".

Malidthu (Ma-leed-thoo) – Malidthu is a Canaanite Goddess of love, fertility, childbirth, and the fragrant myrrh-tree.

Marai bin Ahu (Muh-rye ben Ah-oo) – Marai son of Ahu.

Mtoto Metauhetep Akaru Sef (Muh-toe-toe Meh-t'ow-tep Ah-kah-roo-seff) – Regional ruler of Qustul Amani and Qustul.

Menhit (Men-Heet) – A Nubian war goddess in ancient Egyptian religion. Her name depicts a warrior status, as it means (she who) massacres.

Miw (Me-yoo) – Egyptian word for cat, a breed of Egyptian domestic cat.

Naibe-Ellit (Nah-ee-bay El-it) – Name means "Calls My Lady" or channels the goddess Inanna or Ashera.

Nefer Nebty (Nef-her Neb-tee) – Ancient Egyptian feminine name meaning *"beautiful lady"* used as name for belladonna herb.

Nefet (Ne-fet) – Fan on a stand, used by servants to fan their employers.

Nefira (Neh-fear-uh) – Beautiful one from the word Nefer.

Nekhen (Neck-hen) – Hierakonpolis, the City of the Hawk, ancient Egyptian Nekhen, important in Old Kingdom society.

Nemes (Neh-mez) – Symbol of ancient Egyptian regalia. Striped rectangular cloth of blue and gold worn by the kings. Originally a wig cover the tail in the back represent ted a lion's tail.

Neters (Ntr) (Nit-ur) – Kemet name for Children of Stone.

Pyr Akh (Pyr Ntr, Pyr Mer) – All terms for pyramid.

Qustul (Kuh-stool) – Kingdom seat in prehistoric Ta-Seti or Nubia.

Raet (Ray-ette) – Raet-Tawy or (Rattawy) solar goddess, female expression of God Ra. Also considered a wife of Montu.

Ra-Kedet (Ray-ked-et) – The ancient name for the region where Buto (Alexandria) was located.

Sanghir (Sang-hear) – Ancient Middle-Eastern tribe.

Sebek (Seh-Bek) – Human with a crocodile head. Sobek was also associated with pharaonic power, fertility, and military prowess, but served additionally as a protective deity with apotropaic qualities, invoked particularly for protection against the dangers presented by the Nile River.

Seref (Sair-ef) – Alternate form of word saref or seraphim – angel with fiery wings.

Sesen (Se-sin) – A lotus or water lily. Lotus Points; Chakra.

Sesh (Sesh) – A scribe. In the Wisdom schools, a stage of priest candidates often lasting 10 years.

Seshat (Se-shat) – Egyptian goddess of wisdom, knowledge, writing accounting, architecture, astronomy, astrology, building, mathematics, and surveying. Wife and or/daughter of Djehuti.

Shendyt (Shin-dit) – A kilt-like garment worn in ancient Egypt.

Shenti (Shin-tea) – A loincloth under-kilt.

Sheol (She-oll) – Underworld, Hell in Canaanite.

Shinar (She-nar) – Babylon.

Shur (Sure) – Name of the arabian wilderness outside Egypt.

Ta-Seti (Tah-se-tee) – Land of the Bow, Nubia.

Tauret (Taw-ret) – Protective ancient Egyptian goddess of childbirth and fertility.

Tjemehu (Chjim-e-hoo) – Libya. Egypt's western neighbors and usually considered enemies, contained several races, some fair skinned.

Tyre (Tear, Possibly Tire) – Phonecian ancient trading outpost, Lebanon.

Wdjat (Wu-jot) – The Wadjet or Eye of Horus is intended to protect the pharaoh [here] in the afterlife and to ward off evil. Also called Udjat.

Wepwawet (Wep-wah-wet) – Originally a war deity, whose cult center was Asyut in Upper Egypt (Lycopolis in the Greco Roman period). His name means, opener of the ways and he is often depicted as a wolf standing at the prow of a solar-boat. Some interpret that Wepwawet was seen as a scout, going out to clear routes for the army to proceed forward. One inscription from the Sinai states that Wepwawet "opens the way". Also possibly spelled Upuwat.

Made in the USA
Middletown, DE
03 April 2022